is it casual now?

EADA FRIESIAN

is it casual now?

"Some people like to be wined and dined, I like to be fajita'd and margarita'd." The voice was smooth, seductive, and there was no mistaking its purpose. This was a pick-up line—tried and true. But Siena wasn't sure how effective it was on her.

Curious about who would use such a tacky line on her, Siena looked up from her table at the tapas bar and directly into washed-out blue eyes surrounded by dark, perfectly-drawn charcoal lines.

"Excuse me?" She pursed her lips, a deep line forming in the center of her forehead.

"I couldn't help but notice the way your date left, with all this food untouched and a quiet goodbye settling over the table." The woman waved at the table to indicate that the food had just arrived and not been touched. That had been Siena's fault, really. Her *date* was anything but. A young potential client of hers who had too much attitude and not nearly enough grit to handle constructive criticism. It hadn't been Siena's first choice to have the conversation here, but she had neglected to eat all day and the woman wouldn't take tomorrow for an answer. Siena had never been one to hold off on hard conversations, and by the time the food arrived, she finally had some peace to eat.

Siena cocked her head and lifted a single eyebrow. The heated conversation had seemed to fly under the radar for everyone in the restaurant. Except for this brazen woman. "And you are?"

"Oh. I'm sorry." The smile that burst across the woman's face took Siena by surprise. It turned those washed-out eyes into sparkling jewels and, oh goodness, were those dimples? "My name is Julie, Julie Andrews."

"You've got to be kidding." Siena took the offered hand, but she didn't hesitate. She had always been a sucker for forward women, and the obvious lie about the name was probably the most amusing part of her evening so far.

"What can I say?" Julie shrugged. "My mom was a big Mary Poppins fan."

"Right." Siena smiled, though she looked closer at this woman, her eyes dropping to the V cut at the top of the dress that wrapped around her luscious curves and folded across her body exactly the way it should to show everything off. "And what does she think of Victor/Victoria?"

"It's in the fabulous category, but it's one of my favorites." Julie's smile stretched wider as she met Siena's eyes on their way back up to her face from her cleavage.

"Well," Siena leaned back in her chair and waved a hand at the recently emptied chair. "It seems a pity to let all this food go to waste. Care to join me?"

What the hell was she thinking? It had been ages since she'd been so forward with someone, since she'd allowed the freedom of a good time to transform into whatever was going to happen next.

"If you insist." Julie smiled, already slipping into the chair.

Siena loved tapas bars. No matter which one she went to, the sound wrapped around her in a familiar blanket of noise. The clatter of glass and crockery, the chatter of excited voices, and the constant shuffle of movement reminded Siena of the rush of a concert, or backstage at a play. The calming chaos washed over her, and she breathed in the heavy aromas rising from the table just as she was served another plate—the last one that Krissy had ordered.

"So," Julie purred as she leaned forward and plucked up a piece of chopitos. She took her time slipping it between her lips, and Siena's mouth went dry in an instant. "Do I at least get a name?"

"A name?" Siena's brain had been too focused on those full lips sucking in the morsel of food.

"Yes." Her laugh was full bodied, and Siena smiled instinctively. Julie leaned forward, her cleavage on full display.

"Right." A name? Siena's brain struggled to reconnect synapses. Eventually images of running her tongue over the swell of those breasts were pushed aside enough for Siena to remember how to play this game. "Well, Julie, Julie Andrews, why don't I be your Dick Van Dyke for this evening?"

"Oh my God." Julie threw her head back and let out that laugh once more. "I am not calling you Dick, but I might be convinced to call you Van, or would you prefer Dyke?"

Siena chuckled low. If only Julie knew just how amusing that truly was. But there was no way she would be telling this forward buxom woman she was Siena Frazee of D.Y.K.E. Management. She didn't mind keeping the joke to herself, it always ended up being safer that way.

Especially if the road the evening had turned down was the one Siena thought. And Siena was rarely wrong in these situations.

"I could answer to Van." Siena smiled and wet her bottom

lip with the tip of her tongue. How much of this attraction was mutual? With the way that Julie locked her gaze on Siena's tongue, it was certainly going both ways. Because Julie barely raised her gaze back up in time to be considered cordial.

"All right then, Van." Julie's cheeks darkened ever so slightly beneath her makeup, the rouge painting across her skin in a stunning show of arousal.

Siena smiled and gave her a quick wink.

Oh, this was going to be an excellent evening after all. The woman wasn't just deliciously curvy in all the ways that drove Siena wild, but it seemed she could play the game for what it was. And enjoy it just as much.

Dropping her hands from her chin, Julie leaned further forward, ensuring the V on that cherry wine dress strained to contain the generous breasts within. "I'm sorry, but I've got to ask. You don't seem upset by the breakup—not serious I'm guessing?"

"Not upset, not serious." Siena smiled.

Very observant, confident, and forward.

Siena slid a meatball into her mouth and drew the toothpick out slowly, giving herself time to indulge in how Julie shifted around in her chair.

"But I'm not really interested in discussing that any more tonight." Siena took charge of the conversation.

"No?" Julie smirked.

"Oh no, I'm definitely more curious about you."

"Little old me? I'm not the interesting one here." Julie leaned back. Her hand fluttered to her breasts, her fingers splayed out over the cleavage.

Oh yeah, this woman definitely knew how to play the game. And Siena had no complaints, though she did bite back her sigh at losing the sight in front of her. But she wasn't at all ready for that yet. She liked the game. It was a thrill that she had always enjoyed. And her body needed more than a few minutes to warm up.

Siena laughed and shook her head. "Oh, I don't think for a minute you're someone without a very interesting story."

"What makes you say that?" Julie's hand fell from her chest, and she tilted her head, curling her fingers delicately through her hair and putting it behind her ear. For a moment, Siena saw a glimpse of the real person. Not the seductress who had sauntered over with hips delicious enough to hold onto, but a person with genuine curiosity and a brain that piqued Siena's interest, and her libido.

The thrill Siena had been enjoying since Julie had first spoken to her went from stroking her ego, to skittering down over her chest and teasing her clit.

Oh hell. She hadn't expected to be this turned on already. But she couldn't deny there was something about Julie that excited her. And clearly her body concurred.

If she were honest with herself, as she was trying to be more these days, it really had boosted her ego when Julie had come over to her.

"A woman as young as you with this much confidence isn't likely to have had a boring life."

Siena surveyed the table and the damage the two of them had wreaked on it. She hadn't remembered ordering more plates, but there they were, with only remnants of the food remaining. The food had melted in her mouth and made her groan more than once. Those sounds had elicited chuckles and smiles from Julie. And so far, Siena had enjoyed the conversation and company far more. She couldn't even remember the last time that had happened.

"And you know many young confident women then, do you?"

Siena smirked. "Oh, I know my fair share."

"Like the recently departed?" Julie laughed at her own joke.

"Hmmm." Siena pondered the question. "I wouldn't say she had your level of confidence. But she definitely has the potential to get there if she finds herself able to get out of her own way. Is that a problem?" Why on earth did she find it so easy to talk to Julie? And to say things she normally wouldn't, not to anyone. All right, maybe to Tori, but that had always been such a different experience, a different Siena.

"A problem?"

"A problem that I know many young, confident, and sexy women?" Siena took a sip from her glass wondering if she truly were as confident as she liked to present. "Like you."

"Sexy, huh?"

Siena nodded and looked pointedly down at Julie's cleavage. "Is that a problem?"

"That you like younger women like me? No. The only problem I can see is if you don't follow through on what your eyes are promising."

"Oh really?" Siena lifted her eyes and raised the single eyebrow again. She knew the effect it had on many women. Especially the young, confident, and sexy ones. Julie didn't know that most of those women were clients of hers. Playing the player had an enticing pull to it.

"Definitely." Julie's voice was lower than it had been just moments ago, and Siena squeezed her thighs tight together.

Oh hell, they had to get out of here, and soon. The last thing Siena wanted to do was disappoint Julie by coming the moment they touched.

"Well then, we can't break our promises." Siena stood up, walked over to where Julie still sat and offered her a hand. "Shall we get going?"

Julie looked up at Siena, those clear blue eyes twinkling. How had Siena ever thought of them as washed out? They were as blue as the bright sky on a warm summer's day. Something so rarely seen in Portland, but Siena lived for those days.

"I'd like that." Julie's cheeks darkened a little more as she slid her fingers into Siena's hand.

Siena gripped those fingers and pulled Julie up from her chair with a little more force than she had meant. Julie's body brushed against her.

Siena barely bit back the groan as breasts brushed her own.

"Don't we have to pay?" Julie whispered, and Siena's skin prickled with goosebumps at the touch of her breath.

"Already done." Siena felt very powerful being able to say that. There was no need to explain she had a credit card on file with the club, because she too often had to run out in the middle of meals or grab takeaway with no time to wait in line and pay. Or the fact that she could pay for this meal and not worry about finances. It wasn't going to affect her, not like it would have fifteen years ago.

"Fantastic." Julie met Siena's eyes as she stepped back, just enough for air to slide between their bodies.

"I think so." Siena swallowed down the lump in her throat and waved at the counter as she left.

Blair nodded, and Siena knew the meal would be charged to her account by the end of the night. She'd never been so glad to have so little free time in her life.

If it wasn't work, it was usually Harley.

Tonight though, she let her responsibilities fade to the background. She held on to Julie's arm as they stepped out of the bar and onto the rain-slicked sidewalk.

The soft mist of rain that lingered in the air cooled her warmed cheeks. She had expected a sizzling sound like when cold butter hits a hot frying pan. But relief washed over her as the night filled solely with the whoosh of car tires over puddles, and indistinct conversations of other people walking in the rain.

"Where are we going?" Julie asked.

"To my car." Siena took charge, and while she had enjoyed Julie's confidence and forwardness, she wasn't sure she would be able to relinquish the control again. At least not until she had enjoyed the pleasure of making Julie come at least twice.

With a sideways glance at Julie, Siena mentally corrected herself.

Maybe three times.

two

Siena hesitated when she reached the highway, automatically making the turn toward her home. Narrowing her eyes, she took the next exit and found the closest hotel that she could, immediately pulling into the parking lot.

"You're not taking me to your place?" Julie's voice was calm and curious, but something in the undertones said that she was nervous.

Was this something she didn't often do? Despite the confident way she had begun their entire evening together?

Not that Siena had one-night stands often either, but she did have rules, and she didn't want everyone in the world to know where she lived. Even if it was a one-night stand she would never see again.

"No offense, *Julie*"—Siena made sure to emphasize the name she knew wasn't a real name—"but I'm not comfortable bringing strangers back to my home for sex."

"Your loss," Julie answered with a wink. "I can't be as loud here."

"Or, you can be even louder," Siena challenged back, leaning across the center console of her car and getting even closer to Julie. Their lips nearly brushed like this, but neither of them made the move to touch. "Because I don't give a flying fuck what these people think."

Julie's lips curled upward, her eyes alight with mischief. "Well then, *Van*, I do think you have yourself a rebound."

"Thank fuck." Siena didn't hesitate or bother to correct Julie's assumption. What did it even matter really? And yet the lie felt like worms twisting in her stomach.

Meeting Julie's eyes again she shook the thoughts away and wrapped her hand behind Julie's head, pulling her in closer. Their mouths pushed against each other. The kiss was sloppy, fast, and full of heat. Siena didn't care if she made it good. Not this time around. Right now, she wanted to know if the sexual tension between them was just driving her mad or if it was actually tangible like she thought it was.

Julie whimpered, the sound sending waves of pleasure through Siena, and she couldn't stop herself from diving back in and pulling at Julie's lower lip, scraping her teeth along it with a bit more pain than pleasure. Julie hissed when she pulled back, raising her fingers to her mouth and then looking at them, as if expecting blood.

"Don't like it rough?" Siena asked.

"Oh I do." Julie flicked her gaze up to Siena's. "Just give me a little warning next time."

"Fair." Siena kissed Julie again, briefly, and then pulled back with a grin. "Stay here."

She jumped out of the car and ran directly into the lobby to book them a room. Hopefully Julie wasn't a nosy person and wasn't rummaging through the glove compartment to find Siena's actual name somewhere. That would ruin the night flat out. Surely, she'd have questions about the car seat in the back of Siena's car, but maybe she'd be so into tonight that she wouldn't have the gumption to ask.

This wasn't personal.

It was all heat and sex.

With the room card in her hand, Siena went back out to the car and was pleasantly surprised to find Julie on her phone and not rummaging through the paperwork in the car. Biting her lip, Siena slipped behind the wheel and handed Julie one of the two cards she'd gotten.

"Ready for tonight?" Siena asked, but it was more for herself than anyone else. She wasn't prepared for this. She hadn't expected it, and despite wanting to get lost in the carnal pleasures of another woman, she still hesitated.

"Absolutely, Van. I can't wait for tonight."

Siena forced her lips into a grin as she pulled into a parking spot. They didn't have anything with them, so this would be relatively easy. Siena took Julie's hand as soon as they were outside. She laced their fingers together, the warmth from Julie's skin heating her hand.

"So in terms of rough, how exactly do you like it?" Siena tugged Julie down the hall toward the elevator. She was going to take as much command and control as she could tonight, keep everything perfectly happy between the two of them.

"I like my clit to be sucked until it hurts." Julie's cheeks pinked, and it was honestly adorable. The words were loud and confident, but underneath it all, Siena sensed there was a lack of confidence on Julie's part.

As soon as they were inside the elevator, Siena turned to push Julie against the wall. She lowered her mouth to Julie's ear, bending to reach the much shorter woman. She nipped her earlobe and closed her eyes, listening to the shift in Julie's breath, the small sounds she would or wouldn't make. They would tell her a whole lot about how comfortable Julie was with everything going on between them.

"What else do you want me to do to you?"

"With me," Julie corrected. "We do this together or not at all."

Siena hummed as she scraped her teeth along Julie's neck, pushing her thin blonde hair over her shoulder. Julie's skin was so hot. Siena could fall into her and stay there for a very long time. Wrapping a hand around Julie's waist, Siena held onto her, tugging their bodies together and holding Julie firmly.

"You'll have your chance." Siena sucked Julie's neck just above her collarbone and swirled her tongue.

The elevator doors opened, and Siena glanced at them before focusing back on Julie's pale skin and the mark she'd left. Oh she was going to have fun with this one. Julie's skin made it perfect to see any marks left behind. Would her skin redden as she moaned in pleasure? Siena was damn sure she was going to find out.

Tugging hard on Julie's hand, Siena led the way down the hall toward the room in silence. Her heart thudded against her rib cage, anticipation and nerves filling her. She wanted this for sure, but that didn't mean that it wasn't also anxiety-inducing. Maybe she should just give up on love altogether and focus only on the physical pleasures of life.

She had Harley, her daughter, so she had the family she'd always wanted. What else could she possibly need? She wouldn't make the same mistake twice, that was for sure. Marrying Tori, while it gave her the family she wanted, had been a mistake in the long term. They'd rushed into something they weren't ready for, and they hadn't thought out.

But she really didn't want to think about that tonight.

Finally in the room, Siena stood awkwardly by the bed. Julie smiled at her, but there was that same undertone of inde-cisiveness that Siena had witnessed earlier. This start-and-stop needed to end so they could get naked and between the sheets together. Everything between them had been smooth until they'd entered into the physical realm, and then they'd both been forced to question whether this was what they really wanted.

That had to be it.

Siena reached up for the belt on her jacket and pulled it through slowly. She raised an eyebrow in Julie's direction, hoping that she'd do the same thing and start to undress slowly. Or quickly—Siena would take that too.

When Julie didn't make a move, Siena reached forward and cupped her cheek. She stepped in closer when Julie raised her chin up, obviously searching for a kiss. Siena had to change tactics, while she might want a really quick fuck and to forgo the undressing rituals, it was clear to her at this point that Julie wasn't quite ready for that.

Kissing Julie, Siena skimmed her hands down Julie's arms to her fingers and wrapped them together. Pulling away slightly, Siena whispered, "I wasn't expecting you tonight."

Julie hummed, her lips curling upward. She finally moved, reaching up and pushing Siena's jacket off her shoulders so it could fall into a heap on the floor. Nipping Julie's lower lip, Siena let her take control for now. Build that confidence back up and they'd be right back to where they were before. It seemed neither of them was very familiar with one-night stands, but Siena was certainly going to make the most of this one.

"Can I take this off?" Siena murmured against Julie's neck as her fingers slipped beneath the material covering her shoulders.

"Yes." Julie moved to help, sliding her arms from the sleeves and pushing the tight bodice of the dress over her stomach and her chest, revealing perfect breasts and smooth creamy skin. Siena wrapped her arms around Julie's back and pulled her in tight, dropping gentle kisses against the top of her chest, along her collarbone and to her shoulder. "More."

"Bra?" Siena asked.

Without saying anything, Julie reached up behind her and flicked the clasp on her bra. The material fell away from her skin, revealing gorgeous large breasts. Her nipples were a dusky pink, already hard, and begging for Siena to cover them with her mouth. Julie tangled her fingers in Siena's hair and moved Siena's face right down to where she wanted to be.

Shivering, Siena parted her lips and opened her mouth, taking Julie's nipple. She was slow at first, sucking gently before she flicked her tongue hard and used her teeth lightly against the sensitive flesh. They had talked about being rough, and perhaps Julie would want that as soon as she was a little more comfortable.

Fuck, Siena was going to lose herself completely in this woman tonight. It was exactly what she needed. A distraction from the reality of the world spinning around her, from her personal responsibilities, from the mountains of work that she still had to do. It was a break from the ever-ringing phone that ruled her world.

Here they had built an oasis where none of that existed. Where she could simply be a horny woman who wanted to feel good physically. Someone who could throw herself into her desires and pretend like the world outside these four walls never existed.

Siena moved down, getting on her knees. She put her hands on the bundled material at Julie's waist and looked up at her, waiting for confirmation to continue. When she got the nod, and the slight quirk of Julie's lips upward, Siena pushed the dress over Julie's hips—hips that seemed to go on for days. She had that definite hourglass figure, but her thighs were thick, her stomach curved, and she had dimples on her skin. Siena immediately pressed her lips against Julie's hip and one of those dimples, closing her eyes and reveling in the heat of her skin.

Julie plopped onto the edge of the mattress, her knees parting enough for Siena to get a good whiff of her arousal. It sent waves of anticipation and pleasure coursing through her.

This was exactly what they both wanted, hands down. And Siena was going to give it to them. She placed another kiss, this one at the top of Julie's mound, right on the edge of her panties. Siena didn't hesitate as she hooked her thumbs into the fabric and tugged it down.

Her heart thundered, rapping hard against her chest and stealing small increments of her breath. Scraping her teeth, Siena followed the trail of cloth as she pushed it down Julie's legs to her ankles. She pulled off Julie's flats and then completely removed all of her clothing, so she was bare, naked as the day she was born.

"Stunning," Siena whispered, not quite sure if she said the word out loud. She closed her eyes, her mind flipping through all the different scenarios, deciding exactly what she wanted to do first. She finally settled on the easiest one. "May I?" Siena asked, her hands on Julie's knees with a little pressure, indicating exactly what she wanted Julie to do.

"Fuck me, *Van.*"

Siena chuckled, her voice low as she moved in slowly. This wasn't going to be fast. It wasn't going to be quick. She wanted to savor every moment that she had with this gorgeous woman, eyeing her like candy in a candy shop and then devouring her one lick at a time.

One kiss to the inside of Julie's thigh wasn't enough. The second one only made her want even more. Siena slid her hands under Julie's thighs and lifted them up, resting them on her shoulders as she leaned in even closer to where they both desperately wanted her to be. But she wasn't ready—not just yet. She wanted to tease herself into this more.

With a scrape of her teeth, Siena listened for the echoing moan she wanted to hear. But Julie was quiet. For someone who had boasted about being loud, she was suddenly so quiet. It sent a wave of unease through Siena, that she wasn't doing something right, that Julie wasn't ready or didn't want to be here. She tried it again and caught the sound of Julie's breath catching. It was slight, but just enough for Siena to hope that she was doing this right.

"If you want to scream, then scream," Siena said against Julie's skin, going back for another kiss and another nip.

Julie whimpered, the flat of her palm on the top of Siena's head. Siena pulled away enough to be able to look up into Julie's sky-blue eyes. Her full lips were parted, her face slack.

"What is it?" Siena asked.

Julie shook her head, those stunning locks of bright blonde hair falling over her shoulders.

"Do you want me to stop?"

"No," Julie said, breathless. "No, don't stop."

A frown formed on Siena's face, a line deepening in the center of her forehead. The mixed signals were almost too much, and she was about to pull the plug on everything. She would if she had to. She wasn't going to do this if they both weren't into it.

"Don't stop," Julie repeated.

"What's wrong?" Siena asked, hoping for an actual answer to what she wasn't specifically asking this time around. She needed more to go on than what Julie was giving her.

Julie bit her lip, her breathing coming in quickly and making those stunning breasts rise and fall with each inhale and exhale.

"Julie?"

Julie shook her head, cringing. "Don't call me that."

"That was your suggestion for the game." Siena was about to move away, but Julie clamped her legs down on her shoulders and tightened her thighs. When Siena looked up at her again, her look hardened, filling with determination. "What do you want me to call you?"

"Nothing." Julie sucked in a deep breath and let her legs slide off of Siena's shoulders once more as she cupped Siena's cheek. Half sitting now, meeting Siena halfway, she brought their lips together, tangling their tongues.

Siena lost herself in the embrace, in the forwardness she was finally seeing come back to life in Julie. She was pinned down, forced to remain where she was by Julie's legs now wrapped around her body. Julie nipped at her lip, sucking it into her mouth and biting. Siena winced but then grinned. That must have been payback for earlier.

"I want you to fuck me," Julie said, putting her hands behind her and thrusting her chest into the air, her nipples calling to Siena like a moth to flame.

"Are you sure?" Siena asked, needing that verbal confirmation now.

"Fuck me, *Van.*"

three

Siena shivered.

This woman, whatever her true name was, had captivated her the moment they'd met. She was full of energy, tenacity, but also an edge of confidence issues that seemed to arise when least expected. Yet they didn't seem to be making an issue of themselves. Siena moved fully onto her knees, sliding her hands up and down Julie's thick thighs that still rested on her shoulders.

With one glance up into Julie's sky-blue eyes, Siena was ready. She raised an eyebrow, her lips thinning as she swallowed and prepared herself for exactly what she wanted to happen. "How rough?"

"I'll tell you if it's too much."

"Any no-go areas?"

"I'll tell you to stop if I don't want it."

"Very well." Siena pressed an open-mouthed kiss on the inside of Julie's thigh, the skin there smooth and soft, probably untouched except in moments like these. She scraped her teeth, a little harder than she had done so far. Julie's echoing gasp, the slightest sound coming from her lips, was exactly what Siena wanted to hear.

She did it again and again, moving closer to the scent of arousal that threatened to overwhelm her, to consume her. Siena shifted her body, pushing harder between Julie's legs. She nuzzled her nose into the blonde curls. She was so ready for this. It was exactly what she needed.

She didn't wait again.

Siena parted her lips, she covered Julie's clit, and she sucked. It was exactly what Julie had told her she wanted, suck her until it hurt. Digging her fingers into Julie's glorious thighs, Siena pushed her face harder into the warmth between Julie's legs. She closed her eyes, focusing on every sensation she could find. The slight roughness from Julie's hair against her cheeks, one that tickled her nose a little annoyingly, the wetness that bloomed with each swipe of her tongue.

Julie opened, her body parting with as much anticipation as Siena felt. Sliding her tongue through Julie's folds, Siena gathered up her juices, savoring the flavor, the sweetness that she had hoped for. Siena hummed as she moved straight back to cover Julie's clit with her lips. Sucking. That's what she was here for—at least this time around.

Three orgasms.

That's what she'd promised herself she would give Julie before she even dared to let Julie touch her. And that sounded like an amazing plan. Julie's hips bucked, and when Siena looked up to see her face, she was stunned by the pure pleasure that had cascaded across her face, the rise and fall of her breasts as she dragged in ragged breaths.

Siena wanted to speak. She wanted to say words of kindness, or anticipation. She wanted to tell Julie exactly what she wanted to do. It seemed that Julie responded to that, desired it even. But Siena had her lips locked around Julie's supple clit, and when Julie wrinkled her face up in pleasure, Siena knew she couldn't abandon her current path just to say something.

Julie moaned, though the sound was so soft, Siena nearly missed it. So much for being someone who screamed—or perhaps Julie was still holding back on her because they were in a hotel and not at either one of their homes. But this was the safer way to do this. Siena had to protect what was hers at all costs, and she'd never put Harley in any danger if she could avoid it.

"Ah!" Julie cried out. She shifted on the edge of the bed, wiggling as if she couldn't control her movements. Perhaps she was close, perhaps she wasn't. But Siena wasn't going to stop, not until Julie told her to. She was trusting that Julie knew exactly what she wanted and that she was confident in her own body.

Siena moved her hands from Julie's thighs to her hips, dragging her closer to the edge and closer to Siena's mouth. She sucked in a sharp breath, pleasure sliding through her own body at the way Julie reacted to everything she was doing. She dug her fingers into Julie's hips, her nails biting into the skin. She hoped it was adding to more of what Julie had requested —rough, hard, an edge of pain.

Julie moved her hips, finally in time with Siena's sucks. The rhythm was slow at first, but then sped up. She must have been getting close. Siena held her tightly, keeping Julie's body right where she wanted her. She wasn't going to lose traction, she wasn't going to let Julie lose sight of the ending they were both here for.

When Julie jerked, her thighs tightening around Siena's head, Siena knew they were at the brink. She closed her eyes, feeling through the moment with Julie against her face, the sounds of her breathing easing from the tension of her orgasm, the heat of her skin that overcame her, the weight of her legs on top of Siena's shoulders as she no longer held them up. Arousal coursed through Siena even more.

She had done that.

She'd made this woman jelly in her arms, helped unwrap everything that had been holding her together for a few moments of pleasure. A few moments that weren't yet over—Siena would make sure of that. The dampness between her own legs had become a wetness, her own pussy vying to be touched in any capacity. But she wasn't going to allow that to happen just yet.

After all, there were still two more orgasms for her to give Julie before they could get to the next stage.

Siena shifted up, pushing Julie backward onto the bed and moving her knees to her chest. Julie cried out in surprise, her eyes wide open as Siena towered over her for a brief second before she moved down and covered her clit again with her mouth. This time, she slid two fingers straight inside Julie's hot pussy and nearly moaned herself at the heat that surrounded her, the tight grasp of Julie's body on her, the pulsing that hadn't completely stopped yet.

Not waiting, Siena started a furious rhythm. She wanted to catch the last tendrils of pleasure still washing its way through Julie's body and pull them together for a rapid-fire orgasm that would leave Julie breathless. The only problem was that the more she moved against Julie the more the pulsing between her own legs intensified.

Julie moaned, louder than before but still not as loud as she had promised. Siena put all of her focus on what she was doing, pressing into Julie's body and following every sign she gave that Siena was doing something right. Julie flung her hands back behind her head, her chest rising up to meet the sky in all her stunning glory. This woman really was beautiful. She was confident in her looks, in her actions, in everything she'd done so far, and nothing was sexier to Siena than that.

"Oh God," Julie cried. Her thighs tightened around Siena's head, squeezing her ears against her skull, the sharp points from her earrings digging into the soft skin.

But Siena didn't let up. She was going to see this orgasm through until Julie told her to back off and give her a break.

"I can't—" Julie's voice broke on the words. Her face scrunched up, contorted with pleasure as she clenched her eyes shut tight. "I—" Julie's hand flung down on top of Siena's head, tightening in her hair and pulling hard as her shoulders came up.

The pull against Siena's fingers, sweet and strong, was exactly what she'd wanted to feel. Siena slowed her movements, easing everything down to give Julie the break she no doubt needed. She wasn't quite willing to push them beyond this point just yet. They needed to know each other better for that.

Julie sucked in a ragged breath, her skin pink from chest to cheeks, little red dots all along the way calling to Siena. She wanted to kiss each one, so she did. Bending forward, her fingers still planted deep within Julie's body, she pressed her lips delicately right between Julie's breasts. Then on the soft mounds, then to those peaked nipples.

Julie gasped, once again tightening her fingers in Siena's hair and scraping her nails against her scalp. She murmured, "So sensitive."

Siena stayed right where she was, letting the rough part of her tongue cause ripples of sensations through Julie's body.

"Another finger."

Siena's brow wrinkled as the words Julie said clicked in her brain. She wanted another orgasm. She was ready for more already. Siena parted her lips and took Julie's nipple fully into her mouth. She teased her breast and kept her hand still between Julie's legs.

Would Julie start to move against her? Demanding more?

Siena moved up, pressing her lips to Julie's neck and scraping her teeth against Julie's heated flesh. She left another mark just at the top of her breast before moving back up to her neck and starting over again.

"*Van!*" Julie said firmly. "Another finger."

Chuckling, Siena stayed right where she was. She wanted to drag this out a little longer. She wanted Julie to beg for more, which Siena would gladly give her.

Slowly, Siena added another finger, stretching the tight opening of Julie's body. Julie sucked in sharply, her hips raising up to meet Siena's movements. Julie was dripping wet, and Siena's skin was soaked. Finding the right amount of pressure when everything was so slippery was tough enough, but she was determined.

"More…" Julie cooed.

Siena added her last finger and pressed the heel of her hand against Julie's clit. With every thrust of her fingers, her palm would push against Julie's clit and create a sensation that would take her through yet another orgasm. Siena knew it would. She loved it when someone else did this to her.

Julie's legs fell to the sides, opening her up even more for Siena's perusal. Standing at the edge of the bed still, Siena leaned over Julie and pressed kisses to her chest and neck and lips. This was the best part about this position. She could kiss and touch all at the same time.

Julie nipped Siena's lower lip, and a wave of her own pleasure pooled between her legs. Her own clit tingled, and if she could just focus on her own body a little longer, she might be able to get off without Julie actually touching her.

"Harder," Julie whispered.

Siena complied. She jerked her fingers harder, firmer, faster. Julie rewarded her, moaning as she wrapped her arms around Siena's shoulders and tugged Siena into her even more. Julie crashed their mouths together, stealing Siena's breath.

"Fuck me, *Van.*"

Siena did exactly as she was told. She closed her eyes, listening to the signs from her own body as she continued the same rhythm and pattern as before. She lost herself in the moment, in the risk of sleeping with a stranger, in the joy of finding nothing but pure physical release with another person, without the complications of a relationship or emotions.

"Fuck," Julie muttered.

Siena felt the same. She was so close to careening through her own orgasm, still fully clothed but within the grasp of the woman underneath her. Siena was losing control though. It was harder and harder to focus on what she was doing to Julie as her mind and her body fully tuned in to the sensations floating through her own body.

"I'm close," Siena whispered against Julie's neck.

"That's hot," Julie answered, drawing in a breath at the same time. "That's so hot."

Her voice broke on the last word as she came. Relief flooded Siena because now she could really focus on herself. Biting into Julie's shoulder, Siena closed her eyes and let pleasure flow through her freely. She was washed with it as it consumed every thought, breath, and cell she had. Julie touched her shoulders lightly, running her hands over her and under her shirt.

When had she pulled that up?

Siena didn't want to move, just yet. It was so hard to catch her breath after that whirlwind, and her legs felt far more like jelly now than they had in ages. She was going to have to move at some point, because she was sure she was crushing Julie, and Julie would want to stretch out her legs.

Finally, Siena moved. She shifted to the side, pulling herself up on the bed. She reached for the blanket and wiped her wrinkled fingers on it to clean them quickly. She lay on her back and stared up at the ceiling, her eyes wide open as she listened to Julie's rhythmic breathing next to her.

"I'd say meeting you tonight was well worth it," Julie said with a giggle in her tone.

"Yeah," Siena answered, her lips curling upward. She turned her head to catch sight of those sky-blue eyes and tousled blonde locks. She hadn't really wanted another relationship after Tori. She'd made enough mistakes in that one to stay away from relationships, deep ones, for the rest of her life. She wouldn't put someone else through that.

"Are we done for tonight?" Julie asked.

"Do you want to be?" Siena raised an eyebrow and locked her gaze with Julie's.

"You're still dressed!" Julie's lips curled upward. "I'd very much like more."

Siena smiled back. "Let's take a shower first to clean up and have a bit of a break."

"And a bit of a tease?" Julie winked at her.

"Ha. Sure." Siena stretched her hands above her head, easing her muscles. She could go at this for a few more hours before she'd need to catch some sleep before morning.

Julie, however, popped right up. She bent down and planted a loud kiss on Siena's lips. "Meet you in the shower."

She stood up, planting her feet on the ground just as a loud crash echoed through the room. Siena sat up right away, finding Julie's purse spilled out all over the floor.

"Shit."

"I'll pick it up," Siena drawled. "You go get in the shower."

"You sure?" Julie glanced at her curiously.

"Yeah." Siena bent down. "I'm sure you're getting cold."

Julie laughed lightly. "Are you going to warm me back up?"

"For sure."

With that, Julie walked naked to the bathroom. Siena bent down and started picking up the spilled items. Julie's phone was first, and she checked to make sure the screen wasn't cracked, not that she would know if it hadn't been cracked before, but it looked to be in good shape. Her wallet was flopped open, and Siena snagged it next, narrowing her eyes when it opened to Julie's driver's license.

Jamie.

Kettlehouse.

"Holy fuck." Siena's heart thudded. Her chest tightened. She stared at the driver's license, wishing it was wrong, but the picture matched the woman she had just fucked for the last hour. "Holy fuck," she repeated.

Jamie Kettlehouse was a notorious gossip writer, someone who had irked Bunny, Siena's biggest client, nonstop over the last five years with some of the crap she wrote. She came up with all out lies half the time, and the other half, everything she wrote was flat out truth. Not only did she write for a reputable magazine, but she also had at least one blog site and social media that haunted Siena's every step.

Siena was fairly certain she wrote under at least two more unconfirmed pseudonyms.

"I'm waiting!" Julie—no, not Julie—Jamie called from the bathroom.

But Siena couldn't. There was no way she was going to be able to walk into that bathroom and continue where they left off. She was done. Putting everything into the purse, Siena dropped it into the center of the bed. She grabbed her jacket and threw it on.

Her mind raced.

Her body was still a puddle and on fire.

But she was so fucked.

She couldn't have made a mistake this stupid.

It was going to ruin her.

With her jacket on, Siena walked straight for the door and out of the hotel room. She went straight for her car, got in, and drove out of the parking lot. She was going to have to fix this. She was going to have to find some way to make this not blow up in her face.

But that was going to be impossible.

So much for casual.

four

The shower knob squeaked as Jamie turned the handle to shut the water off. Her legs were absolute jelly still, and she couldn't wipe the grin from her lips. The happy little butterflies of energy kept dancing through her body, and she couldn't remember the last time she was this happy or this excited for something.

It had been such a hard year.

The steam in the shower filled her senses. She'd sworn that *Van* was going to join her in the shower, but maybe she was too distracted by what they'd just done. Jamie pressed her palm to the handle and twisted it open, stepping naked and dripping wet into the…empty…hotel room.

"What the fuck?"

The room was cold now, where it had been warm and full of energy before. Her purse was strewn out on the middle of the bed, the contents spilled out and in a mess of a pile that was beyond disorganized.

She stood still, blinking as though the next minute to pass would suddenly make sense of the scene in front of her. But it didn't matter how many times she blinked—nothing was tracking in her brain. Had she just been robbed? Fucked hard and then her information or credit card that was maxed out stolen? Three orgasms had turned her sharp mind into a sludge of thick thoughts that weren't entirely clear.

Turning on her heels, she marched back to the bathroom and quickly dried herself. Finding her clothes was easy enough, but as she slid the soft fabric of her dress over her body, the fog over her mind lifted.

Jamie shifted through the items on the bed quickly, finding nothing missing. So this wasn't a robbery. Van must have found something in there that had scared her. But what the hell could it have been? It wasn't like Jamie carried around illegal drugs or child porn in her purse. She shuddered at that thought —*never* on either of those.

So what had Van found in her purse that had her running out without so much as a goodbye? Was the woman closeted? If so, she'd done a poor job of hiding that at the restaurant and an even worse job on the bed.

"It's not that," Jamie muttered to herself confidently as she riffled through her bag. Nothing incriminating, just the usual things—phone, wallet, tampons, pen, notepad, lipstick, business cards from people she'd talked to.

"Fuck." She went back through the items and flicked open her wallet. "Well so much for anonymous."

Her driver's license had slipped around in the tumble off the bed and the horrid photo of herself stared back. Her real name stared up at her in large bold print along with her birthday and address from three apartments ago. A stark reminder that even in her mid-thirties, she still hadn't figured out what the hell she was doing with her life and was still living paycheck to paycheck. She wasn't the favorite kid in her family, that was for certain.

But why would knowing that send the woman running?

Was she married? Because there had been no damn ring on that finger. Jamie had checked, multiple times.

"Unless she knows who I am." Biting her lip, Jamie rifled through the items again before shoving them all back into her purse. That excited pull she got at the start of a new story built inside her chest. It was the adrenaline she lived on. If Van had found out who she was, then Jamie could do the same. She wasn't an idiot, and she knew exactly how to find the information that she wanted.

And her tenacity and stubbornness for finding that information was what made her so good at her job, and a royal pain in her boss's ass.

She had long ago gotten used to being called a hack or a liar. But she knew the truth of things. And she never made up something she couldn't prove. People simply refused to give her the chance to show her proof. And showing her cards without being made to had never been something she was willing to do.

Taking her time and laying out her plans, Jamie stood up and smoothed her hands over her dress. She could do this. She could figure out exactly what had sent Van running and then she could decide what she wanted to do with that information. Or not—she could do nothing for all she cared, or she could do absolutely everything and destroy Van with a few clicks of her fingers against the keyboard.

Jamie smiled, pulling the strap of her bag over her shoulder and stretching her lips wide as she pulled the door closed behind her, key card firmly in her grip. Her face, reflected in the closed elevator doors, still held her telltale blush of sex, but she could use that to her advantage as well. A girl well fucked just wants to be well fucked again, doesn't she?

Stepping up to the counter, Jamie plastered on the softest smile that she could. She could play girl next door like she lived it. "I'd like to check out."

"Okay," the young gentleman behind the counter said. "What's the room number?"

"Room 312." Jamie rattled off while she twirled her still damp strand of hair around her finger and leaned over the counter to give the young man an ample view of her cleavage. She would use whatever means it would take to get this information.

"You're all checked out." He grinned up at her, his gaze definitely dropping to her breasts.

"Oh, here's the card." Jamie slid the card across the desk and moved her fingers right before he could accidentally touch her. "Do you mind if I get the receipt? I like to keep records of what goes on my credit card statement." She gave a gentle chuckle to him. "My daddy always told me that I should be as fastidious as possible when it comes to finances."

"He sounds like a wise man." The man bent his head and typed away on the keyboard.

Jamie had to swallow that lump. Her dad wasn't a bad guy, but they certainly didn't always get along either. She was the screwup kid, after all. And she'd live into that role for as long as she could, because someone had to be the scapegoat.

"Here you are." The paper was curled at the top and the bottom from the printer.

Jamie grinned at him, taking the paper between two fingers as she skimmed it for the name. Her stomach plummeted. Cold washed through her. That had to have been it. Her screwup personality had lost her a good fuck again. Breathing heavily, Jamie looked up and nodded at him, still keeping that same soft smile plastered on her face, although she was no longer feeling it.

"Thank you so much. I really appreciate it."

He nodded at her and stopped paying attention. Taking the paper and shoving it into her purse, Jamie walked out of the hotel lobby and into the chilly, damp air. Her heart hammered against her ribs, nearly to the point of pain.

Fuck.

Fuck. Fuck. Fuck.

Whipping out her phone, Jamie debated whether or not to call the only person who could calm her down, but she stopped herself. Nope. This was her own screwup, and she was going to deal with it on her own. She didn't need someone else telling her how bad she was.

Biting her lip, Jamie stepped into the parking lot and headed for home. She never would have imagined that she would pick up *the* Siena Frazee at a tapas bar. Not the big name, open queer, powerful and professional-to-a-fault Siena Frazee who repped the biggest queer outing story that Jamie had been trying to uncover for years now and failed miserably every single time.

"Really?" Jamie laughed, edging toward maniacal. "Siena Frazee?"

Who'd have thought that would happen?

———

"Earth to Jamie!" Jessie's voice filtered through to Jamie, and she jerked her head toward her sister.

"What?" Jamie asked, a little snippier than she meant. She scanned the classroom to see if there were any hints as to what she had missed.

"What?" Jessie laughed again, shaking her head as she pressed the corners of an alphabet poster onto the wall beside the whiteboard of her kindergarten room. Jamie couldn't understand why this particular poster had to be changed every year since it was basically exactly the same, but she went with whatever her sister told her to do. It was their tradition to set up Jessie's classroom together—it had been for the last ten years since Jessie had started teaching, and Jamie had only missed the chance once.

"I was saying how much I appreciate you taking time off to come help me."

"You make it sound like I never help you with anything." Jamie's cheeks flushed with the familiar shame she felt about how little she really did to help her sister. But this was something she wouldn't give up if she had to. This was their tradition, and if they did something together like this, then they wouldn't argue as much.

"Noooo," Jessie pulled the word out as though giving herself time to find the right words. "You try to help when I ask, but you rarely take time off in the middle of a workday to do it. And by rarely, I mean never, except for this."

"I..." Jamie fumbled for answers. Only her twin sister could ever hit directly on the point and have her entirely flabbergasted for words. Words were her life, but that skill was rendered useless when it came to Jessie.

"You what?" Jessie dropped her hands and tilted her head as she turned her full attention and body toward Jamie.

"I wrote a blog post, and I'm pretty sure it's going to hit hard for a..." Jamie swallowed back the lump in her throat. "...a few different reasons, and particularly for a few specific people."

"Okay." Jessie shrugged her eyebrows creasing together. "But that's sort of what you do half the time."

"Most of the time," Jamie muttered in correction. At least she wanted it to be most of the time, but building up a blog that was full of gossip, and gossip that was mostly true, was far harder than she'd anticipated. And while she was good at blogging and finding out information, she was really crappy at being a business owner.

"Exactly." Jessie nodded, relief washing over her face. "So why would this time be any different?"

Jamie's face burned, and she knew without a mirror that her face was flaming a deep pink. They might as well have been Irish-born with how their emotions flared up their ivory skin.

Jessie raised her eyebrows, nodded toward one of the small chairs behind a just-as-small table and sat on one opposite it.

"Ugh. I totally should have bailed on helping you," Jamie growled out, but the corners of her mouth lifted, and Jessie smiled softly at her.

"Tell me what happened."

"It doesn't matter."

"Yes, it does." Jessie laughed. "Don't make me pull out the big sister card."

"Two minutes. You're two minutes older than me."

"Exactly." Jessie pursed her lips, lifted her chin slightly and pushed back her shoulders. "So it's time you tell your older and far wiser sister what shit you've gotten yourself into this time."

"That's just it." Jamie ignored the "wiser" comment, and its implications, and slumped into the uncomfortable tiny furniture. "Normally, it's just me getting into shit because I'm exposing other people's dirt, but this time my own shit might actually bite me in the ass."

"Oh my God." Jessie's mouth opened in an O, and her eyes sparkled with a little too much enjoyment.

"You look far too pleased about this." Jamie pouted.

"I am." Jessie chuckled. "I've been waiting for you to finally get caught up in one of your stories. What did you do? Get a restraining order put on you or something?"

"I wish," Jamie muttered before she could help herself. A restraining order would be easier than a night of really hot, amazing sex and then finding out that the woman you fucked would consider you her mortal enemy.

"Holy crap." Jessie sat back in her own chair, all humor lost from her face. "What happened, James?"

And so Jamie told Jessie without going into too much fine detail, like how the woman rocked her world only for her to find out she was one of her biggest nemeses in her career life.

"Wait." Jessie leaned forward in the chair, legs crossed, and arms folded over her raised knee. "*THE* Siena Frazee? The woman you curse every other week. The one who somehow manages to get on top of half your stories and all the ones that would bring your name out of the trash column and into the real-journalist sphere?"

"Hey," Jamie shot back. "It's not a trash column."

Jessie's reply was those raised eyebrows once more, those ones that Jamie was fairly certain she used on her students every single day, probably multiple times a day.

"Fine. But not everything I write is salacious and about the shock factor."

"I know, but it's all about the drama of other people's lives."

"Exactly." Jamie shot up out of the tiny chair, unable to feel her butt any longer sitting in the furniture designed for kindergarten kids. "*Other* people's lives. Not mine."

"Then why did you write about it?"

"Because I had to." Jamie shrugged as though the answer should have been obvious to everyone, especially Jessie. "I can't just ignore stories when they pull at me."

"But now you're scared of the backlash?"

"Yes." She hissed and shoved her fingers through her hair. "But how was I supposed to know that goddess was Siena *Fucking* Frazee?"

"Goddess, huh?" Jessie's voice filled with implied mischief. "She must have been pure magic to have gotten under your skin this much."

"Hardly." Jamie scoffed. But of course, Jessie had hit yet another nail right on the head. Jamie turned away from her sister, knowing her face continued to deepen in color. "Where do you want the bookshelf?"

"Nice change of topic." Jessie laughed behind Jamie.

Jamie turned back and met Jessie's eyes. Silently, she begged her sister to move on, at least for now.

With a nod, Jessie stood and pulled out some books from one of the bags the two of them had dragged into the room earlier.

"I think under the far corner there. I'll put a nice rug and cushions, and it can be a quiet-time reading area for those that finish work early."

"These kids are so lucky to have you." Jamie grabbed at the opportunity to move the conversation off of her, but she also meant the words. She would make a horrible teacher in any form, but Jessie was brilliant at it.

"Thanks. I hope so. Open house is next week, and I'm looking forward to meeting the kids and their families."

Jamie let the rest of the afternoon be consumed in rearranging furniture and taking direction about poster placement. But despite enjoying the time with Jessie, her mind kept drifting back to her article that had dropped earlier that day. Which, of course, made her entirely too aware of Siena still being on her mind. And *that* idea was completely stupid in and of itself.

Jamie was in the prime of her life, she wouldn't be settling down anytime soon, if she chose to settle down at all, ever. And besides, even if Jamie was looking for a relationship, which was the last thing on her mind, Siena wasn't even near the list of partners. She probably was still married, not that Jamie had managed to figure that one out. There had been a wedding announcement years ago but never an announcement of a divorce, and Jamie had been too chicken to look up the public records.

She hadn't wanted to spoil her one hope of that yet.

Besides, she and Siena were in the same world but on

entirely opposite sides. Siena was all high and mighty about celebrities, expecting the people to throw money and praise their way but never giving any of their true selves back. Everyone has a right to know who exactly they looked up to, who they spent their money on.

No matter how mind-blowing the sex had been, Jamie wouldn't change her mind about this. No matter how often she had brought herself over the edge again and again as she remembered Siena's touch. Jamie sighed and shook her head as she drove away from the school. She just never dreamed she would have to deal with being this close to the actual subject matter of any of the drama she wrote about.

That's what was unnerving her.

Nothing else.

Not. At. Damn. All.

five

"What the hell is this?" Bunny flopped a printout of a blog post onto Siena's desk loudly.

Siena, however, had already seen it, read it at least three times over, and was hating herself for that one night of weakness even more. She couldn't believe that she'd made such a stupid rookie mistake.

No matter how good the sex had been.

And it had been damn good.

"That is the latest gossip drama from none other than Jamie Kettlehouse. JK for short." Siena rolled her eyes. Jamie was an absolute joke. The fact that she continued to put out this shit and try to pass it as actual journalism was the true joke. Or perhaps it was the fact that people actually read it and thought it was all truth.

"This is ridiculous," Bunny said, again pointing at the printout. As if she couldn't just email it over to Siena. Siena stopped at that. Bunny would never just email a link over, that wasn't her style at all. "She should be in jail for writing this horseshit."

"Well, not quite." As much as Siena hated to admit it, it wasn't like JK was crossing the line of libel. Though she had come close to it several times. Running her fingers through her hair, Siena rested back and closed her eyes. "But it doesn't exactly paint *me* in a good light, does it?"

"You read it?" Bunny plopped down across from Siena, finally calming down slightly.

"I was alerted to it right after it was posted." Siena sighed again. She needed something stronger than water for this one. Reaching into the bottom drawer of her desk, she pulled out a rarely used bottle of whiskey and filled a couple of small cups. Handing one over to Bunny, Siena took a sip before she eyed one of her oldest friends. "I'm going to have to change a few things around and head out with you and Piper on the next tour."

"What? You can't. You already explained you wouldn't be with us this time."

"I know." Siena ran her hands through her hair once more. She had gone through the options over and over, and every single time she came to one conclusion. "But if we ignore this then *JK*"—she spat the name. It must be in those initials. She'd never met anyone with them who wasn't a snake in the grass—"will turn this molehill into a fucking mountain."

Bunny stared wide-eyed at her, and she closed her eyes and took a deep breath.

"I'm sorry."

"Fuck that." Bunny shook her head. "I'm not your client right now, Siena. We'll find another way."

"There isn't another way." Siena smiled softly at her friend. She appreciated how Bunny could work with her and still maintain the friendship they had developed over the years. Siena prided herself on her professionalism. She was good at her job. Damn good. Hell, she was the goddamned best. But sometimes, moments like this, she wondered if all this professionalism was really worth it.

She shook off the idea as soon as it entered her thoughts.

Of course it was. But sometimes the cost wasn't.

"Have you told Tori and Harley yet?" Bunny asked, the hint of a wince in her voice, as though she expected to be yelled at for asking.

"No." Siena's shoulders dropped forward, and for a moment, she let the last of her professional demeanor sag. "No, I haven't told either of them that I'm going to miss Harley's open house. I've been avoiding it, hoping some miracle will appear and I don't have to."

"Then don't miss it," Bunny said again, earnest and sincere. Not many people got the privilege of seeing this side of Bunny. She was either the rock star or the consummate professional where work always came first. Well, maybe not always professional, but always focused on work. It was one of the many things the two had in common that had moved them from a manager-client relationship into true friendship.

"You know as well as I do that I have to stop this ball rolling any further."

"I know." Bunny leaned back in her chair and nodded. "I just wish I really did arrive with the miracle you needed."

Siena and Bunny shared a soft sad smile, mirroring each other. She often understood where Bunny's thoughts were, even if she didn't always agree with her reasoning or justification. She did always understand it.

The silence settled over them for a few minutes.

"I'll tell you what, though," Bunny broke the silence with a little more of her well-known force, "if I ever find out what that snake looks like, she'll be getting more than just a little piece of my mind."

She got loads more than a piece of my mind.

Siena opened and closed her mouth, heat rising to her cheeks.

"Sorry." Bunny rolled her eyes at herself. "I just hate that you're going to have to disappoint Tori and Harley because of her bullshit."

"I know. And you aren't the only one who's going to hate me just a little right now."

"She won't hate you."

"Maybe neither of them will, but that kind of makes it worse." Siena forced her shoulders back, putting her professionalism back into place like a suit of armor.

"You'll make it up to her. Harley will forgive you. You're a great mom, Siena."

"Thanks." Siena rarely felt like a great mom, but she also knew she tried her best and really would do anything for her daughter. Including making sure she didn't fuck up her job to the point of not being able to support her and Tori. Not that Tori needed the financial support as much as she used to.

"Good luck." Bunny stood and gave Siena a consolatory smile.

"Thanks. I'm going to need it." Siena picked up the phone as soon as Bunny closed her office door behind her. She had to rip the Band-Aid off immediately or she'd end up fucking it up worse by not telling them and just missing the open house without explanation.

That would have been a thousand times worse, and absolutely not the parent Siena ever had been or would be. The disappointment in Tori and Harley's voices would be hard enough without extra anger mixed in.

———

"All right, what the hell has got the great Siena Frazee in a bar at three in the afternoon drinking?" Ingrid's voice sailed over to Siena where she sat at a table at their bar.

They had been coming here since they met at management school and whenever shit got to be too much, they would call on each other to meet and bring the other back to the real world.

"I've fucked up," Siena said, the whiskey she had already drunk having loosened her tongue.

"Well shit." Ingrid pulled her handbag around to her front and sat down on the chair opposite Siena. "This isn't some petty little shit who has pissed you off."

"Nope." Siena shook her head and then narrowed her eyes. "Actually. She is a petty little shit who has pissed me off, but I can't say I'm surprised or even that I entirely blame her."

"Her?" Ingrid lifted a hand and got the attention of the waitstaff. "This sounds like I'm going to need a drink as well."

"Oh yeah." Siena leaned forward and chuckled. It was the first moment of lightness that she'd felt since hanging up with Tori. The call had been a bad one. Tori hadn't screamed or yelled or anything like that. It really wasn't in her nature. She had even tried to be understanding and give Siena a break from the guilt, which of course only made her feel that much worse.

She'd even offered to tell Harley for her, but Siena didn't want Tori to take the blame for Siena's parenting fuck ups. That had never been something either of them would do to their darling daughter or to each other.

"I have to miss Harley's open house at school next week. Her first one."

"What? Why?" Ingrid pulled the straw from her drink and took a healthy gulp of the amber liquid before she snuggled into her chair, clearly getting ready to settle in for the long haul.

Siena gave a small snort. Not the most attractive of her

moments but fuck it. What else could go wrong right now? "Because I fucked up and have to tour with Bunny and Piper so the accusations can't stick."

"Ah fuck. You're talking about the JK blog?" Ingrid nodded and took another gulp of her drink.

"Oh yeah." Siena lifted her eyebrows and nodded. Despite the heaviness in her chest over the entire situation, the corners of her mouth curled up just a touch.

"She has really fucked over a lot of us managers with that one. And it looks like it's getting a bit of traction as well."

"Exactly."

"So then, how come your cheeky grin is showing?" Ingrid gave her own half grin and raised a single eyebrow at Siena.

No wonder they had become fast friends and stayed that way. They didn't catch up all that regularly, but when they did, they slipped into the easy friendship of a history and understanding that few others could grasp.

"Well," Siena chuckled, a self-deprecating sort of hard chuckle that made no secret of the desolation and stupidity she felt. "I fucked her."

"What?" Ingrid's eyebrows knitted together, and her glass stopped halfway to her mouth. It hung in midair, and Siena focused on her friend's fingers as they warped through the thick glass, instead of meeting Ingrid's eyes.

"I didn't know it was her at the time."

"Oh my God." Ingrid's hand lowered and the glass landed with a *thunk* onto the tabletop, the next gulp forgotten. "You're serious? You slept with *Jamie Kettlehouse?*"

"Ssshhhh." Siena quickly looked around the space.

She really didn't know why she bothered. It wasn't as though this was a popular hangout joint. It was nothing more than a dive bar really, but it was theirs.

"What the hell happened, Siena? You don't just sleep with people."

Siena cringed as she thought about the words that she planned on saying next. "Apparently, I do now. And with my impeccable taste and timing, the person I decided to change my entire personal vow for is none other than the demon spawn of my entire fucking career."

"Wow." Ingrid shook her head as she took that previously forgotten drink. "Just how did this even happen?"

"She hit on me, and she has delicious tits." Siena groaned and dropped her head forward as memories of sucking those tits rushed to her mind.

"Wow."

"That's it? That's all I get?"

"Well, until you explain a bit more." Ingrid held up her hand. "And no, I don't mean more about the tits and whatever has got your face flaming red again. But how do you go from mortal enemies to fucking?"

"I need another drink for this," Siena said.

"I've got it." Ingrid raised her hand again, slugging back the last of her current drink as she did.

Once fresh drinks were ordered and had arrived, Siena dove into the events of the evening when her strength and resolve had disappeared beneath blue eyes and soft lips.

"Holy shit." Ingrid hadn't touched her drink as she listened to Siena's story and now sat with a strange look on her face—a look Siena was certain she didn't like.

"What?"

"What do you mean what?"

"Don't play with me, Ingrid." Siena lifted her eyebrows and gave her best stare-down. Even with a few drinks in her, Siena was still in complete control over her faculties and knew how to use the power of her stare to her advantage. "What is that look about?"

"This look is still processing."

"Bullshit." Siena chuckled, shaking her head. "You've

never taken time to process anything. You're a friggin' speed processor."

Ingrid laughed and finally took a sip of her fresh drink.

"Fine. I'm wondering if JK—pfft, why would anyone want to use that as their persona nowadays—" Ingrid rolled her eyes and shook her head. "—but anyway, I'm wondering if she knew it was you."

"Yeah, I'm pretty sure she does."

"I mean the article is about managers in general. I mean, she's done a number on all of us."

"Yep. That's true." Siena nodded. "But you can't tell me the little details and examples she's talking about didn't have you thinking exactly of me."

"Hmmm." Ingrid's lack of response told Siena exactly what she thought. "You really just walked out while she was in the shower?"

"What the hell else was I supposed to do?"

"Be a grown up and confront her!" Ingrid smiled as though that could minimize the sting of her words.

"It was a nightmare, all rolled up in unreleased arousal, and I panicked. Okay?"

"Yeah, you did." Ingrid agreed with a nod. "And now you're going to have to deal with it and not keep running away."

Siena rolled her eyes and shook her head. "Easy for you to say. And I don't plan to do anything but my job in relation to that woman. Ever again."

"Sure." Ingrid laughed. "You keep telling yourself that."

"All right Miss Know-it-all." Siena laughed. "My time's up. What's going on in your world?"

"Well, funny you should ask." Ingrid smiled and began to regale Siena with the things that had happened since the last time they had caught up.

By the time they left, Siena felt a little lighter. She was no closer to working through her guilt about missing Harley's open house, or understanding how Jamie fucking Kettlehouse had so easily gotten under her skin, but she was determined on one thing.

She would do her job and avoid the tabloid hack just like she always had.

There would be no more contact with JK.

None whatsoever.

six

"Kettlehouse!" Her boss's voice boomed through the open plan office the moment she stepped out of the elevator at work. "My office. Now!"

"Oooh, someone's in trouble." Scott, the typical misogynistic journalist who hadn't quite made it to the new century, smirked as Jamie stepped past. She wished those cigarettes he acted like no one knew about would get to killing him already.

What the hell had she done now?

She didn't let the thought smear her features. She had been at this too long now to make such a rookie mistake. Instead, she pushed her shoulders back as she walked through the sea of desks and cubicles. It might as well have been a gauntlet.

It wasn't as though she hadn't had to run it before, but usually she knew what the hell the soon-to-be ass chewing was all about. Right now, she didn't have a clue. In fact, she had even gotten an almost-grin and nod in relation to her last story.

The eyes that watched her as she passed bored into the back of her head. She'd been on the other end of this situation, so she understood the desire to stare. It had always been a schadenfreude deal—that complete relief it wasn't her in trouble.

But still, couldn't they at least pretend like they were too busy to want to know what was going on?

"Shut the door." He didn't look up as she stepped over the threshold.

She let the door fall closed behind her with a loud click. What was the point of trying to close it gently? The entire office knew she was in trouble.

"What's up, boss?"

"*What's up?*" Now he did look up, and how she wished he hadn't. His eyes were filled with complete fury. "Are you fucking kidding me?"

"Ah." She couldn't keep her eyes on his as she tried again to work out what was going on. "No."

"I've had call after call about you and your blog."

"*My* blog?" That was the last thing Jamie had expected him to say. Sure, she hadn't any clue what the problem was, but it never crossed her mind that it might have anything to do with her blog. "What about my blog?"

"You've really put me in the shitter now, Kettlehouse."

Damn, that was twice he'd used her last name. That didn't bode well at all. She had to figure out the issue and find a resolution immediately.

"I told you about my blog when I first started it. You didn't have a problem with it then. What's happened to make it an issue now?"

"This happened." He held up a stack of phone messages and flicked them across the desk. Some fell to the floor but most scattered over the surface in front of Jamie.

Tilting her head, she picked up some of the names. Her blood ran cold.

"How did they know to call here?"

"For a journalist, you can be a real dumbass sometimes."

He growled. "You've got a unique voice, kid." Kid? Kid was a good sign. Now she just had to get him further away from Kettlehouse so she could feel like breathing easy might be possible again.

"They figured out it was me, I get that. But why bother harassing you? I've got all the right disclaimers on there, stating that the opinions and facts were on me and me alone. That I wasn't associated with any paper or publication in relation to what's written on my blog."

"Come on, Jamie." *Jamie* was good as well. This could be okay. "You aren't that stupid. Yeah, I know you have all the right disclaimers, but that isn't how the world works."

"Yeah." She rubbed her palm against the back of her neck, beneath her hair. "I know. But what are they hoping to achieve by harassing you?"

"What do you think?" His eyes met hers, and what little relief she had been clinging to fled away.

She swallowed the lump in her throat but couldn't answer.

"Siena Frazee isn't the kind of person to let herself be smeared and turn a blind eye."

"Siena?" The lump hadn't completely been swallowed, and her voice came out in a croak.

Her boss snorted. "Do you really think anyone in the industry didn't know exactly who you were talking about?"

"I was talking about the entertainment industry as a whole." Her defenses were up, and it was going to take some work to get them back down.

"And how the managers were the secret faces behind the stars, keeping the truth from the public while doing things like lining their pockets and taking advantage of their clients."

Fuck. She had said that. The article had been well-researched and all the information she cited was accurate.

However...

Shit.

Her cheeks burned hot in spots, and she dreaded to think how splotchy her face now looked.

However, she had put the last touches on the article after Siena had run out on her and her fury had known no bounds—apparently.

"Okay. So what happens now?" Jamie asked hesitantly.

"They want you gone."

"Gone?" Downgraded or reprimanded sure, but gone? "As in fired?"

"Out on your ass." He nodded to reinforce his confirmation.

"You can't…" Jamie trailed off, not seeing any weakness in his gaze. "This wasn't anything that bad. I swear it wasn't." She didn't have it in her to beat around the bush any longer. What the fuck? It was a single blog post. "What do I need to do?"

Sure, it had gotten a whole lot more traffic than previous blogs but still.

She shook her head, still trying to process the information. Surely, he wouldn't just fire her.

Then again, it wasn't the first time she'd pissed him off, but he'd never been harassed by entertainment managers either. Not like this. Were they all asking for her to be sacked? Were they all coming to Siena's defense?

"You need to fix it!"

"Fix it?" The fear of being fired was nothing compared to the anger that rose in her chest. "You mean rescind it. Fuck that. I didn't write anything that wasn't true."

"I'm sure you think using a *theoretical* example somehow makes it true that you didn't lie. But that means shit in this industry, and you should have figured that out long before now."

"I'm not rescinding it." Jamie wouldn't back down. She knew it wasn't the smartest thing to do, but she had regretted doing the smart thing too many times in her life. No way in hell would she take that path with her blog. She'd worked too hard to get it to where it was and rescinding now would ultimately mean the death of her baby. She might not be the most business savvy, but she sure as shit knew this would be the nail in the coffin.

"You don't want to rescind it, that's your choice. But you better find some other way to fix it if you want to keep your job here." He pointed at her as if to make his point even more clear than before.

"Like how? Getting an interview with Siena Frazee herself?"

"For that…" His eyes lit up like beacons, the idea sending thrills through him that made Jamie shudder. It didn't help that a colleague had once commented that she bet he made the same eyes during an orgasm. "…I'll run the article here, parallel with it on your blog."

"Are you kidding me?" Jamie's own eyes widened at the very idea. If she could get him to run a story alongside her blog, that could be just what she needed to get some real traction of her own.

If she could get the interview.

As if reading her mind, he smirked over his desk at Jamie. "If you can get her to agree, then absolutely."

"Right." That sobered her in an instant. But still, she had to at least try.

She'd managed to get Siena in bed, surely an interview wasn't completely out of the realm of possibilities. Even if they hadn't known each other's names when they'd gotten to the bed, and she was damn sure of that because Siena Frazee never would have fucked her three ways if she had.

Jamie walked out of the office in a stupor. Had that really just happened? She'd been fired before, but this felt…worse. In so many ways and so much more devastating than any of the other times. She *needed* this job. And she was going to hit middle age before she knew it, and it was about damn time that she become an adult, right? At least that's what her parents kept telling her—comparing her to Jessie every single second.

"Cleaning out your desk, then, JK?" Scott sneered.

"Now, why would I do that?" How she wished she hadn't been so quick to use her initials on the blog. Seemed too late to change it now, despite the association with another JK who would not be named—ever. She refused to be guilty by association.

"Give you enough rope to hang yourself, did he?" Scott scoffed.

"Oh to be so insecure as to have to badger someone just to feel like a man." Jamie rolled her eyes and looked over at the other two female journalists on staff. They sniggered, and Scott all but stomped his foot in a tantrum.

"Yeah well. Won't be long before you fuck up again and the gay woman card only gets you so many passes."

Jamie bit back another retort.

She could only fake that much confidence while her heart thundered at the idea of calling Siena's office. But what the hell other choice did she have?

Sure, she'd been angry and had stupidly let that affect the last edit of her post, but didn't she at least owe some of the entertainment managers a chance to defend themselves? She had asked for their comments before she published but none of them had gotten back to her. Amusing that so many wanted to talk about her now.

Well, not so amusing from her end.

And not really to her, but to her boss.

"Ugh. Just do it," she muttered to herself, forcing her thoughts away from the spiral she was creating and making herself crazy over. "Stop being a chicken shit."

It was easy enough to find the number. She already had it in her files for the post to begin with.

Quickly, before she talked herself out of it again, she opened her files, found the number, and dialed.

"Good morning, you've reached Siena Frazee's office. How may I direct your call?"

"Hi." Jamie used all her charm even as she knew it would get her nowhere. The receptionists for these media managers were warriors in their own right. She would have been impressed if she hadn't been so damn frustrated with the walls they put up to stop her getting through to the managers themselves. "I was wondering if Ms. Frazee was available?"

"Do you have an appointment?"

"For a call?" Jamie wrinkled her nose and cringed.

"Yes."

"No, I don't."

For a moment, all Jamie could hear was the click clack of fingers on computer keys. The sound washed over her and sent a pleasant sort of electric thrill over her skin.

"If you give me your name and reason for the call I'll see if she's available at her earliest convenience."

"Um…" Ever articulate, Jamie rolled her eyes and mentally chastised herself. "My name is Jamie Kettlehouse, and the reason is—" *personal* "—regarding an interview."

"Let me put you on hold."

Music filtered through the phone, and Jamie blinked, pulling the thing slightly from her ear to get a better view. She wasn't sure what she thought the plastic receiver might be able to tell her, but somehow, she expected an explanation for having gotten through the first gate of the manager barricade so easily.

"Are you fucking kidding me?" The voice came down the line a mere second after the hold music was abruptly cut off. "You're calling my office regarding an interview?"

"Well, nice to hear your voice as well, *Van*." Jamie knew she should have stayed professional. Kept their history, no matter how recent, pushed to the awkward margins of the conversation. But the tone in Siena's voice had put Jamie's defenses up instantly, and the pain and anger at being fucked and dumped burned fresh.

"Well, *Julie*, I wish I could say the same about you." There was something in the petulant tone of Siena's voice that made Jamie snort laughter before she could stop herself.

"Charming," Siena muttered.

"Well, apparently not nearly charming enough to require an explanation, but that's not why I called."

"Ah, yes." The way Siena said it, Jamie imagined the woman dressed to kill, legs crossed as she moved her chair back and forth with the heel of her pump. The queen in her domain. "The interview."

"I was hoping to get on record—"

"No!"

"You didn't even let me finish."

"I'm pretty sure I did. Several times." Siena was quite fucking pleased with that response, Jamie could tell in her tone. Heat pooled between her legs—damn why did she like the icy ones with quick tongues and sharp wits the best? "But whoever it is you're wanting to interview—forget it."

"I want to interview you," Jamie rushed the words out as quickly as possible. She had to at least get the ask out there before Siena hung up on her.

"Me?" The shock was genuine, and Jamie's lips twitched slightly.

"Yes. Seeing as you and all of your entertainment friends have such an issue with my piece about the corrupt nature of the music industry, even though when I requested a comment from more than a dozen of you, they went without a single reply, I thought I would offer *you* the opportunity to have your say on the matter."

"Seriously?" Siena's snarl came through as clearly as though she had pressed her forehead against Jamie's.

Damn it, it was still morning, and Jamie already wondered if her clothes showed just how much she had been sweating through this conversation. She hadn't been prepared for this. But she wasn't about to let anyone else know that.

"If you don't want to, I can always request the interview with one of the many other managers who have been in contact since my article was published. Ingrid Bauer for example."

Siena snorted again. "Good luck with that. And it was hardly an article."

"Oh." Jamie wished it didn't delight her to know that, yes, Siena had read the piece herself. "So you have read it?"

"Yes. I've read it." Siena's voice was tight, and she spoke with barely contained anger or frustration.

"Would you like to be the one to set the record straight then?" Jamie chuckled, seemingly unable to antagonize the woman. "So to speak, at least."

"Fine!" Siena snapped. "Hold the line, and I'll transfer you back through to reception, and they'll arrange a time."

"Oh." But the hold music had already returned, and soon, too soon, Jamie had an interview organized, and she sat staring at the phone that was now back in the cradle on her desk.

"What the hell are you staring at, Kettlehouse?" The boss's voice so close behind her made her jump and turn in her chair.

"I have an interview with Siena Frazee."

"No shit?" The boss's eyebrows disappeared beneath his shaggy fringe.

"No shit." Jamie knew she wore her *this is insane* grin, but soon it was wiped from her face as the boss did nothing more than humph at the confirmation and tell her to get her ass onto the work he actually paid her for.

She did, though her mind was never entirely forgetful of the fact that in two days, she would see Siena Frazee again.

And of course, she didn't at all wonder if she would finally get to see the delicious skin that hid behind the power suit Siena would undoubtedly show up in.

Nope.

That didn't cross her mind for a single moment as she worked well into the evening.

seven

Siena eased into one of the last empty parking spots at the school. She'd made it and found a parking spot before the bell to end the day had rung.

With a relieved sigh, she quickly checked herself in the rearview mirror and stepped out of the car.

She finally had a chance to meet Harley's new teacher for the first time and apologize for having missed last week's open house—thank God Paula had been able to arrange the meeting while she'd been tied up with the Jamie drama. The guilt still wormed away in her chest, and the desire to overcompensate by spoiling Harley itched closer to the surface.

Tori had already warned her not to, knowing how Siena thought after all these years. And still, she ached to show Harley just how much she regretted not being there. But Tori was right. As she far too often was, having explained how the more Siena made a big deal out of it, the more it would be imprinted on Harley. It had made absolute sense the moment Tori had said the words.

Smiling, Siena stepped away from her now locked car and

toward the school building. It was nice to have something other than Jamie Kettlehouse to think about.

Her mind still reeled over this morning's conversation. What on earth had inspired her to give in? And to give in so easily? She knew it'd be a disaster, but maybe it'd help rid her of the Jamie Kettlehouse effect—the one that had kept her mind returning to those eyes and tits.

She shook her head as though that could rid her of the memory. She knew it was useless, but at least she could force it to hide at the back of her mind for now.

Now was all about Harley. She loved her weeks with Harley. They were always a little more busy, unexpected, and hectic, and she wouldn't change that for the world.

Tori's directions led her perfectly through the maze of the school. Stepping through the door, the first thing Siena heard was the sweet sound of her Harley's voice. The room was filled with color and a buzz of children and adults talking as parents came to pick up their kids from school.

But all Siena cared about was the wild child running full steam toward her.

Crouching down, Siena scooped Harley into her arms and squeezed her.

"Mommy!" Harley squealed a little too loud in Siena's ear as she wrapped her arms around Siena's neck and legs around Siena's waist.

"Are you sure you're Harley?" Siena spoke into Harley's ear. "*My* Harley?"

"Of course, I am." Harley giggled, and no matter what else was going on in Siena's life, everything now settled inside of her, all right once more.

"Really?" Siena adjusted Harley in her arms and lowered her back to the ground. "Because you look far too big and grown up to be my baby."

"'Cause I'm not a baby." Harley stuck out her lip in indignation.

"Oh no?" Siena tilted her head, fighting to hide the smile pulling at the corners of her mouth.

"Nope." Harley shook her head adamantly. "I'm Batman!"

"Well, of course you are." Siena couldn't hold back the smile anymore and gently brushed her short nails over Harley's soft hair on her head. "Now before we go, I'd love to meet your teacher."

"Ms. K is the bestest teacher ever!" Harley grabbed Siena's hand and pulled her over toward a small crowd of parents and children.

Looking around the room at the other parents, Siena felt the weight of her years press a little on her shoulders. Some of the other parents were so young, and instantly she regretted the decision to look closer.

"Ms. K," Harley's voice loudly announced as the crowd of parents parted with goodbyes.

Siena stopped in her tracks. Not even Harley's yank on her arm got her feet moving again.

Had she thought so much about the woman that she had actually manifested her in real life?

"Jamie?" Siena choked out over a lump that had formed instantly in her throat—dry and painful. The panic that had hit her earlier in the day when she'd been on the phone with this very woman came right back into her chest and multiplied exponentially.

"I'm sorry?" The woman tilted her head and looked at Siena like she was crazy.

"Harley, why don't you run and grab your things and get ready to head home?"

"Okay, Mommy."

As soon as Harley was out of hearing range, Siena turned back, fire in her veins and poison in her words.

"What the hell are you doing here, Jamie? Here to write some fabrication about my daughter? Is nothing sacred to you?"

"Oh." The woman's face fell. "You know my sister."

"Your…sister." The words fell hard from Siena's mouth, the bile taste on the top of her tongue and the back of her throat intensifying.

"Yes."

Siena studied the woman closer. It was Jamie, but it wasn't. There was something a little bit off about her, although the features were basically identical. This woman was softer, warmer—easier and less hard edged. Maybe jaded? Was that it?

"Your twin sister is Jamie Kettlehouse?"

"Yes. I'm Jessie Kettlehouse, and I'm Harley's teacher this year. The kids call me Ms. K because my name is too long and hard for kindergarteners to pronounce sometimes." Jessie stuck out her hand. Siena noticed the slight tremble in the woman's fingers.

"Like hell you are." Siena stepped back from the offending appendage and turned away, pulling her phone out of her pocket as she did.

Harley stood beside her, looking up with wide eyes filled with confusion and a little sadness.

"Mommy," Harley whispered. "You said the H word."

H word? Siena knitted her eyebrows together, trying to remember what she'd said. But all she could hear in her brain was the buzz of anger, and it took everything in her to focus.

"Oh, I'm sorry, baby. I shouldn't have said that."

"That's okay." Harley instantly beamed a smile, the naughty word already forgotten about.

"I need to talk to Ms. *Kettlehouse* for a little bit longer before we can leave." For good. Because she damn well was going to pull Harley from this school as soon as she had a word with

Tori. "Can you draw me one of your favorite things about the week?"

"Okay." Harley's face beamed as though she'd just been given a pony for her birthday and raced off toward a low table. For a moment, Siena basked in the sunshine her daughter brought to her life. She supposed the mission she'd just sent Harley on was as important as anything else she could have requested.

"I'm sorry. I didn't catch your name. And I don't think I should be calling you mommy." Jessie smiled, trying to shake away the tense air that lay thick between them.

"My name is Siena Frazee. I'm Harley's other mother, and I have no intention of having my daughter in your class."

"Oh." Jessie's face splotched red as her mouth dropped open in a wide O so similar to Jamie's, it was more than just a little unnerving.

Fucking fantastic!

"Great. So you've spoken to your sister lately." Siena couldn't look at this Jamie who wasn't Jamie anymore. She turned her back on the teacher and began typing a little too hard on her phone.

Siena: *There is no way in hell our daughter is going to this school. It's not happening, Tori. If it means I have to cut back on my own things to ensure she goes to a better school, it's what I'll do, but there is no God damn way this woman is teaching Harley.*

Tori: *What are you talking about?*

Tori's instant reply had no emojis or personality, and Siena knew she really would have to fight for this one. But she would fight. She would do anything for her daughter, and her daughter wouldn't be taught by Jamie—no, by Jessie—Kettlehouse.

"Siena?" Jessie's voice was nothing like Jamie's confident flirtatious tones. Still, it sent an uncomfortable shiver racing up Siena's back.

"My name is Ms. Frazee. Not Siena. Not to you," Siena snapped back.

"I understand this must be incredibly strange to you, but I think we've simply gotten off to a bad start."

"You don't understand a damn thing." Siena hissed. She had to pull herself together, she knew that, but just looking at this woman made all her self-control and professionalism fly directly out of the window. "Did you know I was Harley's mother? Did you and your *sister*," Siena hissed the familial word, "have a good laugh over how this would play out? And to think I was going to give her a chance to redeem herself after that blog post. Unbelievable."

"I promise that's absolutely not the case. I wasn't aware that you were Harley's mother. And I'd really like the chance to sort some things out before any major decisions are made."

"The decision's already made." Siena didn't want to hear any more. The heat in her neck was enough. "You won't be teaching my daughter."

"Mommy?" Harley's small voice came from beside Siena.

She closed her eyes and took a deep breath, forcing her rage to simmer down into the pit of her stomach instead of letting it spark in her eyes.

"Yes, baby?" Siena turned, a smile as good as she could force out at the moment pressed on to her lips. Her phone buzzed in her hand, and Tori's name lit up the screen, but she ignored the call. She had to finish this conversation before she could have the next one.

"Why are you being rude to Ms. K?"

"What?" Siena reeled back slightly.

"Ms. K is nice, and I don't want another teacher." Big tears pooled in the corners of Harley's eyes, and Siena had the mental image of her brain in one corner of a boxing ring while her heart pumped ready for a fight in another. And she had the distinct feeling her heart was beyond pissed off with her, shaking itself back and forth in disapproval at making her daughter cry.

"Harley, it'll be okay." Siena softened her voice in a way nothing else could have done except for the sight of her breaking child.

But Harley continued to shake her head even as she buried her face into Siena's shoulder and let the tears out. Siena quietly made the soothing sounds that had always helped her and Harley both during the harder days together. There had been less and less lately and this feeling of going backward tore at Siena.

Behind her, she could hear Jessie's quiet voice. But she couldn't quite hear what the woman was saying or any reply from whoever she was talking to.

After a quick glance over her shoulder, she saw Jessie pull a phone away from her ear and slip it into her pocket.

Had she called security?

Siena had to admit that if someone had barged into her office and started snipping at her or any of her clients or staff the same way, a call to security wouldn't be far from her thoughts.

She had overstepped. She knew it the moment the words had left her mouth, but the importance of that truth began to truly register. Her phone buzzed in her hand where her fingers ached from how hard she clutched the damn thing.

Tori: Siena. Would you please answer me? Is Harley okay?

Siena: Yes. She's okay. I'll call later. I'm going to start looking for new schools immediately.

Tori: Come on over and talk to me about it before you start doing that.

Siena wanted to scream at her phone. She wanted to scream at herself. She knew what Tori truly meant behind those words. *Come on over before you waste time being stupid.* But of course, Tori would never say it like that.

To be fair, the part of Siena's brain currently not in control knew Tori would never even mean it that way. Tori would hear Siena out and find a way to make her feel good about whatever they decided, together. Because of course she wouldn't be able to just move Harley from the school. She would never do something like that without being on the same page as Tori first.

But that didn't mean she had any intention of backing down from getting Harley as far away from this shit as possible.

This shit that you created. Her mind unhelpfully added.

"Ms. Frazee?" Jessie said, and it was obvious in her tone she had tried to get Siena's attention more than once.

"What?" Siena snapped far harder than was necessary. Seriously, she needed to pull herself together, to reel back her anger and frustration. But for the first time in her life, or at least the first time in more years than she could remember, she struggled to find that control she'd always been so proud of.

"I'd like to show you some things Harley has done over her first few days at school."

"Why?" Siena asked, not buying into the sweetness that radiated from this woman's eyes. Though she did feel like she had just kicked a puppy. "So you can convince me to keep her here?"

In true Siena style, when she fucked up, she went all in.

Sisters, identical on the surface, but they were unequivocally opposite in many other ways. But that didn't change any of this. Siena needed to keep Harley away from it all.

Dread uncurled in the pit of her stomach.

Her divorce with Tori had been so ridiculously amicable, even if she'd never touch tequila again thanks to their divorce sex, but amicable during and since. She hated the idea of fighting with Tori now. But when it came to Harley, she would clamp down and do what was right for her daughter.

But was this right?

Yes.

She argued silently with herself as Jessie looked at her, a softness in her eyes and around her mouth. She was gorgeous, in a far more sweet and innocent way than Jamie had been.

Siena looked over to see Harley focusing her entire attention on the piece of art she was creating.

"Fine." Through clenched teeth, Siena agreed to be shown around the classroom.

After every piece of art or photo Jessie showed her, Siena would look over at Harley, checking she was still happily drawing. After the third item, she turned and noticed Harley's seat at the drawing table now empty.

Her heart screamed in her chest. It was so loud in her ears, she wondered how everyone could continue as they were as though they heard nothing. Her breath caught and the panic set in.

"She's over with her friends at the building blocks." Jessie's voice cut through the panic, and with a quick look where Jessie pointed, Siena located her daughter laughing with several other children.

"Thank you." Siena turned to Jessie, the first real smile on her face.

It didn't last long, when over Jessie's shoulder, she saw the person responsible for all her current problems step into the room.

"What the hell is *she* doing here?"

Jessie threw a look over her shoulder before turning back to Siena.

"I called her. I think you and Jamie need to sort out some things so that Harley and I aren't caught in the crossfire."

Jessie had seemed such a soft pushover. The quintessential kindergarten teacher. But the tone in her voice brooked no argument, and Siena wondered how much she needed to reevaluate Harley's teacher.

Jamie's eyes widened as they landed on Siena. After a beat, her head gave a single solid nod and she walked toward Siena and Jessie.

This is going to be a shit show.

eight

The phone call from Jessie had given her no clue as to the shit show she would be stepping into. But the tone of the call was enough to have Jamie rushing out of the office and heading down to the school.

The drive had all different scenarios playing out in her head, but not one of them came anything close to what she stepped into.

Her eyes met Siena's, and her blood froze in her veins, while heat rushed to her cheeks.

And between her thighs.

What the hell was Siena doing here?

Was it revenge and payback for the blog? Wasn't trying to get her fired enough? Trying? Hell, she had gone beyond trying. But this was next-level crazy person.

She had known the phone call was going to be rough, but she honestly believed that she'd made a truce with Siena. A tentative one, but still. They'd both waved the white flag in a sense.

Hope of interviewing Siena and the more wistful future hope of then one day finally getting a real interview with

Bunny and Piper flew out the window—the window that was covered in art pieces she herself had helped her sister stick up only last week.

The memory of the panic that had filled Jessie's voice came back to Jamie, and she pushed away her own ambitions for the sister-protection mode she'd had to engage very rarely so far in her life.

She would if she needed to.

But first she had to find out what the hell was going on. And the only way to do that would be to force her feet to finally move forward.

Taking a deep breath and giving herself a single solid nod, her feet obeyed, and she walked toward Siena and Jessie.

"Jessie." She stared at her sister first, wide eyes that promised a beat down on whoever needed it. Jamie just wasn't sure who that would be. "You didn't tell me exactly why I had to rush down here in the middle of my workday. So, what's happening?"

"Jamie, this is Siena Frazee. I believe you two have met. Maybe not, though. Did you know she had a daughter who just started school this year? In my class?" The wince for Jessie was enough to tell Jamie far more about what was going on than any other words she could manage to get out.

"What?" Jamie's fears of keeping her job just kept plummeting even farther as she registered the rage that vibrated beneath Siena's very skin.

"Wait. You have a kid? And she attends here?" Jamie's luck really couldn't get any worse, could it?

"She won't be a student here for much longer." Siena's face was a hard-edged mask of barely contained fury.

"What?" Jamie couldn't have heard that correctly. "Why won't she be here much longer? Has something happened?"

Siena scoffed and rolled her eyes, pointing to Jessie with

one long finger—and Jamie knew exactly what she could do with it.

Jamie turned to Jessie for an explanation, but her sister gave her a familiar *I'm as flabbergasted as you* look.

"I don't understand." Jamie didn't like admitting that. *Ever.* But her brain hadn't quite caught up, all the pieces refusing to fit together to make any sense.

"Did you know who I really was before you hit on me?" Siena leaned in, hissing the words quietly into the space between her and Jamie.

"What? No. Of course not. This is insane. You can't have a kid."

"Just like you can't possibly have a twin sister teaching my daughter." Siena's voice was low, a warning or a threat?

But was Siena threatening Jessie's job as well? Jamie would never be able to forgive herself for that, or to live it down with any of her family. The rest of her life would be punctuated by conversations around "that time Jamie got Jessie fired because she couldn't keep it in her pants or stay out of other people's business." God, she could hear the conversations over Sunday night dinners already.

"Mommy!" A small girl's excited squeal made Jamie step back and blink, happy enough to be pulled out of her thoughts. "There's two Ms. K's. Are you sisters? I have a sister named Rebel, but she's not really my sister. She's my cousin, or my niece. Maybe? I'm not sure on that."

"Cousin," Siena mumbled.

"That's right! Sister-cousin!" The girl giggled loudly.

"Harley, this is Ms. K's sister, Jamie." Her eyes still held the fury Jamie had seen in her face, though her features softened, and the woman, Van, Jamie had slept with peeked out as she spoke to her daughter.

Harley's eyes widened, and Jamie felt her lips twitch up into an involuntary smile. The twin reveal always gave her a little thrill. Her entire life, being a twin had always brought out the strange and curious, but seeing the excitement in a child's eyes was a nice change.

"We're twin sisters," Jamie added, a smile spreading over her face. She wasn't all that keen on kids. Well, truth be told she hadn't much thought about them individually, but she couldn't deny that this kid was a bit of a cutie.

"Twins?" Harley's excitement seemed only to grow, her smile taking up half her face and dancing in her eyes. Her small body twitching with energy as though she was moments away from bursting.

"Yep." Jamie nodded for emphasis.

"But I'm older," Jessie said, a grin on her face. Most of my students don't get to meet Jamie, so that makes you special."

"What, you're older?" Harley turned to Jessie, and Jamie rolled her eyes as Jessie squatted down as she talked to Harley.

It gave Jamie the chance to focus again on Siena.

How the hell did the world keep fucking her over like this?

"I swear, I had no idea. About any of it," Jamie rushed out in a lowered voice, hoping to do some kind of damage control with this absolutely insane situation.

"Yeah, right." Siena scoffed in return.

"I wasn't the one who ran off halfway through because I found your license," Jamie hissed. So much for damage control.

"And I wasn't the one who decided to throw her career under the bus publicly by implying I'm corrupt and abuse my clients. And not at all subtly, if that was what you were going for, and I suspect subtly was never even on your mind. I don't even think it's a word in your vocabulary."

"No, you're just the one trying to get *me* fired. Did you really have to rally all your manager friends to harass my boss and threaten my livelihood? So your name might get a bit of a hit, but bad press is better than nothing."

"What?" For a moment, Siena's confusion flooded her face.

"Yeah, I know. You're all about keeping your precious celebrities squeaky clean, but guess what, that's a total load of bullshit. If they want the fame, then maybe they should let people know they aren't perfect. All it does is give their fans shame and guilt when they don't measure up."

"No." Siena shook her head, features squeezing together in frustration. "What do you mean about my manager friends?"

"Now who's full of shit? My boss has gotten so many calls he's stopped answering his phone. All of them threatening him and telling him to fire me."

"I don't know anything about that." Her face seemed so genuine, but Jamie wasn't buying it. She didn't trust this woman. How could she? She had left her alone in a hotel room after fucking her senseless.

Nothing about Siena Frazee made sense. And nothing she said or even did could be trusted.

"Well, so much for never seeing each other again," Jamie muttered.

She closed her eyes and tilted her head back. Opening them, she stared at the ceiling, counting the imperfect blemishes she hoped Jessie didn't notice. Because no doubt Jamie would be pushed up on a ladder to scrub them off, especially after this debacle.

"How the hell are you two even related?" Siena asked.

It snapped Jamie out of her current thoughts as she dropped her head back down and turned to see what had inspired the outburst from Siena.

Following where she looked, Jamie found Jessie and Harley laughing together. The pain of never being enough, never being the *good* child rang dull and familiar in Jamie's chest.

"Yep. She's all sunshine and rainbows. It's why you should be grateful she's teaching your kid."

"Right, as if you didn't already know about this." It was an accusation, but Jamie was sure she sensed a small hint of doubt at the words' sharp edges.

"All right," Jessie spoke as Siena opened her mouth as if to reply. "Jamie, I really need some more sticky tack."

"Sticky tack?" Jamie gave her sister the best petulant look she could muster.

"Yes," Jessie hissed in reply, even though her smile remained on her lips. "In my storeroom, now please."

"Of course, summarily dismissed." Jamie rolled her eyes as she turned toward Jessie's closet, but not before she caught the look on Siena's face. She had no idea how to interpret it, but it twisted uncomfortably in the pit of her stomach.

She stomped off, refusing to focus on that look any longer, even if her mind seemed to have other ideas. The sticky tack was in plain sight, but she hesitated before leaving the small claustrophobic area again. She wanted to give Jessie a chance to get through to Siena. If anyone could do it, it would be Jessie.

Did Siena truly think Jamie was some kind of criminal mastermind, setting up these pieces just to fuck with her? To what end?

With a heavy sigh, she knew exactly what she might get out of interviewing Siena and hopefully Bunny and Piper.

But she didn't premeditate any of it. She had just always been good with taking advantage of the situations that arose in front of her. Siena would never believe it though.

This entire situation had become nothing more than a royal cluster fuck.

Jamie made a slow return back to where Jessie and Siena stood talking. Looking around the room, Jamie was relieved to see only a handful of children remained. Currently there were no other parents besides Siena.

Siena's shoulders had lost some of their tightness, and they rolled inward as her hand rubbed small circles on Harley's back. The kid didn't look much like Siena. Jamie focused on what she had learned over the years about Siena—not much about her personal life to be honest. Jamie had always been more interested in getting to Bunny and Piper—but Siena had been given a little more credit in Jamie's eyes when she confirmed her sexuality publicly as though there were nothing salacious or newsworthy about it.

Oh Fuck!

She was married—married with a kid whose birth mother was Siena's wife. That had been the thing she had read about Siena. One of the only pieces of personal information. Everything else she knew about the woman had to do with the business.

Or at least until she discovered firsthand that the woman was wicked with her tongue and could make her scream louder than thunder.

Harley leaned into her mother's leg, head resting on Siena's hip. What mattered was the way she clung to Siena. The idea that this woman, so eager to call her posse down on Jamie for calling out shit behavior, had engaged with Jamie in a goddamn affair.

Jamie's stomach roiled with queasiness at the thought. She wanted to call Siena out on her hypocrisy, but she didn't want it to be true. And she certainly didn't want to be the asshole to do it in front of Harley. The girl looked sweet enough. As far as kids went, Jamie felt for her. She seemed little, but maybe not. Jamie had no idea.

It didn't matter. What did matter was the drama that was unfolding in Jamie's life. She loved other people's drama. But this was definitely not the shit she had signed up for.

"Pulling Harley out will do little but cause another big change far too soon after she's just settled in. If you're really concerned, I'll be happy to discuss having her go into another teacher's class. But I promise Jamie can be a bit of an idiot at times, but she never has a long-term plan. To my parents' chagrin."

"Gee thanks." Jamie had stood, silently listening until her mouth as usual got her in trouble. She turned to Siena. "And this way you don't need to have to explain to your *wife* why you suddenly want to pull your daughter out of the school."

"Excuse me?" Siena's cold words might have hurt Jamie if she wasn't filled with fury.

"Come on, Harley." Jessie wide-eyed Jamie as she veered the child away from the two women about to go toe-to-toe. "Let's double check you have everything before you head home."

"I remember reading about your wife giving birth."

"Not that it's any of your business," Siena said, though Jamie heard her swallow audibly. "But my *ex-wife* and I share custody of our daughter. And explaining to her about my desire to change schools is none of your business."

"You're still pulling her out of the school?" Jamie's mouth dropped open.

"No." Siena's shoulders slumped forward, and for the first time, Jamie saw an exhaustion hidden behind the dark eyes and beauty of this woman. "I don't know. I'm not doing anything now. But this sure is one hell of a coincidence."

"Tell me about it," Jamie muttered.

To her surprise, Siena offered her a small smile, and after a moment assuring herself she really had seen it, Jamie returned it with her own.

Siena stepped closer, and Jamie caught a whiff of Siena's scent. It was so familiar at this point because Jamie couldn't get it out of her head. "Write anything about my family, and you're going to wish that getting fired was the only thing I could do to you."

Jamie put her hands up in the air, shock running through her. "I don't do that."

With one last hardened look, Siena turned away and strode over to where Jessie helped Harley with getting her backpack on. "Time to get going, Harley."

Jamie tuned out as the adrenaline drained from her. What the hell was the world playing at? Finally alone with Jessie, she could let her guard down a bit.

"Well, this better not appear on your blog." Jessie stepped up beside Jamie and crossed her arms over her chest. "Especially after the disaster of your last post."

"Seriously?" All the fury Jamie had built inside that hadn't been given a release burst from her mouth before she could stop it. "Couldn't you ever be on my side? Just this once?"

"Wow." Jessie lifted her hands up, palms facing Jamie as she took a step back. "That's not fair."

For a moment, Jamie stared silently into her sister's eyes. Just because they were twins didn't mean they got along all the time. Sometimes Jamie wondered if it wasn't worse than being normal siblings.

"Sorry," she muttered. "It sucks always being the evil twin."

"You aren't evil, Jamie." Jessie put her arm around her sister's shoulders. "You just approach things differently, and I'm just lucky my way has parental approval."

Jamie scoffed but kept her thoughts out of her mouth.

"Come on." Jessie jerked her head toward the door. "Let's get a coffee, and you can tell me all about what happened. Did you say you're being fired?"

"Most likely." Jamie nodded and let Jessie walk her out of the classroom. "Especially after today."

"Well, I think that coffee just upgraded to getting drunk."

Jamie laughed and leaned into Jessie.

Maybe being twins wasn't always a bad thing.

nine

"All right, but if you have tequila, I'm out." Tori chuckled and brushed a kiss on Siena's cheek as she opened the door.

"I'm never living that down, am I?"

"It wasn't just you." Tori patted Siena's back as she walked past, shutting the door behind them.

"Where's Miranda and Rebel?" Siena asked as she sat down at the kitchen table.

"They're over at Miranda's parents. Tierney and Miranda are trying to spend more time with them. Want wine?"

Siena laughed and nodded. What she actually wanted was something much stronger, but she also needed as clear a head as she could muster.

After a call to Tori, Siena had rung Aili. She'd called in a favor once Harley had fallen asleep. Aili would have preferred to have spent time with her goddaughter awake, but she was consoled with a home cooked meal and Siena owing her a favor.

"All right." Tori slid one glass in front of Siena as she slipped into the chair opposite, her own still in her hand. "So spill. What's going on?"

"Where the hell do I start?"

"At the beginning." Tori smiled, and Siena remembered how easy it was to let Tori be the person in her life to give her Harley. There wasn't judgement or condescension, just open goodness that radiated.

"Some people like to be wined and dined, I like to be faji-ta'd and margarita'd."

"What?" Tori sat back, eyes blinking in confusion.

Siena laughed. "That's what Jamie said to me the first time I met her in person."

"Jamie?" Tori raised an eyebrow in suspicion. "And if this involved margaritas which means tequila, then I think I know how this turned out."

Fuck, her reputation really did precede her, didn't it? Siena's cheeks burned as she went into the complications and coincidences that had happened since she heard that god-awful pick-up line.

Tori sipped her wine. "Well, I have to admit. That's an interesting situation you've gotten yourself into."

"So," Siena prodded. "Do I go ahead with this meeting tomorrow or not?"

"First…" Tori put the glass down carefully on the tabletop. This wasn't going to be something Siena liked, she knew that much. "I need to ask some questions. Is that okay?"

"Yes." Siena sighed. "It's why I'm here. You've always been better at the life stuff. I mean look at you. You've not only made your business into a booming success, but you made your own dreams come true, despite the opposition you got from everyone—including me."

"It's just about being brave, Siena. You know that. But back on topic… I can't help wondering why this woman has gotten under your skin so much."

"Of course, she's gotten under my skin. She writes trash that makes my life harder. And then just conveniently finds me in a bar and picks me up? And then her twin sister is teaching Harley?"

"It's a load of coincidences, I get that. But you aren't exactly known for your one-night stands."

"So?" Siena's defenses rose up, and she grasped for them.

"Well, there was obviously something about her that pulled you to her. Beyond the history in work lives that you didn't even know you shared at that time."

"Tequila! You said it." Siena crossed her arms and glared at the wine on the table. Tequila would be nice right about now.

"Be truthful—and serious—right now. You need to hear it from yourself more than I do."

Siena winced. She hated and loved when Tori called her out like that. "Fine. She's beautiful and charming. No doubt it's how she gets information she shouldn't have access to and why she's so damn good at her job."

"Oh, now it's information?" Tori picked up her wine glass and brought it to her lips. It didn't fool Siena, who still saw the smile around the rim of the glass.

"What do you mean?"

"First you called it trash, now it's information." Tori waved her hand out in front of her, as if that would be enough of an explanation to get them to where they were going.

Siena groaned. Trust Tori to pick up on that.

"Fine. I haven't found a lot of what she writes to be complete bullshit. And the stuff that is bullshit is always framed as questions or things she's wondering. But she's fucking with people's lives. They have a right to their privacy—celebrity or not."

"I know." Tori nodded in agreement. "So despite the history and her sister teaching Harley, which by the way—I love Ms. K. She's wonderful. And no wonder Jamie is getting under your skin if they really are identical."

"Only in looks," Siena added, far too quickly. She gulped at her drink as though that would stop Tori from noticing.

"Yes." Tori chuckled. Of course, she noticed. "So despite these things. Why wouldn't you go to the meeting tomorrow? Wouldn't it be better to have someone like that on your side instead of always fighting against them?"

"Not sure she has a side to get on, at least not one I could trust." Siena tossed up the idea.

"Trust is just another brand of bravery."

"Why did I come here again?" Siena smiled so Tori knew she was joking—or at least half joking.

"Just think about it, Siena. Having someone in the press on your side might come in handy in the long run. Especially if you're telling me you haven't read anything that was entirely bullshit."

"No." She hated this truth. It would be so much easier if Jamie had spouted unfounded shit. "I haven't found any outright lies, but she uses her platform to plant the seeds."

"Okay, sure." Tori nodded. "But what if you gave her the right seeds to plant?"

"What?"

"Surely there's something you could offer her?" Tori raised her eyebrows not subtly leading Siena down the path she obviously assumed made sense.

"No." Siena shook her head. It might make sense on the outside, but there were so many more dynamics than people realized. "Giving her access to me is one thing. I'm not giving her access to Bunny and Piper."

"Wouldn't it be a positive thing to have the person who's written so much bad speculation be the one to actually write a story of truth?"

"You're assuming she can be trusted."

"And you're assuming she can't."

Siena chuckled and shook her head as she looked down into the depths of her half-gone drink.

"What's so amusing?" Tori asked, her lips in a soft smile though confusion filled her eyes.

"Just thinking no matter how much things change, I'm glad that some things remain the same."

"Us bickering is a good thing that's remained?"

"No. The fact we can have different opinions and not turn them into a screaming match."

"I like that, too." Tori smiled and sipped from her glass.

The silence was comforting until Tori brought the discomfort right to Siena's face.

"So you are attracted to her still," Tori said.

"Shouldn't that be a question?" Siena wasn't ready to admit that openly to anyone, not even herself yet.

"Definitely not." Tori laughed. "So what do you plan to do about it?"

"I guess I'll go tomorrow. Get this interview over with."

"Not what I asked. And you know it."

"Of course it is." Siena smirked and breathed a sigh of relief as Tori rolled her eyes but let the conversation go. They talked a little longer, and by the time Siena left, she felt a little lighter. Not exactly better, but at least decided.

———

Sleep teased Siena all night. It never stayed long enough. She would wake again an hour or so after finally drifting off, feelings of control slipping away from her.

Tori had been right. Again.

With all the bad press Jamie had given to Bunny and Piper over the years, she would be the only one who could truly make a dent in any of those questions she had posed article after article.

It took Siena twice as long as normal to get ready. She changed out of her black pin-striped pencil suit and decided on loose black pants, a long-sleeved shirt, and a vest. She kept debating on whether or not to take a jacket. Uncharacteristically running a little late, she grabbed the jacket off the hanger before she raced out of her front door. Well, she was late for her liking. She heard her mother's voice in her head. *If you aren't ten minutes early, then you might as well be late.*

The cozy cafe she had chosen was only a few blocks away from her place. Close enough for her to feel as though they were meeting on her own turf. But far enough away that it wasn't Siena's locale. And Jamie wouldn't know precisely where she lived. The weather outside already promised to be a drizzly, bitter affair, which meant that winter would soon be upon them.

Siena looked down at her outfit and worried her bottom lip. Since when had she ever felt so concerned about what she wore when meeting the press? She scoffed at the thought as a rideshare pulled up. After getting inside, she settled into the back. Her mind wandered without her permission.

She had never willingly met with any sleazy journalist before. The only time she'd encountered them, it'd been unexpectedly at events where she had directed security to get her clients through safely. She'd met with real journalists all the time, but Siena wouldn't classify Jamie as one of them.

Siena loved her job. There was a thrill in it. A rush she lived for. But it had never been her desire to be the face of anything.

Scoffing, she noticed the driver flicking his eyes to the rearview mirror and checking on her. She met his gaze and gave a small smile, cheeks warming with embarrassment. It always seemed such a private space in the back of a cab, too easy to slip into alone mode, when in reality you were still in public.

As far as she knew, her face had never been publicly circulated with her name. There were photos of her in the background. Not many but a few. But whatever deity, if any, that looked after the entertainment industry had found her worthy of remaining unrecognizable.

She mulled over this fact as the driver pulled up two shops away from the cafe. Siena could have kissed the grizzled man for not pushing for small talk as nerves already tingled beneath her skin. When Siena had started managing, she had been able to project confidence in public with an ease that had been lacking lately. She never struggled to remain professional or polite, but it didn't fill her with the same excitement or energy it once had.

Not like the joy she got when helping a new artist get their foot further into their dreams. She enjoyed working one-on-one with her clients, even the more challenging ones. At least they helped her appreciate other clients. Especially the ones who had turned from client-only to also friends—like Bunny and Piper, and Siena sensed that was going to be no truer than this winter. Bunny was running Piper into the ground, and they were both exhausted and needed a really good break.

Stepping up to the door, Siena knew she had to force down the butterflies in her stomach and smother the tingling anticipation of sitting down with Jamie again. This wasn't about her and Jamie.

She would put on her business face, and she would be the hard-ass manager she had become known as. They may not recognize her face, but she would be stupid to think many journalists in this town, or in any media reporting, wouldn't recognize her name. Years and sacrifices, sweat and tears had gone into this outcome.

The bell above the door tingled as she pushed it open and stepped inside.

Like hell she would allow a moment of weakness to undo

all that she had worked for. No matter how screwed up and complicated the moment was turning out to be.

The warmth of the cafe washed over her, and she took in a deep breath to center and settle herself. Her stomach grumbled as warm sugar and cinnamon from the pastry case joined the comforting aroma of coffee. She gave herself to the count of ten to indulge in the warm hug of the place before coming back to reality. Hopefully this meeting wouldn't make it impossible for her to return and enjoy the ambience again.

When she opened her eyes, her manager mask was firmly fixed in place once more. This was a business meeting. And it had been more years than she cared to count since a business meeting had made her nervous. She wasn't going to let this one change that record for her.

She spotted Jamie sitting with her back to the corner at a small round table that looked far too intimate to be for a business meeting. Despite her suddenly dry mouth and her need to lick her lips, Siena pushed her shoulders back and lifted her chin ever so slightly. Each step sent a shock ricocheting up her legs, making her body tremble and heat pool between her thighs.

Business meeting! she reminded herself.

Though she couldn't deny it would be a lot easier to focus on that point if Jamie didn't look so deliciously sinful in that knitted green dress that rode up on her thick and squeezable thighs. Jamie stood as Siena approached.

Siena bit back the groan that threatened to rumble up her throat.

Why was this woman so damn sexy? And why couldn't Siena see past that? She had to focus on the post that had made her look like a sleazy villain manager from the bad old days.

Of course, it didn't help that as she drew closer it became harder for her to keep her eyes from those delicious tits and remember the taste of this delectable woman on the tip of her tongue.

"Siena, I honestly wasn't sure if you would show." Jamie smiled nervously, and Siena thought she might die on the spot.

The sex had been amazing. Jamie had been so present, reacting physically and verbally at every touch and stroke Siena made as she explored her body.

Why had the sex been so good, especially when Siena hadn't even taken her clothes off? Hadn't even been touched the way she craved?

"I'm a professional, Jamie. And this is a business meeting." Despite the crisp tone she used, Siena noticed the tiniest of smiles pulling up the corners of Jamie's lips.

She wanted to kiss that smile into oblivion.

No, she didn't.

She wanted this meeting over with and wanted to get something positive out of the entire situation. Some good press for Bunny and Piper would never go astray.

Siena simply hoped she could keep her thoughts on track and that she wasn't putting her faith in the wrong person.

ten

Jamie's legs jiggled under the table as she sat, hands wrapped around the now cold coffee mug. She'd shown up early, which in hindsight seemed rather masochistic on her part.

After the encounter at the school, she had little faith in Siena showing up for their planned meeting. All morning, she had expected a phone call from her receptionist, telling her that Ms. Frazee would have to cancel their meeting indefinitely.

And yet, here she sat early for a meeting that might not even happen.

"Anything else I can help you with?" The waitress smiled, the curve of her lips an interesting flirtation. But Jamie didn't react in kind.

"No, thanks." She smiled, but she didn't meet the waitress's eyes or lean forward to use her best assets for the cause.

"Okay, well. If you need something, just give me a wave."

"Absolutely." The interaction was false, but one she had engaged in many times over the years.

This time it didn't boost her up or flatter her. She knew waitresses flirted for tips—it's what she'd done before she found the job at the paper. She shuddered at the idea of having to go back to being a waitress. If anyone would even hire her now.

No wonder the interaction didn't hit the same as usual. Her livelihood currently rested in the hands of a woman she barely knew, except by reputation. But she knew what her hands and mouth felt like on her skin and inside of her.

"Damn it," Jamie muttered as she crossed her legs under the table, not only stopping the jiggling motion but trying her best to minimize the pressure that was building between her thighs. She could already feel her own wetness and ached to relieve the tension before having to deal with this meeting.

Quickly, she leaned down and grabbed her phone from her bag and checked the time. She had five minutes. It wasn't like she regularly masturbated in a public bathroom, but the cafe had their own stalls, and she needed as little pressure between her legs as possible. And this was just at the memory of Siena's touch—what the hell was she going to be like when the woman actually showed up?

If she showed up…

As if summoned by her thoughts, Jamie felt eyes on her. More specifically, eyes on her cleavage as she moved back up into her seat proper.

"Oh Jesus, Mary, and Joseph," Jamie whispered.

Was Siena seriously wearing a vest?

Fuck!

Jamie jumped to her feet as Siena drew closer, trying to ease some of the discomfort that sitting had caused against her swelling clit.

"Siena, I honestly wasn't sure if you would show," Jamie rushed out the moment Siena was close enough for the words to be considered a private conversation.

"I'm a professional, Jamie, and this is a business meeting." Siena's words were crisp and to the point. She actually sounded exactly how Jamie would have imagined the famous

Siena Frazee to sound. Before she'd eaten out Jamie's pussy, that is.

"I didn't mean to imply anything else. But the situation is quite… unusual."

"Yes, it is." Siena pointedly looked at the chair and then back up to Jamie. "Are we going to sit or have the meeting standing up?"

"Sit," Jamie's voice choked out. She forced a small cough to clear her throat and tried again. "Please, take a seat."

Siena nodded and slid into the chair with ease.

They waited for the waitress to return. Jamie noted that she didn't bother flirting with Siena. Relief washed over her at knowing the waitress didn't flirt with everyone. It should have given her a confidence boost. Not relief.

Because the relief wasn't about the waitress.

No! That couldn't be right. What could she possibly be relieved about then?

Jamie's breath hitched for a moment as she watched their interaction. She hadn't even noticed the waitress's dimples earlier. She had always been a sucker for dimples. But even now, noting their attraction, she still felt nothing toward the waitress.

She turned to watch Siena finish her order.

Fuck, no.

A mix of emotions she refused to analyze swirled in her chest.

Nope.

This wasn't happening.

"Are you having another coffee?" The waitress turned that flirty full-beamed smile back to Jamie.

Not a single flutter washed over her. It was just the stress of it all. Of course it was. And Siena caused a reaction because three orgasms in an hour would do that to a woman.

"I'll have another coffee, thanks."

"Of course, cutie."

Jamie felt her cheeks flush, and from the corner of her eye, she saw Siena's amused smirk and raised eyebrows.

"Now that *that* charming display of hormones is over, we need to get down to business."

"What?" Very articulate, Jamie mentally scolded herself.

"Business. I believe we have an interview to organize?"

"Organize?" For God's sake, she needed to up her game before Siena wrote her off as a moron. "I was under the impression this would be the interview."

"I believe a change of circumstances is in order."

"Seriously?" Jamie knew she should bite her tongue, hold back her frustration and annoyance, but being around Siena made that impossible. It had from the very moment she'd approached her in the tapas bar on that fateful night. Not that she could genuinely find herself regretting it.

"It'll be in the best interest of all involved. "

"Except for me!" Jamie sounded like a petulant child, and she knew it. But she'd had enough of this crap. Living on tenterhooks for days had already done a number on her.

"Including you."

"Yeah, right." At least Jamie found herself able to relax as she leaned back in her chair and the waitress returned with their drinks.

"Thank you." Siena smiled and gave the waitress a nod. The waitress looked startled for a moment before returning the smile.

"Look." Jamie sat forward again as she added sugar to her coffee. "I don't even like this job, but I need it. Thanks to you and your friends staging a harassment tag team on my boss, I'm going to lose it if I don't get this interview with you."

"You don't like your job?" Siena looked so startled by the confession that Jamie burst out laughing before she could stop herself.

"You look like this is a strange thing."

"It is."

"Maybe for you." Jamie stirred her coffee, unable to completely process the idea that someone could love the job they were actually getting paid to do. "But most people in my world get paid to do jobs they don't like because bills have to be paid and passions don't pay the rent."

"And writing a trashy celeb column is your passion?" Siena sneered.

"It's not." The heat rose up Jamie's neck and covered her face. She would look like a beet, but she no longer cared. How dare this woman sneer at her? Just because she'd given her mind-blowing sex didn't mean she knew Jamie. Not at all. That comment made that perfectly clear.

"Then what's your passion?"

"My blog isn't a trashy celeb column." Jamie's words were hard, and she threw them out like javelins. She noted Siena's sharp jerk back in her seat, but she didn't care.

Okay, she cared. She cared more than she wanted to and that was an entirely different problem all together. One that was pissing her off even as she refused to examine it.

"Have you even bothered to read any of my blogs all the way through? Or did you just read the parts that affected you?" Damn it, why did she have to get all defensive now?

Siena's stern face fell away, and for a split second, Jamie saw the woman she had picked up at the tapas bar. But just as quickly, she vanished again. The same feeling of abandonment washed over Jamie as it had when she had stepped out of the shower.

Jamie didn't wait for Siena to verbally respond. The look was enough for her to go off of. "Maybe if you did, you wouldn't be so quick to call it trash."

The silence spoke volumes as Jamie slumped in her chair, sipping her coffee.

"What is it you're actually passionate about then?" Siena ever-so-slowly lifted her coffee mug to her lips, those perfectly shaped lips that could—nope. Jamie had to focus.

"About the power of role models. About having someone who's like you, someone who's brave and in the spotlight when the rest of the world makes you feel so very alone."

Siena nodded, a small sad smile on her face. She set her mug down, and the silence between them was deafening. Jamie just needed her to speak with that fire and rage she'd witnessed in the classroom. Not this calm, cool, and aloof professional that she was already despising. "I think you'll like my alternative plan to interviewing me."

Jamie looked up, eyes narrowed, but didn't say anything. She wouldn't beg. She wouldn't ask. If Siena wanted to tell her, she would have to do it on her own.

"What if I let you have an exclusive interview with Bunny and Piper?"

Jamie instantly regretted taking the mouthful of coffee as it sprayed out of her mouth, and she choked on the dislodged liquid. As the coughing fit ended, she opened her mouth to apologize until the sound of soft laughter reached her ears. She looked up and saw Siena, *her Siena*, smiling back.

When Siena caught her gaze, she quickly covered her mouth with those long slender fingers.

"Oh God, I'm so sorry. I didn't mean for that to happen."

"But it felt a little good after my blog post about managers?" Jamie smiled, letting Siena know that it wasn't out of anger or defense that she brought this up. Jamie couldn't deny her own surprise at bringing up the elephant in the room.

"Maybe a little bit." Siena looked sheepish, and Jamie wanted to kiss those lips.

No, she did not. She did. But she couldn't.

This was business, and Siena had made that more than clear the moment she'd stepped through the door. She didn't realize she had a smile on her face while Siena helped her clean up the mess from her coughing fit, enjoying the comfortable silence of the act until she sat back down and noticed Siena examining her with an expression she hadn't seen before.

"What?" She asked as her smile turned into something more self-conscious.

"Nothing." Siena shook her head and flicked her eyes away.

But there was no denying the coloring that brushed her cheeks.

Jamie would make it easier on Siena. After all, this was for the sake of her job. A job she didn't even like.

But I do like having somewhere to sleep and food to eat. She hushed the contentious voice in her head and pushed on.

"Why would you give me an exclusive interview with your top clients?" Jamie's fingers shook slightly while she asked. Was she looking a gift horse in the mouth? Would Siena take the offer back? She wanted to say yes, but it didn't make any sense to her.

"Because," Siena paused as though weighing which words to use. "Despite the shitstorms you've created for me when you pose questions about their lives, you've never directly said something that you couldn't prove."

Jamie's mouth might have fallen open. She couldn't be sure. Her entire face felt numb from Siena's words.

It was true. She would never knowingly publish a lie. Posing theories was one thing. And theories she knew were true on good authority but didn't have actual proof of was the line she had been determined not to cross.

Jamie wasn't stupid. She knew people took from her blog what they wanted, knowing that the question wouldn't be posed if there weren't some genuine possibility of it being the truth. And it was a thin line at times. But despite what everyone thought, and her own desire to get her name out in the world, she did have some semblance of integrity.

"Are you interested in the interview?" Siena's brows were knitted together, concern flashing across those dark pools Jamie would happily get lost in.

Jamie shook her head to get rid of the idea.

"You aren't interested?" The concern turned quickly into anger.

"Oh yes! No." Jamie never got this flustered. The Siena effect had her in a world of confusion. "I would love to interview them."

"Okay?" Weariness crossed Siena's eyes, and Jamie wondered how anyone could write about the cold businesslike manner of this manager.

"I'm just blown away."

"There will be conditions about the interview. But you'll get an exclusive two-on-one with Bunny and Piper once I approve the questions you intend to ask. And those will be the *only* questions you're allowed to ask."

"Approve the questions?" Jamie's heart sank. "So this'll be more like a press conference in the form of an interview?"

"No." Siena's mask, the one that was all cold and businesslike, had returned, and Jamie's chest ached with longing to find the real Siena beneath once more.

"But you aren't going to let me ask anything about their private lives, are you?"

"The focus will be on their music."

Jamie nodded.

"Do you still want the interview?"

"Yes."

"Send through the questions, and I'll be in touch shortly to go through them." Siena moved her coffee to the corner of the table, the liquid sloshing toward the top rim. Jamie was entranced for a brief second, her brain working quickly to try and catch up with everything that had just happened.

"Fine." Jamie wanted to say no. But she didn't want to lose her job.

No.

She didn't want to never see this woman again.

Damn it. So much for a no-strings-attached one-night stand.

"Just call me Pinocchio," she muttered to herself as she watched Siena saunter out of the cafe.

She was in trouble.

And she wasn't talking about her job.

eleven

Siena blew out a puff of air, stirring strands of loose hair that had fallen across her face during the day. Sitting back in her chair, she rolled her neck in slow circles hoping to hear that pop followed by the release of at least one of the multitude of knots the day had given her.

What she really needed was a deep-tissue massage. The lack of popping from her neck confirmed this fact.

The light on her intercom system lit up, and she pressed it automatically.

"Siena, your five o'clock will be here in ten minutes. Did you need anything?"

"Coffee, please." She let her finger slide from the button and lifted both hands to her head. She rubbed small circles around her temples.

After a moment, she shook out her fingers, sat up and rolled her shoulders back. Clicking into her calendar, her movements stopped as she stared at the name.

"Of course," she muttered and closed her eyes.

Only one word was written in her five o'clock appointment.

Jamie.

"Your coffee." Paula handed over the mug of steaming coffee, the scent wafting in Siena's direction putting her instantly at ease.

"What would I do without you?" Siena asked with a grin.

"Starve and forget to go home." The small smile that pulled up the corner of Paula's lips made Siena laugh.

"Most likely."

With a smile, she left, and the door clicked with a popping sound similar to the one Siena had failed to achieve through her earlier neck roll.

Time ticked down and one minute before five, the intercom chirped this time with clipped words.

"Your five o'clock appointment has arrived."

"Please let her in," Siena replied, her finger holding the button down a little too hard, turning the tip of her fingers white.

The door opened, and for a moment, Siena and Jamie simply stared at each other. Siena wanted to muster the same professionalism she had managed to enter their previous meeting with, but the sight of Jamie framed in her open door was a sight not even her late-night imagination could have captured.

Not that she had been having late night imaginations, especially about Jamie. Nope, not at all.

"Good evening." Jamie finally broke the string that held them both in place and stepped into the office properly. She closed the door behind her, the spell finally broken.

Siena was on her feet and professionalism took over from the arousal that had already warmed up her lower belly.

"Thank you for coming here for this meeting, Jamie." Siena stepped out from behind her desk and waved a hand over to the small meeting area in her office. She barely refrained from rolling her eyes as she felt like some kind of game show host with the swing of her hand. Really, Jamie Kettlehouse had been nothing but a pain in her ass since her blog posts had been brought to her attention years ago. There was no need for Siena to feel like a schoolgirl.

"Please take a seat. Would you like coffee or something to eat?"

"Ha." Jamie chuckled as she sauntered over to the low couches. She sat on one as she shook her head. "No, thanks. Your ever so kind receptionist offered as much as well." The stress Jamie placed on the word kind told Siena all she needed to know about the frosty reception Jamie must have been given.

"Fine. Then let's get into this." Siena pulled the pieces of paper from the printer she passed on her way to sit on the couch opposite Jamie.

"Can we find a time for the interview with Bunny and Piper first? My editor is on my ass about nailing it down."

"Unfortunately, no." Siena shook her head, the sincerity of her words lacking even to her own ears. "These questions are entirely unacceptable."

"Excuse me?" The casual air around Jamie sparked as she shuffled forward on the couch, perching on the front, her shoulders squaring as though preparing for a fight.

"These questions have absolutely nothing to do with either of their professional work."

"So asking about how they first started playing together…" The innuendos dripped from Jamie's lips, and Siena's stomach tightened, "…has nothing to do with their careers?"

"Fine, but ninety-percent of these questions are absolutely ridiculous and not at all what either of them will answer." Siena's face morphed into something else entirely, and she knew she was putting on a cold, hard front. They both probably needed it there.

"Because they don't want to, or you don't want them to?"

"Ms. Kettlehouse," Siena reminded herself of who she was dealing with, "your reputation of coming to outrageous conclusions continues I see."

"It's entertaining how those with secrets always jump to assuming my conclusions are outrageous." Jamie squared her shoulders, her face hardening at the accusation.

"Because they are. You have no proof, and no credible facts to point anyone in the direction of your theories."

"If you bothered to look, you would find all of my information there." Jamie hissed.

Taking a deep breath, Siena rubbed circles once more over her temples. She was going to have a headache by the time this ended, wasn't she?

She needed to reel this conversation back in to where she could control it. "We're getting off of the point."

"And what is the point?" Jamie asked. Siena was certain it was supposed to come out defensive, but there was a quiet sadness in the words.

"You need to come up with different questions—interesting questions. They'll answer anything about their careers. They won't answer the trash column questions you've sent through." Siena was going to hold to that. It wasn't just what she knew Bunny and Piper would actually answer, and it was going to be a pain in the ass to convince them to meet with Jamie to begin with, but that was a problem for future Siena. Right now, she just needed to get Jamie to ask good and reasonable questions.

"They aren't trash column questions." Jamie's voice rose as she leaned farther forward, as if she could reach out and touch Siena and make her point heard all the more.

Siena shuffled herself forward on her own side and put the papers she was still holding on the table between them—well, threw might have been a more accurate description. They stopped at the edge of the table where Jamie immediately snapped them up. She scanned the colored ink that took her one page of questions and turned them into four pages with Siena's comments and snarky rebuttals. There were also strong hints and downright suggestions about questions that would actually work at different points.

"Are you kidding me?" Jamie looked up, her eyes narrowed, and her top lip quivering into a small scowl.

Despite Siena's determination to remain professional, she had to bite the inside of her cheeks to stop herself from laughing. Not only did Jamie's feistiness cause a slight ache between her thighs, but her twitching top lip gave her the image of Elvis in his heyday.

"Take the suggestions, Jamie."

"They aren't suggestions. They're controlling information."

"They're appropriate questions, and they're focusing on what all you trash columnists seem to forget about."

"For fuck's sake." Jamie was now so far forward that her generous ass barely remained on the edge of the couch. She leaned forward, her fingertips whitened as they pressed down hard on the coffee table between her and Siena. "I know how to do my job."

"Ha." Siena scooted herself as far forward on her own couch as Jamie was on hers and placed flat hands on the table. "I hardly think so. Considering you doing your job is why you're in this precarious position in the first place."

She hadn't meant to drop her eyes to the delicious cleavage Jamie now had on display in front of her, but as the word *precarious* slipped from her mouth, her eyes did what they wanted. The tightness in Siena's lower stomach increased and the throb turned into a wetness on her underwear.

Damn it.

This was the exact fire that had stirred when Jamie had approached her, confident and cocky in her swagger in the middle of the tapas bar.

She couldn't think about that. Her body was already going too far down that line of reaction.

"Precarious positions are exactly what gets me off, and why I do this job." Jamie licked her lips and Siena shivered a little as Jamie's eyes dropped to Siena's lips, lingered way too long, and moved back up again.

Those beautiful blue eyes had turned from a summer sky into a storm-filled sea before Siena registered exactly what her body had in mind. Her breath was loud, her chest moving more rapidly as she leaned further toward Jamie.

"You do this job to piss people off," Siena lobbed in her direction, needing to say something, anything to keep Jamie right where she was—or better yet, move her closer.

"No." Jamie moved closer, and Siena's breath shuddered out between her slightly opened lips. "I do this job because the truth is worth searching for."

"The truth isn't always what it looks like. The truth is even celebrities deserve to have their lives kept private if they wish."

"Are you saying there's something that is being kept private?" Jamie's eyes lit up like she'd hit the jackpot.

"Of course. No one wants their full lives on display. This isn't *The Truman Show*."

"But what secrets are you helping to hide?"

"You never give up do you?" Siena scoffed. For a moment, her self-control tried to kick back in, but then Jamie's eyes sparkled and one side of her mouth lifted into a smirk.

A small groan rumbled its way up Siena's throat and escaped her mouth before she could stop it. A responding catch of breath from Jamie thrilled and tightened the last remaining loose muscles in Siena's body.

The sound of Jamie's breathing joined Siena's near panting in the otherwise silent office.

The warm touch of Jamie's breath caressed her lips. Memories of the soft touch turned hungry and eager flashed through Siena's mind. Her mouth opened, to say something or to cuss, Siena wasn't entirely sure. She never got the chance to do anything more when a loud buzz drowned out the sound of their panting.

"Ms. Frazee." Paula's voice was almost as effective as a bucket of ice water thrown over the pair.

Siena's eyes widened as she realized how close she was to Jamie. She could see the fine lines and details of Jamie's eyes and the dark arousal that sparkled within them.

"Fuck," she muttered under her breath as she pushed with her wrists against the table and shoved her body back deep into the couch she'd abandoned for the temptation of blonde hair, blue eyes, and the memory of the most addictive taste on her tongue.

"Would you and your *guest*"—the sneer at the word gave no doubt as to Paula's opinion of Jamie. Not that there had been any doubt up until this moment. The tinny sound of the voice continued to fill the room—"like something to drink or eat?"

Jamie chuckled as she sat back down on her own couch. She sat down with a calm that Siena usually prided herself on. Siena pushed the sensation of heat in her cheeks to the back of her mind as she stood back up and paced to her desk.

"No, thank you." Her voice was a rasp that caused another faint chuckle from behind her. "We're just finishing up."

She removed her finger from the intercom button and turned slowly around, her ass pressed as hard into the edge of her desk as possible.

"We are?" Jamie's eyebrows furrowed as she stood up.

"Yes." Siena nodded, forcing her legs to take her weight. She pushed her shoulders back and ignored the wet pulsing of her clit. "We're definitely done."

"An interview time?" Jamie asked, though little hope showed in her face.

"Take the notes, go through them. And when you come

back with questions I can actually present to Bunny and Piper, then we can schedule a time."

"Do they even know?" Jamie asked, looking at Siena from the tops of her eyes, her chin down and almost touching her chest.

Damn. This woman was going to be the death of her if she didn't get herself under control.

"My clients know everything they need to that concerns them. Especially in relation to media opportunities."

"Wow." Jamie's laugh bordered on a sneering scoff. "You really can play this diplomatic game better than any agent I've ever…come up against."

The pause in Jamie's words made another groan rumble its way up Siena's throat. This time however, she managed to bite back the sound before it escaped.

"I'm good at my job." Siena gave her own half smile back. "Isn't that why you *came* to me?"

Two could play this game. And while Siena had already begun to scold herself for the unprofessional near kiss, she wasn't above making sure Jamie left as uncomfortably aroused as she was.

"Hmmm." Jamie's smile was all flirt and amusement. She snatched up the papers and fluttered them lightly in the air. "Challenge accepted."

"Fantastic." Siena barely got the word out.

"Thank you for a very enlightening meeting, Ms. Frazee." Jamie made a slow walk to the door. She moved with an obvious swing to her hips, and Siena's eyes followed each movement. She ached to get her hands on that gorgeous ass once more.

"You'll be hearing from me soon," Jamie said as she opened the door.

Framed behind Jamie stood Paula, standing tall with her

hands planted on her hips. It was once again as sobering as her voice had been when it filled Siena's office earlier.

"I look forward to seeing what you come up with in response to my feedback."

With a small laugh, Jamie turned away again. "Make sure you think about what I said, Siena. Just like I'll think about what'll happen the next time I come against you."

That phrasing had to have been intentional. Jamie wasn't an idiot when it came to words. And they both knew that.

Siena's eyes were drawn to the woman's amazing curves until Paula blocked her view by stepping into her line of sight and filling the door frame.

"Is everything all right, Ms. Frazee?"

Siena blinked and her mind whirled. But she was, after all, one of the best in her field. If she had been able to fake her emotions during her divorce, she could damn well keep her professional mask in place despite the throbbing between her legs and the warmth that remained in her cheeks.

"Absolutely." Siena nodded, her professional mask easily slipping back into place. "Please escort Ms. Kettlehouse out of the office. I'll be heading home in a moment."

"So early?" It was a thrill to see that Siena could still shock her rarely rattled receptionist.

"Yes." Siena needed to leave as soon as possible. "Take some time to enjoy the early night, and I'll see you tomorrow."

Siena returned to her desk. As she sat, biting her lower lip to hold back the groan the movement of sitting had caused, her door had already been closed, without another word or sound. The temptation to take care of her ache right then and there teased at the edge of Siena's mind. But being caught in such a state had her quickly tidying her desk and shutting down her computer instead.

As she did, her eyes flicked over to the meeting area and the image of laying Jamie out on the coffee table and taking her every way her mind and body could imagine washed over her.

Her movements of tidying up quickened, and she wondered if she would manage to make it home before her fingers found their way to her need and relieved her of the pressure.

twelve

"Kettlehouse!" Her boss screeched out her name as he stood at his open office door.

"For fuck's sake," Jamie muttered before she stood up from her desk and started yet another walk of shame toward the office.

She had been on a high since her rather interesting meeting with Siena last night, but the reality of not getting any further with the interview had hit the moment she stepped into the office.

The office pariah—she even considered ordering herself a joke name block with the title on it for her desk. Which of course wasn't hers because all the desks were hotspot desks since they never wanted anyone at the paper to forget they were replaceable in a moment.

She used to love the thrill of being one shit story away from getting bumped down to a shittier shift. But now, it did more to piss her off than to hype her up.

And all because of a damn blog post that she had every right to publish and share with the world. Damn Siena and her manager horde. Siena still hadn't apologized, or even acknowledged just how much she was fucking with Jamie's livelihood. And while that pissed her off, Jamie couldn't help but be impressed by the woman's ability and power.

She supposed she deserved it, at least a little bit. But Siena deserved to be used as the example of shitty managers as well. Not because she was a shitty manager, but because Jamie was still too damn raw about being fucked and left.

She closed the door behind her before her boss could tell her to. He sat behind his desk, flicking through papers as though her presence was nothing more than a mosquito buzzing around annoying and distracting him from his real work.

"You got a date for the interview?"

"Um, not exactly."

"What does that mean? Not exactly?" He looked up, the pretense of more important work forgotten about for the moment.

"She's pushing back on questions. I'll get the date soon."

"Make it sooner." He held up a stack of messages. To be fair, they were a lot smaller than last time. "I'm sick of these bastards. They're freaking rottweilers with a bone."

"I'm working on it."

"You're on thin ice, Kettlehouse. Get a date soon or get ready for graveyard shift." He looked up again. "If you're lucky."

"Sure." Jamie forced the word out over the instant lump in her throat. With a nod, she turned and returned to the door.

"Close it behind you when you leave."

It was an odd request.

The door was never normally closed unless he was in there screaming at someone for fucking up. As she pulled it closed, she caught a glimpse of him lifting his phone. Must be something unusual because he often delighted himself in letting his editors overhear conversations with big names, or his particular method of dealing with assholes who threatened to take him or the paper to court.

Jamie shrugged as she headed back to her desk.

It wasn't as though she actually cared. The only reason losing this job would suck was the bills that needed to be paid. And being blackballed at yet another news outlet.

But the blog had started taking a hit as well.

The comments section had to be more closely monitored as the controversy of the topic turned into the controversy over Jamie herself. She had a feeling she knew how her job being at risk had found its way into the comments, but Siena didn't really seem like that kind of person. And Jamie had always prided herself on being able to read people.

Of course, she hadn't read that Siena would be the kind to fuck and run but that was before everything got complicated and Jamie had been dragged into the drama she loved to hide behind her byline from.

At her desk, she nodded and did what she had to do. It would have been nice if she had been able to successfully convince herself that she hated having to contact the woman again. But the flutter in her stomach belied any such tales.

Jamie: I sent over some more questions. I'd like to pin down…

Jamie looked at the words, smirked, and tried again

Jamie: Siena, the questions have been sent through. Please contact me with potential times for an interview with Bunny and Piper.

She was tempted to put an *x* at the end, but after typing and deleting it twice, she kept it professional and hit the send button instead. It was far too easy to mess with Siena, but at this rate, it was much better for her livelihood to do that without any kind of paper trail.

Moments later, the delivered message turned into a read message. No bubbles appeared on her phone, and she scolded herself for the disappointment that washed over her.

With an effort, she placed the phone face down on her desk and got back to her email on the computer. The day dragged with her checking her phone far too often and growing more despondent with each time the message remained unanswered.

"Heading downstairs, want anything?" Jamie stood and asked Scott.

He looked up at her, startled. Surely it hadn't been that long since she had offered to buy him a coffee. She tried to remember and came up blank.

"Um, sure." He pushed back his chair and bent down to fumble with the bag at his feet.

"My treat." She smiled, and he looked even more like a deer in the headlights.

"Is this because you're going to be fired?" he asked.

"What?" She stared at him, open-mouthed as she regretted her initial offer.

"Sorry." He lowered his head and rubbed the back of his neck. "You've just never offered to get coffee before."

"Never?"

He shook his head. "Sorry."

"It's okay." She sighed. He was just a kid. His first job, and this paper was a pretty rough example of a workplace. "Guess I'm just a shit co-worker."

"Nah." His smile was nice. A kindness she hoped wouldn't be entirely killed with his chosen occupation. Journalism could be a tightrope gig. It could also be the best rush a person could ever experience. "You're nicer than most of the others. You didn't laugh when I tried to hand in a piece about the new generation."

"Oh." A light turned on in Jamie's head.

"Yeah." He looked concerned for a moment before shrugging.

"All right. I'll be back soon, Scott."

"Thanks." His smile made her feel better about the silence from Siena.

At least until she got to the counter and ordered two coffees the way she liked them because she hadn't even thought to ask Scott what he liked. What the hell was wrong with her? Had the job turned her into a bad person? A self-centered asshole just like Siena had accused her of, not in so many words, many times before? Maybe she had always been a self-centered jerk. She'd ask Jessie, but how would she handle Jessie's tactful way of saying she had always been a brat?

With relief, she heard her name being called, taking her away from these thoughts that made her question far too much about herself. As she got to the counter, her phone began to trill from her pocket. She looked at the coffees as she pulled out her phone.

Fuck! How did people buy others coffee and still manage to keep their day flowing?

"Need a tray?" the barista asked. Her smile was lovely. Jamie even considered giving her a flirty smile and response back. But as soon as the idea came to her mind, it skirted off as the image of Siena smiling up at her from between her legs flashed into Jamie's mind.

What the fuck was that about?

"A tray would be great."

After a quick thanks to the barista who had now moved away to call out another name, Jamie pulled the phone from her pocket. She answered without looking at the caller ID and jammed the phone between her shoulder and ear. She scooped up the tray from the counter and wove around people toward the exit of the coffee shop.

"Hey, it's Jamie."

"Hello?" The voice was silk to her ears, but Jamie must have been imagining it, surely.

There were curses behind her as she stopped dead in her tracks and pulled the phone away from her ear to look at the screen.

Siena.

Fuck!

The tray of coffee balanced precariously in her other hand wobbled as she blinked at the name.

She reshuffled her hold, put the phone back between her ear and shoulder, and walked forward once more.

"Ms. Frazee." Jamie's voice was too loud for her own liking, but there was little choice with the surrounding voices and clattering that continued around her.

"Is now a bad time?" Was that a smile, perhaps even a chuckle in Siena's voice?

Jamie couldn't be one-hundred-percent sure as she finally stepped out of the busy cafe.

"No, not at all. Sorry, I was just grabbing coffee." Jamie scowled at her own lapse. Why on earth had she apologized?

"Do you have time to talk now about your latest round of questions?"

"Latest round of questions?" Jamie seethed as she stepped back into her work building. She walked up to the elevators and stopped. She didn't bother stabbing the button, and her mood right now would definitely end up with her stabbing it. But if she stepped inside the elevator, the connection would undoubtedly be cut off as they moved up the building to her floor. She usually wouldn't have cared. People called back if they needed to. But she didn't know if Siena actually would.

Why she cared so much obviously had to do with the new threat once again hanging over her head about losing her day job.

"Yes." Siena's response held no humor this time. "The questions are a lot better, I'll give you that, but there are still some I won't allow you to ask."

"You'll give me that?" Jamie scoffed at the woman's audacity. Did she truly think Jamie didn't know what she was doing? Or worse, did she think of Jamie as some kind of green rookie?

"My question, Ms. Frazee, is where and when Bunny and Piper would want to answer them?"

"No!" Siena's response was too quick—too sharp.

Despite the frustration that had been building inside Jamie over the entire conversation, Jamie smiled.

"Have you asked them yet?" Jamie wouldn't let Siena keep all this control. It was sexy, but Jamie wouldn't let that distract her from taking back the reins. The idea of fighting over them gave Jamie a new thrill.

"If you want this interview, Ms. Kettlehouse, then all questions must be approved by myself. And these are not them. There are several here that will not be allowed to be asked of my clients."

"Fine." Jamie huffed. The way Siena could have her emotions pinballing made Jamie's head spin. "If we set a date for the interview, I can finalize the questions over email before then."

"I'm not finalizing anything, especially a date and time for an interview with my clients, until all questions are seen and authorized. Approved. By. Me." Siena's voice gave no room for argument.

Jamie loved the challenge. She sat down on the uncomfortable green excuse for a sitting bench in the building's foyer and crossed her legs.

"Then let's settle them." Jamie put the tray with the coffees on the chair next to her and leaned forward, her elbow on top of her knee.

The sound of paper flicking came through the phone line.

"I can meet you in a few days. Friday at two. Does that work for you?"

"Oh my, Ms. Frazee." Jamie really was enjoying this far too much. Especially considering how frustrating it also was. "If I didn't know better, I might be tempted to think you were just trying to spend more time with me."

A beat of silence gave Jamie all she needed to know—that her words had, at the very least, knocked Siena off her sure footing—at least a little.

"Are you available or not?" Siena's voice was strained, and what Jamie would have given to see her face in that moment, to be able to see her warring with her own mixed emotions.

"For you, always," Jamie purred out, surprising even herself with the ease and truth she felt behind them.

"Fantastic." Siena coughed into the phone as though having to clear her throat. "I'll send through the details of where we can meet, and I'll see you then, Jamie."

"Looking forward to it," Jamie replied, even though the sound of the phone being hung up already echoed in her ear.

For a moment she remained at her seat, despite how uncomfortable it was. She wanted to feel in control of this entire situation but never in her adult life had she felt so at the mercy of others.

With a determined huff, she grabbed the tray of coffee and headed back upstairs.

She would get these questions sorted and spend the catch-up with Siena finding out just how much she could get the woman to falter in her professionalism.

thirteen

"You'll get here on time, won't you?" Tori's question was filled with the same sad doubt Siena had heard so many times during their marriage. Somehow it hurt more now, knowing it was a sadness for their daughter and not for themselves.

"Yes." Siena would fight hell itself to get to Harley's first school social event. Especially after missing her open house.

"I hope so." Tori's voice calmed Siena's rushing mind. She always held onto hope, even after the number of times Siena had let her down in the past.

"I'll do everything I can to make it on time." Siena smiled down the phone line as she shuffled through the papers she would take home to work on after the school Halloween party she had promised to help out with.

"Excellent," Tori chirped happily. "We'll see you then."

"What did she end up dressing up as?" Siena was eager to know which of the final costumes won out.

"She wants to surprise you."

Tori and Siena chuckled and spoke a little more before Siena hung up to find a message and an email waiting for her from Jamie.

Her chest tightened, but of course, that must have just been from her anxiety about getting to the party on time.

After scanning the questions, she picked up her phone and dialed Jamie's number. She had called so many times that she nearly had the thing memorized already. Moments before she was about to hang up, sound exploded on the other end of the phone.

"Hey, it's Jamie." At least that's what she thought was said. Even Jamie's voice sounded different with all the background noise.

Or maybe it wasn't Jamie at all?

"Hello?"

After a moment, Jamie's voice returned, and the conversation bounced from enjoyment to professional, to downright shocking.

Siena's head reeled from the conversation with Jamie. It barely lasted a few minutes, but for the rest of the afternoon, it lingered in her mind, and she replayed every breath and chuckle, smirked at every snarl and sneer, and couldn't get Jamie's words out of her mind.

"Ms. Frazee?" Paula stood at Siena's open door, eyebrows raised and papers in her hands. "Is everything all right?"

"Absolutely." Siena smiled as she looked up.

"It's almost two. If you don't leave now, you won't make it to the school on time."

"Oh." Siena's heart kicked up a beat, and she was on her feet, shutting down her computer and grabbing her bag. "Thank you."

"You're welcome." Paula gave her a rare warm smile. The woman was always professional, a smile on her face when needed, but only one thing ever washed her in true warmth. "Can't have that gorgeous child of yours disappointed."

The Harley power.

Siena returned the smile and nodded. No, they couldn't do that.

Parking at the school was much easier this time. She wasn't late, she was sure of it. She double checked her watch and then the details about what time they needed her to show up.

"Ten minutes early." She all but fist pumped in the air. The fact she considered it made her chuckle to herself. It wasn't like she was twenty anymore, but lately she had definitely been feeling a lot more energized for life. All of life, not just her work.

But as she stepped into the buzz of the hall where the school dance would be held, the young energy she had been filled with drained away.

They were all so young, and that was just the teachers and other parents dotted around the hall, working on various tasks.

Someone busied themself with setting up a table of snacks, while several others wove streamers around poles and even more blew up balloons. The buzz of people talking and arms flying as they directed others to finish or begin tasks filled Siena up.

She had always thrived on the busy life of events. It had been one of the things she loved most about the many roles she had as an entertainment manager.

"You made it!"

She heard Tori's happy squeal before she saw her. Turning around, Siena caught her breath seeing Tori and Jessie approaching her.

"Oh, Ms. K, right?" Siena slid her nice and safe parent smile on her face, only for it to slip the moment she met those eyes.

"Not quite." Jamie chuckled.

"Ms. K is over there." Tori pointed, and Siena followed the gaze to see the truth in the matter. "This is Jamie. Who, I believe, you've met before."

"Yes." Siena turned back and looked at Jamie, barely aware that Tori was still there despite her being the one talking. "What're you doing here?"

"I'm here to help my sister. Is it going to be a problem?" Jamie was feisty as her fingers curved around her hips. Siena was certain it was supposed to be an attempt to intimidate her, but her body pulsed at the stance.

"Of course not." Siena smiled, knowing the parent smile was long gone, replaced by the one she hoped let Jamie know just how delicious she looked.

"Alll riiight." Tori clapped her hands together and grabbed both Jamie and Siena's attention. "School party."

Siena's mouth opened and snapped shut again.

"Our daughter's school Halloween party."

"I'm all here." Siena smiled and gave Tori a firm nod.

"Excellent. Well, the children are going to be heading in soon so let's get the rest of this place set up."

"You didn't tell me your ex-wife was head of the PTA. She's even more of a task master than you." Jamie smiled, a dusting of pink on her cheeks shining through her makeup.

"And you don't want to get on her bad side, trust me." Siena gave Jamie a conspiratorial smile. It felt good, and that in itself sent a wave of confusion through Siena.

"No," Tori interrupted, "You don't. Though I'm not the president of the PTA yet. But chop-chop."

Siena laughed, and Jamie's own chuckle threaded harmoniously through the sound.

True to her word, the children showed up shortly after, and the Halloween party was soon in full swing. The music played, and the children played in that carefree way only small children could.

"You would think they'd never seen twins before in their lives." Tori sidled up to Siena as she leaned against the wall, chaperoning the children on the gym floor from activity to activity.

"I suppose some of them haven't before now." It had been easy for Siena to do her allocated task of supervising while also getting to watch Jamie in all her glory as children seemed to swarm around her and Jessie most of the evening. They'd dressed up as *Thing 1* and *Thing 2* for the party, which was perfect for them.

"I suppose you're right."

"Mm-hmm." Siena wasn't going to dive into what she assumed Tori was hinting at. If Tori wanted to get into anything, she would have to specifically ask the questions.

"I think Harley is getting more than a little tired," Tori said.

"Oh." Siena pulled her eyes away from the crowd of children pointing out all the similarities between the twins and asking questions Siena couldn't hear from the distance.

"It's okay." Tori smiled when Siena's eyes met hers.

"Where is she? I should have taken her home already."

"Nope." Tori shook her head. "I'm going to take her home. You need to stay a bit longer to help clean up."

"Oh. But don't you need to be here until the end, Ms. PTA-going-all-out-as-parent-of-the-year?"

"Nah." Tori shook her head and gave a small laugh. "That's what delegating is all about."

"Since when?" Siena asked, a smile creeping over her lips.

"Since I have someone waiting at home for me."

"Ah." Siena looked at Tori a little closer.

"You okay?"

"I'm happy for you, Tori. I really am. You finally got your happily-ever-after." Siena wrapped her arms around her ex-wife.

"And maybe you could get yours someday soon, too." Tori pulled back and gave Siena a wink.

With a laugh, Siena shook her head. "I don't think so."

"Just do something for me, okay?" Tori used the tone Siena had never been able to say no to. "Don't dismiss the possibility."

"Okay." Siena had no other words. She could face down angry and arrogant musicians, parents and partners demanding her clients' details or royalties, event or record managers who tried to renege on contract deals. But all it took was for Tori to ask her a favor, and Siena would do anything for the mother of her child.

"Good. Now I've put you and Jamie down as the cleanup crew. I'm sure that won't be a hardship for either of you."

Before Siena could respond, Tori skipped away. Siena watched her approach, the cutest little eighties punk rocker Siena had ever seen. It had brought her near tears when Harley had excitedly explained that she wanted to be one of Siena's rock stars.

"Your ex is a sweetheart." Jamie had wandered toward Siena while she was entranced watching her daughter animatedly talking with Tori, wriggling out of Tori's arms and walking beside her like a big girl.

"Mommy!" Harley squealed and raced toward Siena before she could respond to Jamie's comment.

"Hey, my little rock star." Siena scooped Harley up in a hug before putting her back down onto her feet. She crouched down to Harley's height as they spoke. "I hear you're getting an extra night at mama's tonight."

"Yep."

"You're okay with that?"

"Yeah. Mama said I'll get to spend some time with Rebel in the morning. And you've got lots of extra stuff with work, so this is better."

"Did she now?" Siena looked over Harley's head and caught Tori's eyes.

Tori smiled and shrugged, innocence personified.

"All right, Batman."

"No, I'm a rock star!"

"Of course. All right, rock star. Have a good night. I love you."

"Love you, too." Harley wrapped her arms around Sienna's neck and squeezed.

Taking in a deep breath of her daughter's unique scent mixed with sweat and sugar, Siena allowed all stress to fall away from her shoulders. At least for that moment.

"All right, gotta go now, Mommy. Arms are too tight."

"Oh!" Siena chuckled and let her daughter go. "Sorry. I just love you so much."

"I know."

Saying her goodbyes to Tori and again to Harley, Siena didn't miss for a second Jamie's presence remaining beside her. Tori then gave them their shutting-down instructions, who to go to if they got stuck, and left with a wave over her shoulder.

"For a powerhouse of a manager, you're decidedly soft and adorable with your daughter."

"Thank you?" Siena wasn't sure if the compliment was genuine, or even a compliment at all.

"Oh, I mean it as a good thing. It means you do actually have a heart." Jamie smiled and started walking back across the floor. The last of the children had filtered out, directed by teachers and other parent volunteers. Jamie reached the first table and began packing up the trash left behind, tossing it into a large plastic can beside the table. "I wish I had half the patience with kids as other people do."

Siena laughed, taking the tablecloth from the now empty table and bundling it up.

"For people who look identical, you and your sister really are nothing alike, are you?"

"Absolute opposites, I'm afraid." The self-deprecating smile that stretched Jamie's lips caused an unusual ache in Siena's chest. "She's kind, patient, and a nice person."

"You don't really think that, do you?"

"Of course, I do," Jamie said, her face contorting in an affronted manner. "My sister is one of the best people I've ever met in my life. And sure, I might be biased, but other people see it too. It's not just me."

"She is a nice person. I wasn't asking that." Siena's voice was nearly a whisper as she spoke. "I meant you think you aren't those things."

"Oh." Jamie didn't respond. Instead, she continued to move table to table until all the trash had been taken care of. Without the need of any verbal communication, the two retraced their steps, tipping over the tables and folding them down as though they had done this all a thousand times at a thousand different events.

"Can I ask you something?" Siena asked, hoping enough time had passed for the thickness of the air to clear for Jamie as much as it had for her.

"Sure," Jamie said, not looking up.

"Will your boss really fire you if you don't get a date for the interview set?"

"He's threatening it. And he's not one to threaten lightly." Jamie shrugged as though it wasn't of any concern.

Siena's stomach twisted uncomfortably. She'd never been one to take on the consequences of other people's actions. The situation Jamie found herself in now was a result of her own choices. Siena couldn't help stupid or impulsive.

"I think that's everything on your ex's to-do list." Jamie surveyed the large space. "I'll go let Jessie know."

"I'll come with you." Siena smiled. For a moment their eyes met, and Siena's stomach tightened.

"Well, that would be a nice change." Jamie smirked and winked wildly.

"Oh my God." Siena laughed despite the heat in her cheeks that swiftly moved down into her chest. She shook her head and followed Jamie out of the gym. There were still far too many people around for Siena to feel comfortable lingering very long, but she wouldn't just leave before she had spoken to Harley's teacher—to Jessie—Jamie's twin sister. It still felt far too surreal to be true.

"All finished then?" Jessie smiled, her voice still carrying the bubbles of energy that should have been illegal this far into the evening when Siena knew full well she'd been dealing with a horde of small children all day. Not that it was all that late. But the sun had set, and the last lingering rays stretched over the school buildings.

"Yeah. All done to Tori's directions," Siena answered, wondering what the conversation between the twins was as they stared at each other, their eyes flicking slightly.

Whatever it was, Jessie recovered first, and for a few minutes, the three of them spoke with an ease that Siena found herself genuinely enjoying. The tension between her and Jamie remained, tightly wound in a delicious way.

"Do you want me to wait and walk you out when you're done?" Jamie asked.

"No. It's fine. We've got a few more things to get done before I can take off for the night." Jessie threw a look over her shoulder to some other people behind her.

Siena assumed they were other staff.

"No worries. Well, I'll see you later."

"Sure." Jessie nodded.

"Yep," Jamie said with a nod and turned on her heel. "You heading out as well, Siena?"

"Yeah, I'll walk with you," Siena replied on autopilot, her curiosity about Jamie growing beyond the desire to taste her once more.

"Great, see ya, Sis."

"Bye."

They headed away from the gym and toward the street where Siena had parked.

"I didn't set anyone on your boss." Siena spilled the words before she realized they were on her tongue.

"I know." Jamie surprised her by saying.

"You do?"

"Yes." Jamie laughed as the incredulous look that must have been plastered on Siena's face. "I told you. I'm good at my job."

"You checked it out?"

"Yep. Seems the ones continuing to harass my boss are the ones where the information has hit just a little too close to the truth."

Siena laughed and nodded as she stopped walking at the trunk of her car. Jamie took one more step before turning back around and smiling at Siena.

"Yours?" Jamie jerked her head slightly to Siena's vehicle, the Lexus that she had scrimped and saved years for, and she was damn glad she'd been able to afford it.

"Yes."

"Nice ride." Jamie stepped back toward Siena, the air between them thickening once more as the space decreased.

"Do you still think I'm like that?"

"Like what?" Jamie's eyes dropped to Siena's mouth and back up again.

Siena licked her lips, the pulse between her thighs growing the more she took Jamie in.

"Using my position in unethical ways?" Siena's voice dropped.

"I don't think it for a moment. Never did." Jamie stepped closer still, the toes of her shoes meeting Siena's. "You wouldn't need to use any unethical means to get into any position you wanted."

Siena's breath caught as the lightest touch of Jamie's fingers danced up her arm. Was she really going to do this? Was she going to kiss Jamie Kettlehouse out in the open and fully knowing exactly who she was?

"Is that so?" Siena asked.

"Mm-hmm." Jamie's eyes danced as her smile tempted Siena beyond her control.

Siena snaked her arm around Jamie's waist and pulled Jamie into her. Her breath caught, and she struggled to tear her gaze away from Jamie's full lips, from the confidence that she seemed to always ooze when in Siena's presence. As their bodies collided, Siena took Jamie's lips. Jamie's groan as Siena teased open her mouth and slid her tongue in made her underwear wet and her pulse get heavier and faster.

Siena cupped the back of Jamie's head, tilting her backward and pushing her against the trunk of the car. Her entire body heated in the chilled air, and she slid her hand down Jamie's side from her breast to her hip and back up again.

"Fuck." Siena's curse was a breath between kisses as Jamie's hands found Siena's breasts, rolling her already erect nipple through her clothes. Her knees went weak at the barest of touches from Jamie. She was so touch deprived, and that wild and crazy night in the hotel room had proven that fact over and over again.

"This time, I get to play," Jamie murmured as she turned Siena and pressed her back against the trunk of the car, taking more control than Siena had thought she was willing to give. But there was something delicious about Jamie taking and doing rather than just receiving. Siena had shorted them both the pleasure of that experience before, hadn't she?

Siena pressed her shoulders into the trunk of her car and jutted her hips out, giving Jamie access to anything that she wanted to touch. She couldn't stop threading her fingers through Jamie's long blonde hair, against her skin and clothes. She moved in for another heated kiss when light washed over them, the head-lights effectively throwing the metaphorical bucket of cold water.

"Oh shit." Siena laughed as Jamie stepped back.

"This was, um…. This was fun," Jamie said, her breath coming out as hard as Siena's.

"Fun?" Siena raised an eyebrow. She wasn't nearly done yet, but if Jamie didn't want to do more, she'd respect that. She could always take care of herself when she got home if she needed to.

"Well, while I'd like to follow through on playing." Jamie quirked up one side of her lips. "I have some questions I need to sort out before a meeting with a really sexy and powerful production manager in a few days."

"Oh." The reality of who Jamie was in her working life hit hard, and Siena pushed herself up from her car. "I have another proposal."

"Really?" Jamie's smirk deepened and her eyebrows rose.

"Not that kind of proposal, unfortunately."

"Oh." The eyebrows remained high on Jamie's forehead.

"Tell your boss you'll interview me in response to your post. He can run it, or you can put it on your blog." Siena swallowed down the thickness that remained in her throat.

She wanted Jamie more than anything else. She wanted to taste her, fuck her, make her come again and again and again, just like she had before. But she wouldn't be the reason Jamie lost her job.

"Seriously?" Jamie looked stunned, as though not willing to believe her luck quite yet.

"Yes. It's what you wanted originally, right?"

"Yeah." Jamie's face clouded over as an emotion as far from arousal as possible filled her eyes. "So does that mean you are taking the interview with Bunny and Piper off the table? Is that what all this was about?"

"What?" Siena asked as Jamie waved her hand between the two of them. "No. That interview will happen once we agree and I approve all questions. You said you believed that I wasn't like those other managers," Siena said. "Were you bullshitting me?"

"No," Jamie shook her head. "It's just…" She trailed off. Then with a huff, she stopped searching for words.

Siena smiled and stepped forward, taking Jamie's hips in her hands and pulling her close, but not too close. If their bodies slammed together again, Siena wouldn't be able to pull away again. But she wanted to make her point very clearly to Jamie, and it seemed that Jamie needed precise words in order to understand what Siena wasn't saying.

"I want to fuck you, Jamie. Over and over again. I want you to fuck me. But I'm not going to be responsible for you losing your job. That's an entirely different thing from this."

"Oh."

"So. Maybe once these interviews are figured out, we can um…" Siena felt like a twenty-something again. "…continue where we left off?"

"That could definitely be something we can look into, Ms. Frazee."

Siena laughed, throwing her head back. She caught the flickering lights of stars in the sky and wondered how she ever thought things in her life could be simple.

"All right then." Siena nodded. "Do you have a ride home?"

"I've got my car."

"Then I'll see you in a few days. Yes?"

"Yeah." Jamie nodded and stepped out of the way of Siena's car.

As quickly as possible, Siena got herself buckled in and drove away, sticking her arm out of the window and waving at

Jamie as she pulled away from the curb. She tried not to look back, but it was impossible.

The Kettlehouse effect had firmly taken ahold of Siena again.

The last thing she saw in the rearview mirror was Jamie standing in the circle cast by a streetlight. Siena hadn't felt this hopeful in a long time. And maybe, just maybe, that one-night stand might turn into something a little longer than she had expected.

fourteen

Jamie worried her teeth on her bottom lip as she finished reading through the article one more time. It read well, and she liked it. It had been a while since she had liked an article this much. The editing stage had been more pleasant than ever before. Still her stomach tumbled with nerves.

The interview with Siena had been quick and easy. Far easier than she had anticipated. The questions were in essence asking Siena about thoughts and comments on Jamie's previous post, her articulation doing nothing to quell Jamie's desire to get arrested for public nudity.

The tension between them hovered beneath the surface of the professionalism neither of them would drop. Despite the need for them to lean over the coffee table in the crowded cafe in order to hear each other.

Siena's eyes had wandered on more than one occasion to Jamie's cleavage. Jamie had done nothing to dissuade her from looking. The woman's precise answers and calm voice told nothing of the darkening of her eyes.

Jamie had listened to the recorded interview a few times more than she technically needed.

Tapping her fingers on her mouse, Jamie bit the bullet and pressed the number. She had been debating video calling Jessie for a little over an hour now.

"Hey, Sis. What's up?" Jessie answered after a few rings. Her hair was a mess and her eyes still glassy. That jealous side of Jamie snickered at the idea of Jessie's students and parents seeing their perfect teacher disheveled like this.

"I have an article I want to post, and I'm not sure about it." Jamie dove right in, squashing that darker thinking.

"Okay?" Jessie answered as she moved around her kitchen. "So what's the issue?"

"I was wondering if you could read it and let me know what you think."

"Since when did you ever second-guess yourself or bother to ask me for my thoughts?" Jessie smiled.

Jamie knew her sister meant the words in jest, but they hurt, and she couldn't muster the energy to hide the pain.

"Hey." Jessie stopped moving, a spoon of ground coffee held in the air above her machine. Her voice was gentle. "I was joking. But you have to admit it's unlike you to second guess yourself. Is this because of your dumbass boss?"

"Probably," Jamie replied, grabbing ahold of the easy out. It was about so much more than that, but she wasn't really ready to dive into that yet. There was too much for her to be thinking about as it was. And these interviews were literally capable of tipping her career progress one way or the other. She knew which one she would prefer.

"Of course, I'll read it. Send it over, and I'll get to it as soon as the coffee's ready. I'll call you back soon."

"Thanks, Jessie."

"Of course." Jessie smiled before the call disconnected.

Thirty minutes later and Jamie was certain she was going to climb the walls at any moment. Each minute had felt like hours since she'd hit send on the email to Jessie. She had made coffee, paced the floor, eaten some toast, and now had resumed pacing once more.

Still Jessie hadn't called her back.

"It wasn't a fucking novel, Jessie," Jamie muttered, running her fingers through her disheveled hair. She jumped in the middle of her pacing when the sound of knuckles on her door echoed through her place.

The kids asking questions about the similarities between Jessie and Jamie at the Halloween party hadn't bothered her. Their innocence and curiosity were genuine and sweet. But usually, the questions that probing adults asked would annoy her at the best and become downright creepy at the worst. Eventually everyone would ask about telepathic links and mental abilities between them as twins.

Jamie and Jessie had never known anything quite like that. The conversations they had with a mere glance had far more to do with their similar lived experiences versus them being twins.

They did, however, always seem to know when the other one was around. That feeling washed over Jamie now as she stared at her closed door.

"Open up. I know you're still home, JJ." Jessie's voice so alike and yet so different from her own.

"I hate that nickname," Jamie called out loud enough for her voice to reach through the still closed door.

"I know!" the call came back.

Jamie wanted to scowl, but her smile won out. As jealous as she was at times with Jessie's easy perfection, she understood why everyone loved her. She loved her sister even more than the rest. Her playfulness with Jamie had saved her sanity countless times while they were growing up.

That aside, she still needed to steel herself for her sister's unexpected presence. Jamie pushed her shoulders back and channeled her remaining anxious energy in a vain attempt to control the situation.

"Well, it's about time," Jamie said as she flung open the door.

Jessie laughed, rolled her eyes and stepped inside. "You didn't have a clue I was heading here."

"Nope, but in the story I tell in the future about this, I'll be all in tune and shit. It's what the people want."

"True," Jessie said. "Just make sure you add that I was already up and ready, exercised and beautified enough for the runway when you called."

Jamie laughed and wrapped her arms around her sister before they shuffled themselves inside.

"Of course. You're always the prettier one in all my stories." Jamie chuckled even as the truth of the words missed Jessie.

"You're nuts." Jessie laughed as she headed to the small kitchen and grabbed herself a mug and another cup of coffee.

"So?" Jamie asked tentatively. "What do you think?"

"Can we maybe catch up a little first?" Jessie smiled, those big baby-blue eyes of hers better than any puppy dog Jamie had ever seen.

"Of course," Jamie said. "It's been a bit hard catching up lately."

"Lately?" Jessie sat at one end of Jamie's couch, pulling her legs up and folding them underneath her as she used the arm as a backrest.

Jamie mostly mimicked her sister's position at the other end, though she left one leg down, her toes bouncing her leg as they moved up and down on the floor in front of the couch.

"I know." Jamie rolled her eyes. She was sure they communicated better through eye rolls than anything else. "I'm a shit sister who never has enough time for her older sibling."

"Two minutes older, and don't you forget it." Jessie nodded before sipping her coffee.

"So, what exactly do you want to catch up on?" Jamie asked, dreading the answer as she asked the question, feeding directly into Jessie's agenda.

"Did you realize I was the one leaving the parking lot the other night?" Jessie was eyeing her carefully, definitely waiting for Jamie's reaction. And Jamie really needed to control her shit right now. But she was also damn sure that wasn't going to happen.

"What? What other night?"

"The Halloween party."

"Halloween par…" Jamie's mouth dropped open, and realization dawned in a heated flush of her cheeks. Her hand slapped over her mouth in a vain attempt at hiding the shock. "The headlights," Jamie murmured behind her hand.

"I didn't think so." Jessie smiled as if she'd caught Jamie in her own little lie.

"Well, fuck."

"I know you did a while ago, but again?" Jessie asked, her smile turning up into an all-knowing grin.

"No, I didn't fuck her again. Especially in the school parking lot."

Jessie shrugged, her face expressing shock at Jamie's outburst. "It's not like it was during school hours."

"No." Jamie jumped up and paced again. "Oh my God. I know you have issues with how much I like sex, but do you really think I have no uncrossable lines?"

"Hey, I don't have issues with it. And you're both consenting adults." Jessie stopped for a moment and pinned Jamie with her eyes. "Aren't you?"

"Of course." Jamie was disgusted that her sister had to even ask. "Consent is sexy."

"Okay, so you didn't fuck again." Jessie sipped her drink as though she had mentioned nothing more interesting than what she had for breakfast.

"No. We did *not* fuck again." *Unfortunately*, Jamie's mind unhelpfully added. "But can we please get back onto the actual topic?" Jamie's voice was a little harder edged than she had meant.

"Seems to me this topic is pretty much related to the one you called me about," Jessie replied, seemingly unaffected by Jamie's snapping.

Jamie shook her head. "No. It's not. I fucked her before I knew who she was." *Or she fucked me.* "This interview is nothing about that."

"So then why is it so different from everything else on your blog?" Jessie's eyebrows rose as though she had just pulled out the smoking gun in the middle of a courtroom.

"You've read my blog?" Jamie could have been knocked over with a feather. She stopped pacing and turned to her sister as she blinked slowly, trying to process this information.

"Of course I've read it," Jessie replied, her face filled with hurt. "I'm one of your subscribers. I figured you must have known that."

"I didn't." Feeling like she had kicked a puppy, Jamie shook her head and wondered how she had missed that. To be fair, she rarely bothered to look at the details of the subscribers, focusing almost solely instead on the number. And by focusing, she meant being utterly obsessed with every movement the numbers made.

"I also read all the bylines of yours I find in the paper," Jessie said. "It's the only reason I read the newspaper."

"Oh." Jamie was suddenly lost for words.

"Did you really think I wouldn't?"

Jamie closed her mouth, trying to find her words again. She searched for a truth that wouldn't be carved on a dagger. "I guess I just never thought you'd bother. You've never mentioned them, so I just didn't think about it, I guess." The lie came too easily to Jamie's lips. Of course she had thought about it, thought about how uninterested her family was in her passion for the truth, for her growing skill in writing.

Jessie pulled her face into a look Jamie knew all too well. The look she had named Jessie's enhancing-her-calm expression. "I do. I've always read what you get published. And this is different from what's usually on your blog."

"How so?" Jamie grabbed onto the safer topic, easily pushing away the idea of her sister following her life far closer than Jamie had ever followed back.

"It's not…" Jessie's lips pursed together for a moment, the telltale sign she wanted to find a more diplomatic way of saying what was on her mind. Jamie supposed they weren't one hundred percent opposite as she had told Siena they were the other night. She guessed it might be more like a ninety-percent average.

"Just spit it out, Jessie." What little patience Jamie had remaining throughout this unexpectedly confronting conversation vanished. But that wasn't Jessie's fault, not really. So Jamie added. "Please?"

"It's better written, there's absolutely no doubt about that. But it's not the same level of snark and bitchy observation as your usual stuff. It doesn't have that same hate-for-the-world angle you usually take."

"Oh." Whatever Jamie had expected the answer to be, apparently, it hadn't been that.

"It's not bad. It's just different." Jessie smiled and lifted her shoulders.

As close as the two of them were, that connection had become more distant over the years as Jessie threw herself into caring about other people's kids and Jamie focused on getting her own career on track.

"You think the difference is something my audience will see

as bad." It wasn't a question. What was worse was that Jamie couldn't even entirely argue or even disagree with Jessie's assessment. It had felt good writing something without such a negative spin on it for once. Was that why the writing had come so much easier? Why the words flowed and she had smiled as she edited it?

Or did that have more to do with the subject?

No, Jamie dismissed that idea. For now.

"I guess that depends," Jessie said.

"Depends?" Jamie narrowed her eyes at her sister. "What do you mean *it depends*?"

"Well," Jessie put her mug down on the coffee table and straightened her back, wriggling in her pretzel pose on the couch. "I guess it depends on who you actually want your audience to be going forward."

"It's taken me this long to get to the number of subscribers I have now. Why would I want to change that? I might finally be getting somewhere. I don't want to live my whole life relying on other people for my income, especially when being a grunt at a paper isn't exactly filling me with joy."

"Does the blog fill you with joy?" Jessie asked.

"You just have to ask the hitting questions, don't you?" Jamie teased. "And honestly, not usually."

"But this one did?"

"Yeah." Jamie's smile was easy and real. She felt it in every part of her. "It really did. It felt good giving the other side of the argument."

"It's a good piece, Jamie. You should be proud of it."

"But?" Jamie asked, feeling that two-minute age difference as though it were years. She sat on the couch next to Jessie. Her sister twisted around, her legs still crossed though her position righted so her thigh touched Jamie's.

"But…" Jessie said as Jamie rested her head on her shoulder. "I just want to know what's going on with my sister behind the writing."

"I don't really know," Jamie answered honestly, knowing Jessie would listen no matter how little any of it made sense.

"Okay, so start anywhere, and we can figure some of it out. If you want, that is."

"I hate my job. I do it to pay the bills. I wrote that first piece with information I had gotten ages ago, but never thought I would ever use." How would Siena react if Jamie actually explained that to her? Instead, Jamie had done what she normally did and pushed to get exactly what she wanted— or at least what she thought she wanted and what she thought the world wanted of her.

"Until she left you high and dry on a Friday night?" Jessie's voice carried a hint of mirth with a larger helping of understanding.

"Yeah. And I'm not proud of it."

"You've written far more damaging articles."

"I know," Jamie whispered, fearing the words that danced on her tongue. "And I think maybe every word of it makes me a bad person."

"You aren't a bad person," Jessie replied quietly, not quite matching Jamie's whisper.

"But I'm not a good person." Jamie knew that truth deep in her heart, and she wasn't ever going to be able to escape it.

"I think you are," Jessie answered.

"You think everyone's a good person."

"Nah, I just think everyone has the potential to be."

"Even me?"

"Especially you," Jessie replied. "If you think you aren't the person you want to be, then maybe it's time to change things."

"I want the interview to be good, but I don't know if she'll let me ask the question."

"Oh, not the interview you sent me?" Jessie picked up her phone as if to show the interview she'd sent over.

"No. This interview is just to placate the day job until I get the questions approved for the big one."

"The Bunny and Piper one? And Siena has to approve all of them?"

"Yeah." Jamie smiled. She should have known. Jessie always listened to her work rants and remembered. Jamie needed to work harder on listening to Jessie's work talk. She had to learn to ask. Because she did care, whenever she could get her head out of her ass long enough to look around. And she needed to do that way more often than she had been.

"So, what questions don't you think Siena will approve you to ask them?"

"She's approved most of them. But honestly, there's only one question I really want to ask them now."

"What question is that?"

"What made you choose Siena as your manager all those years ago?"

"Oh, Sis. Looks like you might have met your match."

"I know," Jamie said. "I'm fucked."

"So what are you going to do?"

"Get my head back on and stop fucking around."

"Hmmm." Jessie pursed her lips. "I'm not sure I'm going to like where you are heading with this, am I?"

"Nope." Jamie smiled, though it mustn't have reached her eyes as Jessie's own face deflated like the metaphorical kicked puppy once more.

"You know having feelings doesn't have to be a bad thing."

"It does if it stops me being the kick-ass journalist I've been working so damn hard to be."

fifteen

Ms. Siena Frazee,

Thank you for sending back your notes on the latest set of questions I have sent in relation to the interview with Bunny and Piper.

I've decided to go in another direction, and there will be only one question I would like to ask them. While I know you have made it clear that you would like to screen all questions before setting a date to sit down with them, I think this question will only work if both women are given the opportunity to answer it honestly.

I can assure you the question relates solely to their careers as musicians.

Awaiting your reply,
Jamie

"What the fuck, Jamie?" Siena muttered again as she scanned the words for the tenth time. Everything about this gave Siena the feeling of trying to walk on the deck of a ship in the middle of a storm, a stomach-churning thrill she wasn't sure she liked.

There had been a third round of questions, and now there were only two questions of the dozen Siena didn't approve of. The other ten would allow Piper and Bunny to answer as much or as little as they felt comfortable.

The woman had so much spunk and fight in her, but this was too far.

After their impromptu make-out session at the school, Harley's school, Siena had been filled with a small spark of hope that maybe, just maybe, she and Jamie could at the very least finish what she had cut short the first night they had met.

She hadn't heard from Jamie since the concessional interview with Siena a few days later, only for this email to ping into her inbox this morning. She'd been expecting the interview to be read prior to publishing. But this…this wasn't that at all.

Taking a deep breath, Siena started typing.

Ms. Kettlehouse,

As you have mentioned, no questions can be asked that have not already been approved by myself. This is non-negotiable. If you're no longer interested in interviewing my clients, I'll remove you from my calendar.

If you're still interested, I suggest you send your question through for my approval.

Siena

The email reply came almost instantly, and Siena frowned as it popped into her inbox. Surely, it'd be quicker if Jamie would just text her the question. Why was she even withholding it? There was no point to this. Growling, Siena clicked open the email and read.

Ms. Frazee,

I was under the impression negotiating terms for your clients was part of your job. The interview can be unrecorded in all forms, and you and your client may be given the opportunity to read my final edit before publication.

I will, however, not be sending through any more questions for your approval. I do not have time, nor do I need to be babysat in doing my job. I'm a perfectly capable journalist.

Jamie

"What the hell?" Siena muttered under her breath. What was Jamie playing at? She hadn't questioned Jamie's abilities at all. All she'd done was try to protect her clients. She was about to call Jamie up and give her a piece of her mind, but she didn't want any misunderstanding in what was being exchanged between them.

Jamie,

What the hell are you doing?

.   .   .

Okay, well that might not have been exactly what Siena was going for. She wished she could click the unsend button, but there wasn't one in her email. And she'd definitely allowed herself to be goaded into responding purely based on emotion.

She had to be better than this. She was just about to type another email out and apologize for her irrational behavior when another email popped into her inbox.

Ms. Frazee,

My job. I suggest you do yours.

Ms. Jamie Kettlehouse

Siena's breath sped up, and her cheeks burned hot. Was she fucking kidding? Do her job? What the hell had happened between their kisses and now? What the hell could the one question be that Jamie would sacrifice the opportunity to interview Bunny and Piper in person?

"Siena?" Paula's use of her first name wasn't entirely unheard of, but the concern in the tone snapped Siena out of her angry haze. At least enough to look up from her computer screen and blink away the red rage that had covered her.

"Sorry, Paula, what was that?"

"I asked if you were all right." Paula frowned, and Siena could easily see all of the concern in her shoulders and face now. *Shit.* She really needed to get herself under control.

"Of course. Why?"

"Because if you keep typing the way you have been, I'll

need to start researching a new keyboard for you. And we both know I don't have time for that."

Siena looked down, expecting to see keys missing or at the very least finger-sized divots in them.

"Should I put it on my calendar?" Paula asked, slight exasperation filling her tone.

"No." Siena wouldn't let herself break down or lash out in front of her receptionist, no matter how long Paula had been in the position. "It's fine. Thank you, Paula."

Siena turned off her computer and stood up.

"Are you heading out?" Paula's furrowed brows and flustered expression gave Siena a small vindictive spike of glee. She could still surprise her at least. Though she definitely didn't need to take up that challenge every day.

"Yes. I don't have anything else scheduled for the rest of the day, right?"

"Correct."

"I need to manage some things for Bunny and Piper."

"Oh, okay." Paula's confusion eased slightly as her brows relaxed and her forehead smoothed out once more. There remained some lingering concern on her face. Undoubtedly from Siena's change in schedule combined with the behavior that had brought her into Siena's office in the first place.

"It'll all work out in the wash." Siena leaned back on one of her well used statements and gave Paula the best smile she could manage. Losing Paula was the last thing she needed.

"Must be a pretty intense situation for it to get you frazzled like this." Paula rarely fished for compliments, but the comment made Siena twitch. "I hope it's not any more insane media dramas." Paula smiled, unaware she was hitting the nail right on the head.

"Nothing we can't handle, right?"

"You mean you." In control of what happened in the office once more, Paula smiled and resumed being the relaxed receptionist Siena adored. "If it were up to me, all those jerks would be turned away and kicked off a bridge—a high bridge."

Siena laughed, trying hard to ignore the lump that formed in her throat as she grabbed her things and walked out of the office.

It wasn't hard to find Jamie's address. Siena couldn't help but acknowledge the small flutter of worry for the journalist who had so often pissed her off in the past. Jamie was on quite a few managers' shit lists and Siena wondered if Jamie hadn't had problems with her home being so easy to find.

Shaking off the concern, she remembered why she had sought out Jamie's apartment in the first place. The climb up the stairs pulled at Siena's rarely used muscles. It had been far too long since she had seen the inside of her gym or taken someone home for some fun acrobatic adventure.

Her night with Jamie didn't count. She hadn't used nearly enough muscles in that hotel room.

Taking a deep breath, she shook out her hands before lifting one and knocking on the red steel door.

"What the hell?" Jamie started speaking before she had even pulled the door open, her voice and annoyance obvious.

For a moment, Siena stood stunned into silence at the sight of Jamie. She stood natural and real in a sleeveless shirt that didn't quite reach the band of the small shorts that hugged the tops of her thighs.

"Uhhh..." An incoherent gurgle came out of Siena's mouth.

A small flicker of a smile crossed Jamie's lips until they turned down, arms crossing over those delicious breasts. The movement snapped Siena out of her haze, and she swallowed the lump that had remained since she left the office.

"What the hell is the question, Jamie?" Siena didn't wait for an invite, stepping past Jamie and inside. She barely caught a glimpse of the small space before the door lock snicked behind her, and she turned to see Jamie with her hands on her hips in front of the closed door.

"Seriously?" Jamie laughed, the sound nothing like that infectious noise Siena had been dreaming about whenever her mind wandered off over the last few weeks.

"Why have you gone back on our agreement?" Siena didn't like the hint of hurt that leaked out in her words. She ignored it as best she could and only hoped Jamie would do the same.

"It wasn't an agreement. It was a dictate," Jamie spat back.

"Dictate?" Siena snarled. She was many things—driven, workaholic, detached at times—but she was *not* a dictator. She had never been accused of being one either.

"Yes. You decided where and what." Jamie marched over to a small kitchen and pulled open the fridge door as she spoke. "I even went against my own ethical code and allowed you to *dictate* this interview, but not anymore."

"Ethical code." Siena snorted. Jamie clearly had picked up on the fact that Siena was perturbed by the word *dictate* and was using it to her advantage. Clever woman.

"Yes." Jamie returned with two bottles of water. She shoved one in Siena's hand as she opened the other one and took a gulp before continuing. "Despite what all you money hungry managers think, I *have* writing and journalism ethics. I'm not a hack making up sensational news for shits and giggles."

"No, you just make it up for likes and chaos. For your own sick pleasure of seeing the chaos you sew multiply as the gossip is passed around."

"Well, it sure isn't for the money." Jamie scoffed as she lifted her arms to indicate her home.

"Then why bother pissing everyone off for shit you can't even prove? Is that why you won't tell me the question?"

"It's called censoring. You need to protect your clients, sure. I get that. But there's a difference and this is well beyond protecting them."

"Are you kidding me?" Siena's fingers tightened on the bottle of water, and she was glad she hadn't opened it to take a drink. If she had, she would have feared the lid would pop off with how hard she squeezed the plastic.

"No." Jamie met her eyes, and the fire in them was electric.

"You've written vile and wildly speculative things about my clients in the past. You've caused me no end of trouble. Not to mention the time it takes me to put out the fires and fix the problems you create! And you think me checking your questions before you ask them is too much? I shouldn't even be considering letting you interview them."

"Then why are you?" Jamie asked, eyes pinning Siena's. There was a knowledge behind them, a way of telling Siena that Jamie knew more than she was letting on. The intelligence behind those baby blues was intoxicating. Even as anger heated her chest.

Siena opened her mouth and slammed it shut again with a shake of her head.

"You haven't even spoken to them, have you?" Jamie spat the question, the tone so sure Siena knew she didn't have to answer. "You are fucking unbelievable. You told me you were going to talk to them!" Jamie shook her head and paced back and forth in the small space.

Siena felt a tug at the corners of her mouth as she noted the uneven strip of carpet. Evidence of this track having been paced many times before. But with a flick of her eyes back to Jamie's scowled expression, the urge to smile dropped. Even as her stomach muscles tightened at the movement of the feisty woman who continued to confuse her and make Siena's own thoughts and feelings contradict each other.

She stepped closer as Jamie paced back toward her.

"What's the question, Jamie?"

"The question? That's all you care about, isn't it?" Jamie pivoted and turned back before she reached Siena.

"I want to know what question is burning so hard in you that you're willing to jeopardize the olive branch I've offered."

"Olive branch? You've pushed back on everything." She returned, her fingers tangling in her hair, pulling at the strands. Jamie's disheveled appearance made heat pool between Siena's legs. Her body itched to reach out and touch, to stop Jamie's wild and barely controlled movements. "You've made it impossible for me to do my job. To *keep* my fucking job."

"That's not on me." Damn her body. She was angry, not aroused. "You got yourself into this mess—not me."

"By writing the truth!" Jamie snarled.

Angry *and* aroused apparently.

"You wouldn't know the truth if it bit you in the ass."

"Fuck you, Siena." Jamie turned again, hands no longer pulling through her hair.

With a quick flick of her eyes, Siena saw Jamie's hands clenched into fists at her side. What were they playing at? Siena had known coming here was going to be a fight. But she hadn't expected the tension to rise and stay at this level—threatening to get even higher every second.

"There's truth the public has a right to see, and then there's the truth everyone deserves to have kept private to their own lives and choosing. Even celebrities. It's why I care about doing *my* job properly. You don't have a right to slander someone else. You don't have the right to who a person is. It's my job to protect everything that is them."

"To protect them from people like me?" Jamie scoffed and stopped her pacing close enough that Siena felt her warm breath on her face.

"Yes."

"And what about people like you?"

"Me?" Siena couldn't hide the shock at the question.

"Yes. You haven't even told them you're in negotiations

with me for an interview." Jamie poked a finger into Siena's shoulder, making her point.

"I don't tell them every interview I turn down or every avenue I explore. It's not uncommon to just do the work and tell them the results."

Jamie shook her head wildly, that answer not satisfying her anger. Or was that hurt? "Did you ever plan to carry it through?"

Siena sighed, bowing her head slightly so she could look directly into Jamie's baby blues. "What's the question, Jamie?"

"You want to know?" Jamie hissed.

"Yes." Siena shuffled closer, her shoes touching the tips of Jamie's socked feet.

"You really want to know?" Jamie leaned in closer.

"Yes." Her voice sounded like a whisper, hoarse and raw as she leaned close into Jamie's space.

"Do you really hate me that much?"

"Hate you?" Siena shook her head. "For making sure I wasn't putting my clients into a marketing nightmare?"

"But making me think I had a chance to actually talk to them and offer a real insight for their fans?"

"They give enough." Siena's voice grew again in volume, her chest tightening as that tension she'd dissipated a little came rushing right back into her.

"They could give more. They already do. Any adult with half a brain can see who Bunny and Piper are with the lyrics they write and sing." Jamie flung her hand out to the side as if she was pointing to something that would prove her point.

"So why do you care about making them say it?"

"For the teens, for the sheltered ones who've never seen someone like themselves thrive. You think you stopping them talking about who they are is helping anyone? When their coming out can help more people than you can imagine?"

Siena wasn't going to touch that one with a ten-foot pole.

Bunny and Piper's sexuality was theirs and theirs alone. She would never force either one of them to come out unless they wanted to. And she'd kept that secret close for decades. Changing topics slightly was the only way out of this one. "So why hide behind the smear campaigns?"

"Because without pissing you off, I get nowhere. If you ever bothered to read anything of mine further than five years ago, you'd see. I tried playing by your rules. They got me nowhere. But you didn't, did you? No, because it's easier to see me as trash instead of an actual human being. If I became real, you might not be able to use me so easily as someone to be pissed off with."

"You think I can't see you as a human?" Oh God, that was anything but the truth.

"You don't see me at all." Jamie's breath was hot, her breasts rising and falling faster with each word.

"You're *all* I see." Siena moved in so close her nipples hardened at the gentle brush of Jamie's shirt against her chest.

"Yeah, right." Jamie's eyes flicked to Siena's lips.

"*Yeah, right* is right." Siena closed the gap. One hand instantly tangled in Jamie's hair. She pulled Jamie close, so hard and fast that it hurt in a delicious burst of lips slamming against lips.

For a moment, a heartbeat that lasted too long, Jamie's body remained rigid in Siena's embrace. Just as Siena was about to pull back, despite the taste of Jamie's lips feeling like cool water after a desert walk, Jamie's hands were on Siena's hips pulling her even closer. The groan that escaped Jamie's mouth snapped the last of Siena's reserves as she gave in to everything Jamie.

sixteen

The moment Siena's mouth touched hers nothing else mattered. Not the question she hadn't given to Siena. Not even the question that had come out in a rush of anger and heat. Jamie's body might as well have been on fire, and she couldn't concentrate on anything other than Siena's hands on her and the arousal that burst inside her.

No one had ever gotten beneath Jamie's skin like this, and as she got her mind to catch up with her body, her fingers digging into Siena's hips and pulling her pelvis into her own, she scratched the itch that had been there since their night together.

Feeling the heat radiate from between Siena's legs made her groan, opening her mouth as it moved against Siena's lips. Siena wasted no time exploring Jamie's mouth with her tongue, dancing in and out, a little deeper with each swipe.

Jamie shuddered, fumbling furiously until she found the hem of Siena's blouse and slid her fingers beneath. Her skin gave so much more than it had ever promised, tight with a gentleness that made Jamie's hips rock into Siena.

"Bed," Siena mumbled as she slowly traced Jamie's lips with her tongue.

"What?"

"Where is your bed, Jamie?" Siena chuckled.

"Not clear," Jamie said as she pulled Siena toward the couch. She pressed small but urgent kisses along Siena's jaw line, reveling in the rumble that came from Siena's throat.

"What's that mean?" Siena asked as she tilted her head, giving Jamie more access to the length of her neck.

Jamie nipped a path along Siena's collarbone, hands running up and down the skin on either side of her body, tracing the curves that hid beneath.

"It means sit that gorgeous ass of yours down." Jamie stepped back as she gently nudged Siena, chuckling with a smirk on her lips as the woman gave a small yelp and fell into the couch behind her.

Siena looked up at Jamie, her throat bobbing as she swallowed. "I want to touch you."

"Good." Jamie laughed, her eyes boring down into Siena's. "But it's my turn."

"Your tur…" Siena's words trailed off as Jamie dropped to her knees, nudging Siena's legs open as she shuffled into the space she created.

"Mmmmm." Jamie couldn't help the groan escaping her as she pressed her cheek to the inside of Siena's thigh, rolling her face closer to the scent she wanted to bury her face into. Siena's breathing filled the quiet of Jamie's apartment as she took in a deep breath, smelling Siena's arousal even through her clothes.

"Oh fuck." Siena's head fell back onto the back of the couch as Jamie lifted her head and shuffled closer at the same time. Her body pressed hard between Siena's legs, her nipples hardening as they brushed past the warmth.

"You like that, huh?" Jamie moved, aware of Siena's eyes

following her movements as she straddled Siena's lap. Warmth filled her cheeks as her desire grew. Capturing Siena's mouth once more, she ground her hips against Siena's.

Fingers, strong and sure, grabbed her ass and pulled her even closer. Jamie moaned and increased her speed to match the squeezing of her ass cheeks.

"I really, really…" Jamie panted between kisses before she tipped her head, arching her back and feeling Siena's mouth wrap around a breast through her clothes.

"Really what, baby?" Siena's voice was silk.

"…want to fuck you with a strap." Jamie forced the words out in a rush. The hands disappeared from her ass, and the mouth on her breast stopped.

Bringing her head forward, Jamie's stomach tightened with nerves before she saw Siena's face. A wild smile met hers and those dark eyes could have been black with how much desire and lust Jamie saw in them.

"You think I can handle all that power you'll have?"

"Oh." Jamie's eyes widened. Was this what a power bottom was all about? Jamie's lips quirked up at the corner into a smile. Two could play at this game, and play they would. They never got the chance before. "Well, fuck."

"Is that a yes, Ms. Kettlehouse?"

"By the time I'm done with you, you might struggle to move."

"Oh, promises promises," Siena purred, and Jamie laughed.

"I'll be back." She leaned her body against Siena's and kissed her again. Not as hard, but the touch sent sparks through her, igniting every nerve of her body. Jamie skidded to a halt right as she was about to leave the room. She purposely let her eyes roam all over Siena's body, the way she was sitting so confidently on the couch, the redness in her lips from their brutal kisses, and her hair mussed and out of place already.

"You better take your clothes off. I'm not in this for the slow, pleasurable today."

Siena chuckled low and quiet, her lips curling upward as her eyes lit with what seemed to be amused pleasure. "Then you better give as good as you're claiming."

Jamie hesitated, her toes digging into the carpet, her hand on the doorframe to her bedroom, and her heart in her throat. It would be so damn easy to walk over there and fuck Siena with her tongue and fingers, forcing both of them into a sexual oblivion before either of them could think to say anything else. And that was a challenge Jamie would be willing to take on.

But that's not what she wanted.

Not this time.

Jamie raised an eyebrow at Siena, giving her a look that meant all business. "You better be naked when I get back."

She left without a second glance, needing to separate herself before she gave into her baser desires. Siena's delicious laugh met her ears as she reached the drawer where she kept her toys. Her spine felt electrified with just the sound waves coming from Siena reaching her. What fresh hell had she found herself in? She shouldn't be wanting to fuck Siena every second they were in the same vicinity. Should she? Usually she was one and done and over a woman by now.

Then again, she'd always been a little bit obsessed with Siena Frazee, hadn't she?

She made quick work of her clothes, put the medium-sized dildo into its place and stepped into the strap. Nerves swirled in her stomach, and she wondered if this might actually be a dream, but quickly dismissed the idea as she maneuvered the base of the dildo into place. Her own wetness coated the tips of her fingers, and she bit back a groan and the temptation to ease some of the pressure pulsing in her swollen clit.

"Jamie." Siena's voice singsonged her name, pulling it out for several seconds.

"Coming!" Jamie replied, her smile wider than it had been in a while. Much better to let all of this happen with Siena right there with her. It had been amazing the first time, and Jamie had no doubts that this time would be even better.

"You better not be. Not yet, anyway." Oh there was so much seduction in that voice. Siena knew exactly what she was doing, didn't she? And she knew how to use her body, her voice, and her brain to get exactly what she wanted. Well, so did Jamie.

Jamie chuckled, and the nerves of walking out with only the strap on disappeared in the sound of Siena's voice.

"Oh my." Siena's breath caught as their eyes locked. Then Siena's gaze dropped to Jamie's breasts, staying there and lingering long enough to take them in fully. Then she looked farther down Jamie's body, across her wide hips and thick thighs and curved belly to right between her legs. "Fuck," Siena whispered.

"Indeed." Jamie's own eyes widened as Siena, still sitting where she had been but now completely naked, spread her legs out in front of her. She wasn't someone who was lacking in confidence—not in work, not in body, not in sex. Jamie's heart raced, pounding relentlessly as she struggled to come up with what to do and say next. But she couldn't move her gaze from the dark hair between Siena's legs, the curls that covered exactly where she'd wanted to press her face earlier.

It would hold all that scent, all the wetness and flavor that Jamie wanted to consume and memorize. Siena's breasts were pert, stunning, her nipples a dark dusty brown and hard as pebbles that begged to be touched and rubbed and played with. Siena's waist was small, curved inward, and begging for Jamie's touch.

"Do I pass your inspection, Jamie?"

"Of course. Did you think my standards were high?" Jamie winced at that. She hadn't meant that to come out like it had.

"Hardly, but we are on a bit of time crunch, don't you know that?"

"Oh, are we on a timeline now?" The question had meant to be flirty. A way for her to continue the teasing and push away the nerves that had crept up while she stood naked in the room, wondering exactly how they had gone from screaming at each other to her wearing her strap. Instead, something strange and unreadable flashed across Siena's face.

"I work in time, Jamie. Everything is on a timeline." Siena smiled, and the words came out easily enough, but the thick tension in the room grew a little cooler.

What the hell was this woman doing to her?

"Sorry." Jamie shook her head and looked down, instantly regretting her eyes being open as the strap mocked her.

"Hey." Siena's fingers were under her chin, lifting it slowly to meet her eyes.

Jamie hadn't even heard Siena move. And suddenly there was a softness to her that Jamie had been wholly unprepared for. She'd seen it, the soft and caring side, but she'd never expected or even thought she'd be on the receiving end of it.

"No timeline. No pressure. Let's just see where things go, okay?"

"But why? I'm the bad hack journalist."

"And I'm the money-hungry manager who doesn't give a shit about her stars." Siena raised an eyebrow as if to prove her point.

"I don't believe that. If you've read my latest post, you'd know that."

Siena blinked but whatever thought had entered her mind disappeared before she opened her mouth again. "And I don't believe you're nearly as bad as you think you are."

Jamie opened her mouth, wondering why Siena's words stirred such warmth in her chest.

"But maybe..." Siena's chin dropped forward, and she

flicked her eyes down before returning her smoldering gaze back to Jamie's. "A little bit isn't such a bad thing. All of us women in this industry need to be able to hold our own, don't we?"

Jamie could fall for this woman. The way she so easily made Jamie comfortable in moments of vulnerability, how she brought it out in her in the first place. The thought caught her off guard, but the pulse that had returned more urgently to her clit made it easy to push it away.

Before she could say or do anything more, Siena dropped to her knees and licked the underside of the dildo before wrapping her lips around the tip of it.

"Oh my God." Jamie's legs shuddered at the sight. "Lie down."

"What?" Siena pulled back, looking up with confusion and a tilt to her head.

"I said…" Jamie grabbed one of the cushions from her couch and threw it over Siena's head on to the floor over Siena's head. "Lie down. On your stomach."

"Oh." Siena smiled and obliged willingly.

Jamie took her time as her eyes grazed over every inch of skin. A small tattoo marked Siena's left shoulder. It made Jamie's chest warm. Until her eyes roamed down to Siena's perfect ass, lifted up from the cushion she lay against. Her knees were bent, and Jamie could see hints of her wetness in the dark patch of curls.

"Like what you see?"

Jamie took her time moving her eyes back up Siena's body to see Siena looking back at her over her shoulder.

"Oh yes." Jamie nodded and slowly lay her body on top of Siena's. She moved her hips a little to the side so the strap didn't hurt either of them, not ready just yet to use it.

Starting from the base of Siena's neck, Jamie made a trail of open-mouthed kisses down Siena's spine. In perfect reaction to her touch, Siena's body wriggled and squirmed beneath Jamie. Her ass pressed up as Jamie reached the base of Siena's spine.

"Please, Jamie," Siena begged, and damn if Jamie didn't wonder how long she would be able to last if Siena kept begging her.

"Please what?" Jamie knelt over one of Siena's thighs, straddling her there. With one hand, she cupped Siena right between her legs, her fingers parting her and finding the slick wetness she'd been longing to touch and taste.

Siena's reply was little more than a guttural moan as she buried her face into the carpet, her hips moving her harder into Jamie's touch. Jamie smiled as she ran a finger up the wetness and found Siena's swollen clit. Slowly, she circled the sensitive nub, chuckling as the movement of Siena's hips became more erratic. Shuffling so she leaned over Siena once more, she kissed the small tattoo and removed her hand from Siena.

After a groan of disapproval, Jamie wrapped her arm around Siena's hip and found her clit once more. The groans increased, and Jamie's own breathing increased as she pushed herself closer to Siena's ass.

"Can I be inside you with it now?" she asked as she pressed a beat with her finger on Siena's clit.

"Yes! God yes, Jamie."

Jamie guided the strap, making sure to move slowly, letting Siena's body and her reactions gauge how much she could take.

"More." Siena moaned as Jamie rocked her hips, not moving in any farther.

"Are you sure?"

"Yes, Jamie. Fuck me."

"Yes, ma'am." Jamie chuckled and pushed as far as she could, increasing the thrusts of her hips as her own arousal peaked, and Siena's ass pushed harder against her, moving in time with her own thrusts.

Fingers dug into Jamie's ass, and she laughed as she moved faster and faster inside of Siena, her fingers working against her clit as she lay more of her weight against Siena's back.

"Fuck, yes. Yes."

The more she thrust, the more Siena screamed and squirmed beneath her. The movements rubbed the base of the dildo against Jamie's clit, working her up until she thought she might also be tipped over the edge well before Siena got there. But that wouldn't be a bad thing, would it? Jamie bit down hard, holding off her own orgasm for as long as she could. She wanted to know what Siena looked like when she was as unraveled as Jamie had felt in that hotel room. She needed to know.

Siena's body stiffened, and she screamed out loud enough for the sound to bounce around the walls. Jamie let go of the last of the strength that held her up, and she all but collapsed onto Siena as she caught her breath.

"Are you okay?" Jamie asked, her cheek pressed against Siena's skin.

Siena laughed. "Your breath is tickling my spine."

"Oh really?" Jamie breathed out, making more shudders of laughter ripple beneath her.

"Yes."

"I figured."

"No, I mean. I'm okay. Thanks for checking."

Jamie kissed Siena's back as she retook her own weight.

Sadness washed over her as she thought about the lack of meaning in this. Not that she wanted it to be anything more. But she'd never felt so empty after a good fucking before.

Her mind ignored that thought and entertained the idea of what it might be like getting to have more time to touch this woman, to make her scream. And even more to get to know her in a deeper and different way than before. The things the public didn't know—not that there was much out there about Siena Frazee. But Jamie wanted more. She wanted to know the things that had sparked in her eyes, the truth she hid from general consumption.

As she eased herself out of Siena, she steeled herself to the fact that this was nothing more than the end of the one-night stand that had been rudely cut in half—prematurely.

"Where did you go?" Siena asked as she shuffled over, half sitting up now.

"Just glad I finally got to finish what we started." Jamie's entire body tightened. All the ease and looseness she'd had moments ago vanished into the ether.

"Finished?" Siena smirked and lifted a single eyebrow. "Oh babe, we aren't even close to finished."

No words appeared in Jamie's mind as a lump in her throat formed. She was used to people saying all kinds of things during sex, especially before they climaxed and got exactly what they wanted. Hell, Jamie was known for saying unexpected things when she was aroused.

Siena pulled Jamie in for a kiss, and this time, the sweet bliss that washed over Jamie filled her with a strange sort of hope, that maybe it wasn't just sex after all. Maybe it was more and that's what Jamie was pushing against. She wasn't used to the more.

When they got out of their own way, the chemistry between them went beyond attraction. She'd had a taste of it before, and the more she got to know the person behind the manager, the more Jamie liked the woman.

seventeen

Siena's body ached in all the right places. She couldn't remember the last time she had spent a whole afternoon ravishing and being ravished by a sexy woman. And not just any sexy woman, but one who not only understood the need for consent but reacted to the smallest cues from Siena's body.

She had managed to keep her mind focused on work for the better part of the day. She loved her work and enjoyed the thrill of seeing others thrive, despite the prima donnas—those who thought she should do all the hard work while they did nothing but stand still and look pretty. Despite them, Siena still loved her job.

Thank goodness, because it made it a lot easier for her to push the sneaky memories aside.

But as the afternoon wound down to its usual lull, her mind kept wandering back to Jamie and all the things they had done to each other. And with each other. It had been a while since Siena had truly let herself go with another woman. The one-night stands of the past were nothing more than scratching an itch. But with Jamie, she had allowed her desires, her cravings to rise up and do far more than just scratch.

The trilling sound of her phone startled her out of the memories, and she chuckled quietly at herself. Like a teenager caught masturbating, she had jumped at the sound. Placing her hands on the keyboard, she turned her face to her screen. Only now did she realize that she'd been lost in her own memories so long that her screen had grown dark from inactivity.

Rolling her eyes at herself, she realized that it wasn't her work phone.

And no matter which phone it was, they couldn't see her anyway. It wasn't as though Paula stood at the door with her pursed lips, raised eyebrows, and judgmental and concerned glances. Her phone stopped, and she shook her head. It wasn't like her to get so caught up in her head over a one-night stand.

Technically two-night stand really, but Jamie had crawled beneath her skin, and Siena's swirling mix of emotions confused her to no end. She picked up her cell from the desk, turning it over in her hand to check the missed call.

"Ingrid?" Siena said aloud to the empty room. It wasn't unusual for Ingrid to call during the day. It happened regularly. But rarely did it ever happen on her personal phone.

Before she could unlock her phone and return the call, it vibrated in her hand, the sound almost as startling as the first time it had rung.

"Calling on my cell in the middle of the day means one of two things. Did you have lots of salacious adventures you don't want recorded, or is there a world of fury needing to be vented?" Siena answered the call, the smile still on her face. With Ingrid it really could be either. Both of their workplaces recorded all phone calls. And that had saved Siena many lawsuits over the years.

Right now, she really hoped Ingrid's call would be in relation to her former suggestion, but her stomach plummeted as the energy through the phone told her the truth before Ingrid's words came out.

"Definitely fury." Ingrid's voice threatened to scorch Siena where she sat.

"Oh shit." The smile dropped, and Siena instantly brought her computer back to life, clicking up a new file ready to take notes. When Ingrid was like this, Siena always needed to take notes. Her words would flow quickly and were more often than not filled with vitriol. "Tell me."

"That fucking tabloid hack of yours is at it again." Ingrid exploded in a torrent of words. "I have no idea how or where she got her information, but the idea she can make these accusations and I can do nothing about it is bullshit. All because she hasn't made a single statement I can use as solid proof of a defamation claim is fucking ridiculous. She's a sneaky bitch. And I want to know how the fuck she got ahold of any of this information to begin with. Is there someone in our circle being a narc? I want to find these fuckers. Without the sources, she'd be nothing. And why does anyone listen to her to begin with?"

"Ingrid, hey…" Siena cringed as she interrupted the flow of fury, but her heart pounded too loud in her chest. "Slow down for a second, all right?"

"What? Why?" Ingrid's pout could be heard through the phone line.

"Because I need to know who and what exactly you're talking about." Siena used every ounce of her self-control to keep her voice calm and steady.

"I'm talking about that tabloid hack who fucked with Bunny and Piper earlier in the year. The one you're always having to put fires out because of. Well, she's now got her talons into my top client."

"Jamie Kettlehouse." Siena barely managed to get the name out. Her mouth was dry, and her lips felt chapped when moments ago they hadn't.

"None other," Ingrid hissed. "She got some dirt on my golden girl, and now everywhere you turn, she's being targeted as a liar and a fraud. I mean for fuck's sake. This could ruin her! All because that bitch thinks it's her right to call out the hypocrites. We're entertainment managers, of course half our clients are fucking hypocrites, but how the fuck does it affect her? So what if my client wants to act like she does charity work and splash that over the pages?"

"Hang on." Siena's fingers flew over her keyboard, her shoulders dropping and her heart growing heavy with each new article that popped up.

"Wow. They are not holding punches, are they?"

"Exactly. So you see what I mean?" Ingrid's voice still carried the fury, but there was also a smugness in the tone. One that Siena had never minded before. But this time, she wanted to scream and kick shit. Holding back, she couldn't be sure her frustration and annoyance really had anything to do with Ingrid at all.

"All right, so from what I can tell…" Siena had scanned several of the more popular articles, all pointing their sources back to Jamie's blog. "…the slant is definitely on her offstage presence."

"Yeah, but like you've always said, they deserve some privacy as well. They give enough."

Siena saw the difference, but there was no point in high-lighting that to Ingrid. It wasn't her job to justify Jamie's blog. It wasn't Siena's either. And yet part of her wanted nothing more than to form a defense for Jamie.

It was crazy. Her work meant so much to her, and here she was, thinking about Jamie instead of automatically helping her friend with the shitstorm she and her client were facing.

"Yeah, I know." Siena shook her head. Tried desperately to shake off the desire to justify Jamie's actions. "All right, let's get on top of this as much as we can."

"How?" Ingrid sounded deflated, and Siena knew she had to shake off anything to do with Jamie and help her friend.

"How we always do it." Siena smiled, ignoring that small part of her that still clung to the confusion she felt over Jamie. "We use the media against them."

"I don't think the usual stuff will work."

"No, I think you're right. But we can start a dampening campaign and try to anticipate anything else that might come up about it."

"Okay." Ingrid's tone was a lot calmer now.

Siena put her phone on speaker and let her fingers dance over the keyboard.

They spent hours together, and even after Siena had hung up the phone, her mind raced with steps Ingrid could use to help solve this problem. But she refused to let herself feel anything, at least yet. Because she wasn't sure what to think or believe. Her feelings were getting in the way, and she needed to think about this logically.

Siena had seen texts fly in from Jamie throughout the day, but she hadn't read or answered any of them. She wasn't ready for what they had to talk about yet, whether that was an actual interview with Bunny and Piper, a conversation about their second one-night stand, or something to do with the pressure that Siena knew Ingrid was putting on Jamie's boss to fire her.

Finally home and anything but rested, Siena's mind decided she was no longer in control, and it was now time to unpack all the thoughts and worries she had pushed down. She collapsed onto her couch, one leg up and her hand over her eyes to block out the light as she crashed hard.

She and Ingrid had worked for hours on fine-tuning the steps Siena had laid out, Ingrid taking over the details as she knew her client better than Siena could. She had chuckled at Ingrid's unguarded opinion of her client and wondered how her friend could work so hard for someone she obviously disliked. Then again, Ingrid had never had as strong feelings about that as Siena did. It was what had cost Siena her marriage.

Siena knew she wasn't as perfect as Tori in always doing the right thing, but she did try to only represent those she believed in, those who didn't lie to her or outwardly deceive the public. Keeping some things private was far from telling lies, as far as Siena was concerned.

Siena wished it had been her week with Harley. Her daughter was the light of her life. More than work, more than anything else she had ever experienced. And having her daughter here always helped ground Siena. She also had the skill of helping Siena with her grown up problems without even understanding what she'd done.

It had been a selfish thing, marrying Tori and having a child. Because that had been the only reason, when Siena truly thought about all those years ago, that she'd agreed to get married in the first place. That clock had been ticking, and Siena had let it take over her brain. In the end, she hadn't been able to keep it up with Tori, and she'd needed to end it for both their sakes. But despite the guilt that often tried to overtake her, she could never regret those choices.

She didn't want to regret any more choices when it came to Jamie either.

Then again, she wasn't thinking about an actual relationship with Jamie. Siena wasn't going to make the same mistake twice and rush into something when time seemed short. She always had more time.

Jamie's article had definitely stirred up the hornet's nest. But Siena couldn't find herself as angry as Ingrid had been. The truth about Ingrid's client being a spoiled brat behind the cameras was notorious on the manager side of the entertainment industry. It was why Siena had turned her down the first time and the second time she'd tried to leave Ingrid. And yet she was still cleaning up the brat's mess.

Siena had ignored Ingrid's rants about Jamie's source, but she also wondered how the hell Jamie had gotten ahold of the information. Surely it wasn't coincidence that they were spending more time together and suddenly Jamie was publishing more often and with stronger sources and claims than before.

Siena lay back on her couch and the dull throb of her earlier headache built up pressure. This wasn't just a Jamie and Ingrid issue. This was more than that. The first time they'd had sex, Siena could claim ignorance. But not this time. This time she'd walked into Jamie's apartment, and she had known full well what and who she was doing.

The itch beneath her skin wouldn't be satisfied.

Firing up her laptop, Siena found Jamie's blog and read the article properly.

It was incredible the way Jamie used her words to set the entire frame of her article. At the beginning, Siena wouldn't have picked up how well the slant would lean against Ingrid's client.

Three times she read it, and each time her stomach flipped in confusion.

The Jamie she knew, the feisty woman intent on truth and transparency, seemed to clash with the words and the sneaky way she found the information that Siena and her colleagues spent half of their working life keeping out of the limelight.

Who was Jamie really? And did her work show more truth of the woman than the caring and adventurous lover Siena couldn't stop thinking about? Or the sweet woman who helped her twin sister with Halloween parties for kindergarteners?

Either way, Siena knew keeping in contact with Jamie, professional or personal, was going to be nothing short of a roller coaster ride.

She just had to decide if she wanted to buy a ticket.

eighteen

"Well done, Jamie." Scott greeted Jamie as she plonked her breakfast bagel down onto her desk. The white paper bag was scrunched tightly from her grip as she had been down to the wire getting to work on time. Even though she started at noon this week. Her early week. But it didn't matter the shift she was on, she still preferred a breakfast bagel over any other option to start her workday.

"Huh?" She looked up to see Scott beaming over at her. "Well done? For only just making it to work on time?"

"No." Scott laughed and shook his head. "For the blog post."

"Oh." Jamie smiled. It had definitely hit harder than she had expected it to. It was part of the reason she had run late for work. She'd been caught up reading comments and looking at pieces other writers had done, taking her initial article and running with it. She had cringed a little bit as some of the writers might have taken it a little further than she would have, and definitely in different directions. But she had jumped in the shower and forced those thoughts away.

This was a good thing. The kind of momentum she had

been striving years for. She was finally hitting her stride and her website hits had dramatically increased. Including all her other articles. And it served the diva right to be called out on shit she had blatantly lied about.

"Thanks, Scott."

"I've started following your blog. And I've been reading some of your older posts. It's fascinating. And your writing gets stronger all the time." Scott's young, fresh eyes stunned Jamie a little, and she wasn't sure if she was embarrassed or what else it might be that washed over her. Being in the limelight for her writing hadn't ever been a problem. Probably because most people only had something negative to say about her topics, and nothing at all to say about the quality of her writing. The only time they even bothered to point out anything was when a typo or a missed comma had snuck through.

"Oh thanks." Jamie buried her head in the bag to grab out her bagel and hide the pink that had undoubtedly scattered across her now warm cheeks.

"Kettlehouse."

His voice was so close that she just about jumped out of her chair as she whirled around to find her boss standing two feet from her. He loomed over her, and she hissed internally at the toxic masculinity that reeked from the man.

"Good job on the article with that manager chick." He leered as he made no secret about peering down her cleavage.

She silently seethed at his description of Siena. "Thanks."

"What manager woman did you do an article on?" Scott asked, wheeling his seat closer and giving their boss no choice but to step back or be run over.

"It'll be in tomorrow's run, you can read it then." Their boss scowled at Scott before laughing at his own pathetic excuse for a joke.

He turned back to Jamie. "But don't think it gets you off the hook. I still need the interview with the pop stars. You better get a date to me soon or I'm gonna start thinking you're blowing smoke up my ass."

Scott had rolled his chair back to his desk, but she was certain she had heard him mutter something along the lines of that not even being a possibility in his dreams. His commentary was ignored.

"I've given you enough time on this. Get it or move onto something else. You need to be getting more scoops like that blog poster who just blew it out of the water with information about that false-saint celeb. Skinny bitch thinking people can be hot and have brains."

"On it," Jamie muttered, fighting the urge to roll her eyes. He couldn't just tell her to offer him her blog pieces before she posts them. Of course he couldn't. He had to sprinkle on the extra arsehole cologne. He turned away not waiting to see if she had anything else to add.

What she wouldn't give to see him trip over his own feet as he marched back to his office. It was ridiculous how he continued to run this office like it was 1970. But she knew better than to complain.

"What a fucking ass." Scott scowled.

"Yep." Jamie turned to look over at Scott. His face was still twisted into an unimpressed version of the happy young writer Jamie had judged as being too green behind the ears. "Thanks, by the way."

Scott nodded in acknowledgement, but apparently, he was more concerned about the blog comment. "How doesn't he know the blog is yours?" Scott asked. "It doesn't take a genius to see your writing style shine through there and the articles here. Does he even read?"

"He does know. He's just being an extra layer of asshole today." Jamie shrugged. "Besides, people see what they want to, I guess. The whole industry is built on first-appearance judgements. It's why it's so important for fans to know that their idols are just humans as well. They make mistakes, they aren't perfect, and they might not fit into the molds the world expects them to fit into."

But hadn't she done exactly the same thing with Scott? She'd assumed his happy-go-lucky nature made him naive and entirely unaware of the shit this industry could dish out and get you caught up in.

She wondered again why she bothered working there at all.

But of course, it took no time at all for her to remind herself of the benefits that kept her in place. She had a freedom she couldn't guarantee other places would offer and that she couldn't afford to lose. Especially the late shifts that gave her enough time to work on her own website and write those blogs that she would never offer him. He had no idea what she was making off her website, which this month wouldn't be mere pennies. He had no idea just what Jamie was capable of.

Jamie had dragged herself through her emails and kept finding other things she needed to work on instead of calling Siena to set up the interview. They had left on a good note the other day, which had quickly turned into evening. But something akin to butterflies, that couldn't be butterflies, had tied her in knots and stopped her from picking up that phone.

"I think it's my turn for a real coffee. You want one?" Scott said an hour later.

"Oh." She looked up and smiled, grateful for the distraction. "Yeah, that would be great."

With a nod, Scott left, and Jamie realized that at least part of her hesitation to call was also her not wanting to be overheard. Siena had a way of getting Jamie to let her guard down, saying things she hadn't intended on letting slip out.

Waiting for Scott to move away from his desk, she counted thirty seconds as slowly as she could before she lifted the handset on the old phone and tried to call Siena. She couldn't hide the smile or the thrill that raced through her body as she remembered Siena's touch.

The phone rang three times before it went to her voice-mail. Listening to Siena's voice, strong and professional, caused Jamie's underwear to get a little wet, so by the time the sound came for Jamie to leave a message she was already in a head space not entirely professional.

"Ms. Frazee." Jamie's smile grew as she purred down the phone line. "I'm calling in relation to an interview date with Piper and Bunny. If you could please get back to me as soon as possible, that would be fantastic." After a moment, Jamie couldn't resist adding. "I'll make it worth your while."

She hung up and continued through her inbox, feeling less concerned about the drudgery she had to wade through in order to pay the bills. It was all worth it for days like these, for moments when she felt a little less like the failure of the family.

The rest of the day flew by in a rush of words and calls, and she rode the thrill of news and leads. Though *thrill* might not have been exactly what she would describe it. The simple fact the boss hadn't spoken to her any more today was a bonus.

When Scott started packing up his desk and stood, she looked up at him surprised.

"Time for you to have some quiet, huh?"

Jamie looked around to see the rest of her nine-to-five colleagues packing up their things. Some rushed out without a single goodbye or wave, while others dawdled and mingled, chatting with each other as though they were friends. And maybe they were.

It was easy to forget about things like office politics when you only saw most of the others a few hours each day.

"See you tomorrow," Scott said with a smile and a wave.

"Yeah." But Jamie was already distracted.

It was five o'clock, and she still hadn't heard back from Siena. It had only been a few hours, but a few more than she had expected. The previous joy in her belly swirled into a discomfort that made her now regret the bagel she had eaten.

The woman was a busy manager. It was one of the features she liked the most about her. It was definitely a turn-on for Jamie. Not needing someone to blow up her phone daily was definitely a bonus. So Jamie hadn't minded not hearing from Siena for the first few days after she had come to Jamie's apartment.

But now something felt wrong.

Steeling herself for whatever might come, Jamie picked up the phone again and dialed Siena's number. She didn't even need to check her notes. The phone rang and rang. Frustration built within her and just as she was certain the voicemail was about to click on again, the phone connected.

Someone had picked it up, and she gasped a little at the now unexpected situation she had dismissed as happening.

"This is Siena Frazee." The voice was crisp and sharp when Siena answered.

"Ms. Frazee." Jamie recovered quickly and put on her purr for the greeting. "Did you get my message?"

"I did." Siena's tone was crisp and short. A tone that made the hair on Jamie's arms bristle and her back straighten in her chair.

"Are we able to set that date now?"

"No. You haven't sent over the one question you now want to ask." The sound of typing and papers shuffling came through the line, as though Siena were only half-engaged in the conversation with Jamie. So different from the attention she had given Jamie the other afternoon.

"This is ridiculous. I told you I'm not doing the back-and-forth with the questions anymore. I have ethics, whether you believe it or not, and being censored isn't part of that."

"Ms. Kettlehouse." The tone was so cold, Jamie involuntarily shivered despite the heat in the office. "If you wish to have access to my clients, then you will do this my way."

"Way to get the media on your side," Jamie muttered under her breath before she could stop herself.

"Excuse me?" The rustling and typing stopped, and Siena's words might as well have been hissed.

"Nothing for you to worry about, Ms. Frazee." Jamie ensured her address to Siena this time held not a single trace of the purring flirt she had first used at the beginning of this call.

"Are we scheduling a time to meet about these questions or not?" The typing began again, and Jamie wondered why the hell she had ever expected anything else from this cold-hearted entertainment manager.

This wasn't the woman she had picked up or the woman who had spent the afternoon with her, getting to know Jamie in a way no one else ever had.

"I don't suppose I actually have a choice in the matter."

"Of course you do," Siena snapped, and for the first time, Jamie actually enjoyed the fire in her voice. "You have a choice about everything you write and don't write. You have a choice about everything you do. Don't put blame on other people for choices that *you've* made and the things *you've* done."

The silence stretched between them, and Jamie wondered how in the hell her life had gotten complicated. Drama had always been her interest, but not her own drama. When it came to her life, she steered away from drama in all areas.

"When are you free to once again discuss and eliminate questions the public might actually be interested in knowing the answers to?"

"You're impossible." The words were muttered, and pages were flicked with a force that sounded like Siena may have actually torn them incidentally. "Two days. One o'clock at the same cafe as before."

"Fine. Your terms... once again." Jamie didn't need to

check her calendar. She knew she had to prioritize this if she wanted to keep her job. It had never seemed like such hard work before. But she knew having her byline on an interview with Bunny and Piper would help her, both in this job and for her reputation on the blog.

Ever since Siena had learned that she was behind the blog, Jamie had been less careful about others finding out. Anyone paying attention could easily see that she was both of them. The call disconnected without even a word from Siena. Jamie stared at the receiver in her hand.

"Well, fuck you, too." Jamie slammed down the receiver and looked up to find a fellow late shifter standing nearby. They held a full coffee cup in their hands, their mouth open a little and their eyebrows raised.

"This job is filled with shits and giggles, ain't it?" Jamie ignored what else they might have wanted to discuss. She pushed her chair back and stood. Grabbing her coffee off her desk, she decided the coffee offered at the place downstairs might at least get her through the last few hours of her shift without her going full shit fit on anyone else who walked past her desk.

"Truth." They chuckled, taking the hint and giving a nod as they continued on their way.

She didn't have that kind of relationship with any of her colleagues, especially with the late shifters. She never had the kind of camaraderie that seemed to come easy for everyone else. She had never seen the point in it. When she was honest with herself, Jamie had never had that kind of sharing relationship with anyone. Other than Jessie. She'd never needed it.

Even with Jessie, there were times it was still hard for her to open up to her sister. She would in the end, but it had to be on Jamie's timing and based on her sense of comfort. And with more than just a few pushes from Jessie.

Jamie walked to the small kitchenette of the office. She

didn't particularly need the caffeine, but anything to keep her hands busy and give her a sense of control was welcome. She had always been in control, always been on a path she was sure-footed with. It had never mattered that no one else understood it—not even Jessie.

But at the moment, nothing felt sure-footed. And everything kept getting in her way. Including herself.

"And this is why I should never have mixed business and pleasure, no matter how good the sex was."

nineteen

Siena arrived early at the cafe.

The lunch crowd was still in full flow. The noise of muttered conversation, the clatter of ceramic dishware and flatware, mixed with the hiss and churn of the espresso machine. Taking a deep breath, Siena let the bustle of the cafe wash over her. It calmed a fluttering in her stomach that made absolutely no sense at all.

Especially considering what she planned to discuss with Jamie, outside of the interview questions, if such a conversation came up at all. The phone call with Jamie had been terse, and she had been grateful when it was over.

She tried to convince herself that showing up early was simply the professional thing to do. But her time had always been important and expensive. She rarely showed up early for anything. On time, definitely, but her work life rarely allowed her the luxury of waiting for an appointment. Especially one outside of her office.

But professionalism was the theme of the day, and that was why she'd shown up early—the only reason she'd shown up early. It had nothing to do with her needing to seat herself before she saw Jamie again or why she had to choose the table farthest from the door in the hopes of getting to watch Jamie's sashay one more time.

No. None of that mattered. They were just perks of being a consummate professional.

She regretted that her seating meant the cafe clock taunted her, being directly in her line of sight, but she refused to get up and move again.

"This is ridiculous," she muttered to herself as she finished her first cup of coffee. It really should have been her only cup, but she still had ten minutes before she expected Jamie to show up, and she just couldn't concentrate on the work she'd intended on doing while she waited.

After ordering a second cup of coffee and pulling out her calendar to go through next week's meetings she needed to prepare for, her nerves settled. Siena looked up when she felt eyes roaming over her. She was halfway through her second cup and had worked out her schedule for next week within an inch of its life. Jamie smiled and gave a small nod when Siena's eyes met her own.

Siena watched as Jamie eased her way through the cafe crowd, and for a moment, Siena forgot how to breathe.

Jamie truly was exquisite.

Her curves were perfectly wrapped with a long pants jumpsuit with a neckline that dipped down into a deep V. But it was so much more than just her clothes. The way she walked, hips swaying from side to side, radiated a confidence that Siena hadn't dared to dream of having ten years ago.

And the sparkle in Jamie's eyes as she drew closer told Siena that Jamie knew damn well just what effect she had on the crowd. At least this crowd of one. Plum purple had never been a color Siena had ever appreciated on anyone before. She couldn't remember ever seeing anyone wearing it to be fair. But she wouldn't forget it now. Her appreciation had skyrocketed.

"Damn it," Siena muttered under her breath. Jamie wasn't even in range to speak to yet and already she was proving to be a complete distraction.

She had definitely decided on the right course of action. Her work had suffered since the two had met. Siena had been spending less time in the office and had found herself fantasizing about all kinds of things during slow times at work. And each and every one of the fantasies starred Jamie in a leading role. Even Bunny and Piper had noticed. Siena had screwed up their contract renewal and had to run interference with that.

She'd sworn she sent Bunny a copy of it, but she hadn't been able to find it. Not that she'd thought Bunny had even read it or the highlighted changes that Piper wanted.

"Ms. Frazee." Jamie's smile was wide, and as she sat in her chair, she leaned forward. There was no doubt in Siena's mind that the full view she got of Jamie's extensive cleavage was intentional.

"Ms. Kettlehouse." Siena could do this. Curse her body for reacting, and her mind from flashing memories of holding those breasts in her hands and worshipping them the way they truly deserved. The only way they should be treated, with respect and awe.

But she could keep her reactions to herself, and the wetness that coated her underwear could be dealt with later.

"Thank you for meeting me. We need to get these questions sorted out today. It's taking up too much of my time, and I'll have to cancel the interview if we don't come to some sort of conclusion."

"Considering I'm not the one holding up the interview, I can't see a problem with that." Jamie scraped back her chair as she stood. "But right now, I need coffee and some lunch. Would you like anything?"

"What?" Siena had been shocked by the question and looked up, blinking to see Jamie as she looked down at her. Her face soft and gentle, the mask of indifference had slipped away, and all Siena saw was the woman who had picked her up in the tapas bar and tasted like the rest of the world was on fire and she was the last breath of fresh air.

"No." Siena shook her head and looked down. What the hell was wrong with her? She wasn't the sentimental romantic type. Not truly. And yet the thoughts in her mind made her own head spin.

"Fine. Here are my questions. I'll be back shortly." Jamie placed a folder on the table in front of Siena before she walked away.

Siena wanted to stop her, wanted to call out and explain she had been answering her own desire for Jamie. But that would do the exact opposite of what she needed. Instead, after watching Jamie saunter off and stand in line at the counter, she opened the folder and looked at the questions.

Damn it. They're good.

It wasn't going to take very long at all. The last two questions Siena had problems with were reworked and now far stronger and more worth Bunny and Piper's time. She had made a few notes on the pages by the time Jamie returned.

"It's a rather busy time to be meeting here," Jamie said as she slid back into her chair. She didn't lean forward this time, and Siena found she missed the enticing view she had been granted earlier.

"It was the time I had free to get this done."

To get this over and done with. No matter how much she enjoyed looking at Jamie. She needed to put some distance between them, because she *had* to keep this as a one-night stand and nothing more.

"Funny." Jamie smirked as she leaned back further in her chair.

"What's funny?" Siena asked, frustrated at Jamie for still

playing games. And more frustrated with herself for wanting to know what Jamie was thinking and saying.

"It's funny how your timetable can fluctuate so quickly when it's something you want versus something you're annoyed with."

Something or someone?

That was the unstated part of that sentence, wasn't it?

Raising her eyebrow, Siena knew she shouldn't follow this line of conversation, she knew Jamie would take it away from the reason they were here. But again, she didn't really want the meeting to be over. Even if Jamie was the worst person she could possibly become fixated with. Her hours helping Ingrid put out fires made that abundantly clear.

"One day you have seemingly endless free time… say for an entire afternoon and evening, to do precisely what you want." Jamie smiled, and Siena's body betrayed her by reacting to the movement of her tongue as it darted out and licked her lips. "And you're so suddenly busy that all you're able to carve out for a work meeting is the busy rush of lunch and you can't even have the decency of small talk."

Siena opened her mouth to answer, but a waitress appeared and placed a coffee and toasted sandwich in front of Jamie. The woman left after Jamie thanked her. She lifted the coffee to her lips and took a sip.

Siena took a deep breath. It was now or never, and she needed it to be now.

No matter how she had felt with Jamie that afternoon. This wasn't the woman for her to fixate on. Jamie leaned back in her chair, eyes on the folder that still remained on Siena's side of the table.

"My workday can fluctuate at a moment's notice. It's what being a professional in the entertainment business is all about. It's affected by the people I work for, the people who work for me, and it's affected strongly by the media and what ridiculous things they come up with next."

"Right." Jamie's tone made it obvious she understood the pointed comment all too well. "And here you are making sure I'm getting all the right lessons about being censored in the entertainment business."

"It's not censoring," Siena hissed in reply. "It is protecting my clients."

"So you do this with everyone who interviews your precious Bunny and Piper?" Jamie took one finger and ran it around the rim of her coffee mug.

"I don't need to," Siena snapped back. "When Bunny and Piper typically book interviews, it's with people who have a far greater understanding of how this industry runs."

"And that right there is the problem." Jamie shook her head. "You and your manager friends have such a strong hold on your clients, the artists don't even get a real say about how they want to connect to their audience."

"Here we go again." Siena rolled her eyes. "You love to take everything that doesn't cater to you and turn it into some twisted conspiracy. Like I'm controlling absolutely everything that's out there about Bunny and Piper, like I'm fabricating these people who don't exist. But they *are* people."

"Is that how you justify what you do?" Jamie scrunched her nose, but she didn't take her gaze from Siena's face.

"I'm not the one needing to justify my position." Siena was trying not to get worked up, but Jamie was just so damn good at it. And she knew all the right buttons to push.

"There are far more fun positions then sitting here being scolded like a schoolgirl." Jamie hummed, her eyes lighting up at Siena's reaction.

Heat flashed over Siena's cheeks and raced down her body. No doubt exactly what Jamie had intended by her words.

"Then again, maybe being spanked over my knee is exactly what you want."

Siena ignored her. "If you're willing to take my suggestions on these last questions, then we can schedule an interview date." Despite Siena's physical reaction, she had to keep her words at the very least focused on the reason they were actually there. And she had to figure out exactly how she was going to intervene during the interview when Jamie no doubt pushed the boundaries. This was definitely one that she was going to insist on being present for.

"That's it?" Jamie's eyes furrowed even before she looked down at the folder she now held open in her hands. "No comment at all about what position you like the best?"

"No." Siena leaned forward.

She knew it was the right thing to do, to end anything but professionalism between them. So why did she keep balking at saying that? Why were the words thick and hard to force out of her mouth?

"No?" Jamie's smirk wavered a little on her lips, and Siena felt sick seeing this mighty woman doubting herself. She never wanted Jamie to have self-doubt or shame over what they'd experienced together. Because it had been amazing. Siena would never deny that.

"Those..." Siena emphasized the word, "...*positions* you're so keen to talk about are a conflict of interest to our jobs."

"So now you're going to tell me you didn't enjoy them?"

"Of course I enjoyed it." Siena's mouth spoke before her mind could re-engage and shut her up.

Jamie's smile grew wider, more satisfied.

Pushing forward, Siena continued, "Our times together have been extremely pleasurable. But had I known who you were when you first approached me, none of that would have happened."

"You knew who I was at my apartment. You knew who I was at the Halloween party."

"Yes." Siena rubbed the bridge of her nose with her thumb and index finger. "And I enjoyed it. However…"

"However?" Jamie nudged as Siena's silence lingered in the loud ding of customers and cutlery.

"However, as I said, it's a conflict of interest. And I'm not going to risk or give up my career for a good fuck."

"And you really think we can't do both?"

"Yes." Siena pushed her shoulders back and steeled herself. This was the right thing to do. It didn't matter how Jamie made her feel. Not that she allowed herself to fully examine exactly how she did feel. But it didn't matter.

She was happy with her life.

"I don't agree." A shadow passed over Jamie's eyes. Those gorgeous baby blues that were so damn expressive and would no doubt be Siena's undoing.

Siena's own doubt reflected back at her, and while it was somewhat a relief to know that beyond the flirting, Jamie had thought about the reality of it all. She bit back a smile, because Siena had no doubt that Jamie had thought this through. She thought everything through. And Jamie wasn't innocent or stupid, despite the sunshine that radiated from her, the confident swagger of her presence, and the brain people often didn't see beyond it that was incredible and amazing. Most people would take her as a girl next door when they first looked at her.

But Jamie was anything but that.

And damn, Siena desperately wanted more. Somewhere in the back of her mind, she wished Jamie could be the right person. The one that she'd thought Tori was. The one who wasn't just a one—or two—night stand.

But it was impossible. There were too many things stacked against them.

"The conflict is too high, and I suggest we move forward in a solely professional manner—at least through this interview." Siena pursed her lips, hating herself for saying those words. But there was no way she could see that they'd work out. Not right now. Not when Jamie needed her to keep her job and not while Siena kept trying to control every single thing that Jamie published about Bunny and Piper.

"And the great Ms. Frazee has spoken." Jamie's lips pulled up into a light sneer.

"Don't be petulant."

Jamie let out a guffaw as she picked up the second half of her sandwich. "Calling things how they are isn't petulance."

"I'm not interested in anything more." *That's a lie!* Siena's heart screamed at her, but she shut it up quickly.

"Sorry?" Jamie asked, the sandwich returned to her plate, uneaten.

"I'm not looking for a relationship."

"And why would you assume I am?" Jamie looked genuinely confused now.

Siena had misread this entire situation. She'd put all of her pent-up feelings and desires onto Jamie. Which was exactly what she'd done with Tori all those years ago. Fuck, she was making the same mistakes again. Siena opened her mouth and closed it again. "I suppose I did."

"Careful, that almost sounded close to an apology." Jamie smiled, and for a moment, the face that looked at her pulled at Siena's heart.

She was doing the right thing. Jamie was amazing, but she wasn't the right person for Siena.

"Apologies would imply I'm just human after all."

"And we couldn't have that." Jamie chuckled.

Siena watched as Jamie scanned the notes she had made on the questions, the plate with her sandwich pushed to the side.

"All right." Jamie looked up, and the face that had pulled at

Siena's chest had been replaced by the mask of the professional Siena had said she wanted.

"All right?" Siena asked.

"I can work with these suggestions." Jamie nodded as she looked at the papers again and closed the folder.

"Great." For the first time with Jamie, Siena felt a loss as an awkward silence settled between them.

"So can we set a time and date for the interview now?"

"I'll have to talk to Piper and Bunny. I'll send through some potential times for you this week."

"Fine." Jamie nodded and pushed back her chair. "Nice doing business with you, Ms. Frazee."

"And you as well, Ms. Kettlehouse."

Jamie walked away, that confident swagger she'd entered with vanished. Siena had done the right thing. She knew that. So why did it feel like she had just punched herself in the gut?

twenty

"Well, I've had a suck-tastic day. Can I come over and bring pizza and beer?" Jamie spoke into the phone the moment Jessie picked up.

"Oh hi, Jamie. So nice to hear from you. Yes, I'm doing well, how are you?" Jessie's dry humor didn't come out often, but it always amused Jamie to no end when it did.

"Fine." She laughed and mimicked her sister's chirpier tone. "Hi Jessie! I'm doing great. I'm looking forward to the frontal lobotomy later today, which will make the earlier part of my day seem like a bummer. How are you?"

"All right." Jessie laughed, and the sound made Jamie's shoulders relax as she headed toward her car. "Aren't you supposed to be working?"

"I called in sick," Jamie muttered into the phone.

"What?" Jessie's surprise might have made others think Jamie had just confessed to murder. But she supposed it was just as surprising. Maybe even more so.

"I called in sick," Jamie repeated, especially because it was very obvious that she wasn't sick.

"I'll order the pizza now. Grab the beer and head on over."

"Thanks, Sis." Jamie knew she could always count on Jessie. No matter what. Jessie was her rock.

They hung up, and Jamie refused to believe the saltwater that had spilled onto her cheeks was tears. Tears weren't her thing. And besides, what did she actually have to cry over?

By the time she arrived on Jessie's doorstep holding a six-pack of beer, all evidence of the emotional breakdown that had threatened earlier had been wiped away.

"Pizza is five minutes away," Jessie said as she opened the door, holding up her phone to Jamie. The app showed the pixelated pizza, sized bigger than the houses on the map, was just a few blocks away.

"Thank you." Jamie plonked down the beer on the counter in Jessie's kitchen and turned to find her sister standing there with arms open wide.

"Nope, not ready for that." Jamie waved her off, really trying hard to avoid any more displays of emotions she didn't understand or want to feel.

Jessie pouted. "Just give me a hug. You need it."

Jamie trudged forward. Her sister was right, of course. But she hated that she did need it. She hated that she ran off to her sister's shoulder whenever life got too shitty. And of course, it was a shitty situation she had gotten herself into and really had no one else to blame. Siena had been damn right about that.

Sure, she didn't know the article would blow up the way it did. The effect the entertainment managers had on her boss had definitely been unanticipated, but still, she had written and posted the damn thing knowing it was controversial and raw. That was the point, wasn't it? Get attention, move the blog forward, which was what she really wanted to be doing, wasn't it?

She hadn't known this one would be the thing that started her blog getting as much attention as her byline often did. How could she? She'd thought other articles would get her this much attention and they hadn't gone anywhere.

She relaxed into her sister's arms until the threat of tears she refused to shed stung her eyes.

"I need bad food and alcohol."

"Good. They're almost here." Jessie smiled, allowing Jamie to untangle herself from their embrace. "Go get set up in the living room, and I'll wait at the door for the grease."

Jamie didn't need to be told twice. Although, it had been a while since they'd had a sister indulgence night, it came as easily to her as riding a bike. She grabbed two beers, putting the rest of the six-pack in the fridge and snagging the ranch dressing on her way out toward the living room. Jamie plonked herself down on the floor next to the couch and ignored Jessie's eye roll when she came in holding the large box in her hands.

"Fine." Jessie sat on the floor on the other side of the coffee table, sliding the pizza between them. "But really, not even plates?"

"I'm on KP duty. I'm making it easy for myself." Jamie already had a slice of pizza pulled out of the box, the ranch squirted onto the cardboard, and her mouth around the end of the piece she'd dipped into the dressing. She bit off a tiny bit and quickly pulled the piece away, hissing from the burn on her tongue.

"Why are you always so surprised that it's hot?"

"Because the assholes at mine wait half an hour before they bother bringing it to me."

"And you don't heat it up why?"

"Ew." Jamie shook her head and tentatively nibbled at some more of the slice. "You're a savage."

"Yeah, but who's going to believe you?" Jessie laughed as she folded her own piece in half and turned it around, taking a huge bite into the crust.

"You really are a heathen."

Jessie shrugged and smiled as best she could with a mouthful of pizza crust.

With just a few slices left in the box, Jamie closed the lid and lay back on the floor parallel to the coffee table. Jessie didn't comment as she mirrored Jamie's position on the other side.

"I ate too much," Jessie moaned a few minutes later.

"The only way to eat pizza."

"For you maybe." Jessie laughed, and the quiet that settled over them was the comforting blanket of their relationship.

"What happened?" Jessie asked.

"I need to start looking for a new job."

"Oh shit." Jessie sat up, twisting around to stare at Jamie. "They fired you? I should have known. For you to take a sick day."

"They didn't fire me." Jamie stopped Jessie before she could continue any more with the rant. "Yet."

"Yet?" Jessie stared at Jamie, eyes bugged. "What makes you think they're going to fire you?"

"Because I'm never going to get this interview. And my boss told me that if I didn't get it, he'd fire me."

"The one with Bunny and Piper?" Jessie looked confused, and Jamie sat up and faced her sister.

"Yes." She gave Jessie a quick rundown on what happened and then lay back down.

"Why don't you think she's going to follow through with the dates?"

"Because it's what she's been doing for like two months now." Jamie opened her eyes and stared at the ceiling. Even the popcorn plaster mocked her. Her own ceiling at home was stained with spiderweb cracks. But Jessie's was pristine, and Jamie could have even put money on the fact it had been repainted recently.

"What she's been doing?"

"Yep." Jamie didn't move. She couldn't be bothered. "She puts on more and more conditions. She wants one meeting and then another meeting. She even mentioned that soon they'd be too busy for an interview. I read they were doing a Christmas charity event, but they haven't even announced dates for concerts next year. But *she* makes it seem like there aren't going to be any viable times, and I know it'll go back and forth until whoops it's now too late. And as soon as my boss finds out I don't have the interview, I'm going to be gone."

"Is that really such a bad thing?"

"Well, despite what you might think, I like having a roof over my head and food to eat. Beer is also a definite necessity." Jamie pointed at the empty bottles on the coffee table. Another one didn't sound like a half-bad idea either.

"Sure, I get that. But there are other places you could work."

From the corner of her eye, Jamie saw Jessie's head turn toward her. She didn't turn her own, she didn't need to, and she wasn't sure she could meet her sister's eyes with the thoughts in her head and the words that wanted to escape.

"Yeah, I know technically I could. But everywhere I would want to work wouldn't hire me. Not after everything that's happening with the goddamn manager mafia. And even the not as sought-after places know I'm not worth employing." Jamie knew she was being mopey and unhelpful when all Jessie was trying to do was help.

But the afternoon had left her deflated. Everything about Siena had been so different, so off from the woman she had gotten to know since the tapas bar. And it had thrown Jamie, despite how much she had to tried to hide that from Siena.

"And you really think that because she no longer wants to get all freaky with you that she won't send potential interview times?"

"I don't think she ever intended to set up the interview with them. I know she hasn't told them about the opportunity. And now that she's gone all frosty on me since the other day? No, I really don't think she'll allow it to happen. She's too fucking controlling."

"That's bullshit, James. I'm sorry." Jessie yawned, and her eyes turned away from boring holes into the side of Jamie's head.

"Thanks." Jamie closed her eyes again, the beer and pizza helping relax her body. Sleep pulled at her, and the comfort of her sister being close did nothing to dissuade.

"So, what are you going to do about it?" Jessie interrupted the perfect near sleep with her question.

"How do you sound so awake again when two seconds ago you were yawning?" Jamie snorted. "I want a sleepover, by the way. Your apartment is so much better than mine."

"It's problem-solving time."

"Oh fuck off." Jamie groaned as Jessie jumped to her feet and rounded the coffee table to stand at the end of Jamie's body.

"Come on."

Jamie stared at the hands Jessie offered out in front of her.

"There's not going to be any stopping you, is there?"

"Nope." Jessie pulled Jamie to her feet and bounded off the moment Jamie was balanced on her own.

"I don't know what to do, Jessie." Jamie called out in the now empty room. She hadn't paid attention to which direction Jessie had fled. The kitchen or the bedroom?

"Yes, you do. You've known for ages." Jessie returned from the bedroom holding a pencil case large enough for Jamie's head to fit inside, and a lined notepad.

"Oh shit. We've entered teacher mode."

"Don't you be giving my *teacher mode* a hard time. How many times has it saved your butt?" Jessie sat crossed legged on the couch, the note pad in her lap and the pencil case on top.

She pulled out a red pen and ruler and started lining up columns Jamie wasn't brave enough yet to look at.

Jamie rolled her eyes but kept her mouth shut.

Jessie wasn't wrong about Jamie being rescued more times than she cared to admit. But the way Jessie attacked everything with clean lines and logical steps made Jamie's skin itch as though she had brushed up against poison ivy.

Jamie enjoyed organization, but in her own way. And it was nothing like the boxed in idea of how things were supposed to be worked out and followed. The way Jessie did it, which of course was the way her parents had taught both them and their older brother, was so foreign that Jamie had never fully under- stood it.

"All right, time for a plan to get Jamie into a workplace that has moved forward from the 1970s."

Jamie burst out laughing and sat next to her sister, leaning in and resigning herself to letting Jessie create a plan that she may or may not follow. In the next few days, or at all.

———

Turned out it was only five days later when Jamie pulled the ridiculously clean and crisp plan out of her bag and laid it on the desk in front of her. The nine-to-fivers had left about fifteen minutes ago, and the other late shifters had gotten their next caffeine hits.

Jamie would be left alone for at least the next hour, all things willing.

With a resigned but determined sigh, Jamie opened the paper and began with step one on Jessie's plan. Forty-five minutes later, Jessie called Jamie's cell, causing Jamie to jump and curse aloud.

"Hey, what's up?"

"Just checking in to see how things are going."

"Well…" Jamie debated whether or not to keep the information to herself, but really, there would be no point. Jessie knew just about everything in her life. "I've started step one of your master plan."

"Damn it." Jamie was certain Jessie pursed her lips on the other end of the phone line.

"Damn it? I thought you wanted me to follow your precious little step-by-step list of ways to box my life in."

"Hey!" Jessie replied, but Jamie knew she wasn't truly offended, just like Jamie had only half meant what she had said. "And yeah, I did. But seeing as you are only on step one and it's been almost a week, I'm guessing something else happened to push you over the edge?"

Jamie shrugged even knowing Jessie couldn't see it, because she floundered for words to express how she felt about the entire thing. "Yeah. I guess you could say that."

"What happened?"

"I messaged Siena when I still hadn't heard from her and asked about the dates." Jamie continued to scroll through emails, sorting them into the ones she'd attack tonight and the ones that could easily wait a few more days to deal with.

"And no answer?"

"Oh no." Jamie laughed humorlessly as she leaned back in her desk chair. "The answer was the problem."

"Uh-oh."

"Yep. She hasn't been able to find a time that works for Piper and Bunny yet, but will let me know as soon as she *blah blah blah*. In other words, *good luck, I've now wasted as much of your time as I feel like you've wasted of mine whenever you dare to print anything even nearing the truth about my clients*."

"I doubt that's what she's doing," Jessie said softly.

"I love you, Jessie, but you have no idea what this industry is like. It's riddled with the worst people you could imagine."

"Well, no wonder you're so desperate to get work and recognition in the area."

"Oh shut up." But Jamie laughed. It wasn't like Jamie hadn't questioned her own sanity on the matter time and time again over the years. "Besides, I didn't just roll over and say okay. I offered her some suggestions on times that'll work for me, and thought perhaps it might make it easier for her."

"Look, I get it." The smile in Jessie's voice was something Jamie needed more and more lately. Whenever her life tilted and left her scrambling for her footing, the more she needed the safe harbor of her sister's calm gentleness.

"But?" Jamie preempted what obviously rested on the tip of her sister's tongue.

"While I might not know the in-depth details of the industry you're so fascinated and addicted with, I've come to know Siena a little. And I don't think she's that vindictive."

Jamie was about to agree. She'd never seen Siena as the vindictive type. Even when the managers had started hounding her boss. Her phone lit up and she looked at the screen.

A one-line text from Siena.

None of these dates are viable. My clients are very busy.

"No offense, Sis, but I don't think either of us truly know Siena half as much as we might like to think we do." Jamie fought to hold back the true venom she wished to unleash. It wasn't Jessie's fault.

"Uh-oh. Another message?"

"None of the dates work. Her clients are *very* busy. As though I'm nothing but a lazy idiot."

"Stop reading into what's not there, JJ."

"I will," Jamie said, "once people actually tell the truth and don't try to hide it between the lines."

"All right." Jessie sighed on the other end.

The different way they saw the world was an old argument, thankfully one neither was willing to get into again tonight.

"Thanks for checking in."

Jessie got the not-at-all-subtle hint, and they said their goodbyes. Jamie picked up her phone, and after a few colleagues had come and gotten their next hit of caffeine, she looked at Jessie's checklist again and moved on to step number two. If only she could stop herself from messaging Siena with another list of potential interview times, knowing these would be rejected just as readily as the first.

twenty-one

Siena regretted agreeing to one of the times Jamie had sent through on her second list of availabilities. But seeing as it was actually the same time she had already scheduled Bunny and Piper to come to her office for a catch-up, she decided she really did need to stop stringing Jamie along.

She hadn't wanted to cut their ties. Not really.

She hadn't wanted to stop them having sex again. But she knew it would never work out. They were on opposite teams with their own chosen career goals, and that wasn't something as simple as liking crunchy peanut butter or smooth.

Bunny and Piper walked through her door ten minutes early for the interview. Bunny was dressed in loose sweatpants and layered tank tops like she'd just come in from a long run and Piper was all done up and wearing a cute white dress.

"I can't believe you have actually agreed to this." Bunny shook her head as she hugged Siena and brushed a kiss on her cheek.

"I'm curious about how it might help things," Piper said in response as she followed Bunny with her own greeting.

The three sat back in their usual seats at the small meeting area in Siena's office after getting drinks for everyone.

"I'm hoping it helps steer things back toward your actual music, Piper. But yeah, I can't say I had it on this year's bingo card, that's for sure." Siena pursed her lips and glanced toward the door to her office, expecting Jamie to walk in any second now.

Bunny smiled and rested her arms on the back of the couch, one arm behind Piper as she spread her legs and took up space like she owned the entire office. Siena wouldn't ever deny that agreeing to work with Bunny and Piper had catapulted her career into a whole different arena. And now she was considering signing another duo group that she'd caught the attention of. The letter she'd gotten from them had definitely piqued her interest.

"Don't do that in the interview, yeah?" Siena said, pointing at how Bunny was sitting.

Bunny and Piper looked at each other and then turned their confused expressions back to Siena.

"Do what?" Piper asked.

"Your arm, Bunny." Siena jerked her chin in Bunny's direction.

"Oh for crying out loud." Bunny pulled her arm away and leaned forward in the couch, elbows now resting on her knees. "This is one hell of a bad idea."

"She's getting more attention, and it's better to get on her good side before she gets any more traction. She's making a hell of a lot of trouble for some others at the moment. It's what I like to think of as a preemptive strike," Siena said, feeling slightly guilty about the twist to her own story. It hadn't happened in this order, but it made it easier for her to justify the interview. To them, and more importantly to herself.

"Like your interview with her?" Bunny waggled her eyebrows. "That was…unexpectedly sweet."

Siena's cheeks burned. She really hadn't expected the interview she'd given on a whim to turn out as well as it had. Jamie had done a good job on it, which had boosted her confidence that Jamie wasn't only in it for the gossip.

"It was," Piper chimed in. "I read it even."

Piper usually stayed as far away from tabloids or news like that as possible. Siena relaxed back into her chair and glanced at the door again. When was Jamie going to be here? She'd never been late to a meeting before. In fact, she was notoriously always on time or early.

"What crawled up your butt?" Bunny asked.

"Nothing," Siena lied. She and Jamie hadn't been on good terms since their last conversation, that distance between them growing with each passing day, and it didn't sit right in Siena's chest.

"Don't lie to one of your oldest friends." Bunny gave her a pointed look. "You've been distant."

"I've been thinking about the past." Siena sighed heavily and ran her fingers through her long hair. She couldn't get Tori out of her head lately, not that she wanted to be in a relationship with her again, but because of how screwed up Siena had been when they were together. "Did I tell you that Harley went as a rock star for Halloween?"

"What?" Piper said. "A true rock star?"

Siena chuckled lightly and whipped out her phone and pulled up a photo that she'd taken when she and Tori had gone out trick or treating. She handed it over so Bunny and Piper could look at it. "My God, she's getting so big," Bunny mumbled.

"Grew a foot this last year, I swear. She looks so much older now that she's in school. Acts older too."

"Little bug is growing up." Piper pouted her lips and looked like she was going to cry in an exaggerated way. "We've got to find some time to hang out with her again."

"Yes, she's been asking for that." Siena took her phone back and noted the time. Jamie was now officially late. And there hadn't been a text or a call about it either. Jamie was always the professional. Siena had no doubt that she would show up when she said she would show up. Putting her phone onto the arm of the chair, face up so she could see it, Siena looked to the door.

Surely Paula would be in soon, telling her that Jamie was here and ready to set up for the interview.

"So how's Tori?" Piper asked.

Siena frowned. Tori was doing amazing. And it irked her in a way that she hadn't actually said out loud before, but maybe with Bunny and Piper she could. They'd been there throughout the divorce, from Siena's bringing up the conversation to Tori to her plummeting and treating herself like shit afterwards, to slowly bringing herself back up.

"Is something wrong?" Bunny asked.

Shaking her head, Siena tried to mask her feelings. "Tori's doing great. She and Miranda are moving in together. She and I had a whole argument about bunk beds."

Bunny snorted. "Piper broke her arm on hers."

"Hey now!"

"I know." Siena rolled her eyes. "I told Tori as much. It wasn't pleasant. But she won out. There really isn't another option for the room. And lo and behold, Harley broke her arm on it. Remember? I had to race out when we were meeting with Bea and Jo." She sighed heavily. "Do you ever wonder if you keep making the same mistakes because you're not healed or if it's just because you're too stupid to learn from when you did it before?"

Bunny and Piper froze. They glanced at each other, clearly sharing some sort of conversation that Siena wasn't included in. Bunny flung herself back into the couch, her hand along the top edge of it and behind Piper again. She eyed Siena cautiously.

Piper was the one who spoke. "That's pretty deep for pre-interview conversation, Siena."

"Sorry." Siena rubbed circles into her temple and glanced at her phone and the door again. Ten minutes late. Jamie wasn't coming, was she? "I just can't stop thinking about Tori."

"Really?" Bunny frowned. "I thought you were over her."

"I am. I don't mean it in a *I want to get back together* way. I keep thinking about our marriage, and divorce. But mainly why I asked her to get married in the beginning."

"Because you loved her?" Piper asked, her leg bouncing up and down like it always did. She wasn't nervous, it was just the extra energy that the woman seemed to always carry with her.

"Because I loved what she could give me." Siena loosed the words, and she could feel the tension rising sharply. "I love Tori, don't get me wrong, but I was never in love with her. I was in love with the idea of what she could give me that I couldn't give myself. A family. And when she gave me that, I realized it wasn't fair to her to keep her tied to someone who couldn't love her the way she deserved."

"So that's why you divorced her." Bunny lifted her eyebrows unexpectedly. "I never really understood that one."

"But what if I'm doing that again?"

"Siena…" Piper glanced to Bunny before getting an affirming nod to continue. "Is there someone else? You haven't mentioned anyone…"

Because there wasn't anyone. Was there? Siena hadn't worked that one out yet, and no matter how many times she told herself that she and Jamie weren't in a relationship, it did oddly feel like that. Siena was attracted to her physically for sure, but she was also attracted to who Jamie was—the confident blonde who was brilliant at her job and amazing with words.

"Siena?" Piper asked, her head tilting and catching Siena's eye where it still stared at her screen.

"I'm sorry. This time of year is always a struggle, you know that. Especially since Tori wants to start new Christmas traditions with Miranda, so I won't be invited to everything with Harley this year. The wonders of co-parenting, huh?"

"What's really wrong?" Bunny sat forward, ready to take on the world if she needed to. Siena had seen that look in her eyes so many times before, and she loved it every time. Bunny was fiercely protective of those she loved, and Siena was proud to call herself among them.

"It's thirty minutes past the hour." Siena stared at her phone and the door that was still closed. She knew for sure at this point that Jamie wasn't coming. She just didn't know why. Had she chickened out? Or was it because she couldn't stand being in the room with Siena? Or was it worse? Had there been some sort of accident that had kept her from getting there? Was she in the hospital?

"Do you have another appointment?" Piper asked, not immediately catching the meaning behind Siena's mention of the time.

"She didn't show up," Bunny said, mouth dropping open as she put two and two together. "What the fuck is she playing at?"

That anger had been what Siena wanted to feel, but she didn't. She was so caught up in the what-ifs and the worries that she couldn't bring herself to actually focus on how ticked off she should be that she'd spent so much of her precious time setting up this interview and convincing Bunny and Piper that it would be to their advantage only to have Jamie not fucking show up.

Siena swallowed and called back the emotions that wanted to pour out instead of tears. "I don't think she's playing. Not really. It's not her fault."

It was Siena's fault. She'd dragged it out too long. She'd played the game and she had pushed Jamie too far. Siena had just wanted their relationship—sexual at least—to be casual and they'd never managed to pull that one off, had they?

"Are you kidding?" Bunny twisted around to look at the door. "Look, we don't do interviews like this for extra credit. She should have shown up and done what she said she was going to do."

"Bunny, shut up," Piper interrupted.

Bunny angled her body toward Piper, and Siena knew a tirade was about to start but she looked up and met Bunny's eyes. In front of her, the emotions of bent-out-of-shape Bunny morphed back into the ultimate protector Siena had ever known. God how she loved her friend. If this entire situation hadn't involved Jamie Kettlehouse, someone Bunny already hated, Siena might have been far more inclined to actually talk to Bunny and Piper about what was going on.

"Siena, what's wrong?"

Siena swallowed the lump and the tears that wanted to spill. Fuck, she needed to get her shit together. Standing up, she swiftly walked out of her office and into the main office area. Sure enough, Jamie was nowhere to be found.

"Did she call?" Siena asked Paula, already knowing the answer.

Paula shook her head. "No, she hasn't."

"Right." Siena sucked in a breath and calmed herself down. She needed to do something with herself to burn off this energy. And what she really needed was to spend some time thinking of the farthest thing possible to what this could be. Snagging her phone, she called Tori. "Hey, mind if I grab Harley from school today? I wanted to surprise her with Zena's Donuts."

"Oh, that'd be great, actually. I'm running a bit late with this client."

"Perfect. I'll drop her off in the morning at school and we can go back to our regular schedule."

"Sounds good. Love you, Siena."

"Love you, too, Tori." That love had never been a lie, and Siena had never made the mistake of trying to play it off as casual either.

Siena checked her watch. She could do this. It would be perfect timing. But she had to make sure that Jamie wasn't going to randomly show up in the next twenty minutes either. She took her cell and dialed Jamie's number, waiting patiently as it rang and rang and rang.

There was no answer.

Not that Siena had expected there to be one. This was so unlike Jamie—at least the Jamie that she knew. When it tipped over to Jamie's voicemail, Siena closed her eyes and pinched the bridge of her nose.

"Time's up, Jamie. You didn't show, and I can't keep them here. Hope you're not dead in a ditch somewhere." She almost added a *call me* to the end, but she didn't. She didn't even say goodbye as she ended the message and held her phone down to her side.

Walking back into her office, she caught Bunny and Piper's attention. "Want to spend some time with Harley and me at Zena's? I thought she'd enjoy the treat and I need to pick her up from school."

"She's really not coming?" Piper asked.

"Afraid not." Siena had used those few minutes outside to set herself up for what was coming next. It had been enough time to pull her shit together and put her mask back in place. "You coming?"

"Are you driving?" Bunny asked.

Laughing, Siena nodded. "Of course. I don't trust you within twenty miles of a car in downtown Portland."

Bunny threw her hands up. "I'm not that bad of a driver."

"Says the tickets you've racked up. Totally believe that one." Siena strode to her desk and snagged her purse. This was a much better way to spend the next few hours. Far more worth her time than someone who didn't follow through on commitments.

twenty-two

"Can you grab those lights?" Jessie pointed to a box on the stage.

Jamie walked over and pulled them out. They were a tangled mess. "Did you put these away last year?"

"Maybe." Jessie grinned. "I promised Aisha that I'd help her out. I just didn't mention you were going to be my light detangler."

"Perfect." Jamie frowned as she plopped her butt onto the stage and started to unwind the cords. They had an hour until the parents started showing up with their kids for the holiday concert, and Jamie didn't want to be there. But she'd promised Jessie she would be, and there was no way she was going to break a promise to her sister.

Jessie continued to work alongside a few other teachers and parent volunteers, leaving Jamie alone except to snag the next string of lights that they were putting up around the auditorium. Jamie frowned as she worked. Jessie was so damn popular. It sucked. Jamie had never been popular, and while they were in high school, Jamie had hated every single minute of it.

Especially because people she really didn't like would start to talk to her, thinking she was Jessie.

It wasn't that hard to tell them apart, was it?

Jessie was happy and popular, and Jamie was the one that dragged everyone down.

"Seriously, what's wrong with you today?"

"Huh?" Jamie looked up, finding Jessie giving her the evil eye.

"I've called your name like four times."

"Sorry, I was…distracted." What she was actually doing was sitting in the *woe is me, the world hates me* moment that she used to live for when she was younger. She'd managed to process through a lot of that since then, but it still came back to bite her in the ass when she wasn't expecting it. And since she'd missed the interview time with Siena, she'd been right back in that moment.

"Distracted or… something else?"

Like hell was Jamie going to admit that. Not tonight of all nights. "When are we doing Christmas at the house?"

"Christmas day?" Jessie answered, raising an eyebrow up. "You're in the group text."

Yeah, but Jamie had been avoiding her phone like the plague ever since that voicemail had come through. Had Siena really thought she was dead in a ditch somewhere or had she just been trying to guilt Jamie about missing the interview that she had begged for. She'd even gotten down on her knees at one point and begged Siena for it—though Siena might see that particular moment in an entirely different way than Jamie did.

"James."

"What? Sorry." She shook her head again as she pulled particularly hard on the next row of lights she was detangling. "These things are annoying." She nearly threw her hands up in the air and gave up. "Do you really need them all?"

"We need that one, and then we're done."

"Fine." Jamie went back to focusing on the cord slipping between her fingers. She'd hated missing that meeting.

"Oh, the kids are coming," Jessie said. "Hurry up."

Jamie finally got the last knot undone and handed the cord over. Jessie immediately put it up and then started to hug her students as they came in one by one. God, her sister was so popular. There was nothing better than being a teacher of little kids. They always loved their teacher. Meanwhile, Jamie had picked a career where no one would ever like her.

And sometimes she just wanted to be liked.

That was a lie. She wanted to be liked most times. Just sometimes she wasn't willing to accept that she wasn't the lovable twin.

"Ms. K! Your twin is here!" Harley's sweet voice filled Jamie's ears.

Jamie closed her eyes, debating whether or not to make a run for it. She'd known that Siena would likely show up that night, that she wasn't going to bail on her daughter again when it came to something as important as this. But she had thought that she could sneak out before they showed up.

She'd just have to fake it until she made it.

She could pretend she was Jessie, right? Bubbly, outgoing, the one that everyone loved, and didn't care what people thought of her? Yeah. She'd done that before, and she could do it again. Jamie pushed herself off the edge of the stage and smoothed her hands down her tight jeans and the ugly Christmas sweater she'd insisted on wearing so that she could match the kids that night.

She walked close to Jessie, needing to stick by her sister to keep her sanity for the next little bit, and she was pleasantly surprised to see that Siena was nowhere in sight. However, there were two other women standing with Harley. One Jamie recognized as Harley's other mother—although she didn't remember her name at all.

God, Jamie needed to be better with names, but so often she was lost in her own world trying to figure out everyone's drama that she forgot she needed to pay attention to those people around her. "See, Mama!"

"I see, Harley." The cute brunette put her hand on Harley's shoulder.

The other brunette looked like Siena in a lot of ways, except they had vastly different eyes. Where Siena's were dark brown, this woman had honeyed eyes.

"I'm Jamie." She extended her hand.

"Tori. And this is Miranda." Miranda didn't smile at all, and the similarities between her and Siena intensified. She wrangled a wild little child on her hip, a mop of curls on her head that covered her eyes and hung all the way down to her shoulders at this point. The kid, however, was utterly adorable. Even Jamie couldn't deny that one.

"This is Rebel!" Harley chimed in, pointing to the kid that Miranda was holding. "She's my sister-cousin!"

"Right." Jamie frowned when she saw that Harley's arm was in a cast from her fingers all the way up past her elbow and nearly to her shoulder. "What happened, kiddo?"

"I fell off the bed." She frowned and stared down at it. "Wanna sign it?"

"Sure." Jamie waited while Harley dug around in her mom's purse for something and then handed over a permanent marker.

Jamie had never actually signed a cast before. Everyone had always wanted Jessie to do that, not her. She found *Ms. K* written with a heart and decided to write next to it. She printed her name instead of using cursive and she added a heart over the *I* just to make it seem far more kid friendly.

"There you go."

"Thanks!" Harley stared down at it and beamed. "It's almost filled up!"

"It is." Jamie put her hands on her hips and stilled. Even from this side of the room she could feel when Siena entered the auditorium. Looking up and toward the main entryway, she locked her gaze on Siena's.

A shiver ran down her spine. *That* was not a friendly look. Jamie should have known better than to think that Siena wouldn't feel slighted or upset by what had happened. She should have prepared to grovel or beg again or something. But instead, she was stuck right next to Jessie and she didn't hear a damn thing that Harley was chattering on about.

"I didn't expect to see you here." Siena's cool tones rocked through Jamie.

"I was uh… helping Jessie set up for tonight." Jamie threw her thumb over her shoulder, but she didn't turn to look at the stage. She couldn't tear her gaze away from the brooding woman in front of her.

"Figures." Siena leaned in and brushed her lips against Tori's cheek. "Good to see you."

"Mommy!" Harley squealed and raced up to Siena, wrapping her arms around Siena's legs. "You're going to love tonight." She giggled.

"I have no doubt of that," Siena said, but she was cringing. Jamie didn't blame her. She'd helped Jessie with most of the concerts in the last few years, and each time she went home wondering if her eardrums would ever recover. Though it wasn't as bad as the fourth and fifth grade band and orchestra concerts. Those were just hands down brutal.

"Where do you need to go to get ready, kiddo?" Siena asked.

"She needs to go to our classroom," Jessie stepped in. She held out her hand for Harley. "Come on, why don't we go see who else is here already."

Jamie was about to walk away, but she couldn't. Siena's eyes were locked on hers again, and she was frozen in place. Tori took Rebel from Miranda's arms and bounced a little with her. She leaned over, bending down with Rebel and making her squeal with delight.

"Thanks," Miranda murmured.

Siena flicked her gaze to them before drawing right back to Jamie. What the hell was going on? Why couldn't she speak? She wasn't ever speechless. She always had words. Words were her life. And now she was stuck here, staring at Siena like she was dumb, and she couldn't even manage to figure out how to make her feet and legs move so she could get away.

"How long do these usually last?" Siena asked.

Jamie pursed her lips. "Why? Can't spare more than an hour for your daughter?"

Tori tensed, and she looked directly at Jamie. Even Miranda looked uncomfortable with that comment. Jamie hadn't meant for it to come out of her mouth with so much vehemence, but she couldn't help it. Not with the way that Siena had talked about time so often, about how Jamie was wasting her time, about how valuable her hours were.

"So an hour?" Siena answered, raising an eyebrow as her eyes locked on Jamie's in a challenge.

Of course she would be the one to keep her cool during this entire debacle. Jamie was going to make an ass of herself, again, and Siena was going to come out the winner. That was how every single conversation had gone between them so far, hadn't it?

"Yes, about an hour," Jamie mumbled under her breath.

She finally looked around, really needing to escape this entire situation. She definitely should have told Jessie that she couldn't help her tonight. Either that or she should have left while she had the chance. Not to mention, she'd lost her safety blanket of a sister already.

She started to walk away, not saying anything else, but Siena caught her wrist and pulled her back. Siena looked at Tori and Miranda and smiled. "Save me a seat, would you?"

"Sure," Tori answered, smiling as she turned away to find seats for all of them.

Siena pulled at Jamie's wrist and started to drag her down the hallway and away from where everyone was coming in. "Where are we going?" Jamie asked.

"I don't know what that was about." Siena spun around, dropping Jamie's hand and shoving hers into the pockets of her jacket. "But I don't appreciate it."

"Appreciate it?" Jamie scoffed. "So high and mighty, aren't you?"

Siena narrowed her eyes. "Look, we need to talk. But now isn't the time or the place."

"I don't want to talk to you."

"Please." Siena's tone softened then, and it sounded far more like a request than it did a demand. That was something that Jamie could maybe handle. Except she wasn't sure what she'd do or say or how bad it was going to get if she let herself loose around Siena.

"I'll think about it."

"Where were you?" Siena asked, her voice firm and commanding again. "For the interview."

Jamie clenched her molars tightly and shook her head. "You didn't want me to do the interview anyway. So what does it matter?"

"It matters."

"No, it doesn't." Jamie hardened her entire body. "If you'll excuse me, I need to help my sister."

She didn't wait around. Immediately, Jamie turned on her toes and walked away from Siena and toward Jessie's classroom. She was too scared to look as soon as she stepped into the kindergarten classroom to see if Siena was still staring at her down the hallway, but she swore she felt Siena's eyes still on her.

She was playing a dangerous game with potentially ticking Siena off, but she needed to. For her own self-preservation. She'd already kicked off Jessie's plan, and this was her unofficial add to it. She needed to make a name for herself, figure out her own career, and she needed to do it all on her own. It wasn't about favors. It was about skill and passion.

"Everything good?" Jessie said quietly.

"Yeah, everything's peachy." Jamie winced. But more kids were dropped off. Immediately she walked over to the small table that Jessie had set up with coloring supplies and went to entertain the kids until it was their turn to go onto the stage and sing. She could do this. She could be the sister she always wanted to be, and eventually, she could be the journalist that she'd always dreamed of.

twenty-three

Siena clapped one last time as all of the students left the stage after their final number. Harley had been so excited when she'd finally spotted them in the crowd, and Siena had waved enthusiastically back at her.

"Did you want to go get her?" Tori asked.

"Yeah." Siena waited for the majority of the crowd to leave through the door, though. She'd been at plenty of these types of events in her lifetime and in her career. She knew that it was far easier to move around once everyone was gone.

Rebel had fallen asleep on Miranda's shoulder and was happily breathing in and out heavily as she continued to sleep during the final number. Harley would find that adorable. Siena was glad that Harley could at least have somewhat of a sibling relationship because she sure as hell wasn't going to get a sibling from Siena. Maybe Tori…maybe. Though Siena had more doubts of that since she'd fallen in love with Miranda.

"What's going on with you and Jamie?"

"W-what?" Siena stuttered over the word.

"What was that before the concert? I thought you were

going to take her out back and ream her a new one. I haven't seen you that upset in a very long time." Tori pressed a hand to Siena's arm. "What happened?"

"Nothing happened." Why was that always her go-to answer lately? And why was everyone prying? She really needed to get herself under control. Siena clenched her fists at her sides. "Jamie was supposed to interview Bunny and Piper. She didn't show up."

"Really?" Tori frowned. "That doesn't seem like her."

"It's not like her." Siena looked over the dissipating crowd, making eye contact with Jamie as she started to clean up the decorations from the stage. Oh, the joys of being the stage help. That was one job that Siena had never enjoyed.

She couldn't tear her gaze away as Jamie went to work.

"Siena." Tori cleared her throat.

"Yeah?"

"Are you going to get Harley?"

"Oh, right." Siena looked around to find the auditorium mostly empty. She immediately walked out and went down the hall toward Harley's classroom. When she stepped inside, she was greeted with a very excited six-year-old. God, she loved this kid through and through.

"Hey baby! You were amazing!" Siena scooped Harley up in her arms and gave her a big hug and a kiss on the top of her head. "I loved it."

"Were you surprised?"

"I was. You did such a good job keeping the songs a secret." Siena kissed her again and then put her down onto the ground. "Mama and Miranda are waiting for you. They want to see you before they leave."

"Okay!" Harley ran over to give Jessie a hug goodbye and then skipped back to Siena. Siena gave Jessie a sad little wave, but said nothing as she walked out of the classroom with Harley's hand in hers.

They made it to the front doors of the school where Miranda and Tori and a now very awake Rebel were waiting. Harley ran straight up to them. Siena let them talk a while as she looked around. Jamie came toward them, her jacket on and her hands shoved in it. Instead of turning toward Jessie's classroom, she scooted around Siena and Tori and started straight for the door, giving Siena a sideways glance as she went.

Oh, she was doing this intentionally. She was going to walk out without saying a damn word.

"Harley, we've got to get going. Say goodbye." Siena didn't drop her gaze to her daughter. Instead she kept her eyes on Jamie's retreating back. She wasn't going to let Jamie go without a conversation. Because she was afraid that if they didn't talk now then they'd never talk again.

With Harley's hand in hers, Siena walked outside, trying to catch sight of which direction Jamie had walked off in. It took her a second, but she finally saw her at the corner. "Come on, Harley."

Siena walked swiftly with Harley in tow as they went. She was going to have this conversation. She wanted an answer. She needed to know why Jamie had just given up so easily. Was this some kind of game to her? She obviously hadn't been dead in a ditch, but had she been in a ditch?

"Mommy, can we slow down?"

"In a minute." Siena looked both ways before racing across the street and catching right up to Jamie. "Were you just going to leave without talking?"

Jamie spun around, her hair flying around before it settled back down against her shoulders. She looked absolutely confused before she glanced down at Harley. "You're with your family."

"I told you that we needed to talk."

"We did talk," Jamie answered, holding her ground.

Siena shook her head slowly. "No, we didn't. You walked away from me."

Jamie once again looked down at Harley. Siena kept Harley's hand firmly in hers. "We can talk about this some other time."

"No, we can't. It has to be now." Siena straightened her shoulders. "Why didn't you show up for the interview?"

Jamie pursed her lips and then shook her head. "Like I said before, Siena, it doesn't matter. It never mattered to you. My career, my job, what I do for my livelihood doesn't matter to you."

"What the hell are you talking about?"

"Mommy, that's a bad word."

"I know it is, Harley," Siena hissed and then cringed. Her tone was way too harsh with Harley. She'd have to apologize for that later and explain that she wasn't mad at Harley.

Jamie took a step away, half turning her body as if she was just going to up and leave again. "We can talk about this when Harley isn't here. I don't think you want—"

"I want an answer." Siena's voice cracked through the empty street.

"Siena!" Tori's familiar voice reached her ears, and it was the scolding that Siena needed and didn't want. Of course she would show up now.

Closing her eyes, Siena's shoulders drooped. "I know." She kneeled down onto the sidewalk and held Harley by her arms, looking directly into her eyes. "I shouldn't have said that. It is a bad word, and I'm sorry. Sometimes when I get angry and frustrated, I say things that I shouldn't."

Harley nodded slowly, biting her lip, but she didn't say anything. Had Siena scared her that much?

"I also am not mad at you, baby. I promise."

"Are you mad at Ms. Jamie?" Harley's voice echoed.

Siena looked up into Jamie's wide eyes and then at Tori.

She had to answer truthfully. There was no way she could lie to Harley about this one. "Yes, I am."

"But she didn't do anything wrong."

"No, she didn't," Siena answered. "Being mad at someone isn't because they always do something wrong. Sometimes we just…" Siena winced. "You know, I'm just really mad at myself, that's what it is. And I need to figure that out, but I need to figure it out *with* Jamie."

"Okay?" Harley squeaked out.

"I'm sorry, baby. I need to do better next time." Siena moved in and hugged Harley. She was going to have to stand up and tell Jamie that they'd talk about this later, and then she really was going to have to find a time for them to talk. Siena faced Tori. "I'm sorry."

"Do you want her to come home with me for the night? You do owe me a night, and that way you and Jamie can have some time to talk."

"Oh, no, that's fine," Jamie interjected. "We don't have anything to talk about."

"Yeah, you do," Harley interrupted. "Mommy needs to apologize to you too."

Fuck Harley for being so astute. Siena cringed. "Yeah, that sounds like a good idea. Thanks. And sorry."

Tori hummed, giving Siena a knowing look. "I expect my apology in the form of tequila. Not for you and me, but for Miranda and me."

Siena laughed and her cheeks rushed with heat. "Noted."

Tori held out her hand for Harley, and they walked away in the opposite direction that Jamie had been heading.

"Well, at least I know where Harley gets her backbone from," Jamie muttered.

"She's not like me at all." Siena huffed as she watched mother and daughter walking away.

Jamie frowned. "She's exactly like you."

"Nah, she's all Tori."

"If you say so, but I don't see it that way. She's smart, she's outgoing, and she stands up for herself and the people she loves." Jamie frowned. "So she's you."

Siena's breath caught in her throat. This was never casual. Hadn't she told herself that already? Hadn't she tried to figure out what they were doing and who they were to each other? Or had she really tried to keep it casual when it was never that?

"Why didn't you come to the interview?"

"I told you already. It never mattered to you." Jamie jerked her chin up in defiance, and Siena could see the hurt that covered her face. She wasn't going to get out of this one without an apology and that was okay. Harley had been right. Siena owed Jamie an apology, more than one.

Siena sighed, the cold air from the December night biting her cheeks and nipping at her nose. Only this time it didn't come with the warm feelings of the Christmas season. It came with pain and struggle. And it came with shame.

"Come with me," Siena said.

"What?" Jamie took a visible step back. "Where?"

"To my place." Siena wasn't sure when she'd made that decision, but she had. Jamie had already woven herself into her personal life so much that this last step wouldn't be too far to make. "It's cold out here, I'm freezing, and this conversation that we need to have is going to take longer than the next twenty minutes."

"I don't think that's a good idea." Jamie shook her head and then looked around as if trying to find some type of exit.

"Then don't come. It was just an idea. But we do need to talk, and I'd rather do that where I'm comfortable. What about you?"

"You think I'm going to be comfortable at your place?" Jamie looked skeptical.

"Maybe. But it's at least warmer."

Silence filtered between them. It was awkward at first, but Siena wasn't going to push any more. Jamie needed to make this decision on her own, and if she decided they were going to have this conversation right here and now, then that's what Siena was going to do. But they really did need to just talk.

"Fine." Jamie pouted, her full lower lip pushing out. "But you're driving. I don't have enough gas to get anywhere but home."

"Fair." Siena shuffled her feet, trying to remember where she'd even parked. Luckily, they weren't too far away. Jamie followed her, and Siena hopped behind the driver's seat. As soon as the engine was running and both of them were buckled in, she breathed a sigh of relief. She hadn't actually thought that Jamie was going to come with her.

"So what are we talking about?" Jamie asked.

"The interview." Siena pulled away from the curb and started driving toward home. "Why didn't you show up? It took a lot of convincing to get Bunny into that room for you. She's not very happy with you in general."

"You actually got them there?" Jamie seemed surprised by that.

Siena frowned and furrowed her brow. "I told you I would."

The silence was deafening. Siena needed to hear Jamie's voice, to hear something other than her breathing in and out. She needed to know what had happened between them that this had gotten so bad.

"I don't know why we're even talking about this," Jamie muttered.

"Because you wanted an interview, and I set up the meeting for it. You worked hard to get there, and then you bailed. What happened?"

"You! You happened!" Jamie's voice burst through the car.

Siena was taken aback, but she didn't give in just yet. There was still time for them to talk. Siena turned onto the highway and continued to drive. "How did I happen?"

"I don't even know why we're talking. We broke up, remember? You told me that we were done. You told me that this was nothing. You're the one who told me that there was nothing between us."

Siena didn't remember that. She didn't remember saying at least half of those words that Jamie claimed she did. She'd pushed Jamie away, yes. She'd told Jamie that it was the end, essentially, that they needed to keep everything professional. But that had been what she'd meant—professional. And then Jamie had ditched even on that.

"I thought this was a one-night stand, Jamie. Nothing more."

"Two nights," Jamie corrected.

"Fine, two nights." Siena pulled into her driveway. "Answer my question, Jamie."

Jamie shook her head slowly, her eyes wide as she stared out the front windshield at Siena's house. "You're fucking rich."

"I'm not rich." Siena laughed lightly. "But I do make decent money, and I invest well. Sometimes it's nice to work for the stars."

"And sometimes it's nice to expose them when they're asshats."

Siena laughed louder. "I'll give you that one." Then she sighed heavily. "Why didn't you come? You didn't even answer my call."

"I truly believed that you were yanking my chain, Siena. You held off for so long, for months, and I had no promises from you that you'd actually follow through with anything."

"I always follow through on my word." Siena looked her over, eyes wide open to how far she had pushed and how much damage she had done. "I'm so sorry you didn't know that."

"How would I?" Jamie asked. "It was just two nights, wasn't it?"

No.

The word was on the tip of Siena's tongue, but she couldn't make herself say it out loud. It hadn't just been two nights. It was never that. Jamie managed to get under Siena's skin because she meant more than Siena wanted her to. Because Siena wanted more.

"It's warmer inside." Siena's words came out rushed, stopping anything else escaping before she was ready.

They walked in silence to the front door where sensor lights flicked on, reminding Siena she had to find her keys and keep moving. She couldn't lose herself in Jamie, not quite yet.

After they were inside and Jamie argued again about Siena indeed being rich, she led them into the small reading room. It had more records than books, but she had always called it the reading room, despite how it had ended up.

Sitting on the small love seat, Siena reached over to Jamie. She gently placed her hand on Jamie's, but she didn't squeeze, she didn't brush her thumb, and she didn't try to lace their fingers. When Jamie finally looked at her curiously, Siena knew she had her full attention.

"I think we started this wrong."

"Started what wrong?" Jamie frowned.

"Hi. I'm Siena Frazee." She smiled at Jamie. "And I'm a production manager for several local bands in the area. My most famous clients are Bunny and Piper."

"You're ridiculous." Jamie laughed nervously. "This is ridiculous."

Siena shook her head. "No, it's not. I want to take a chance, and I might be making the same mistake twice, but who the hell knows? I'm willing to find out. Get to know me,

Jamie. The real me. Not *Van*. Not Ms. Frazee. Me. Siena. Mom to Harley, completely neurotic when it comes to my calendar and work life, and overly protective of those I claim as mine."

Jamie shook. Her gaze dropped from Siena's face to their hands. Then she bit her lip. When Jamie looked back up, Siena knew the answer.

They were doing this.

twenty-four

"I'm Jamie," she heard herself saying. "And I'm no one's friend, I'm no one's favorite employee, I'm no one's favorite, not even my parents." Jamie swallowed the lump that lodged itself in her throat. "And I didn't come to the interview because I was scared." Her voice cracked. "And I thought you didn't want me."

Not *want me there.* She had been convinced that Siena hadn't wanted her at all.

Siena's lips parted in surprise, her face falling. "Jamie…" she whispered. "I can't get you out of my head. I haven't since that night I met you in the tapas bar, but even before then."

"Before?" Jamie steadied herself, trying to get a grip on what was happening.

Nodding, Siena flipped her hand over and laced their fingers. "I've read every blog post you've written, every news article in the paper, every one-off that you've managed to publish. I know who you are when you write. I haven't been able to get your words out of my brain since well before I saw you, since I met you."

"Siena…" Jamie trailed off, no idea what to say. She hadn't expected this. "None of that's true. Don't lie to me."

"I'm not lying." Siena lifted Jamie's hand, kissing her knuckles. "I never lie. Bend the truth, yes, when it's useful for my job, but never lie."

Jamie drew in a shuddering breath. She dropped her gaze to their joined hands, her heart racing. Why did this feel so right? Every time they'd had sex, it felt right, but everything in between had been a struggle. But something about tonight was different. It made her want to retreat and fall into herself so she could figure it out.

It scared the living shit right out of her.

And yet she stayed. She didn't run. She didn't try to hide. She held Siena's hand in her own, and she dreamed of their lips pressing tighter and their bodies moving in ways that would bring them both to the pinnacle of pleasure.

"I'm not sure I can do this," Jamie whispered, moving her hand from Siena's. "I…I don't think."

"Breathe, Jamie." Siena took her hand back, pulling Jamie's attention away from the panic that was settling into her chest and straight to Siena. "We're not doing anything except talking."

"That's what I'm afraid of."

"Words are your life," Siena responded, a deep line forming in her brow. "How can you be scared to talk?"

Because it's everything I don't want. At least that's what Jamie wanted to believe. But it was truthfully the opposite. She'd always wanted someone who would pay attention to her, who would love her for her and not because they were obligated to love her. And there had never been a single person in her life who had done that.

"Don't lie to me, Siena. I can't handle it."

"I promise you I won't." Siena cupped Jamie's cheek. "What's going on?"

Jamie shook her head. She hadn't thought this night would turn this direction. She'd thought they'd argue and get mad and scream at each other like they always did. But this side of Siena unnerved her—not in a bad way but in a good way. This was maturity. This was relationship. This was everything Jamie knew she wasn't.

"Kiss me," Jamie rushed.

"What?" Siena seemed so taken aback.

"Kiss me," Jamie repeated. If she could get them moving toward sex, then they could be on equal footing again. She would be able to find her ground and trudge forward through life again.

"Jamie…"

"Kiss me, Siena." Jamie demanded it this time.

Siena shook her head, still cupping Jamie's cheek. "You kiss me, when you're ready."

Jamie fell back into the side of the couch, staring at Siena with wide eyes. "What are you doing to me?"

"Learning who you are."

Jamie bit her lip. "No one knows who I am."

"Because you don't want them to know. It's a lonely life to live that way, you know. I did it for years. It's not worth it." Siena brushed her hair over her shoulder and relaxed. "Let's get to know each other, then."

"No," Jamie answered. "I'd rather not." Moving up on her knees, Jamie swiftly straddled Siena, pushing her knees into the couch cushions and staring down at her. Fuck, this woman was sexy as hell. Even in the vulnerable state that she was in, she held all of the power in the room, all of the control that Jamie longed for. She'd never be able to be like that.

"Kiss me," Jamie demanded again. "I want to feel you against me."

Siena moved her hands to Jamie's hips, then her ass. Jamie needed her to take control but in a different way. She needed the physical right now, not the emotional. She needed to be shagged—hard and good. She couldn't think about who they were to each other or why this felt so good and bad at the same time.

But Siena still didn't move to kiss her.

Frustrated, Jamie bent down and pressed their mouths together. Fire lit up her body, and she sank her hips down on top of Siena's lap. She wrapped her arms around Siena's neck and pulled her in close, their lips moving against each other and their breaths happening in sync. Jamie's eyes fluttered shut, and she focused on what she needed to.

Touch.

Siena's hands against her ass, the backs of her thighs as Siena pulled her in closer, the press of their breasts together through the fabric of their clothes. Jamie slid her tongue along Siena's, nipping at her lower lip, cupping the back of her head. She melted into the touch, she let Siena hold that control in her steady hands, and she let herself melt into the puddle that she'd become.

Without Siena, she never would have been able to do this. Without knowing that Siena would catch her when she fell, that Siena would cradle her when she cried, that Siena would fight tooth and nail for Jamie to have equal rights, she never would have been able to let go this much. It wasn't a game anymore. It wasn't a play of who had more power or who had more control. What they had, they had because it was together.

"Fuck me," Jamie begged. "Just fuck me."

"Where?" Siena asked.

"Bedroom."

Siena pressed their mouths together again, her hands firm on Jamie's ass before she shifted and pushed Jamie off her lap. It wasn't long before Siena stood up and held out her hands, waiting for Jamie to take them. Jamie stared at them. This was her one chance to get up and leave, to make the decision to leave Siena alone and continue with the end that Siena had set before them weeks ago.

And while a really big part of her wanted to stand up and walk out that front door, there was another part of herself that really didn't. She wanted to know if it was possible, if there was any hope that with the two of them, they could be together. Jamie bit her lip, and she slid her hands into Siena's.

The walk up to Siena's bedroom was slow, and Jamie's heart rate ramped up, pounding with each step that she took. As soon as they were inside, she spun Siena around and pressed her against the door, covering her. Their mouths were pushed together, and she pulled at Siena's clothes, trying to get rid of them as quickly as possible. She wanted skin to skin, she wanted body to body. She wanted to know if everything that Siena had just promised her was even remotely possible.

Siena pulled the ugly sweater over Jamie's head and dropped it to the ground. "Fuck, that thing's ugly," Siena said with a laugh.

Jamie couldn't stop her echoing grin. "It's all for show."

Wasn't that the truth? Ninety percent of what Jamie did was for show. When Siena had her shirt and bra off, Jamie spun them around and backed Siena up toward the bed. She pushed Siena onto the edge of it and then plucked at the snap and zipper on her slacks.

"God, you're sexy," Jamie muttered. "Fucking perfect."

"Hardly," Siena answered as she helped pull her pants off and toed off her black heels.

She must have gone to the school straight from the office if she was still dressed like this. Jamie had seen her dressed down, and this wasn't it. Before Siena could say anything else, Jamie bent down and pressed her face between Siena's legs. Siena let out a cry and fell backward, her hands holding her up at an angle.

Jamie drew in a deep breath, Siena's scent settling into the pit of her stomach. Fuck, this was what she had been missing. She hadn't gotten a chance to taste the last time or the first time, but she wasn't going to give up the opportunity now that they were doing this again. Jamie scraped her teeth ever so lightly across the soft skin inside Siena's thigh, across the cellulite and stretch marks, across the dark freckles. Then she used her tongue. Siena gasped, her knees parting even more as she threaded her fingers into Jamie's hair and tugged gently.

Jamie shifted, lifting Siena's legs over her shoulders and pushing in even deeper. She kissed the top of Siena's mound, the wiry and curly hair, and she savored Siena's scent again. If only she could bottle that up and take it with her, she would die a happy woman. Siena was amazing. Siena lifted her hips up slightly, and Jamie took that as a sign. She didn't lick or suck at first.

Instead, she thrust her tongue as far inside Siena as she could go. And she groaned as Siena's flavor bloomed on her tongue. Siena cried out, her back arching on the bed. Jamie reached up and snagged Siena's hands, folding their fingers together and pressing them down into the mattress. She held Siena there as she continued to tongue fuck her. She needed this—the sweet reminder that this was what brought them together and this was why they were here. Not because Jamie was someone who deserved Siena, and certainly not because Siena was interested in a deeper relationship.

They were here for the sex, and nothing more.

Weren't they?

Jamie dropped one of Siena's hands and switched her tongue for two fingers. She pressed the flat of her tongue against Siena's clit and started to lick her while fingering her. Siena got louder and louder, her voice reverberating off the walls with each press of Jamie's fingers against her.

"Fuck," Siena muttered, her eyes clenched tightly.

Her breasts moved with her body as she tried to control her

reactions, and a thrill of pleasure ran through Jamie at the fact that Siena wasn't in control any longer. Jamie had successfully taken that from her—or had Siena given it up? Either way, Jamie was the one in charge, even if it was only for a few brief moments.

"Jamie…" Siena's voice cracked. "Jamie, don't stop."

Jamie left her mouth and her fingers exactly where they were. She held on tightly, as Siena pushed her hands into Jamie's shoulders and careened through her orgasm. Jamie continued to lick and taste. She was going to memorize this scent, this flavor. She was never going to forget it. Something about Siena was special, that was for sure, but Jamie wasn't quite sure what it was. Not yet anyway. But she wanted to make sure that in twenty years, she'd remember this moment.

"Come up here," Siena said, her words slightly slurred from pleasure. "It's my turn."

Jamie smiled, licking her lips and the last bit of Siena's flavor from her mouth. She wasn't sure that Siena could figure out what to do with her right now. It'd definitely take her a few minutes to get herself together if her closed eyes and soft smile were anything to go by. Jamie enjoyed the sight as she finished getting undressed. After stepping out of the last of her clothing, she looked back up and met Siena's smoldering eyes.

"Right here," Siena said, indicating that she wanted Jamie to straddle her again. Curious, Jamie crawled her way up. Siena ran her hands up and down Jamie's legs and then tapped her thighs again. "All the way up, Jamie."

"I…" Jamie wasn't used to this position. It was so much more intimate than she was normally okay with. But Siena just waited for her to move. She didn't push, she didn't pressure, she didn't do anything other than smile and say, "Okay."

Jamie climbed up, straddling Siena's head. Siena moved her arms under Jamie's thighs and grabbed hold of her tightly. Fair was fair, right? And Jamie knew without a doubt that

Siena could do wickedly amazing things with her mouth. Lowering her hips down, Jamie waited for the first brush of Siena's tongue against her.

She wasn't disappointed.

Siena sucked in a sharp breath and went full on. She curled her arms around Jamie's thighs, moving her closer and closer. Jamie's eyelids fluttered shut, and she leaned forward over Siena's head and pressed her hands into the mattress to keep herself upright.

Jamie's voice was loud to her own ears. "Fuck." She groaned, clenching her jaw. She couldn't help herself when she started rutting against Siena's mouth, wanting and needing more. She would never get enough of how wickedly amazing Siena was at doing this. No oral that Jamie had received before Siena could compare to this.

Holding herself upright, Jamie stayed as planted on Siena's face as she possibly could. She didn't want to move. She didn't want to get Siena off rhythm. Words floated through her brain, but she wasn't sure any of them reached her lips.

Perfect.

Amazing.

Yes.

More.

Don't stop.

Again.

Again.

Again.

Jamie would take this happening as often as she possibly could. She'd wanted Siena's mouth each and every day since she'd experienced it the first time. There were so many more fun things they could do, but this was what she had lived for since that first night. This was what was going to make her weak in the knees.

"I'm coming!" Jamie cried out, digging her fingers into the

pillow and lifting herself up lightly. The last thing she needed to do was suffocate that beautiful face between her legs.

Siena held her closely, even as she collapsed to the side and flung her leg up to avoid crushing Siena underneath her. Siena rolled with her, and then she brushed her fingers all over Jamie's body in the most tender touches that Jamie had ever experienced. It was light, it was patterned, and it was sensual.

Jamie closed her eyes and caught her breath, slowing her heart rate into something manageable. Eventually she shifted around and lay next to Siena, facing her. Siena tangled their hands together, once again kissing Jamie's knuckles with a smile on her lips.

"Stay the night with me," Siena whispered.

Jamie's voice caught in her throat. What harm would one night do? It wasn't like she had the money for gas for her car or money to catch a ride back to her car or to her apartment. Besides, Siena was so warm and inviting, and they could fuck again and again until they were both so exhausted that they passed out next to each other.

"You swear you have coffee, right?" Jamie asked.

Laughing, Siena nodded. "Yes, I have coffee."

"Then it's a deal." Jamie moved in quickly and kissed her hard. She hummed and closed her eyes again. "Do you know how fucking amazing you taste?"

"Just as good as you do," Siena answered with a cocky quirk of her lips.

twenty-five

Siena had been living on a high ever since she had taken Jamie home.

A gnawing at the pit of her stomach tried to remind her of the morning-after facts. She hadn't heard from Jamie since she had dropped her back off to her car after another round of orgasms, toast and coffee. Not precisely in that order.

But the thrill that bloomed inside her couldn't be quelled.

"Hey, Piper," Siena answered the phone with a smile on her face. Piper didn't often call Siena about business things. That was always Bunny. But things had been shifting. Siena could feel the changes buffeting around her. Even with her distractions, her honed skill at her job had never let her down before.

"I need your help." Piper sounded nervous, her normal chipper and bubbly tones dampened by something that Siena was in the dark on still.

Siena looked over to the dining room table where Harley sat, legs swinging as she sang incorrect words to pop songs while coloring on random paper she'd stolen from Siena's printer in her home office. Harley was insisting on practicing writing with her left hand since her right one was confined by a cast practically up to her shoulder and she didn't want to fall behind in school. Her swinging feet were still far enough off the ground that Siena could push the idea of her baby growing up too quickly from her mind. Most of the time.

She listened to Piper, and even as she told her friend and her client the reality of this backfiring, her mind was already working on getting everything she needed.

"Mommy, what's wrong?"

Siena looked up to see Harley staring at her with big, worried eyes and her mouth slightly open.

"Oh, I'm okay, baby." Siena sat next to Harley and looked at her daughter's drawing and the random numbers and letters that she'd manage to learn how to write littering the page. "Just trying to figure out a problem at work."

"Can I help?" Harley asked before shoving the end of her pencil in her mouth and biting on the end.

"Don't chew the pencils, baby. You'll get splinters in your mouth."

"Mommy." Harley laughed but put the pencil back on top of her paper. "I won't get splinters."

"Good. Because they would be super hard to try and get out with the tweezers."

Harley looked horrified. Siena pulled her head toward her chest and hugged her even as she smiled, a little too amused that her fostering fear about pencil chewing might have worked a little too well.

"Hey, we're going to meet Aunt Piper down at a park. Her and her friend are doing a little dress up for some photos. Did you want to come with me and help take them?"

Harley pulled back from Siena, leaning so far that Siena worried for a moment that her daughter might fall off her chair. But Harley stopped moving once she saw enough of Siena for her liking.

"Really?" Her mouth fluttered between a smile so large it threatened to eat up her face, and the open shock of such an offer.

"Really."

"Yes, yes, yes, yes!" Harley was off her seat, dancing around the table. She made awkwardly jarring movements as she waggled her shoulders and kept going.

The sight was everything Siena needed. She laughed and then jumped up, joining Harley in her dance and chanting.

"Can we go now?"

"Soon baby." Siena laughed and ruffled Harley's hair. "Let's get you cleaned up. And I better change as well."

"Why is it just Aunt Piper and not Aunt Bunny?" Harley asked as she pointed out the dress she wanted to wear at the park. Siena had to think hard about how many times Harley had actually been with only one of them and not both of them, and she had to admit, it was rare. Bunny and Piper were always together.

Siena didn't enjoy lying. Not even when she walked the fine line between bending and crossing the truth at work, she never enjoyed it. And the idea of lying to her daughter made her stomach churn. "I think Piper wants to keep it a secret."

"Secrets are bad, Mommy."

"Not a secret, sorry baby. Piper wants to keep it a surprise."

Harley pursed her lips as she thought, but she must have understood the difference this time. "Did you get Aunt Piper the deal for these pictures?"

"You know about the deals I get my clients?" Siena hadn't realized just how much Harley was paying attention to what she did.

"Nah!" Harley shook her head and sat on the floor of her room, focused intently on scrunching up the sides of her sock with her one good hand to make it easier to put on. "I just know you help Aunties with them sometimes. That's right, isn't it?"

"Yeah, baby. You're right. And so clever."

"Okay, you need to get changed, and I need to put on my socks." Harley looked at Siena until their eyes met. She gave one sharp nod, and then returned all her attention on getting her socks into line, and hopefully on her feet.

Siena wanted to stand at the threshold of Harley's room and simply watch her. But Harley had been correct. Siena did need to go get dressed. She also needed to figure out if what she planned to do was going to be worth the fallout if she made the wrong choice.

Once she'd put on some going-out clothes, Siena sat down on the end of her bed. Memories of being fucked to within an inch of her life threatened to steal her focus. And for just a moment or two, she let herself indulge in them.

But Harley wouldn't be much longer before she came in search of Siena and wondered why they weren't leaving yet. Before she could talk herself out of it. Again. Siena grabbed up her phone and dialed the number.

"Siena. Hi." Jamie sounded distracted on the other end of the line.

"Hey, did I call at a bad time?"

"Nope, not at all. You just got me out of some more confetti making for Jessie. Please, by all means talk away."

"Right." Siena chuckled. She wondered at which of the upcoming Christmas events at the school she would find herself covered in said confetti. "I was wondering if you'd be interested in a different sort of article to write."

"What kind of article?" Jamie had a way of saying so much, even when she said so little. The hint of hesitation Siena heard couldn't hide any of the curiosity and excitement that seeped through the phone.

"It's a fake piece. That's the first thing you need to know.

And it's not going to be published immediately. It might not need to be published at all."

"What on earth are you scheming?"

Siena laughed. She really enjoyed how much she did that when Jamie was around. It seemed more natural than ever before. "It wasn't my idea. I'm simply helping my client make it happen, which is perhaps what I thought you might be interested in."

"Which client?"

"Piper," Siena replied. Was it crazy that while Jamie's excitement remained, there also seemed to be a hesitation, a distance she hadn't anticipated?

"Right. So what would you like me to do in relation to this fake news?" Jamie asked, and Siena couldn't pretend anymore that it was just her paranoia. Everything about Jamie seemed strange tonight.

"Are you okay?" Siena wanted to smack herself in the forehead as the words slipped out as they entered her mind. There had been no process between thought and tongue.

"Absolutely," Jamie replied in the voice that told Siena that something was definitely not okay. "What do you need in a professional manner from me?"

"Profession..." Siena's heart seized in her chest. They had talked. Well, she had talked. She had ended on such a high after her night with Jamie she hadn't checked. She hadn't made sure without a doubt that they were on the same page.

She was fucking it all up again.

But this time, she wanted the person and not just the idea of what they could offer her.

"Right." Siena wiped at her cheeks as Harley came into the room, socks and boots successfully on her feet. Even on the correct feet, Siena noted, wondering why she would even notice the detail when inside her chest everything was slowly tumbling down. "I'd like you to meet us, if you're able, and write a piece about what you see."

"That's it? Do I get any kind of hint as to what I'll see?"

"I think it'll be better if you see it for yourself."

"Right," Jamie said, and Siena could imagine her nodding and tucking a pen behind her ear. Which was a stupid image. As far as Siena knew, Jamie might not even use pens to take notes. She might be a complete technological junky. She rolled her eyes at herself and then quickly beamed a bright smile to Harley who was looking at her with her brows furrowed.

The smile had done the trick though, and Harley returned the gesture in kind before walking farther into Siena's room and standing in front of the full-length mirror that stood at an angle in the corner of her bedroom.

Images of watching herself fuck Jamie in the reflection filled her brain, and she quickly coughed to shake it away.

"So, will you make it?"

"I'll try. Send me a text with the details, and I'll do my best to be there."

"Thanks, Jamie."

"Bye, Siena."

The way Jamie said it had sounded so final. Not *see ya*, or *later*. But *bye*…

"Is someone else coming to the park? Will I take pictures of them too?" Harley stopped the pain in Siena's chest from entirely taking over.

"I invited them, but I don't know if they'll have the time to show up."

"Who is it?" Harley asked twirling in front of the mirror. "It's Ms. Jamie, isn't it?"

"Yeah." Siena laughed and scooped her daughter up in her arms mid-twirl. Harley squealed and then laughed. "It's Ms. Jamie."

"I hope she comes. She's pretty, and I want to take pictures of her."

"She is pretty." Siena's words threatened to stick in her throat. "But even if she does come, she might not want her photo taken."

"Oh." Harley furrowed her brow. "And I can't take pictures of people if they haven't said I could, right?"

"That's right." Siena nodded, pride swelling her chest.

"Okay." Harley nodded, already taking on the seriousness her role as photographer deemed.

"Well then, let's get going, munchkin."

"Nope, I'm Superman."

"What happened to being Batman?"

"Superman takes pictures for the Daily Planet." She affected a tone that Siena was certain she'd hear more of as Harley became a teenager. "So I'm Superman today."

"So does Lois Lane."

"But Lois Lane keeps getting caught and needs to be rescued. I don't need to be rescued."

"No." Siena smiled, shuffling herself and Harley out of her house as she grabbed snacks and bottles of water at the last minute. "You definitely don't need saving, Superman."

At Siena's words, Harley's chest puffed up a little more. She pushed her shoulders back and strode away slow enough for Siena to whip out her phone and take a picture before Harley got too far away.

It didn't take Siena very long to get to the river and the bridge. Piper and Jo were already there, standing very close to each other. Siena had to rush to get Harley out of the back seat of the car. She held onto her as she climbed because it was so difficult to see in the dark and Harley's arm was still in the damn cast.

They made their way to Piper and Jo, and Harley had already started doing what she was there to do. Taking pictures. Siena stayed back a little, giving Harley the space as Piper played into everything for her. Harley's squeals were such a delight to hear—Siena loved that Piper and Bunny had fallen so in love with Harley when she was born.

"Are you kidding me?" The sound of Jamie's voice was music to Siena's ears. They'd already taken a few photos of Piper and Jo. "You're telling me these two aren't actually together?"

"Hi." Siena looked over at Jamie as she sidled up beside her. They stood a few feet away as Harley moved places and angles, getting photos of the women who talked as though they weren't about to enact a fake engagement.

"Hey. So, what's the fake news? Because I'm finding it a little hard to believe that these two aren't just a little more than friends."

"Honestly…" Siena sighed and tried not to scream and tell Jamie that whatever was happening to stop and come back to her. Stop moving away. "I'm not entirely sure."

"All right. But what's the fake news then?"

"Hang on." Siena placed one hand on Jamie's forearm as she raised the other to get Piper's attention. She hadn't taken much notice of the movement, not until Jamie's arm stiffened beneath her touch. "Are you ready?" Siena called out to Piper, her breathing coming a little faster than it had moments ago.

"All good." Piper smiled to Siena and then turned her eyes back to Jo.

Oh, there was definitely more than just a little something going on there, but Siena wouldn't pry. Not into her client's life, or her friend's for that matter. She just hoped Piper would tell her when she was ready.

"This is the fake part. It's a long story, but if you can write it up so it looks as real as possible, that would be for the best."

"You want me to lie and purposely feed false information

to the people?" Jamie looked a little green about that statement.

"No." Siena shook her head. "Well, not exactly. I don't want it published in any traditional papers." She'd thought this through many times over, and while she could have easily written something up on her own and made it seem real enough for what Piper needed, Siena wanted to see Jamie again. And she wanted to know exactly what Jamie would do— she was the expert in all of this, wasn't she?

"What do you want?" Jamie asked, moving her eyes away the moment Siena tried to meet them.

"You have several blogs."

"What?" Jamie looked startled, and the thrill of getting a reaction not focused entirely on her being an uptight professional was intoxicating.

"Everyone knows about the JK one. But I'm not the only one with secret sources." Siena hated herself for the smirk on her lips and the teasing lilt in her voice. But fear made her desperate.

"All right. You want me to post it up on one of my other blogs. To what purpose?"

"For someone else to believe it's real." Siena swallowed the lump in her throat. She should keep it to herself. But seeing as Jamie was determined to be professional, Siena might as well see how strong that ethical line Jamie insisted upon mentioning really was. "For Bunny to believe it's real."

"There's issues with the duo?"

"Not really. It's Piper's way of trying to get Bunny to stop standing in her own way, as well as in Piper's way I think."

Jamie looked confused, but she didn't say anything as her mouth dropped open as the proposal on the small bridge in the park played out in front of her. Harley took photos, Jamie scribbled in a notebook, and Piper and Jo spoke words that

Siena couldn't hear. All while Siena's heart slowly cracked along fissures that might actually be irreparable.

"Wow." Jamie nodded as she closed her notebook and looked at Siena. For a moment, Siena saw *her* Jamie. The one who sparkled and strode through the world like nothing could ever have the power to damage her. But just as quickly it disappeared once more.

"So, you're okay with the rules? Do you need anything clarified?"

"I understand. You want it published on a no name blog, where few if any people might actually see it. I'll send you the link so you can show Bunny."

"But don't post it yet." Siena rushed to add. "Please. I'm hoping Piper and Jo realize how absolutely absurd the entire thing is before we need to actually show Bunny. But yes, that's where it would be best to be posted."

"All right." Jamie nodded and straightened her back as she squared her shoulders. "Thank you very much for this opportunity, as strange as it is. I'll hear from you if and when you would like me to publish it."

"Jamie." Siena tried, despite the cracking sound of the growing fissure within her.

"Professional. That's all we can be," Jamie answered the unasked questions that had filled Siena all afternoon. "I'll let you know the link once you give the go ahead. Bye Siena."

Jamie started walking off before Siena could even say goodbye.

She didn't want to say goodbye.

The cracks in her chest grew louder and she watched Jamie disappear along the path that headed back to the parking lot.

twenty-six

Why was the noise so damn loud?

Jamie kept furtively looking around the office like she would somehow find the answer. But it wasn't just the voices that were bothering her. It was the slamming of drawers, the ringing of phones, the slide of Scott's chair wheels against the plastic floor mat.

Her head was going to explode.

"Kettlehouse!"

Jamie jerked with a start as her name rang through the room, piercing her ears. Pulling herself to stand, she snagged her phone, saw a message from Siena on it, and shoved it into her pocket. She wasn't sure what to respond to any of the messages that Siena had sent so far. And each time another one popped up on her notifications, Jamie's stomach sank even more.

She dragged her feet toward the boss's office, shooting Scott a sympathetic expression as she walked by his desk. She had no idea what she'd fucked up now, but she was damn sure that the boss's tone meant business.

"Shut the door," he said as she stepped inside.

"Sure." Jamie cringed as she pushed the door closed behind her. She didn't sit down. She stayed upright, feet shoulder-width apart, and waited for whatever reaming she was going to get next.

"Where's the article with the interview about Bunny and Piper?"

Jamie's stomach sank. She'd never thought that Siena would actually make that happen, so she'd avoided it and hadn't gone. Meaning, she now had no article for her boss, and this was going to be her undoing.

But…

She had her notes from the fake engagement, and that would probably satisfy him enough in terms of the pop culture drama that she always told him she had, although he never believed her. Jamie licked her lips, and the muscles in her shoulders tensed sharply. "I'm working on writing it up now."

Why the hell had she said that?

Money. Right. She needed to pay rent this month, and it was already going to be close whether or not she'd manage to do that. If she could even afford the gas to get to and from the office that week. Fuck, why was she in her early thirties and still unable to be an adult?

"You are?" His voice cut through Jamie's inner monologue of fears.

"Uh…yeah, I am. I'll have it ready to you by the end of the week." Now she was just digging herself an even bigger hole. Jamie needed to get her shit together. She needed to stop lying, and she needed to figure out what it was that she wanted in life. Because this job definitely wasn't it.

"Good." He leaned back in his seat, his mustache moving slightly when he wiggled his lips and looked her over again. "Your last article about Siena Frazee was well-received. I'm sure you can deliver again."

"Right." Jamie bit her lip this time. "Uh… I'm going to go work on that right now."

He nodded at her and focused back on whatever was on his computer. Jamie slipped out of the room, shutting the door behind her as the panic set into the top of her chest. What the hell was she doing?

Jamie typed at her computer, staring at the screen as the pounding headache continued to get stronger and stronger. It was so bad that the nausea forced her to run to the bathroom and lean over the toilet bowl. Standing upright, Jamie pressed her forearm into the wall of the stall and took slow breaths.

This didn't mean anything.

Sex with Siena had never meant anything.

At least it wasn't supposed to.

It was only ever casual between them—they were only ever there for the fun and the damn good sex. Their lives had gotten tangled up outside of that because of Jessie and Harley and all the random in-betweens that seemed to pull them together because fuck the six degrees of separation. Jamie hated it. This wasn't what she wanted for her life. She'd never wanted anything like this.

Jessie was the one who was always trying to fall in love and find a partner. Jamie wasn't. She was so focused on her career and her job that nothing else mattered. She wanted to dig deep into the drama of the world around her and forget that the world despised her.

"Jamie, you okay?" Scott's voice rang through the bathroom.

Jamie groaned and closed her eyes. The last thing she needed was that poor kid coming to check on her. She steadied herself, put her hand on the stall, and opened the door. Scott stood at the main bathroom door, his head peeking around the corner. He looked so worried.

"I'm fine," she answered. "At least for right now. Will you tell boss man I'm going home sick? It's just a bad migraine."

"Yeah, sure. You need me to drive you?"

Jamie shook her head. "No, I'm good, thanks."

Though he wasn't wrong. She really shouldn't be driving. She pulled her phone out of her pocket, groaning again when she saw a second text from Siena. The problem was that Jamie had no one to call. Jessie was at work and today was the Christmas party, so Jamie couldn't call her to come pick her up, and there was literally no one else that Jamie trusted to do that.

But what about Siena? Her stupid brain brought up that question, and Jamie cringed. What about Siena? They were keeping it professional, right? And this would definitely be crossing that line in a way that Jamie didn't want to.

"I'm driving you." When had Scott come into the bathroom? Jamie squinted at him as he put a hand on her back and started to guide her out of the bathroom.

"You don't even know where I live."

"Pretty sure I can figure that out," he said. "I'll take you home and then come back. Just an early lunch."

"Boss won't like it."

"He can suck a dick."

Jamie's lips curled upward at that. "It's just a migraine. I promise. My sister gave me some drugs for it because she gets them. I'll take that when I get home."

"Good idea."

Jamie tried not to let the embarrassment take her over entirely as she allowed Scott to lead her out of the building and to his car. He had her home in record time, and Jamie flopped herself carefully onto her couch. Scott set her up with some water and a bowl in case she puked again. She could have laughed at his adorable care of her if she wasn't feeling so miserable.

"I'll call you tonight to check in, okay?" he said.

"Yeah, sure." Though Jamie doubted he would actually do that. She closed her eyes as he stood in front of her, the light from the windows so bright she couldn't stand to keep her eyes open. "Thanks, Scott."

"Anytime."

When the door was shut, Jamie groaned loudly. She hated this. She hated her life. She hated everything about who she was right now. This wasn't who she wanted to be. It never had been, and yet she was trapped in this cycle where she was stuck at one job in order to do the other job that she really wanted to because the one she wanted didn't fucking pay. Even Jessie's very detailed plan hadn't helped her to climb back out of this hole she'd stepped into willingly.

She sent an SOS text to Jessie and then curled into a ball to sleep. She had no doubt that Jessie would show up as soon as she could and baby her until she was better. That's what big sisters were for, right?

———

"Jesus, Jamie." Jessie sat down on the coffee table and eyed her over.

"It's better than it was." Jamie frowned and stared at all the things she had around her. She had only moved once while she waited for Jessie to show up, and that was to take a very cold and very dark shower because her head was still pounding. "Did you bring the good stuff?"

"Yeah." Jessie pulled a pill container out of her purse and took one out, handing it over to Jamie.

"Oh magic, how I adore you." Jamie snatched it and took it quickly with a swallow of ice-cold water that Jessie had already brought her. This stuff was better than the over-the-counter stuff that Jamie could get anywhere. She'd only needed it two other times, but hell, she definitely needed it now.

Lying back down, Jamie covered herself up with the throw blanket all the way up to her chin. She clenched her eyes shut and then just waited. She got lost in her thoughts, in the pain and the ignoring of the pain, so when Jessie sat back down again, Jamie was startled.

"How are you feeling now?"

"Better. I think." Jamie pried her eyes open, finding Jessie still looking at her with concern. "What time is it?"

"Well, I just cleaned your entire apartment for two hours."

"Two…?" Jamie pushed herself to sit up a little, a frown forming on her lips. "It wasn't that gross."

"Sure." Jessie rolled her eyes. "You must be feeling better, you're upright and you don't look nearly as pale as you did before."

Jamie ran her fingers through her still damp hair. She did feel better. "Those pills are magic."

Jessie laughed lightly. "So, what happened?"

"What do you mean *what happened*?" Jamie so wasn't ready for any kind of conversation. At least not with this being the topic. She didn't want to talk about it.

"You only get migraines when you're stressed. So what happened?" Jessie crossed her arms and glared at Jamie. "Spill."

"Ugh, I hate you sometimes."

"Yet you beg me to come take care of you and clean your apartment."

"Hey, I didn't ask you to clean up." Jamie pointed at her. She really must be feeling better if her brain was kicking up this much of a fuss. "I told my boss that I was writing an article for the interview that I never went to."

Jessie wrinkled her brow. "So you're going to make it up?"

"Nope. I hadn't thought about doing that, though that's a much better option." Jamie curled her legs under her and sipped at the lukewarm water that Jessie had brought her before. "I really should have just made up a story."

"What story were you thinking about writing?"

"One that Siena asked me not to publish anywhere." Jamie frowned into the glass. It would be an ultimate betrayal, wouldn't it? Jamie filled Jessie in on the fake engagement scheme, at least what she knew of it—it still didn't make a whole lot of sense, especially since Siena had been involved, but whatever. Jamie wasn't going to think about it too hard. She had information, and that was more valuable than anything.

"So let me get this straight, Siena trusted you—someone she never trusted or even liked before—to help her with something super sensitive and you want to backstab her by printing it in the paper so you can keep your job."

"Well when you say it like that…" Jamie trailed off. "I'm a jerk, I know I am. I never claimed not to be."

Jessie growled at her, full on growled. Jamie jerked back, her eyes wide in surprise.

"What the hell did I do now?"

"Look, you aren't a jerk. You aren't an asshole. You aren't unlikeable." Jessie stood up, fists clenched at her sides. Jamie couldn't remember the last time she'd seen her be this mad about something. "I'm sick and tired of you believing that about yourself."

"It's true!" Jamie fired back. "No one likes me. I know that, and I fully accept it. The only reason you put up with me is because you have to."

"That's the only reason I'm sitting here right now." Jessie rolled her eyes. "That and I love you."

Jamie narrowed her gaze. "Don't get all mushy now."

"Oh my God. You're impossible sometimes. Do you really want to do this to Siena? You like her, James. I know you do. I've seen it in your eyes."

"I said no mush." Jamie narrowed her gaze and crossed her arms over her chest. "It's gross."

"You're ridiculous. You like her. She likes you. Stop trying to ruin it all because you think that you're the pariah of the planet, the scourge of the earth."

"Now who's using hyperbole."

"Jamie!" Jessie screeched. "I'm going to give you another damn migraine if you don't shut up."

Jamie sighed again and deflated. "Fine. I'll listen."

"Siena trusted you with this. That's huge for her, James. Don't you realize that? And you just went in and told your boss about it and planned to write an article? If you ever want a chance of being with her again, you can't do that. This isn't just about the ethics of love, it's about ethics of being a decent human being. You will hurt her so much if you do that."

"I know," Jamie whispered. It had been why she'd immediately regretted saying anything. "I'm so…tangled up in her that I can't think straight anymore. And everything's crumbling down around me. I don't know what to do, but I do know that if I continue this with her, I will hurt her."

"Not if you start being a decent human being again."

Jamie snorted lightly. "What makes you think I ever was?"

"Because I'm your older sister, and I've been around your entire life. You are not an asshole. Most days." Jessie's lips curled upward into a sweet smile.

"But I need my job. I'm short on rent this month as it is."

Jessie rolled her eyes hard. "I'll loan you some money. But you can't compromise your ethics for cold hard cash. That's a very lonely life to lead."

"She's rich you know." Jamie wrung her hands together. "Well, she said she's not, but she has a house in Eastmoreland, and it's fancy."

"She works hard for her money, just like you do. She just has a job with a higher ceiling than writing the gossip column at the local paper and running blog websites that generate zero income but use all your time."

"Time is valuable." How much Jamie hated hearing that again, especially in this context. She hated that Siena was right. What Jamie was spending her time on wasn't life-giving or money-giving. And she needed to do something different.

"It is." Jessie gave her a soft smile. "So what are you going to do now?"

"I'm going to end it with Siena."

"Not quite what I meant, but that can't be the only thing that you're doing."

"I'll figure that out tomorrow. My head still hurts."

Jessie gave her a pitying look. "Fine, tomorrow. But I'm going to expect an answer to that question."

"I'll get to working on it."

twenty-seven

"Did you see what JK is up to now?" Ingrid's voice was so full of energy.

Siena cocked her head to the side, staring at Ingrid as she stood in the doorway to her office. "What are you doing here?"

"I thought you might need two brains to work through this problem."

Problem? Siena frowned and shook her head slowly. What problem was Ingrid even talking about?

"You don't know, do you?" Ingrid sauntered into the office, her long legs sliding through the high split in her skirt. Siena's gaze dropped before picking right back up. "How do you not know?"

"What am I missing?" Siena pressed her lips together hard. She really hadn't been expecting an impromptu visit today. And the fact that Ingrid looked so perturbed by the fact that Siena hadn't heard whatever this big news was irked her even more.

"Piper's engaged."

Siena frowned. Piper wasn't engaged. But she and Piper

and Jo and Harley were the only ones who knew that. And Jamie.

Shit.

Jamie.

Had she posted it on her blog yet? The small one that no one was supposed to know about?

"Here." Ingrid walked to Siena's side and leaned over the desk to pull at the keyboard and the mouse. She typed quickly and pulled up a website. This wasn't one of the ones that Siena knew was connected with Jamie, but Jamie did have so many that she wasn't sure she'd tracked them all down.

Siena skimmed the article, which included photos of Piper proposing to Jo. They didn't have Jo's name though, just Piper's. Siena read it again, this time in far more detail. There was very little information actually provided in the post, just the photos, Piper's name, and when and where everything had happened.

"You better get on top of this before it breaks in the big outlets," Ingrid murmured in Siena's ear. "Bunny's going to flip out."

"Yeah, she is," Siena muttered under her breath. She was reading other articles on the website, but they seemed to all be ripped from other places, which meant that Siena had no clue where the original was posted. She was going to have to dive deep into researching that as soon as she had a minute.

Siena pulled open a new search tab and started to look and see where else the information had been leaked. Jamie wasn't supposed to post about it yet, but the information was already out there. Siena glanced at her phone, trying to figure out what exactly had gone wrong. Had Jamie done this just to piss her off?

Everything had been so odd between them in the last few weeks. Siena wasn't even sure what to do about it.

"There." Ingrid leaned over Siena's shoulder and pointed at the screen.

Siena clicked on another website, finding the original posting of photos. Except it was just a social media page that was fan run. She scrunched her nose up. She wouldn't put it past Jamie to be in charge of a few of those either.

"This is going to blow up," Ingrid whispered. "Almost as bad as that thing for me last month."

Siena couldn't argue with her. "Give me a second."

Snagging her cell phone off her desk, Siena walked out of her office. She didn't need Ingrid overhearing this conversation. She pressed the phone to her ear as she dialed Jamie's cell and waited as it rang.

And rang.

And rang some more.

Cursing under her breath, she left a voice message. "Jamie. Call me back. I don't know what you did, but it's bad. And I need to know."

Because she didn't want to believe that Jamie did this on purpose. That she'd taken the information that Siena had given her and leaked it everywhere. Siena had trusted her, and not only was that going to lead to her own demise, she was going to have to deal with the long-lasting consequences of breaking the trust of her clients. Piper had questioned Jamie being there, and Siena assured her it was fine.

But it wasn't.

This was going to go down in history as one of Siena's worst mistakes. Bunny would have her head over this. And Siena wouldn't be surprised if there was at least some threat of a firing. Shit, she'd really fucked this up.

Ingrid was sitting at her desk, still looking at things on her computer when Siena stepped back in. "It's already been picked up."

"You're kidding me." Siena's heart dropped.

"I'm not."

"Fuck me." Siena ran her fingers into her hair and pulled at the strands until it hurt. She really needed to get hold of Jamie. First, she needed to smoosh out this insane rumor, and then she needed to yell at Jamie, or fuck Jamie. She wasn't sure which she wanted to do first but both of them were in there.

Walking out of her office again, she turned and looked at Paula. "If Jamie calls, put it through. She's going to get a piece of my mind."

"Oh okay." Paula furrowed her brow. "Is something wrong?"

"She leaked something she shouldn't have. I need you to put in a call to Diamond Enterprises so we can run a counter article that we can control. And when Bunny calls, because she will call, it's not going to be pretty. I promise you donuts afterward."

"That bad?"

"That bad." Siena stalked back into her office and threw her hands up in the air. "Where do we start?"

"Diamond." Ingrid grinned at her. "I already started drafting an oppositional article."

Except they couldn't really do that either, but only Siena knew that. The photos weren't faked, but she was going to have to figure out a really good spin on why Piper was down on one knee in front of another woman and then it looked like they were happily kissing afterward.

Fuck.

She really needed to think this one through faster. Not only was she potentially going to lose Bunny and Piper, but she had to deal with the fact that they'd dragged Jo and Bea into this mess too. Two up-and-coming stars that Siena hadn't even officially signed yet, though she wanted to. She was working up the contract that morning to present it to them as a possibility, but like hell would they want to sign with her now.

Siena typed furiously on the computer, listing bullet points of how she could potentially spin this.

Practice for a friend.

Fake engagement all around.

Not actually Piper and Jo—mistaken identity.

Ignore it and say nothing and it'll go away.

Siena snorted at that last one. Jamie would never let this go. She had the power now, and she was going to ride it out for as long as it was useful to her. That's what all the gossip columnists did. They never thought about the damage that they could do to the celebrities they were writing about or the people behind the scenes. The ones who would get fired, the ones who the rumors actually hurt. There was a value in the gossip writers when it came to drumming up business and support and sales, but beyond that, Siena didn't see very much worth in their jobs.

And Bunny hated them.

Bea and Jo at least seemed to handle them a bit better.

Siena winced again.

"You're going a mile a minute," Ingrid commented. "I don't think I've ever seen you this flustered before."

"This is personal." Siena bit the inside of her cheek, already knowing that she said too much.

"I can call her boss again and make another complaint, but if he hasn't fired her already, I'm not sure that he will."

Siena's stomach twisted hard. The last thing she wanted was to be the direct cause of Jamie's termination. Especially when it was because she was technically only doing her job. "No, don't call."

That also answered the question about who kept calling and threatening Jamie's job. But Siena wasn't ready to start that conversation with Ingrid, not right now anyway. She had bigger fish to fry at the moment, starting with protecting her client's privacy.

She called Piper, trying to give her a heads up about the leak, and so that she could get an opinion on which direction Piper wanted her to take it. Because like Jamie had said, the two of them certainly didn't seem like they were in a fake relationship. It had felt so real. Even Harley had commented on it.

"Ms. Frazee, there's a call for you on line one."

"Who is it?"

"Jamie Kettlehouse." Paula gave Siena a serious look.

Siena's lips parted in surprise, and she looked to Ingrid who had now been there for several hours helping sort things. "Is she…" Siena trailed off. She wasn't quite sure what she'd wanted to ask. "Did she say anything relevant?"

"No," Paula said, shaking her head.

"Ingrid, give me the room, will you?"

"Oh, but I want the juicy drama." Ingrid frowned, lines forming right around her mouth and by the corners of her eyes.

"Not this time." Siena was going to stay firm on this. What she had to say to Jamie couldn't leave these walls. Except the fact that Jamie, for some god-awful reason, had called on the office number instead of Siena's cell. So she'd have a recording to listen to for the rest of her life if she wanted to. She'd label it *Siena's Downfall.*

Jamie would get a kick out of that, wouldn't she?

"Just give me a few minutes."

Paula held the door open for Ingrid, who finally decided to follow without throwing around more of an argument. Once the door was closed, Siena slowed her breathing and centered herself. She had no clue what she was planning on saying to Jamie, but she did know that she wasn't happy with the situation.

Picking up the phone, she put the receiver to her ear and clenched her jaw. "Jamie."

"You called?" Jamie sounded so fucking cocky, and Siena wished they were in the same room so that she could wipe the look off her face.

Perhaps the switch to the office number had been intentional on Jamie's part. This would just be the picture-perfect moment to break everything off completely, wouldn't it? Siena tried to find that calm center again.

"You leaked it."

"If you're referring to the fake-engagement photo shoot and exclusive interview that you took me on for Piper and Jo, I did see that it has hit the world wide web and that there are two media outlets that have picked it up."

"Including yours?" Siena wanted to know. Would she be staring at those grainy images on the front page of the newspaper and plastered all over their website in the next day or two? Or would she be spared that added embarrassment?

"Yes, including mine."

Siena's heart clenched hard. All along she had hoped that Jamie wasn't going to do this, that she wouldn't betray Siena like this. She fought the tears as they rushed to her eyes. Because she honestly didn't even have time for that. "This wasn't supposed to get out into the world."

"Then you shouldn't have picked such a public place."

"You're blaming this on location?" Siena's voice rose, anger pulsing through her words. "Like if we'd done it at my house with just the five of us there, you never would have posted it? Where do you get off thinking that you have the right to their personal lives? They're human."

"I'm human!" Jamie shouted back.

Siena pulled the phone away from her ear slightly at just how loud Jamie had gotten. "You're not famous."

"Famous people are famous for a reason. They wouldn't be there without people like me."

Siena couldn't refute that. She'd had the thought so many times and it was such a part of her job. But that didn't mean that she liked it. Bunny and Piper and Jo and Bea, hell, every single person on the planet deserved to keep some of themselves just for them. And that was a truth Siena refused to compromise on. Ever.

"Stop trying to ruin my career," Siena muttered.

"Me? Why not you? You stop trying to ruin mine. All you've done from the beginning is jerk me around, toss me bones, make promises, and never deliver. Fuck you, Siena. You deserve the bed you make."

Siena dropped the phone. She thought about picking up the receiver and finishing the call with Jamie, but she just couldn't handle it anymore. She hadn't signed up for this. And she wouldn't stand for it. Picking up the receiver, Siena hung up.

Her priority had to be her clients, and not some journalist with a vendetta against her. She'd thought Jamie was different, she'd thought that she'd seen under the hard shell that Jamie seemed to wear everywhere she went, but she was wrong.

"That didn't seem to go well," Ingrid said, coming back into the room.

"Jesus." Siena scrubbed her face, finding tears on her cheeks. "Were you listening in at the door?"

Ingrid shrugged. "I don't trust her."

"Yeah, well, that makes two of us." Siena had had enough of her trust being broken. She wasn't going to let it happen again.

Ingrid softened her tone as she stepped back over to Siena's desk. "Was it more than just a quickie?"

"Yeah. Yeah, it was."

"Was it love?" Ingrid said the words slowly but honestly, no judgement in her tone.

"No. It clearly wasn't." Because if it hadn't been love, then this wouldn't hurt so damn much. Siena wouldn't have to face the fact that Jamie had willingly gone behind her back and done something as egregious as this. "Come on. We've got some press releases to write."

"You sure you don't want to talk about it?"

"I don't." Siena squared her shoulders. "Right now I want to make sure that I still have a job at the end of tomorrow."

"Deal. You saved my ass. I'll save yours."

"Thanks. What would I do without you?" Siena smiled. She'd forgotten just how brilliant Ingrid could be, and that she really needed to rely on her as a friend more often.

"Cry alone in your office."

"Oh, fuck off," Siena said with a laugh and a roll of her eyes.

twenty-eight

Jamie's stomach churned and everything seemed harder and sharper as she stepped into the elevator at work. After the call with Siena, she knew it was the last straw for her. She couldn't keep living this way. Jessie had been right. Not that she would admit that to her sister. But once she looked around at her clean apartment and admitted at least to herself how bad she had let it get, she couldn't keep fooling herself.

And then to top it all off, she had opened her phone only to find photos of the fake engagement splattered across the internet. With a hollow pit in her stomach, she had brought up her workplace's paper. And the rock of truth plummeted into the cavernous pit of who she had become.

Her phone rang, and she watched as Siena's name flashed across the screen before her voicemail finally picked up. Because like hell was Jamie going to answer *that* call. That wasn't a personal call. That was a call where she was going to be screamed and yelled at, and that was a call that was going to be dangerously painful.

Tentatively she had listened to the message and knew that no matter what she said, Siena was going to play it the way

Jamie had feared. She was the bad guy. But Siena had been the one person who had seen beyond the hate and dislike and assumptions about who Jamie was. At least, Jamie thought she had. But now the writing was on the wall.

After she'd called back, on Siena's work line, Jamie had been done.

Done with everything. But she wouldn't just scurry off into the darkness like Siena obviously hoped she would.

The elevator stopped, and the rush and bustle of the workday at the paper whooshed into the quiet elevator, trying to drown out the intrusive thoughts and spirals that had been going on in her head all morning. Usually it worked. It was one of the perks of working in a loud and busy office. It was why she hadn't opted for a place with a true graveyard shift. She needed the bustle at the start of her shift to get through the quiet of the rest of it.

"Hey." Scott looked up and smiled.

Jamie returned the smile but feared opening her mouth right then would result in her vomiting. She continued past her desk and pretended not to notice Scott's furrowed brow and the concerned pout on his lips.

She knocked on the boss's door as soon as she reached it, not allowing herself to hesitate or second-guess this move. It would mean everything she worked for would be gone, but she couldn't live with herself anymore. Not like this.

"What?" The grunt from within was all she needed to open the door, step in, and close it behind her before he could argue.

"Kettlehouse, what the hell?" Bossman scowled, but he leaned back in his chair and looked her up and down.

Jamie's skin crawled. It had always crawled, but like so many other things she had pushed it aside for her career goals.

Or you accepted it because you think you deserve to feel bad, her mind added unhelpfully in her sister's voice.

Jamie pushed it back. She could spiral later. And she knew

she would. But right now, she had to stick to her plan. And hope for the best. Except what hope she may have had in the past flitted away as she opened her mouth.

"I didn't get the interview with Bunny and Piper." She had thought about how to approach it—with an excuse or a justification. But none of that mattered.

"What?" His face grew instantly red as he leaned forward in his chair, using the momentum to push him to his feet. His hands, tobacco-stained and wrinkled, pressed hard enough into the top of his desk to turn their backs white.

"And the scoop I was preparing to present to you has already been leaked and published on our website."

"Are you fucking kidding me?" He sat back down, picking up a pen from his desk only to throw it back a moment later.

"No."

"Well, that's it." He looked up and narrowed his eyes at her. "You're done. Grab your shit and get out. You've had too many chances as it is."

"Yep." Jamie nodded. She had anticipated this, but the reality still stung.

"That's it?" Bossman scoffed.

"You're right."

"What?" He scowled as he looked her up and down again. His gaze might as well have been a grater. It tore away the very essence of who she was and turned her into nothing more than an object to glare at. "You've lost your grit, Kettlehouse. I suspected so, but gave ya a chance. Now I see it's really gone. You're no good to anyone without that spitfire attitude."

Jamie didn't say anything, because she had nothing to say.

When he scoffed again, he wheeled his chair back into his desk properly and started working on his computer. She turned and left his office. Dismissed. Terminated. Sacked.

Without a word, she went to her desk.

She'd expected this. She really had. She knew she was

walking in to end her career here, and when she'd stepped into that elevator, it had felt okay. But now? Now the devastation and reality were crashing down around her, and she wasn't going to be able to hold her head high any longer.

Where was Siena's fucking confidence when she needed it?

Jamie sneered at herself for that thought. She really shouldn't be thinking about Siena at a time like this. That would just drag her down into the pits of hell and the spirals that she was avoiding.

"Everything okay?" Scott asked, looking up at Jamie as she remained standing at her desk, ignoring her chair.

"Take it easy, hey, Scott?" Jamie turned a smile to the kid. It wasn't real or happy, and she knew it, but it was the least she could do. He hadn't done anything wrong, and he'd always been kind to her when they'd worked together. She couldn't take her frustrations out on him.

Her trip home was a blur of the spiraling thoughts she had been pushing back to try and force herself to be the better person she wasn't sure she could ever truly be.

As soon as she got inside her apartment, she collapsed into a heap of tears and snot and misery. The pressure of her closed front door against the small of her back the only thing stopping her from flying away altogether.

But none of the breakdown had anything to do with losing the job. At least, not really. It had become little more than a crutch she'd been using to keep herself from doing exactly what she wanted and taking the risks she'd have to in order to achieve her dreams. And she'd used it for far too long as an excuse or justification to avoid being a better person. It had allowed her a plausible excuse not to chase dreams she was too scared to fail at.

The tears and subsequent misery were all around Siena.

And betrayal.

She had never been so wrong about someone in her life.

The one person she had let her guard down with, the one person she might have actually been able to believe and trust. Maybe not love. Never love. That was well beyond Jamie's capacity. But that one person had ended up being the one she should have avoided and been the most wary of. She was the one who had fucked her over in the end.

For what?

Revenge?

Or was it more than that?

Had this been her entire plan from the start? A way to get the notorious Portland gossip writer out of her hair once and for all?

And what better way to do that than to break her? And Jamie was broken, both professionally and personally.

Jamie sobbed harder, a fresh wave of tears racking her body.

Scrubbing at her face with her hands, she sniffed and scanned her coffee table.

She always left a box of tissues on it somewhere among the clutter.

"Goddamn it, Jessie." She had forgotten about Jessie's rampage of cleaning while Jamie came back from the edge of migraine hell.

The table was pristine, with not a tissue box in sight.

Jamie sniffed and resigned herself to getting up. She pulled herself to her feet, using the closed door she had been leaning against. After finally finding the tissues on the windowsill of the kitchen, she grabbed the box and returned to her living room.

Everything weighed her down—mentally, emotionally, and physically.

With a sigh, she flopped down on the couch and heard a strange crinkling noise. It took a bit of wrangling and doing couch squats to find out exactly where the crinkling had come from but when she did, her mind momentarily failed her.

In her hand, she held the photos from the proposal and the notes she had so far written up for the article for her lesser-known blog. She held the now crinkled papers and blinked, unsure what the hell the pile of paper was doing under her couch. It wasn't like she ever hid any of her story information. Who exactly would she hide it from? She told Jessie more than she ever should, but Jessie would never jeopardize anything for Jamie.

And no one else ever came to her place.

Well, not ever.

Memories of Siena's visit tormented her as she remained standing in front of her couch gripping the photos. But they hadn't even existed at the time of that visit.

She pulled her phone from her back pocket and dialed without needing to check the number or truly looking at the phone. Her mind was missing something, but she wasn't going to jump to any conclusions. There might actually be a reasonable explanation.

Even if for the life of her now she couldn't figure it out.

"Jamie, what's wrong?" Jessie's worried voice came down the line. Only then did Jamie think about what day it was, and the time.

"Oh shit, Jessie I'm sorry, I didn't realize the time. I just have a really weird question for you."

"Okay, ask away." Jessie's voice was slow and filled with caution.

"When you cleaned up my place the other day, did you put any of my notes or photos under the cushion on the couch?"

"What? No. You were passed out on it. I wasn't touching you." Jessie's reply was filled with the chuckling Jamie had expected. But hearing it made her chest tighten and an anger flare within her. "Why would I?"

"Right, of course. Sorry to bother you."

"James, what's wrong?"

"I'm not sure, well I'm not completely sure. Not yet. But I'll tell you when I can. Right now, I've got to chase down a lead."

"All right." Jessie's smile came down through the line, and before she realized it, Jamie was smiling in reply. "It's nice to hear you distracted with a story."

"Yeah, it kind of is," Jamie agreed. She wasn't about to explain her day so far to Jessie. That would take way more time than Jessie had right now. After saying their goodbyes, Jamie paced her apartment, the well-worn track a comfort beneath her feet.

It had been nice to be focused on a story and a mystery. Because really what else did a story do but answer a question she had to find the answer to?

At first, as the idea bloomed in her mind, she dismissed it immediately. Swatting it away like a mosquito looking for her blood. But the more she paced, the more her mind got back into the game she had always been so good at playing, that idea grew.

It was going to be tricky. And she would only have so much control over it actually happening. Giving anyone else power over her stories had never come easily. It had been the reason she had started the blogs in the first place. She hated being censored.

The shit she wrote for that paper really did border on the trashy side of things. At the beginning she had written them with everything she had. She would find the angle to make the most mundane thing interesting and ensure her writing capti-vated the reader's attention. But it hadn't taken her long to write the pieces moments before she flicked them over to the boss's inbox.

She hadn't cared, and until she had met Siena, she hadn't quite realized just how much her passion had died, suffocating beneath the vile side of the industry and refusing to fight back due to her own inferiority complex.

But still, this was going to be hard.

She sat down on the couch, letting her notes and photos flutter to the floor.

It was a risk, a huge risk.

And she had no idea if she had the strength to put herself on that line again. No, further out on the line.

Her palms grew sweaty at the very thought of it. And what if she was wrong? With a sigh, Jamie went to her bedroom and grabbed her laptop. Before she did anything else, she had to do her due diligence with her research.

She powered up her computer, ignoring the papers that still lay on the carpet. With her legs crossed and her computer in her lap, she started down the rabbit hole in search of the truth.

She didn't realize just how much truth she would end up finding.

twenty-nine

"Hey baby." Siena smiled as Harley opened Tori and Miranda's front door and jumped up into Siena's waiting arms. "I'm so glad to see you."

"Me too, Mommy," Harley replied as Siena stepped over the threshold.

After a quick hug, Siena put Harley back on the ground with a smile. Harley raced off down a hallway without a glance back.

"Hey, you're early." Tori came out from the kitchen and brushed her lips along Siena's cheek.

"Hope that's okay."

"Of course it is. When has it ever not been okay?"

"Well." Siena felt her face grow warm as she rubbed the back of her neck and looked around at the place she had never been able to afford the equal of during her and Tori's marriage. Miranda, in some ways, was doing so much better than Siena. That or they were just at different places when the relationships started.

"Oh for goodness' sake, Siena." Tori rolled her eyes, but that smile, always so sweet and understanding, danced on her lips. "You are always welcome here. And I never have an issue with you seeing our daughter more. And I never will."

"But does Miranda mind?"

"No, why would she?" Tori asked as she led the way back into the kitchen.

It was easily double the size of their old one, but still Tori waved her hand toward the table, and Siena took a seat in the place as she would have back there—back then.

"I'll put the water on, and you can tell me why you look like you've gone ten rounds in the ring with your hands tied behind your back."

"Oh my God." Siena laughed and relaxed down into the chair a little more. "That's one hell of a metaphor."

"I know, right?" Tori laughed as she puttered around, getting things ready to make them both a cup of tea. "Tierney is dating this gym owner, and everything he says is a boxing metaphor or some other workout thing. He seems nice enough, though, if a little dull."

"That's good." Siena smiled, and she couldn't deny how much she enjoyed Tori's stories and knowing how happy her ex-wife was.

"It is," Tori said as she placed one cup in front of Siena and slid into the adjacent chair with the other cup. "Now will you tell me what the hell's going on with you?"

"What do you mean?" Siena lifted her cup and sipped, instantly regretting the distraction as the hot liquid scorched the tip of her tongue and her lip. "Shit."

"I'd be tempted to say instant karma, but I know how you hate that." Tori smirked and made a show of blowing on her own liquid to cool it before taking a tentative sip. "So I'll ask again. What's going on with you?"

"What makes you think anything's going on?"

"You really want me to do this?"

Siena blew on her drink and took another sip, forcing

herself not to wince as the liquid touched the small burn she had already given herself.

"Fine." Tori settled her cup back onto the table and counted on her fingers as she continued. "You've been taking more time off work. I know this because more than once in the last few weeks you've called to have some spontaneous time with Harley. Which I love, and if it were just that, I would be even more thrilled. But then you chased down Jamie, and you snapped at Harley. Now you're showing up early for exchanges, and you look like a lost little puppy."

"A lost puppy?" Siena lifted a single eyebrow as she looked at Tori over the rim of her cup. "Really?"

"You're more offended at being called a puppy than being told you look like you've been beat up?" Tori laughed and shook her head before she leaned over the table and gently put a hand over Siena's. "Please tell me what's happening. Maybe I can help."

"It's me, Tori." It was as though that simple touch had broken the dam holding back the emotions she'd been failing to convince herself weren't there. "The problem is me."

Tori got up from the table and returned with a box of tissues. She held them out for Siena to take one before sliding back into place and pushing the tissues close enough for Siena to reach.

"Thank you." Siena dabbed at her face. "But I swear to God if you start in on a Taylor Swift song, I'm leaving right now. Besides. I shouldn't be a mess with Harley here, and I'm about to take her home for pizza."

"Pizza's already on its way," Tori said, taking another sip of her drink.

"What?"

"Don't go getting mad, but while I was making our drinks, I messaged Aili."

"Fuck."

"She's on her way with pizza and games to keep Harley occupied enough until you're ready to take her home. Then you'll have two of us to gang up on you."

"Great. I'm such a shit parent."

"Seriously?" Tori's tone snapped Siena out of her spiral into intrusive thoughts before they could even begin.

"I know. I'm a great parent. Harley proves that," Siena recited.

"Yeah, and when you say it like you mean it, I'll know you're doing better about yourself as well. But come on, quit stalling, and tell me what happened."

"Fine." Siena caught Tori up on the fake engagement and the leak.

"All right," Tori said slowly. Her eyebrows were slightly furrowed as she thought about the words before she spoke. "So stuff at work has really gone haywire. But these things have happened before. Why is it affecting you so much this time?"

"Because of Jamie."

"So there *is* something with Jamie?" Tori asked. The lack of surprise in her voice should have offended Siena, or at least made her feel something.

"Yes."

"And more than just some casual fun?"

"It was never just some casual fun." Siena hated admitting that, but it was impossible with it all staring her right in the face. She'd wanted it to be. Because it'd be so much easier if it was.

"And you think she betrayed you?" Tori asked.

"She did betray me. And I should be furious with her. Instead, I'm just sad and broken. I can't keep making these kinds of mistakes."

"What kind of mistakes?"

"Love." The word caught in Siena's throat, and she looked up, prepared to face hurt and anger from Tori. Instead, her ex-wife's face radiated the same kind understanding Siena had always loved about her.

"Love isn't a mistake, Siena."

"Maybe not." Siena could have left it at that, but she had been a coward for too long. "But I screwed up with you. I should never have asked you to marry me. I should have never put you through what I did. I'm so sorry, Tori."

"Excuse me?" Tori now sounded affronted, and the relief of being seen as the true villain of their relationship was a relief. "Don't pull that shit on me, or on yourself."

"Myself?" Siena looked up, and while Tori's face did show hints of anger, it wasn't the anger she was expecting.

"Yes." Tori pinned Siena with her stare. "Do you think I'm completely blind about everything, Siena?"

Siena opened her mouth and shut it again. "No, I suppose not."

"And yet you think I haven't been able to figure out the complications of our past?" Tori put her hand over Siena's once more and squeezed lightly before pulling back. "I know you loved me, and I know you still do. But we were never truly in love with each other. You weren't the only one convinced that near enough was good enough."

Siena blinked and tried to fit this information into her own world view, of both her own actions and of Tori.

"Of course, I was upset and angry when I first realized, but I know you, Siena. You believed in love, and you believed the love we had for each other was enough to get us what we both wanted. Not just you, but I wanted it too. I still did even after we got divorced. That's the difference. You gave up on it, and I didn't. Not our marriage, but the dreams of family."

"Yeah, but that doesn't excuse me. That doesn't mean I'm not making the same mistake that I made with you again."

"Then do something different," Tori snapped out before Siena could continue further down the self-flagellation road.

The doorbell rang, and Tori was on her feet and heading out of the kitchen before Siena had taken in her words, let alone her tone.

Throughout their marriage and subsequent friendship, Tori had so rarely used that tone with Siena that she genuinely couldn't remember the last time or the reason for it.

It did its intended job, though. By the time she returned to the kitchen, pizza in hand and Aili and Harley in tow, Siena was ready to talk properly, and to ask Tori for her help and guidance.

"Hey there." Hugs and kisses were exchanged.

Once the pizza had been put onto plates, Aili led Harley away, pretending to tiptoe in secret as she took the food out of the kitchen. Harley's giggle filled Siena's body with a lightness that had gotten her through more days than she could ever count.

"Nothing that brought her into our lives could ever truly be a mistake, Siena," Tori said.

Siena turned from where their daughter had disappeared and watched as Tori pulled her own eyes from the same place to look back at her.

"I could never see her as a mistake."

"And our relationship wasn't either. It was precisely what we needed, for as long as we needed it to be."

"Love's made you an even bigger sap," Siena joked, smiling at Tori.

"Yep. And what are you going to let it do to you?" She took a bite of her pizza slice as she nodded and waited for Siena's answer.

"She doesn't want me like that, Tori. I can't stop thinking about her. And she doesn't even want me like that."

"Oh my God," Tori exploded as she slapped her pizza slice back onto her plate. "Are you kidding me?"

"What?" Siena took a big bite of her own slice, having realized how hungry she was only when the smell of grease and cheese had made her stomach growl.

"Siena, I love you. I will always love you. As the mother of our daughter and as someone I've shared my life with." Tori leaned back already, shaking her head. "But for the love of God, would you finally stop overthinking every single little thing in your life?"

"Just because I don't like rushing into things—"

"There's taking things slowly, and then there is becoming a sloth with your emotions."

"I'm not a sloth."

"Yeah, you really are." Tori chuckled and picked up her pizza again. "You might get naked easy enough, but not with your heart."

"You want me to get naked with my heart?"

"Yep. And sooner rather than later."

"Yeah okay, let me just schedule that in." Siena's voice dripped with sarcasm. "My first free time would be in three years' time."

"You're impossible sometimes. You know that."

"It has been mentioned." By Tori herself, actually, during one of their many arguments over the past years. Though this time it didn't quite carry the same tension that it used to.

Tori laughed and got up from the table once more.

Siena busied herself with eating until a heavy *thunk* jerked her head up again.

"Go see her. Go take this to her place, and for the love of God, just get out of your own head long enough to let her into it."

"Oh my God." Siena laughed as her eyes flicked from the bottle of tequila, to Tori's eyes, and then back to the bottle. "I don't think that's going to be as helpful as you think. Besides, I owed you a bottle, not the other way around."

"I have a theory about that." Tori sat back down, and the air between them had grown warm and comfortable again.

"Oh yeah?"

"Yeah." Tori picked at her food. "Tequila doesn't make people get horizontal easier."

"Oh, I beg to differ." Memories of their post-divorce fucking flooded Siena's brain. It had been sloppy, drunk, dizzying, and had wrecked her all at the same time.

Tori shushed Siena, who quickly mimed zipping her lips.

With a nod, Tori continued. "It helped us…" She flicked her fingers between herself and Siena, "…get horizontal because that was what we needed."

"Really?"

"Yep. It seems to have the effect of getting rid of the bull-shit walls and making you do what needs to be done."

"We needed to shag one last time?" Siena asked, amused by the entire conversation.

"Apparently." Tori smiled.

"Hang on." Siena narrowed her eyes. "If that's the case, then what did it make you and Miranda do?"

"That…" Tori pointed a finger at Siena as she stood up and quickly busied herself with tidying up the empty cups and plates, "…is something no one else ever needs to know."

Siena laughed and helped by wiping down the table as Aili stepped back inside. God, Siena missed her. With Harley not being in daycare except in the evenings, Siena barely saw her old friend anymore.

"What problems are we solving?" Aili put her hands on her hips. "Harley's sufficiently entertained."

Siena furrowed her brow and wrapped her arms around Aili's neck in a tight hug. "Tori already solved them."

"You're kidding." Aili frowned. "You mean I don't get to use my amazing deduction skills?"

"No, sorry."

Aili's gaze dropped to the bottle of tequila on the table. "Who's trying to get laid?"

Siena broke out into a laugh, right along with Tori. Siena wrapped her arm around Aili's waist and pulled her in for a slight hug. She really needed to not forget her friends so often. She needed them, just like they needed her.

"Tori," she said as Tori was about to head out of the kitchen, undoubtedly to go check on Harley.

"Yeah?" She stopped and turned around.

"Are you really not mad at me for wasting your time?"

"Oh, no." Tori wrapped her arms around Siena's neck and held tight. "I'll never be mad at you for that. We have a relationship I wouldn't trade for the world and a daughter I'd kill for."

"Not die for?"

"Well, sure." Tori untangled her arms and stepped out of Siena's space. "But that's easy. Anyone can die, but killing takes deliberate action."

"You know, I think I should be worried about how much you've obviously thought about this. But it's strangely comforting." Siena laughed lightly, already noticing the ease that she was feeling compared to before.

Tori laughed and looped their arms together. "I think you need a bit more time to relax with friends. What do you say?"

"Yeah." Siena didn't resist this time. She did need this, and she was going to take the offer. "Yeah, I do."

"Perfect, because Tori promised girl time with no partners." Aili clapped her hands together. "Just like the old days."

"Not quite like the old days," Siena confirmed, glancing at Tori. "I don't need to go back to the drama of dating either of you again, thank you very much. I have enough dating drama in my life right now."

"Oh, do fill me in." Aili snagged a slice of pizza and sat down at the table, expectedly waiting for Siena to spill. Laughing, she obliged.

thirty

Jamie's heart beat out a samba in her chest as she stepped into the ground floor foyer of the building that housed D.Y.K.E. Management. She didn't quite manage a chuckle at the name. She had always found it amusing, but now, after getting to know Siena, the name made her even more amused.

But not today. Her palms were sweaty, and she had turned around three times before finally getting up the courage to step over the threshold.

The first time she'd stepped foot in here had been for entirely different reasons. She'd come to seduce, to fuck, to play a game of flirting with Siena because she knew without a doubt that Siena was evenly matched with her on that front. And Jamie hadn't been disappointed.

But now was different.

This time Jamie was there fully knowing what Siena was like, in bed and out of it, and that something needed to change —and it wasn't Siena. Steeling herself to be brave, not the false bravado she often presented but true bravery, she strode toward the elevator and jabbed her pointer finger into the button.

She stepped inside and straightened her clothes, pulling

down the green sweaterdress that she'd chosen to wear that day and trying to make herself look far more professional than she felt. This wasn't a personal call.

At least, not entirely.

But this was her new start on life, and Jamie was going to take the bull by the horns and make it right. Even if she was booted out on her ass in the process. But she had to do this, no matter what. Siena deserved an explanation and Jamie deserved the airtime to let her know what had happened.

The office was pristine, just like the last time Jamie had been there. The walls were a light white-gray, the couches in the waiting area were all modern, and the front desk was devoid of any type of clutter. It was the exact opposite of what Jamie's office would ever look like.

"Hi," Jamie said, plastering on a smile. "I'm here to speak with Ms. Frazee."

The woman at the desk looked up at her curiously. Her eyes were dark, her hair cut into a sharp frame of her face with bangs that went right across her forehead. Jamie didn't remember that look from her.

"Did you get a haircut?" Jamie squinted with a smile on her lips. "Because that looks fabulous on you."

"Thank you." The woman smiled sweetly. "But placations won't get you in to see Ms. Frazee without an appointment."

"Oh! That's not… I wasn't… I genuinely meant that. I really like it. I could never pull off something like that. My sister and I were forced into bangs when we were kids, and it was all the rave of the nineties. Never again."

The woman laughed lightly. Jamie tried her best to remember her name, but for the life of her, she couldn't pull it out of her brain. She really needed to do better at that. Jessie remembered everyone's name, and it always made them smile when she did. Maybe that was why she was so damn popular.

"Oh, those were the days, weren't they?" The young

woman—she had to be younger than Jamie, right?—smiled up at her from her desk. Then her smile faltered. "You don't have an appointment with Ms. Frazee."

"I know I don't. I just…" Jamie pressed her lips together hard. "I need to talk to her about the engagement drama. I have some information that she'll want." This had to work. It wasn't just getting to Siena, it was getting past the bulldog at the gate. Not that this woman was anything like that, but she had no doubt that she could be if pushed in the right way.

The woman furrowed her brow and picked up the phone on her desk.

SCORE!

Jamie withheld doing a little victory dance. She hadn't quite made it into the main event yet, but she was at least one step closer. The words spoken were so quiet that Jamie couldn't quite hear what was being said, but when the woman put the receiver down, she stared up at Jamie with a placating smile and nothing else.

"So…?" Jamie asked, hoping that would get her some kind of answer as to whether or not she was invited in.

"What the hell are you doing here?" Siena's voice cracked through the main office.

Jamie jumped, spinning around and facing down the one person she'd never been more scared to confront. Not because she was scared of Siena, no. It was because she was scared of what this would mean for her.

"I need to talk to you," Jamie said, her voice only wobbling a little. She was actually impressed at how she managed to keep that under control.

"A phone call would suffice."

"You know, I did think about that." Jamie pressed one finger to her lips and then shook her head. "But it wasn't going to suffice."

Siena narrowed her eyes at Jamie, as if debating what to do

with her next. Jamie held her breath. She was only a few steps away from getting to the main event, and now it was Siena who was blocking her path, the one person that she really needed to talk to.

"This better be good." Siena pointed at Jamie and then focused on the woman still sitting at her desk. "Push back my two o'clock."

"Yes, Ms. Frazee."

Siena squared her shoulders and turned around, not giving Jamie any indication as to whether or not she should follow. Jamie balked and watched as the woman went to work. "Uh… what was your name again? I'm so bad with names."

"Paula."

"Oh! Cool. Thanks for uh… getting me in." Jamie flashed her a smile and tried to make herself seem softer, but it definitely didn't work. She'd get better at that with time, wouldn't she?

Skipping a step, she raced after Siena and headed straight for her office.

As soon as she stepped inside, Jamie shut the door. The last thing she needed was for Paula to overhear this conversation. When she looked up, Siena was seated on the edge of her desk, arms crossed, and a very pissed off look on her face.

"You really do have some nerve showing up here."

"I know." Jamie put her hands up. "But I couldn't guarantee that you'd take my call, and I wanted to explain this to you in person."

"Then explain."

"I didn't leak the fake-engagement stuff."

Siena raised an eyebrow at her, but didn't say anything beyond that. Was she listening? Was she accepting that this might be a possibility? Hell if Jamie knew, but she did have to push forward and finish out her explanation.

"I was at home with the worst migraine on the face of the

planet when it went live. Jessie will tell you that. I didn't even know about it for a while until you left me that… oh so lovely message on my phone." Jamie rolled her eyes and then caught herself. "Sorry. I just… I was puking my guts out from the pain, and I promise you, Siena, I didn't post it."

Siena still didn't speak or move. The hard look gracing her face was so difficult for Jamie to distinguish and understand. Normally Siena would be screaming at her by now, right? That's how their normal conversations went.

Nervously, Jamie tugged down the edge of her dress again and continued her explanation. "I had a young colleague at the paper, Scott, and he sort of befriended me in the last few months. Well, I befriended him because I realized I didn't have any friends and you kind of pointed out that I was a bitch, so I was trying to not be that and change who I was."

Siena waved her hands before stopping them. "What are you going on about?"

"Nothing. That's not relevant. Anyway, Scott drove me home that day because I couldn't drive. It was that bad." Jamie bit the inside of her cheek. "Scott is the one who leaked it."

"You left sensitive information out where anyone could access it?" Siena put her hands on her hips and stood up. She stretched her back and closed her eyes, raising her face to the ceiling. "Are you really stupid enough to do that?"

"Well, no one paid attention to me until…" Jamie stopped. "Until I started being nicer to them and then they did." Fuck, this really was her fault, wasn't it? She'd worked hard to be nicer and more likable and that had led her to right where she was now. Betrayed and betraying. "I know it's a fuckup," Jamie said. "I shouldn't have done it, but I did, and in my migraine state, I didn't even think about it until I found the packet under my couch cushion."

Siena frowned, shaking her head in confusion.

Jamie shook her head. "It doesn't matter. Yes, this is on me, but no, I didn't intentionally leak the information." She held her hands in front of her, wringing them together as she waited for whatever judgement Siena was going to rain down on her.

Because surely there had to be some.

Jamie had fucked with people's lives for years, but she'd never faced the repercussions of that quite like she did now. And now it hurt. God, it ripped her to bits to see Siena standing there looking like the world was on her shoulders, the weight of fixing everything, the pain of knowing that Jamie had been the one to cause all of that. It hurt her too.

"I'm so sorry," Jamie murmured, her voice gentle into the office as she continued to watch every inch of Siena's body for a sign that she was doing something right. "I'm so sorry that I hurt you."

Siena sighed and then pinched the bridge of her nose.

The silence was damn unnerving.

"Do you know how much my life has been a living hell lately?" Siena's tone was filled with unrestrained anger. "How much damage I've had to repair and fix and deal with?"

Jamie shook her head, locking her eyes on Siena's. "No. But I can imagine."

Siena blew out a breath, ruffling the hair that fell around her face. She straightened her shoulders and suddenly strode toward the door, locking it. Siena spun back around, pressing her shoulders to the door and staring Jamie down.

"It hasn't just been because of the leak."

"I-it hasn't?" Jamie stammered.

"No." Siena pursed her lips, staying right where she was. Was she scared to get any closer? "You."

"Me?" Jamie raised her eyebrows in surprise. She pressed her fist to the center of her chest.

"Yes. You." Siena strode toward her, her long legs carrying her across the room in a matter of seconds. "You're what I've been dealing with."

"I don't understand." Jamie stared up into Siena's dark eyes, her gaze flicking down to Siena's full lips. She wasn't here for that, but she couldn't deny that the sexual attraction between them had never been the actual problem. It was always something else that came between them.

"Fix it."

"Fix what?" Jamie shook her head, not understanding or tracking where Siena was going with the conversation.

"Fix the leak."

"I…" Jamie paused, her heart in her throat. She'd thought about several ways to do that, but she'd never thought that Siena would go for any of them. "I can't fix the leak. I can't take it back."

"Help me with damage control. I can't do this without a contact in the media." Siena shoved her hands into her pockets and rocked back on her heels.

Jamie's breath caught. "I'm not… in the media anymore, Siena."

"What?"

"I was fired." Jamie frowned. "I never got that interview with Bunny and Piper, so my boss fired me."

"Yet stole the leaked information?"

"There's not a whole lot of ethics in the media—well, not that side of things, anyway." Jamie rolled her eyes. "He probably would have fired me anyway because it wasn't the interview that I'd promised him. Or maybe he would have kept me on so that I could continue to be at his beck and call. I don't know. But yeah, I was fired this week."

"Jamie…" Siena's voice dropped. She closed her eyes and bit her lip. "I'm so sorry."

Jamie shrugged. "It's not the first time I've been fired in my life. I doubt it'll be the last with my track record."

They stood awkwardly together. Jamie wasn't sure what to do or say next, because she'd come there to say what she had to, and yet, there was something else on the tip of her tongue that was itching to get out. But she definitely didn't have the courage to say that.

"Help me," Siena whispered.

"I can't help you." Jamie shrugged. "I'm sorry, but I can't."

"You can." Siena stepped closer, right into the space in front of Jamie. "I know you can."

"How?"

"Just because you don't have a job and access to a professional media outlet doesn't mean that you can't start a media storm. I've seen you do it before. Do it again." Siena curled her hand around Jamie's cheek. "Do it for me."

Closing her eyes, Jamie tilted her face into the touch. Why did this feel so amazing? She wanted to say yes. She wanted to do anything for Siena, but she feared she wouldn't be able to pull through on this one. Creating a media storm with that first article she'd written after their one-night stand had been pure coincidence. Jamie hadn't done anything special with it, had she?

"Jamie," Siena murmured. "Help me."

"Okay." Jamie closed her eyes and pressed her forehead into Siena's shoulder. "Okay, I'll try. But don't get mad if I don't manage to do it."

Siena hummed, her chest vibrating. "I have full confidence that you can do whatever you put your mind to."

"You might be the only one." Jamie couldn't stop the comment, but it was how she truly felt. She'd never been able to pull her head out of her ass, and now wasn't any different.

"We have one more thing we need to talk about before we get to work," Siena said, cupping the back of Jamie's head and keeping her right in the circle of her arms.

"What's that?" Jamie muttered, really not wanting to step back at all. She wanted to stay right here for as long as she could. And that was the problem, wasn't it? She never wanted to leave Siena's embrace. She wanted to live here.

But she had to move.

Pulling away, Jamie took a step back and looked up just as Siena's lips covered hers. The kiss was soft, a gentle plying of lips against lips. Jamie breathed in Siena's scent, remembering those moments of being surrounded by her. On the few times that she'd allowed that to happen. Siena tilted her back slightly, tracing her lower lip with her tongue.

Jamie sighed. Her eyes fluttered shut, and her entire body rocked into Siena's. She just needed Siena to catch her, just this once. Jamie gripped onto Siena's sides, fisting her hands in the soft, silky fabric of her blouse under her jacket. And she held on with everything that she had. She couldn't let go.

Siena pulled back, breathing a little harder than before, and she pressed their foreheads together. Jamie held onto the silence, scared of whatever words were about to happen. But she knew them even before Siena said them.

"Us. We need to talk about us."

thirty-one

Siena hadn't expected this. Not today of all days. But when Jamie had walked in, all that false bravado she carried with her gone, she couldn't help herself.

"This isn't casual," Siena started. She knew she'd have to be the one to do this. Jamie wasn't ready for it, not fully, but Siena needed some kind of conversation between them. Backing away, she looked down into Jamie's baby blue eyes, her parted lips that were so damn kissable and were beckoning her to kiss them again. "And I don't want it to be casual."

"Siena…" Jamie had been abnormally quiet. "I don't know what to say."

"Tell me what you feel and what you want." Siena hated backing away, but she also knew that Jamie likely needed the space to think. Holding her, caressing her during this conversation was only going to slant it in a way that Jamie might not want it to go.

"I can't stop thinking about you," Jamie whispered, pulling a face like she hadn't expected to say that. "I can't stop thinking about fucking you, that's for sure." She grinned up at

Siena again, and there was the woman that Siena had fallen in love with.

That thought had never felt more right. This was far from the convenience of her relationship with Tori. Siena had to work for Jamie, not just for her but with her. But she wanted to, and she could only hope right now that maybe Jamie did too. Tori was right—again—Siena had to stop pushing her feelings to the side and actually deal with them up front.

"Like if I had my way, I'd take you on that couch right now." Jamie gave a nervous laugh.

Siena flicked her gaze to the couch. The thought had occurred to her, on more than one occasion. And she'd definitely had sex there before, though it had been years and a divorce ago. But right now wasn't the right time.

"And then what?" Siena asked. "Leave it at sex?"

Jamie shook her head before she frowned. "No, I don't want to leave it at just that." Jamie took an intentional step forward, wrapping her arm around Siena's back and pulling her in closer. "I want more than that."

"What exactly do you want?" Siena whispered the question, almost afraid to voice it out loud. She'd wanted this moment for weeks now, for them to actually talk about what their relationship might mean or what it could mean in the future. She'd tried before, but Jamie hadn't been ready.

Was she now?

"I want you." Jamie bit her lip. "I want to not be a bitch."

"You're not—"

"I can be," Jamie countered. "And so can you. We all can, but I didn't care before if I was. Now I do."

"Why?" Siena lifted Jamie's chin up with a finger and her thumb, gazing into those eyes. The ones that could come off as so cold, but instead Siena found them absolutely alive with energy and joy and life and passion.

"Because someone pointed out that people care about me."

"Someone? Jessie?"

"No. You." Jamie's lips curled upward, and her gaze decidedly dropped to Siena's mouth. "You did, and I tried to avoid you and I just… can't stop thinking about you. You vex me most days, but I think there's a reason for that."

"Is there?" The tension in Siena's shoulders slipped away, easing the ache that had started in the center of her back.

"Yeah. I like you." Jamie grinned broadly. "And I do still really want to fuck you on the couch."

Laughing, Siena shook her head. She was about to step back and walk away but Jamie pulled her back with a sharp tug on her hand. This time when their mouths met, it was all heat.

"I wasn't kidding."

"Jamie," Siena said against Jamie's lips. "It's the middle of the day."

"You cancelled your next appointment."

Siena groaned. So this wouldn't even be a quickie. "But I still have work to do."

"Won't it be easier if you're relaxed?" Jamie nipped at Siena's lower lip, sucking on it, scraping it with her teeth.

Groaning, Siena moved in closer. She put her arms against Jamie's back and held on tightly, not quite sure what to do next. But fuck if she didn't think that Jamie was right. Not that she'd admit that, and definitely not now. Jamie didn't need to add to her cockiness in any way, shape, or form.

"We have work to do," Siena muttered.

"Tell Paula to set up a meeting with Bunny and Piper. I'll interview them with the questions we'd talked about before, and then we'll publish that. Immediately."

Siena pulled away slightly. "You want to go back to that?"

"Well, I want to ask one question, but you told me no."

"What question?" Siena asked.

"Now why would I tell you that? Give me permission to ask

it, and you'll find out what it is. If not, the others will be good enough to get done what we need done."

We. That word felt amazing coming out of Jamie's mouth. They were actually working together on this. Like they did on the fake engagement. This was what that should have felt like.

"God, you're sexy." Siena covered Jamie's mouth with her own. She tilted her head back and started to walk toward the couch, pushing Jamie along with her as she went. Siena dropped her hand down Jamie's front and over her scrumptious breasts. "And whatever put it in your head to wear this today?"

She found the edge of Jamie's dress, which rode up high on her thighs, and she tugged it up. Jamie moaned, intensifying her kisses with a fury that Siena hadn't been prepared for. It stole her breath the instant Jamie started.

"It was the only thing clean," Jamie mumbled against Siena's mouth before pulling back with a glint in her eye. She put her hands on Siena's shoulders and pushed her backward.

Siena let herself fall onto the seat of the couch with a little bounce. She grinned up at Jamie as she pulled her dress up and over her ass to her waist. The thong she wore was black and lace, and it framed Jamie's body perfectly.

"Is that also because it's laundry day?" Siena couldn't move her gaze from between Jamie's legs.

"Wouldn't you like to know?" Jamie straddled Siena's hips, her knees pressing against Siena's side as she sat fully on top of Siena's lap. "When's the interview?"

Siena sputtered for words. Thank fuck Jamie hadn't tried this method of getting her to agree to stuff before today, because it was absolutely working in Jamie's favor. "They have a concert coming up."

"When's the interview, Siena?" Jamie took Siena's hand in her own and purposely moved it to the inside of her thigh.

Siena's heart raced. Jamie's skin was so warm and smooth.

Her breathing came in ragged gasps that she definitely couldn't control. Jamie pushed Siena's fingers under the swatch of fabric, and Siena groaned at just how warm and wet she was.

"Fuck," Siena mumbled. She'd missed this. She'd wanted this. She took over the touches, sliding her fingers against Jamie and pressing her clit between her middle and pointer fingers. Siena started to scissor them back and forth, catching Jamie as she rocked into Siena when the sensations hit her. "Fuck, you're dripping."

"All for you, baby," Jamie mumbled against Siena's ear before nipping at her lobe. "Fuck me already."

Siena peppered Jamie's chest with kisses, the sweater fabric rough against her skin. Jamie undulated her hips back and forth against Siena's hand as Siena continued to scissor her clit.

"When's the interview?" Jamie hissed out, her head falling back as her hips jerked suddenly.

Siena couldn't think. How the hell could Jamie? She was so damn focused on what she was doing, on what was happening. Siena bit her lip, looking down at her hand and the way Jamie's body moved against her.

"Siena…" Jamie said. "When's the interview?"

"I don't know," Siena answered, trying to pull Jamie's dress up higher. She wanted to touch and taste her breasts, to see the way they moved with each rut of her hips. But the damn dress was in the way, and Siena couldn't get it up and over Jamie's delicious body with only one hand, and not even her dominant hand at that.

"I thought your time was valuable," Jamie teased, dropping kisses onto Siena's neck. "Don't want to be wasting it."

"Fuck this." Siena moved her hand from Jamie's thong and used both her hands to pull the dress up and over Jamie's head. She was greeted with her glorious breasts, tightly confined in a similar black lace bra. "I don't believe for a second you didn't plan to come in here and fuck me senseless." Not that Siena minded. A good fucking was always worth it.

"I didn't," Jamie said with a squeak when Siena put her on her back and hovered over her. "I came in to apologize and tell you what happened."

"With a hope of a fuck."

"Always a hope," Jamie shot back, her cheeks red with arousal. "What day, Siena?"

Siena wanted to curse her out. "I don't know." She just wanted her mouth to be busy with Jamie, not with putting shit onto her calendar.

"Can't think?"

"Don't want to," Siena growled. She hooked her fingers in the sides of Jamie's thong and tugged it down. "Do you want me to? Or do you want my mouth on you?"

"Mouth. Definitely mouth." Jamie grinned at her, but she parted her knees, and oh, that scent. Siena nearly collapsed face-first into Jamie right then and there.

"Good." Siena pressed open-mouthed kisses against the inside of Jamie's thighs. She prayed Paula didn't choose this time to try to get hold of her, because like hell was she going to answer that call. Siena nuzzled her nose into the curls at the apex of Jamie's legs, and she breathed in that glorious scent in its fullness. "I'm so glad you came." She cringed at her phrasing.

Jamie, however, laughed. The sound gurgled up from her and left her lips, echoing through the room. Siena couldn't stop the smile on her lips as she corrected herself.

"I'm glad you came to talk to me today."

"Sure." Jamie gasped when Siena nipped at her hip. "Next time, you get to find me."

"Mm-hmm." Siena pressed her nose back between Jamie's legs and licked her. She would never get over that flavor. Siena loved her. The more she thought about that, the more it settled into her chest as exactly right. And Jamie had come back to her. Not to ask for anything, but to give.

Curling her tongue up and gathering Jamie's flavor on it, Siena swallowed. She was never going to forget this moment. Jamie reached down and tangled her fingers in the hair at the top of Siena's head while Siena pushed her shoulders into the backs of Jamie's thighs to get as close as she possibly could. She would never get tired of doing this.

Siena sucked in a sharp breath filled with nothing other than Jamie, and she stopped holding back. Days like today weren't meant for long slow touches or teasing and then pulling back. They were meant for quick, hard, and dirty. Siena pressed into Jamie even more, flicking her tongue in just the way she knew Jamie would love, the way that would get her to keen and cry out.

Sure enough, just as the thought entered her mind, Jamie groaned. She was getting so loud, but Siena didn't have it in her to ask her to be quieter. This was for them, a reconnection, a new starting point. Siena stayed where she was, teasing and tasting and bringing Jamie up to new heights. Jamie pushed down on the back of Siena's head as if she was trying to get even closer, impossibly closer. Siena had to brace her forearms against the couch just to make sure that Jamie wasn't going to move her off of where they both wanted her to be.

"Fuck…" Jamie said, throwing her hand over her face. "Oh God."

Siena said nothing, eyeing Jamie's breasts as they heaved with each of her breaths and watching as Jamie came apart against her mouth. She stayed there until Jamie slowed and her body eased the tension away. Finally Siena started to kiss her way up Jamie's body until she reached her breasts.

Pulling down the cup of one side of her bra, Siena covered Jamie's nipple with her mouth and teased the hard little nub. She would never get over Jamie's tits and just how perfect they were. Moving on up, Siena pressed their mouths together as she covered Jamie with her body.

"I can't take the rest of the day off today."

"Wasn't asking you to," Jamie answered. "But I have all the free time in the world."

"Except for an interview you need to prep for." Siena nibbled on Jamie's neck, scraping her teeth and marking her. Siena hummed, wanting another go with Jamie already. "Tuesday."

"What?" Jamie gasped.

"Tuesday at ten in the morning. I'll have Bunny and Piper here. You show up with your questions. I'll even let you take a cute picture to add to it." Siena licked Jamie's nipple again.

"Five pictures."

"Three," Siena countered.

"Deal." Jamie clasped her hands on Siena's cheeks and pulled her up, kissing her hard. She curled her legs around Siena's hips and pulled her in so that Siena was lying fully on top of her. Their mouths melded together in a deep kiss. Siena slowed it, eventually pulling away.

"Paula's going to come in here any minute."

"How do you know?" Jamie asked.

"Call it a sixth sense." Siena pulled away, standing up and staring down at Jamie, newly fucked and definitely wanting more. "My place or yours tonight?"

"Yours." Jamie frowned. "Always yours."

Siena would talk to her about that later, but now wasn't the time. She checked the watch on her wrist before wiping her fingers around her mouth. "Six?"

"I'll be there." Jamie moved, sitting up and fixing the cup of her bra. "You uh… need to check your lipstick."

Siena laughed, but instead of going to the mirror, she bent down and kissed Jamie hard, squeezing her breast for good measure. "Well worth it."

"Hmm, I'd say so."

Siena made quick work of her makeup and hair while Jamie finished getting dressed again. She'd ask Jamie to wear that little number again soon. It was stunning on her. As Jamie stood at the door, a knock came quickly. "Told you."

"She's been five minutes." Jamie pointed. "It doesn't take me five minutes."

"It would take me five minutes to get my head back on straight." Siena unlocked and opened the door, knowing full well that the entire office smelled like sex.

"Ms. Frazee, there's uh…" Paula trailed off, her eyes widening ridiculously huge. "There's a problem with Bea."

"Right. I'll be there in a minute. Let me just finish up with Jamie here." Siena smiled at her and then focused back on Jamie when the door was shut. "Tuesday?"

"Tonight," Jamie answered, reaching for Siena's hand. She leaned in and pressed their mouths together in a sweet kiss.

"Tonight," Siena promised.

thirty-two

"I just have one more question." Jamie leaned forward in the small seat across from Bunny and Piper on the couch. She was trying her best to not flip out and fangirl over them, and so far, she thought she was holding her own. The way Bunny exuded so much confidence was outstanding. Jamie wished she could do that.

Sliding forward in the chair, Jamie put her pen to paper to wait for this response. It was going to be a good one. Bunny's gaze dropped from Jamie's face to her breasts before flicking back up. Definite queer vibe, even if Bunny wasn't ever going to admit it to the world. Still, Jamie would love to be the one to break that story.

But not today.

She glanced at Siena, waiting for permission to ask the one question that she hadn't gotten permission for. She held Siena's gaze and waited explicitly for her okay to continue. When Siena gave her a small smile and held her hand out in front of her, Jamie had it.

She nearly couldn't believe this was her life right now.

She'd been trying to get an interview with these two, an

exclusive, for years. And now she was finally getting it! The little kid inside her danced for joy. She just had to contain it a bit longer so she didn't look like a complete loon while Bunny and Piper were in front of her.

"The suspense is killing me," Bunny muttered, but her lips curled upward slightly at the corner.

Had she enjoyed this interview too? Or perhaps Jamie's charm was just too much for her to resist?

"Jamie," Siena said, a slight warning in her tone. "Ask the question."

"Are you sure? Don't need to censor it?" Jamie asked, teasing.

Bunny's eyebrows went up immediately, as did Piper's. Jamie might have just outed them entirely. That would be an interesting conversation later.

"I'm sure." Siena nodded again. "Ask away. I'm fairly sure that Bunny and Piper can hold their own against you."

"Then you're here to…watch me work?" Jamie winked at Siena, her grin growing wildly.

"Uh… I think we can skip the last question and talk about this." Bunny pointed between the two of them. "What the hell is going on?"

"Now you got her one-track mind started. Appreciate that." Siena's cheeks pinked, and she looked away from Jamie and at her clients on the couch. "We'll talk after the interview is done."

Bunny narrowed her gaze. "I'll hold you to that. All right, Jamie, what's the question?"

"What made you choose Siena as your manager all those years ago?" Jamie kept her pen to her paper, but she didn't look at it. Instead, she looked directly at Siena. She wanted *that* reaction. No one else in this room mattered.

"That's an… odd question for an interview about us," Piper said, smiling as she leaned forward slightly.

Jamie smiled, seeing the same shock across Siena's face that she was hearing in Piper's voice. "It is. But it's the only question that I've wanted to ask you for months now."

"Months, huh?" Bunny guffawed. "I would have texted you that answer in one word."

"Really?" Siena snapped her attention to Bunny.

Jamie also turned to face down the rockstars on the couch. "What word?"

"Perfect."

Jamie couldn't have agreed more. Siena was perfect for this job in more ways than she could count. And she was perfect in more ways beyond just the job. Jamie wrote the word down on her notepad.

"She really is perfect for us, isn't she?" Piper added, her foot bouncing the entire time. Jamie had noticed in the past that she did that during her interviews. But she didn't get the sense that it was a nervous habit, just a way of restraining the immense amount of energy she had.

Jamie waited. She knew that there was more to come, that Bunny and Piper weren't done yet. Because this was the way that they were going to talk without stopping. They were going to get so engrossed with talking about Siena that she would learn all of their secrets.

"We first met Siena when she was new to the business and so were we." Bunny put her hand on Piper's knee and squeezed before releasing it. "It was a risk for us and a risk for her, and we all knew that going in, but Siena knows how to negotiate a contract."

"So does Bunny!" Siena chimed in.

Jamie sent her a scolding look, telling her silently that this interview wasn't about her.

"We knew we needed a new manager because our last one was…"

"Homophobic," Piper said loudly. "Sexist. Condescending."

"All those and more," Bunny added, rolling her eyes. "And we'd been doing without a manager for quite some time because we just didn't have the desire to go through that experience again."

Jamie waited patiently, learning more information about the three people in this room than from any other question she'd asked that day. This was one that would open them up and get them talking for hours.

"Siena was down to earth, calm, and had a million and one ideas."

"Oh my God, the ideas!" Piper laughed. "She wanted to take on the world."

Bunny laughed right along with her. "She did. And she had plans and backup plans and backup to the backup plans."

"She even had them colorized and listed out in phases that they were going to happen in," Piper added.

Jamie shook her head. Siena was so much like Jessie in that respect. Jamie was the complete opposite. She had no plan when it came to her business or her blogs or trying to get her name out there. She just knew what she wanted, and she worked her tail off to get it—as chaotically as it came.

"Bunny and Siena can talk business, and Siena and I can talk creatively." Piper smiled over at Siena. "She really is the perfect blend for both of us. And that's worked to all of our advantages."

"It helps that she's hot!" Bunny said, grinning broadly. "And she's not afraid to use her looks to her advantage or to put down the jerks."

Jamie laughed at that. She loved listening to these two talk. It was like they were their own little family together, all of them supporting each other no matter what came their way. Jamie turned to Siena and couldn't stop looking at her. She loved these two so deeply. That's what she'd been protecting. Not their careers, not their lives—she'd been protecting them, and her love of them was what pushed that through.

"I think that's plenty for Jamie," Siena said, but she wasn't looking at Bunny and Piper. She was looking directly at Jamie, their eyes completely locked together. Jamie couldn't look away. She was entranced, completely captivated, and she wasn't sure she ever wanted to look away.

Bunny and Piper eventually left after giving Jamie a pleasant goodbye. She couldn't help but think that Bunny was eyeing her over for an entirely different reason, trying to judge why Jamie had gotten the privilege of being the one to interview them and write up this article, especially when she hadn't shown up the last time she'd had the chance. Jamie had held her own in that conversation though, and she'd gotten looks of praise from Siena for it.

This was more than a client relationship for Siena. This was a deep friendship, perhaps even family. And Jamie was getting to witness a piece of that. She'd definitely add that into her story somehow. It needed to be in there.

That was what would humanize all of them. Friendship and love. Jamie smiled at herself when she had that thought. It certainly had done wonders for her, hadn't it? Even Jessie had commented on how calm and content she seemed to be lately. It wasn't that falling in love with Siena had dampened any of her passions. In fact, it had intensified them. But it had also shown her that with support and hope, she could get whatever it was she wanted in life.

Siena caught her hand just before she was about to walk out the door and pulled Jamie into her, tilting her back and kissing her deeply. Siena held her close before pushing her into the wall next to the door and continuing to kiss her deeply. Jamie wrapped her arms around Siena's back, plunging her fingers into Siena's hair and holding onto her tightly. She curled her ankle around Siena's legs and pulled her in even closer.

If Jamie didn't know better, she was pretty sure that they were about to have another quickie in the office. She started laughing when Siena pulled back slightly and shook her head in response to Jamie's outburst.

"That's the question you were dying to ask them?"

"Yeah," Jamie answered, her voice rough with arousal and deep with tension. "What about it?"

"Nothing." Siena kissed her loudly and then pressed a line of kisses down Jamie's neck to the tops of her breasts, which were exposed in the cut of her shirt. "You could have asked that one before."

"I didn't want you to know." Jamie scraped her nails along Siena's scalp, pulling her deeper into her body. "I wanted you to be surprised. And them." She started to breathe heavier.

"Why?"

"Because I'd get a more honest answer that way." Jamie slid her hand down to Siena's ass and squeezed. "Are we doing this here or at home? Because I'm not sure Paula is ready to walk in on us just yet."

Siena groaned, no doubt annoyed with the reminder that they were still in her office and were definitely not alone.

"I'd rather be able to scream when you want me to," Jamie added, curling her fingers around Siena's cheek in a tender touch. She'd been doing more and more of that lately. And Jamie was surprised, but she loved it. She loved being able to be this close with someone who wasn't her family and who had actually chosen to be this close with her.

"You make a tempting offer," Siena whispered and then leaned in, nipping Jamie's earlobe.

Jamie had no doubt that she was going to torture them both until they really had to decide if a quickie was worth the risk or not. But Jamie hadn't worn a short dress today, which was going to make the quick part brutally hard.

"I heard you're good at negotiating." Jamie moved her hand around Siena's front, trailing her fingers over her breast and then back up, but not before circling her hardened nipple and teasing it with a flick. "What say you… leave work early and ravish me at home?"

"You draw a hard bargain, Jamie." Siena kissed her quickly.

"I do. It's all because I love you." Jamie looked up into Siena's eyes, wanting to hear and feel the reaction that Siena had to that little tidbit of information. She hadn't been sure that she was going to tell her yet, but the moment seemed right. And as soon as the words were loosed, Jamie was glad she'd made the confession.

"You sure about that?" Siena asked, nipping at Jamie's neck and then sucking quickly. "Because you could just be horny. I'm pretty sure that you told me that you didn't need to be wined and dined."

"Oh, I did. But…I think you changed my mind on that one." Jamie gasped when Siena hit a particularly sensitive spot. "I quite like it when you kneel at my feet for me."

Siena laughed hard. She pulled away, unable to stop the laughter from leaving her lips. "I'll see you tonight."

"Fine. Tonight it is." Jamie gave her an exaggerated pout. She was going to be walking around with wet underwear for the rest of the day until Siena made good on her promise tonight.

"We should talk about a job I might have found for you tonight too." Siena sat down at her desk, sliding into the chair like she was all business now. Jamie was jealous of how quickly Siena could go from seduction to work like that.

"Oh?"

"Yeah. Tonight." Siena glanced over the computer. "I'd rather not talk about it here."

"All right." Jamie was curious now, but she knew there was no way to push Siena to get an answer without arguing. And the last thing she wanted to do was start a fight just to get information and then not be able to get out of it later when what she really wanted was a good fucking. "Tonight then."

Jamie opened the door, ready to leave when Siena's voice stopped her.

"Oh, and Jamie?"

"Yeah?"

"I love you, too."

Elation hit Jamie first. Her cheeks burning, not from arousal, but from excitement. She'd never heard those words from anyone before. And they meant so much. She gave Siena a huge wink, one that was over the top, and then she left. There was no way she was going to be able to wipe the grin from her lips now.

This was everything and more.

thirty-three

Siena shouldn't be nervous, but her fingers shook a little as she slid her key into her front door.

She had tried to get out of the office a little earlier, but that had gone by the wayside when more issues arose for some of her newer clients. The beginning of representing someone always carried with it teething problems. But the last few she had put in her books were definitely pushing her to new levels of patience.

Still, she had a little bit of time to get things ready before Jamie was due over for dinner.

And to hear Siena's proposal concerning work. Siena was excited about how logical it seemed, how easy a progression and transition it could be for Jamie. She just hoped Jamie would see it that way as well.

After having a quick shower and changing into something far less professional, Siena ordered in dinner and eventually found the packet of candles she knew she had in the bottom drawer in the kitchen. Only two of them had been used, their blackened wicks not even halfway down the length of them. She grabbed them but quickly changed her mind as she returned them to the drawer and pulled two brand new candles from the open packet.

"New beginnings." Siena smiled to herself as she took them into the dining room.

It was five minutes to seven when Siena's doorbell rang.

"Right on cue." She chuckled as she turned the lighter over in her hands once more. She'd been carrying it around with her, playing with it and refusing to put it down for fear of forgetting where she had put it when she needed it.

She dimmed most of the lights, paid the delivery driver for their dinner, and laid it all out nicely. She chuckled as she looked at the extra little touches she had made and couldn't wait for Jamie to see it all. The bucket with ice held the pitcher she had prepared herself, while the many bowls of food littered the table between the only two seats that had plates at them, opposite each other.

And all of it had been done with the lighter still in her hand.

She really shouldn't be so nervous, but she was.

So many changes had happened this year, and she wouldn't do it differently. Not to risk the incredible future that lay in front of her. But still, her hand shook a little as she flicked the lighter to life. The candles bloomed easily as she touched the flame to them, one after the other. Their light flickering over the walls and the meal she hoped Jamie would enjoy and find as amusing as she did.

She couldn't stop smiling and wondered how she could have ever fooled herself into believing any other relationship she'd had before this could have been confused for being in love.

As she wandered to the front door, forcing her feet to walk and not run, she dimmed the last of the lights and with a flick of her wrist tossed the lighter onto the key table by the door. Her hand felt empty, and the nerves threatened to rise.

"Hi." She opened the door with a smile.

Jamie's smile was brighter than Siena had ever seen it before. Considering how that sexy smile had managed to pick her up in a restaurant, that certainly said a lot.

"You look beautiful." Jamie bit lightly on her lower lip.

"Is that a bad thing?" Siena asked with a chuckle, though she didn't hide her confusion at Jamie's expression.

"Definitely not." Jamie wrapped her arms around Siena's neck as she stepped over the threshold and into Siena's home. "But it does make it a lot harder to focus on eating anything else."

Siena laughed and shook her head. "Careful, or I might start to think you only love me for the orgasms."

Jamie kissed Siena in reply. The kiss, soft and gentle, sent a river of fire racing up and down Siena's body, from her toes to her scalp where Jamie's short fingernails were being dragged.

"Wow." Siena breathed when Jamie pulled away from her just as gently as she had leaned in to kiss her.

Jamie brushed Siena's hardened nipple with her shoulder as she sauntered past, leaving Siena open-mouthed in the frame of her still-open front door.

With a shake of her head which might as well have been her entire body, Siena smiled as she closed the door, making sure it was locked before she quickly scurried after Jamie's swaying hips.

Jamie stopped at the archway into the living room. Siena would have run directly into her back, distracted by those hips and that ass if she had been following any closer.

"You did this for me?" The incredulity in Jamie's voice sent sadness directly to Siena's heart.

"Of course I did." Siena gently wrapped her arms around Jamie's waist, resting her head on Jamie's shoulder and seeing what Jamie saw, and tried to find the thing that put such shock in her voice.

"It-it's beautiful. Thank you." Jamie turned her head and brushed Siena's lips with her own. The angle wasn't the most conducive, but they were Jamie's lips, and it seemed no matter how contorted either of them were, those lips continued to send a spark through Siena's very being.

"You're beautiful. And you deserve to be treated like a queen."

"Because I'm beautiful?" Jamie asked in a tone that suggested she might be testing Siena.

"Absolutely not."

"What?"

"The one doesn't define the other. Who you are deserves to be treated like a queen. And you are beautiful. Both exist separate from the other."

"Hmmm." Jamie's tone shifted to that smirk Siena loved. "It's almost like you are trying to wine and dine me after all."

"Absolutely." Siena chuckled as she unwound her arms from Jamie and moved to one of the places she had set up with a plate and glasses.

"Oh my God." Jamie laughed as she sat in the seat Siena pulled out for her. "Are you kidding me?"

"I would never kid about…" Siena lifted the pitcher from the ice bucket so Jamie could see that as well. "Fajita'ing and magarita'ing."

"You really are perfect."

"Huh." Siena scoffed, but she couldn't hide the smile and doubted the flickering light of the flames truly covered the heat in her cheeks. "Hardly. But I'll do everything to be perfect for you."

"Just be you," Jamie said. "That's more than enough."

"Then dig on in, before the fajita meat gets cold," Siena said as she took her own seat and they both dove in, making fajitas their own way.

"So are you going to tell me what this big job opportunity

is about?" Jamie seemed genuinely curious about it, which was a good sign.

Then again, she was unemployed right now, so she'd probably take anything she could get if there was a chance it would help pay the bills.

"I was going to wait, but all right." Siena took a deep breath and dove in. "Come work for me at D.Y.K.E. Management."

"What?" Jamie's eyebrows knitted together.

"Come and join as D.Y.K.E.'s public relations consultant. Primarily, you'll be in charge of controlling Bunny and Piper's media presence, as well as helping me build up my new clients Jo and Bea."

"Jo?" The shock on Jamie's face was evident. "The same Jo who's fake-engaged to Piper?"

"The one and the same. That's a complicated situation, but I can fill you in on all of that when you start." Siena smiled, unable to get rid of the ridiculous amount of joy and hope that filled her now that her idea was out in the open.

"Siena." Jamie's lips pursed together, and she placed her freshly wrapped fajita back down onto her plate.

"What's wrong?"

"Nothing's wrong." Jamie smiled, but it didn't reach her eyes. "It's an amazing opportunity, and past me would have jumped on it the minute you said, 'work for me.' But I don't want to fall back on bad habits and jumping into things without thinking them through. It's just one of those many habits I want to change."

Siena sat with Jamie's words for a moment, rolling them around in her head. This hadn't been what she expected. Surely working for her and doing this kind of PR would be Jamie's dream job. She'd talked about it more times than Siena could count, and having access to all the gossip firsthand would surely be the perfect job for Jamie.

"I'm sorry. But can I think about it before you jump into getting me sized up for a uniform?" Jamie was genuinely smiling this time, which was a relief to Siena's racing heart and the disappointment filling her.

Siena laughed and the image of Jamie in any kind of uniform presented a whole new option for her to pursue at a later date.

"Of course you can." Siena returned to making her own fajita. After a moment, she looked up to see Jamie hadn't picked her dinner back up.

"You really aren't mad at me?" Jamie asked when their eyes met.

"Mad at you?" Siena blinked, and she stopped wrapping up her first fajita. "I'm proud of you. You're wanting to be a better version of you."

"What if I can't be? What if this is the best I get?" Jamie cringed, her hair falling over her shoulder as she seemed to try and hide behind it.

"This is what I've fallen in love with. And I know you. No matter what, you'll keep trying to be better. You're not a bad person." Siena reached over and touched Jamie's hand lightly with her own, giving her a tender squeeze. When they'd first met, Siena had never expected that Jamie would have this much to be self-conscious about. She hid it well during their initial trysts and conversations.

"All right, enough of all that." Jamie waved her hand and picked up her fajita. "How was the rest of your day?"

And just like that, Siena and Jamie started talking about their days. The margaritas flowed and the fajitas were made.

"Oh my God. You should have stopped me before I ate that last one." Jamie groaned as the two of them moved to Siena's couch.

"I wasn't getting my fingers bitten off." Siena laughed as Jamie pouted. "Lie down and I'll rub your tummy all better."

Jamie laughed but still laid her head in Siena's lap. "Is that a euphemism?"

"Not at all." Siena chuckled, far happier now than she could ever remember being in the last few years. She settled in next to Jamie on the couch, combing her fingers through Jamie's hair and simply relaxing. God, when was the last time she had done this? Yes, her brain was still spinning with work and everything that she could potentially do for Bea and Jo in the upcoming year, but she was simply content.

The sensation was simply breathtaking.

Siena didn't know when they had fallen asleep, but she woke with her bladder screaming at her.

"Jamie," she whispered at first until she realized there was no way to wake Jamie that easily or gently. "Jamie, wake up, baby. I need to pee."

"Hmm?" Jamie stirred and looked up. After blinking a few times, a smile stretched sleepily across her lips.

"Let's go to bed, baby."

"I'm sorry. I'm too tired."

Siena laughed. "Bed, Jamie, not sex. Come on, baby."

Jamie finally moved with a few more nudges from Siena.

Siena took Jamie's hand and led her toward her bedroom. Looking back, she saw Jamie's eyes still closed. The trust she had in Siena to lead her safely filled Siena with the kind of fullness she'd never experienced before.

They hadn't fucked, they hadn't made love, and they had barely even made out throughout the evening, and yet Siena could say without hesitation that tonight had been one of the most beautiful and intimate evenings they had ever had.

Hell, it had been one of the most intimate evenings she'd ever had with anyone.

After she laid Jamie on the bed, Siena went and relieved herself. Hearing Jamie's soft snores from the bathroom, she decided to get changed into a camisole, leaving just her panties on.

"Why did you put more clothes on?" Jamie said groggily as she pushed herself up onto her elbows.

"Because it's been a big week, and we need sleep more than sex."

"Never." Jamie smiled but her eyes were already closing.

"Let's sleep tonight, baby. We have forever to explore more ways to please each other." Siena helped tuck Jamie comfortably into her bed, and then slipped in beside her.

"Hee-hee, big spoon."

"I'll always be your big spoon, for as long as you want me."

"Mmmmm." Jamie's breathing had already slid into the easy slow rhythm of sleep.

Siena snuggled closer and closed her eyes. Who knew that falling asleep clothed and without having had sex would be one of the most incredible nights of her life?

thirty-four

"Good morning," Siena's voice was far too chirpy as she slipped back into bed.

"What time is it?" Jamie groaned.

With a small chuckle, Siena brushed her lips against Jamie's. By the time Jamie tried to react, those lips were already gone.

"Not fair," Jamie muttered. "That was too quick."

"I've made you coffee, if you can bring yourself to sit up." Siena ignored Jamie's accusation.

"You don't play fair at all," Jamie said as she moved, shuffling her body into a sitting position against the head of Siena's bed.

"I never said I was fair." Siena perched on the edge of the bed beside Jamie and gave her another quick kiss on the lips.

"Uh-uh," Jamie said when Siena tried to move back. She captured the back of Siena's head and pulled her back for a deeper kiss.

"Mmmm, you taste like coffee," Jamie moaned when she let Siena out of the kiss.

"And you can too." Siena grabbed a cup from the bedside table and handed it to Jamie.

Jamie took the mug and looked at her warped reflection in the surface.

"Jamie?" Siena asked, placing a gentle hand on Jamie's arm.

"I can't take the job, Siena." Jamie looked up as she spoke the words. Fear and self-loathing filling her, but she had to do this. For Siena, and for herself. She had to be honest and stop hiding behind her walls.

"Oh." Siena leaned back as though the words had physically hit her. "I thought you needed time to think about it?"

Jamie shook her head and swallowed over the lump in her throat. "No. I knew right away that I couldn't accept it. I'm sorry, Siena. I should have told you last night."

"Why didn't you?"

"I wasn't lying." Jamie looked up and hoped Siena could see the truth radiating in her eyes. "I really want to think about decisions, about the big ones, before I simply answer. I want to be moving forward in a purposeful way, not just chasing the bouncy ball that grabs my attention."

"But you're definitely sure now?"

"Yes."

"Okay." Siena's tone was so sad it almost made Jamie reconsider. It almost made her open her mouth and tell Siena she was wrong. Tell her she would take the job, and they could live and work together and skip off into the sunset.

But she knew that wasn't how these things went. "I know you must be mad at me."

"No, I'm not mad." Siena gently lifted Jamie's chin with her fingers. "I'm sad that I don't get to see you walking around all sexy in some more laundry-day outfits. But whatever you choose is okay with me. I love you for you, Jamie, not for what you can offer me."

"For how long?"

"What?"

"How long will you love me when I can't offer you anything? I don't have a job. I don't even have enough gas in the tank or money in my account to get some. And that's not the worst part. I have so much to do to work on myself. I need a lot of time to become the person I actually want to be. And I have been told I'm not the easiest person to be around." God, Jamie was such an idiot sometimes. She really had to stop giving out all the reasons why people shouldn't like her if she wanted to be liked.

"And who says that?" Siena asked.

"Ummm." Jamie let out a small huff of amusement. "Everyone who has ever been around me for any significant amount of time."

"Jamie." Siena stopped her before she could really get on a roll. "I love you. It's not going to be smooth sailing, and there's going to be the ups and downs and the shit that gets dragged in from two lives merging together to become a third entity. Let's be honest, every relationship is a little bit *ménage à trois*."

Jamie laughed, Siena's eyes sparkling as they met.

"None of that stuff is what made me fall in love with you. Not the job you have, not the money you earn, not the things you can offer me professionally. I love you. And that's all there is to it."

The silence lingered and rested heavy in the air.

"Can I ask you a question?" Siena asked.

"Yeah." Jamie took a sip of her coffee and closed her eyes. Whether it was from the blissful hit of her first taste of caffeine for the morning or to prepare herself for whatever the question might be, she didn't know. Perhaps a little of both.

"Why are you declining the job?" Siena asked.

Jamie nodded as she tried to process how to put into words all the reasons.

"Stop overthinking it and just tell me. It's okay, whatever the answer is." Siena's voice was so kind.

"You can't know that until you know the answer," Jamie argued.

"I can," Siena argued right back. "Because no matter what the answer is, I'd still love you, and so that means it's all okay."

"You just love using that word, don't you?" Jamie teased playfully, a smirk on her lips before she lifted the cup once more. This time it was no tentative sip. She gulped down half of what remained as though it might give her the strength to explain why she couldn't take the job. "I love that you think I could do it. I love the offer of the job. And the perk of getting to see you every day at work really would be amazing."

Jamie paused for another sip of the coffee. Siena waited, not butting in but letting Jamie take whatever time she needed to get where she had to go.

"But I can't do that to us," Jamie blurted and knew the rest wouldn't be far behind.

"To us?" Siena asked. "Sorry, please ignore me."

"I could never ignore you. That's sort of how we got here." Jamie smiled.

"True," Siena conceded.

Jamie couldn't believe in the middle of baring her soul she could find herself feeling safer than she ever had with her walls and her distant bitchiness. Then again, she couldn't believe she was baring her soul at all—the truth of her fears and all her faults.

"I don't know that you haven't offered me this job because I know how to make you scream." Jamie held up her hand as Siena's mouth opened. Once Siena smacked her lips back together Jamie continued. "I don't believe that's the reason. But others don't know you, don't know me, and don't know us the way we do. And they'll think it's the reason. Because I won't hide the happiest, most fulfilling adventure of my life. Because that's exactly what you are. What we are together."

Siena looked so confused by that, and Jamie could understand why. "Do you really care so much what people think?"

"Yes and no." Jamie shrugged. She wasn't entirely sure. It was so much harder being honest with herself when she had never stopped long enough to examine her actual thoughts and feelings. "But it's the mosquito effect."

"The mosquito effect?" Siena looked beyond confused, and Jamie never thought she had seen anything more adorable in her life.

"They are tiny, and so seemingly inconsequential, but the buzz will drive you nuts in the quiet dark of the night. And when they land and bite, you'll slap yourself silly just to be rid of them. You'll hurt yourself in order to make them go away."

"Your mind is magnificent." Siena leaned in and kissed her cheek.

"Because I love metaphors?" Jamie laughed.

"Because of how you think, how you use words, how you can relate everything to something the majority of the world would understand." Siena kissed her lightly. "You're fucking brilliant and I'm pretty sure that you don't even know it half the time."

Jamie's cheeks burned, but a warmth settled into her chest that she was loving feeling. Is this what it was like to be loved? To have her own personal cheerleader through absolutely everything? Jamie could get on board with this, although it'd take some serious getting used to.

"So yeah. If we worked together, everyone would know we're also together personally because I refuse to hide this."

"Is that the *only* reason?"

"No." Jamie could have said yes, and the old Jamie would have. But she was already liking the new Jamie just a little more. "I don't want a work Siena and a home Siena. I want all of you. I want you to be able to talk to me about things and not worry that I can't keep my mouth shut or worry that I might change how you or I do something."

"I trust you."

"I know. And I trust you, too. But the little things can hurt more than the bigger things. Remember the mosquitoes." Jamie covered Siena's hand and squeezed gently before interlacing their fingers. She wasn't willing to give this up. Not now and maybe not ever.

Siena laughed and took Jamie's now empty coffee mug out of her hands. When had she finished that? After placing the mug on the bedside table, Siena cupped Jamie's face in her hands.

"I love you more than I thought it was even possible to do."

"I love you, too," Jamie said, peering at Siena through her eyelashes.

"I don't think I truly realized just how much until now."

"Because I'm turning down your offer of a job?" That was nearly unbelievable, but Siena had said it, so it must be true. Right?

"Because you're turning down my offer and choosing me instead. No one has actually ever done that before."

Jamie's face burned hotter beneath Siena's touch and then her kiss. She had to break that tension quickly because it was too much for her to handle. She needed the easiness that she'd found in their relationship, not this intensity that was so filled with emotions she wasn't quite comfortable with.

Jamie smirked. "Well, they are really good orgasms."

Laughing with ease, Jamie pulled Siena in until their lips gently brushed. The kisses were slow at first and then quick. Jamie hadn't had enough, though. She tugged Siena in even closer, deepening their kisses as Siena started to crawl on top of her.

"I love you," Jamie whispered against Siena's mouth. "Come back to bed… I didn't get my dessert last night."

"Always." Siena climbed over Jamie, curling beside her and snuggling into her side.

Jamie inhaled the relief and the comfort. She still wanted more, but she was happy with what they had for right now. She kissed the top of Siena's head and smiled. "Thank you."

"For what?" Siena asked.

"For believing I can be a better human, for trusting me, for loving me when you don't have to."

"No one has to love anyone else."

"Family does."

"Oh no!" Siena's laugh was a mocking sound, and Jamie now had a hundred million questions running through her mind. And she sensed pain there, a deep pain that Siena wasn't prepared to share. Still, she couldn't wait to learn every moment that had formed this incredible woman she got to wake up with. "They don't have to love you."

"Maybe. But thank you, anyway." Jamie shuffled, and Siena sat up.

There had never been any doubt in Jamie's mind that the physical attraction between the two of them had always been electric. From their first touch, the physical contact had magnified that electricity a thousandfold. She had experienced more sexual confidence and exploration with Siena than she had with anyone in her past. And now, she knew this would be yet another new experience for her.

It wasn't time for hard and dirty, or fast and furious.

It was time to use her body to enhance the emotions within her instead of as a wall against anyone getting closer. Slowly, allowing Siena all the time in the world to say no, or to stop her, Jamie shifted and straddled Siena's legs.

"Oh, is that right?" Jamie teased and started kissing Siena's face, over her closed eyes and her cheeks and down to her jawline. Siena tilted her head back, giving Jamie access to her neck.

"I have to make up for last night," Jamie purred between kisses.

"No, you don't." Siena pulled back, gently moving Jamie so their eyes could meet. "You never owe me sex."

"But—"

"No." Siena's voice was firm but not hard. "If sex was all I wanted from you, then we could just as easily still be playing that game. But as crazy as you make me, you never owe me sex."

After a beat of silence, Jamie smiled and shook her head. "How do you do that?"

"Do what?"

"Say exactly what I need when I don't even know what I need?"

"Because you don't see just how amazing and beautiful you really are."

"I'm not. But I'm trying to be."

"Baby, you already are," Siena said, and kissed Jamie again. "You're wanting to show more people the true beauty inside of you, and that's wonderful. But it's already there. It really is."

"Hmm," Jamie said as she slowly moved her hips in Siena's lap.

"Baby, we don't *have* to fuck." Siena tucked a strand of Jamie's hair behind one ear.

"I don't want to fuck you," Jamie said between kisses as her hips moved slowly against Siena's crotch.

"Are you really sure about that?" Siena asked as her chest rose and fell faster and her hands found Jamie's hips.

"I want to make love to you." Jamie stopped the short quick kisses she had been peppering Siena's neck with and captured her lips instead. Siena moaned into her mouth as Jamie's hands found Siena's breasts under the silk camisole.

"Please," Siena whined.

Jamie teased the nipples into erect buds.

"Please, what?" Jamie asked, moving her hips a little faster.

"Please." Siena gasped as Jamie squeezed one erect nipple between thumb and forefinger. "Please make love to me."

"I thought you'd never ask." Jamie removed her dominant hand from Siena's breast, dancing her fingers lightly down Siena's stomach.

"Hold onto me?" Jamie asked.

"I'm never going to let you go," Siena replied.

Jamie couldn't wait any longer. Lifting herself just a little off of Siena's lap, she slipped her hand between the two of them.

"Mmm," Jamie moaned as she brushed her fingers across wet cotton.

"You make me so wet. I've never gone commando so many times in my life, and it's all thanks to you."

"Maybe you should start having a spare pair in your bag." Jamie chuckled lightly, but satisfaction rolled through her. She'd never done that for someone else.

"Maybe," Siena said, catching her breath as Jamie maneuvered her hand beneath the elastic waist band and found the slick folds beneath.

"Or you could just start out commando and save yourself the laundry."

Siena might have laughed at some other time, but Jamie wasn't offended. She was enjoying the feeling of Siena's nails biting into the skin on her back through the fabric of her dress.

"Can I touch you?"

"Yes," Jamie said as her fingers circled Siena's entrance, her hips grinding harder and faster, and her breath keeping up.

Siena didn't bother with trying to rid Jamie of any clothes, thankfully, as she found her way beneath the hem of the dress and into Jamie's underwear faster than Jamie thought possible.

"Impressive."

"Just wait until I fill you up."

"Oh, you already do."

As they worked each other up, Jamie filled with memories, and not just the good ones. Her mind drifted to those moments when her heart had hurt so much from being filled with shame and doubt. Those moments of never being enough, never being the good one. The one everyone despised.

"Hey, stay with me, baby." Siena's soft voice pulled Jamie from the spiraling thoughts, and when their eyes met, the pain she feared would envelop her fled from the truth of her love for Siena, and Siena's love for her.

"I'm here."

"Good girl," Siena purred and Jamie's breath caught.

"Can I be inside you?"

"Yes. Can I return the favor?"

"Oh yes."

As Jamie eased down onto Siena's fingers, she slid her own into Siena. She imagined all the amazing and wonderful things that might happen if she truly let herself believe all the things she saw in Siena's eyes.

She might not have the same complete trust and vision of herself as Siena yet, but she would. She would keep working on it, and she knew without a doubt Siena would keep reminding her just how amazing she was.

thirty-five

"Ingrid." Siena smiled, walking into the restaurant and flicking her hair over her shoulder. She needed to hang out with her more often than she had been. But they seemed to be crisis buddies right now instead of simply just friends. Wrapping her arms around Ingrid's wiry shoulders, Siena hugged her tight. "Let's get dinner, just you and me sometime."

"Uh… sure." Ingrid gave her a worried look. "Is something wrong?"

"No, not at all." Siena stepped away. "In fact, everything is great." Siena squared her shoulders and looked Ingrid over. She looked a whole lot thinner than she usually was, which was saying something, since she was as lanky and wiry as Siena. "Is everything good with you?"

"Mostly." Ingrid sighed. "We can talk about that later." Ingrid nodded toward the door. "Your applicant is here."

Siena spun around to find Jamie coming inside, knocking the water off the umbrella she'd just closed and fluffing out her hair in the entryway. Siena's lips curled upward in a sweet smile. She would never get over the fact that they were together now. It truly was unexpectedly perfect.

Walking right up to Jamie, Siena took her by the hand and kissed her quickly. "Hey there."

"Hey," Jamie said with a worried smile. "You do realize that Ingrid Brett is the one who was trying to get me fired for months, right?"

"Yeah, I do." Siena gave her a smile. "Trust me?"

"Always…except maybe when it comes to this." Jamie chuckled lightly. "But I'll sit through a free meal."

Siena took Jamie by the hand and walked closer to Ingrid.

"I'd like to officially introduce you two. Jamie, this is Ingrid, Ingrid this is Jamie Kettlehouse."

"Good to meet the infamous gossip writer," Ingrid said, extending her hand.

"I prefer notorious." Jamie quirked her lips up in that brilliant smile that made Siena weak in the knees.

Ingrid's voice trilled with a laugh before she nodded her agreement and shook hands with Jamie. They were led to a table toward the back, per Siena's request, and sat down. It hadn't taken Siena very long to toss the idea to Ingrid. It had, however, taken her much longer to convince Ingrid that this would be anywhere near a good idea.

After they'd ordered some drinks, Siena settled in to help facilitate this. Not that she felt she needed to be here for the conversation—or rather interview—but she hadn't seen Ingrid on a more personal level for a while, and it was a good excuse to get out and see her while things were still calm, or as calm as either of their lives got.

"As much as I *love* your CV," Ingrid added an extra snark onto the *love* when she spoke, "I do have a lot of concerns about hiring you."

"Fair," Jamie answered, putting her foot right against Siena's under the table.

If Siena could be there for emotional support, then she

would be. "I'd have the same concerns." She picked up her coffee and sipped it, the hot liquid glorious, especially with that added hit of caffeine in it that she needed after a late night with Harley. Those nightmares about kindergarten were no joke. Tori had tried to warn her, but Siena hadn't quite believed her until she experienced it herself.

Ingrid shot Siena an interesting look, one that was telling her to shut up but was also intrigued. "I read the interview you published with Bunny and Piper. It was excellent. But I don't have the same…sway… as your previous contract."

Jamie grinned. "No, you don't. Nor would I ask you to. I wrote that article in part as a favor to Siena, but also because it was a lifelong dream to have an exclusive interview with Bunny and Piper. I couldn't turn down that opportunity."

"No one could. Exclusives with them are rare." Ingrid again looked at Siena. Was she trying to size Siena up? Or was she simply trying to figure out why Siena had made this proposal? "And it was good timing."

"Yes, it was." Jamie shifted a glance to Siena as well, definitely trying to judge what exactly she should be saying and not saying.

"It was an attempt to sway public opinion, and to turn it back to what we wanted it to be." Siena sipped her coffee again, eyeing Ingrid over. There was definitely something off about her.

"That's definitely something I need, and someone who can think about where those gaps are and where they can be filled." Ingrid thanked the waiter as he brought her a mimosa that she'd ordered. They each placed orders for their brunch and then went right back to it. "How much experience in PR do you have?"

Jamie shrugged. "A bit, but not extensive. My main experience is in the newspaper and media world, the gossip writing you could say. I didn't write the tabloids, but sometimes it was pretty close. Well, once I did, because I needed a few bucks to pay my cell phone bill."

Siena raised an eyebrow at Jamie over that one. She hadn't realized that she'd done that, and now she really wanted to know what that article involved—or rather who. Jamie locked their gazes and shook her head.

"You don't want to read it."

"I kind of do," Siena countered. "I want to know what depths you'll go to for a few dollars."

Jamie snorted and laughed. "It was about a dog, and ninety percent of it wasn't true. But the cash came in handy. I felt so gross after doing it that I refused to even pick up the phone when they called again."

"But you had minutes," Siena said.

"I had minutes." Jamie's eyes twinkled.

Siena would track down the article some other day, or maybe when she got back to the office. She'd just have to figure out what name Jamie had written it under first, because Siena had no doubt that she'd used a *nom de plume*. Especially if she didn't even want Siena to read it now.

"I'm looking to undo the effects of what you did to my client a few months ago. I need to restore her image."

Jamie frowned. "That's going to be hard unless she becomes a little nicer."

Ingrid's lips curled up at that. "That's where good PR comes in handy."

"I won't lie to my readers."

"I'm not asking you to," Ingrid pushed back, a glint in her eye that had scared Siena more times than she cared to admit. Most of the time, it came out all right, though. "I'm asking you to write what's real and what's not. Exactly like you did with Bunny and Piper."

Jamie looked suspicious. And rightfully so. Siena would also be hella suspicious of what Ingrid was saying if she didn't know her. Ingrid's moral standards were nearly as high as Siena's, she was just a little more willing to take on ethically questionable clients and push them to bigger and better things. It was why she was more successful than Siena overall.

Siena thanked the waiter when their food arrived. Ingrid and Jamie were still having a bit of a stare down, and Siena was damn sure that it was not her place to get in the middle of that.

"I think you're walking a fine line in what you're asking of me." Jamie pursed her lips in thought.

Siena resisted the urge to jump in and play mediator. She wanted Jamie to get this job, not just because Jamie needed it but because Ingrid also really needed someone, especially with her current client list. It was getting difficult for her to wrangle them all on her own. It would also be nice to at least have Jamie on their side more often than not.

"How many hours?"

"It's full time," Ingrid responded. "Salary."

Jamie narrowed her gaze. "Then I won't work over forty hours for you, and I get to keep my outside media jobs, the ones I run and my contracts."

Ingrid shook her head. "No."

"Then I won't work for you." Jamie leaned back in her chair with a sigh of relief. Then she bent over her plate and took a huge bite. "I won't be owned by anyone."

Ingrid raised an eyebrow at Siena and pointed at Jamie. "She's good."

"She is," Siena agreed. Watching Jamie in action like this was hot as hell.

Ingrid faced Jamie. "I will approve your other contracts, the people and presses anyway. I don't want you to be working for anyone who conflicts with me. As for your own business ventures. You're more than welcome to continue those."

Siena knew that was what Jamie really cared about. The only other contract she had right now was with her, and that one wouldn't conflict. She and Ingrid did enough business together to make sure of that. Siena ran her fingers through her hair and pushed her leg against Jamie's in support. She wanted Jamie to know that she was there for her no matter what.

"You have to respond to those requests in forty-eight hours. If I hear nothing, it's at my prerogative whether or not I sign a contract."

"One week," Ingrid countered.

Jamie shook her head. "No, this industry moves far too quickly for that. I'm tempted to make it twenty-four hours."

"Twenty-four? Jesus, I do have to sleep you know. Maybe take a piss."

Jamie laughed lightly. "The gossip never ends, and if I miss a story because you're too slow, I'm not going to be a happy employee."

"I'll have to think about the time on that one, and we can negotiate it after you decide if you're willing to sign a contract." Ingrid finally started to dive into her breakfast.

It seemed that Jamie had been hired. Right? Siena wasn't entirely sure, but that's what it felt like with the ping-ponging back and forth between the two of them.

"What's the salary?" Jamie eyed Ingrid inquisitively.

"Seventy-five plus medical."

Siena would refrain from comment on that. She really didn't want to think about why the position was so low.

Jamie hummed a response and went back to eating. "We can negotiate."

"So you're interested?" Ingrid asked.

"I've always been interested."

"Good." Siena grinned at both of them. "Then you two can set up a time to talk more business. Right now, I want to talk about life." Ingrid and Jamie turned on her sharply. She knew that was going to happen. In some ways, the two of them were very similar—bullheaded and single-mindedly focused. But Siena wanted to catch up with Ingrid, and she wanted to share some of her news with Jamie.

"Life?" Ingrid pursed her lips. "I'm single again."

"Are you?" Siena frowned. "Since when?"

Ingrid sighed and closed her eyes. "Since Thanksgiving. I didn't want to mention it and bring everyone else's holidays down."

"It's January."

Ingrid shrugged. "Then I forgot about it."

"You forgot you were single?" Siena looked at her dubiously. "You don't just forget those things, especially you."

"I've been a bit distracted with other things." Ingrid flicked her gaze over to Jamie. "Work things that you'll be welcome to know about once you sign a contract with me."

Well, that ended that conversation. At least for now. Siena really was going to have to find some time to get together with Ingrid again. Because they really, really needed to talk. It sounded like there was so much more going on than she was letting on.

Sighing, Siena glanced to Jamie. "Well, you should know that Jamie and I are officially dating now."

"You thought that was a secret?" Ingrid chuckled.

"No." Siena shook her head. "But if you hire her, things will probably come up in conversation."

"Oh, so you don't want me to tell her all the stories of you from college."

Siena tensed. "They really aren't as bad as that statement makes them seem."

"Mm-hmm." Ingrid winked at Jamie. "I'll tell you those whether or not you decide to work for me. They're just fun."

"I look forward to hearing them." Jamie sipped her coffee. "I always need more information about Siena. Somehow, she's managed to find just about every single blog post and article that I've written. I have no idea how since some of them are on the dark web."

"I haven't found the one about the dog," Siena said. "But I plan to. And it's called just being really good at doing some internet searches."

Jamie rolled her eyes. "Sometimes I think she'd be better at gossip writing than me."

"Hmm, no, I wouldn't be. I have zero tolerance for drama."

"I love the drama." Jamie's eyes lit up excitedly. "I mean all of the drama so long as it doesn't involve me."

"Right?" Ingrid wrinkled her nose. "That's why Siena and I are in management and not on the stage. We couldn't handle the drama even if we tried. The spotlight isn't for us."

Siena wasn't so sure about that. Ingrid had tried to be in the spotlight, and then she'd started working with the manager she was with now, and she swiftly pivoted to the behind-the-scenes work. She'd never gotten the full story as to why Ingrid had given up the limelight, and the excuses she'd gotten had never really sat very well with her either.

"It's really not," Siena agreed. Again, those questions were for another time, when it was just the two of them talking with no one else around, and probably a bottle of whiskey split between them. God knew they needed it after the last year.

Ingrid nodded. "You ever want the spotlight, Jamie?"

"No. My goal isn't awards or accolades. I couldn't care less about those." Jamie finished off her plate and wiped her lips on the napkin in her lap. "I just want people to have access to information and to have the real story behind celebrities and what they claim they stand for. If they really follow through on that or not."

"Hmm, seems we're not all that different then." Siena smiled, then she used the top of her foot and slid it along the back of Jamie's calf. This could all work out exactly how they needed it to.

thirty-six

"Hey, Harley!" Jamie grinned as Harley opened the front door. She'd only just barely knocked, which meant that Harley must have been waiting for her. As soon as she stepped inside, Harley wrapped her arms around Jamie's leg. Wait… arms? "Did you get your cast off?"

Jamie bent down so she could look Harley over. Sure enough, the cast that had encased her arm the entire time Jamie had known her was completely gone.

"Yes!" Harley giggled and raised her arm above her head before attempting to stretch it out. "But I can't straighten it yet." She pouted. "Mommy says I have to go to PT. What's that?"

"It's a doctor that helps you move your muscles better. It'll be fun. Sometimes they make games that you can play."

"Really?"

"Yes, really." Jamie patted Harley's shoulder before standing up to her full height. "Did you get to keep the cast?"

"No! It was so stinky! I nearly threw up."

Jamie laughed. She remembered that from when she'd been a kid and had broken her arm on a trampoline. That was something she'd never wanted to do again, so she'd never stepped foot on one of those contraptions after that. And she still wouldn't, no matter how hard someone tried to make her.

"Yeah, they can get pretty gross. Where's your mom?"

"Kitchen." Harley took Jamie by the hand and led her toward the kitchen, but she didn't let go of Jamie's hand when they got there.

That had been one of the hardest things for Jamie to get used to. Harley was so affectionate with other people, physically affectionate in ways that Jamie had never been growing up. Her parents had always held her and Jessie at a distance, their father especially. And seeing Siena and Harley together was really the first time that Jamie wondered if it truly was just her family that was like that.

She'd have to look into it more and talk to Jessie about it.

"Hey there," Jamie said, catching Siena at the stovetop, cooking something that smelled delicious.

"Hey." Siena grinned broadly. "She was watching from the window."

Jamie chuckled. "I figured." Moving in, Jamie leaned up on her toes and pressed her lips to Siena's. It was a quick kiss as something crackled in the pan on the stove. She glanced down at it and was impressed that Siena was cooking. "I love that you can do that."

"Cook?" Siena looked at her in surprise.

"Yeah. My claim to fame is ramen in the microwave."

"This explains so much," Siena teased as she went back to preparing the meal.

"How was your new job?" Harley asked, her chest puffing out with how thrilled she was to be able to remember something important.

"It's good." Jamie bent down and picked Harley up, popping her on her hip for a quick hug before setting her back down. "I bet not as good as finally being able to scratch your skin."

Harley giggled. "It's so good!" She waved her hand in the air again excitedly. "Is your new boss mean?"

"My new boss is Ingrid." Jamie glanced at Siena. "Do you know her?"

"Mommy's friend."

Jamie nodded. "Yeah, so she's pretty nice." So far anyway, but Jamie hadn't really been there that long yet, which meant she still had time to piss off the boss and run into problems of her own making. Although this job already felt far calmer than any other she'd had so far. Something about the office was odd, but she just put it down to the newness.

"Harley, would you go set the table, please?" Siena asked.

"Sure thing, Mommy!" Harley immediately raced to the cabinet where the plates were, skidding to a halt in her socked feet on the tile floor.

Jamie leaned against the counter, eyeing Siena over. She'd missed spending one-on-one time with Siena, but she also loved this feeling that came over her. It was so…settled. That was the word. It brought a sense of joy into her life, and she wouldn't give that up for the world.

"What are you smiling about?" Siena asked as she plated the chicken and scooped some of the juices onto the plate with it.

"Nothing."

Siena narrowed her eyes at Jamie. "I don't believe you."

Jamie grinned broadly. "I was just thinking that this is nice?"

"Having someone cook you a meal?"

"Well, yes, that." Jamie rolled her eyes. "I was thinking that *this* is nice." Jamie waved her hand out to encompass the kitchen.

Siena looked around, very confused. "The house?"

"The family," Jamie settled on that word. "My life growing up was fairly cold, and I was never really the accepted one. Definitely not the golden child like Jessie, but here… it feels so different. So welcome and warm."

Siena frowned.

"My parents were hard, not just because they didn't really like me but because I don't think they wanted Jessie and me, ever. Dad wanted boys, not girls, and he got stuck with girls—two very girlie girls."

"Ah." Siena scooped the green beans out of the pot and added some butter and seasoning to them before mixing them up. Harley skidded back in for the silverware. "Don't run with those, please."

"Got it!" Harley chimed.

"We're named after Jessie James."

"Really?" Astonishment crossed Siena's face.

"Yeah. Real clever, right?"

"You could say that."

Jamie stood up straight, debating whether or not she wanted to help Harley finish setting the table. "He never really wanted us, and so he never really loved us."

"Surely he did."

"No," Jamie answered simply. "I really don't think he did. Mom did, but not Dad, and after a while she stopped fighting him on that."

"I'm so sorry." Siena touched Jamie's arm lightly. "That's really hard."

Jamie shrugged. She'd talked to Jessie about it many times over the years, and they'd both dealt with it by cutting their parents off around their twenty-fifth birthday. Jamie had gone first, but Jessie had followed pretty quickly afterward. Their lives were much better that way.

"I think I just always assumed no one wanted me because of that." Jamie snagged Siena's hand before she started to bring the food into the dining room. "At least until I met you."

Siena hummed, stepping right up to Jamie and pressing into her side. "You're worth it."

"Some days," Jamie answered, tilting her head up to look into Siena's gaze. "Other days—"

"What happened to not talking negative about ourselves?" Siena teased. "It's a bad example for Harley, remember?"

"I thought some days was a better answer than no days."

Siena rolled her eyes before leaning in for a longer, deeper kiss. She curled her fingers around Jamie's cheeks and held her still while their tongues tangled. Jamie's breathing increased, her nipples hardened, and she tugged Siena sharply into her as she held on for dear life. Suddenly, Siena pulled away, but she stayed so close that Jamie could feel her breath on her lips.

"It's better, I'll give you that. But it's still pretty negative."

"Fine," Jamie mumbled. "But if you're going to kiss me like that every time I say something negative about myself, I might not want to stop doing it."

"Sneaky."

"Will it work?" Jamie moved in swiftly, nipping Siena's lower lip and then sucking it.

Moaning, Siena pushed into Jamie and held her close. "No, it won't."

"Damn."

Siena stepped away as Harley came back into the kitchen. "All ready!"

"Awesome!" Jamie grinned at her, but Harley had a funny look on her face. "What?"

"Were you *kissing*?" Harley said it like it was a curse word.

Jamie glanced at Siena, who just shrugged. Well, this wasn't how she expected the pre-dinner conversation to go. Jamie was nearly at a loss for words, so she just answered honestly. "Yes."

"JJ says that's how babies are made."

"What?" Siena spun around sharply, her voice echoing through the kitchen. "JJ said what?"

"That you make babies with kissing."

"Oh God." Siena's face was beat red.

"What?" Harley asked.

Jamie had to stifle the laugh behind her hand, but she wasn't having much luck. Instead, she decided to grab the plate of chicken and make her way into the dining room. She was going to leave that conversation to one of the parents. She was definitely not a parent. Jamie finished setting up the table while Siena continued to splutter in surprise.

When they all finally sat down, Harley was still asking questions. "But if kissing is part, what's the other part?"

"Oh Jesus," Siena muttered. "Just eat Harley."

"But I want to know."

"There are quite a few ways to make a baby," Jamie jumped in. "There isn't just one, but for some people, kissing is involved. For most people, some sort of love is involved." Did she really mean that though? Especially with what she'd just shared with Siena?

"Yeah, that." Siena plated up food for Harley and then started to cut her chicken.

"I wanna cut it!" Harley squealed and reached for her plate. "I'm a big kid now."

"All right. All right." Siena put her hands up in surrender. "Just let me know if you need some help."

Jamie made up her own plate and was just about to take a bite when she felt Siena's leg under the table on hers. It was so rare for them to be in the same room with each other and not be touching in some capacity. It had been difficult at first, when Harley had first been introduced to the idea of them dating, because Jamie had held back and so had Siena. But now that Harley was far more comfortable with the idea, they had these little moments.

They were halfway through the meal when Harley spoke up. "Are you getting married?"

"What?" Again Siena's voice cut through the din of the room like a whip. "Why would you ask that?"

"Because Mama and Miranda are getting married."

Jamie bit the inside of her cheek. It was a reasonable question for a five-year-old, especially considering the circumstances. And it was why Harley had been at Siena's for an entire week straight.

"Mama and Miranda have been together for a long time now. Jamie and I only just started dating." Siena picked up her wine glass and took a long gulp.

"How long?"

"Oh God. What is with you and the questions tonight, kid?" Siena's cheeks were a gorgeous shade of pink. "We're not ready to get married."

Jamie couldn't have agreed more. She was just figuring out who this new her was. She really didn't need to add a wedding and marriage on top of that. She still wasn't entirely ready to give up all her freedom yet. Or perhaps it wasn't freedom she was giving up but just life as she currently knew it.

"Will you tell me when you're getting married?"

"Yes," Siena answered. "I'll talk to you first thing when that happens."

Jamie smiled down at her plate and then caught herself. Suprise washed through her as she took in the specifics of Siena's words.

WHEN that happens. Not if.

Her smile widened and she had to bite back a small giggle that wanted to make its way out of her mouth. It wasn't from freaking out, there wasn't even the hint of panic in her. It was from the joy of knowing that Siena saw their future together. This incredible woman wanted her and loved her without strings or conditions.

"What happens at a wedding?" Harley's eyes were wide with curiosity as she pulled Jamie back to the table.

"There's kissing," Jamie jumped in, unable to hold her tongue any longer. Siena's glare was enough of a response to get her to bite her tongue on any more though.

"Yes, there's kissing." Siena sighed. "It depends on the wedding. Mama and Miranda eloped, so it's just them and one other person. Very small. They say a few words to each other, usually about love and how they're wanting to stay together for the rest of their lives, and then that's it."

"What about you and Mama? What was your wedding like?"

"We don't have to talk about that now, Harley." Siena slid Jamie a glance, clearly checking to see if this conversation was okay for them to have and trying to protect Jamie from anything uncomfortable.

"I mean, I'm curious too. Don't you have a photo album or something?"

Siena winced. "No."

"Oh, now that's a lie!" Jamie pointed at her.

Harley jumped up from the table. "I know where it is!" She raced out of the dining room.

"Harley Quinn Frazee! You get back in here!"

"In a minute, *Mom*!"

"Oh that attitude!" Siena laughed. "I guess we're doing this."

"We're definitely doing this." Jamie was going to find out every damn thing she could about this woman and her family. She wanted to know everything, and she wanted to be a part of whatever was to come next.

thirty-seven

One Year Later…

"Well, now, this all feels a little bit odd if I'm going to be honest." Jessie smiled as Siena stepped into the classroom and walked across to where Jessie sat at her desk.

With her hands on the back of the chair opposite Jessie, Siena looked around again at the colors and the artwork that surrounded them.

"Considering Harley's no longer in your class, I suppose so." Siena smiled and finally took her seat in the chair.

Harley was growing up so fast. Siena couldn't quite believe how big her baby was getting. Time kept flying past, and she hated imagining how soon Harley would be in the world keeping her mothers awake with worry.

"Yeah, but also you're Jamie's partner." Jessie chuckled softly. "Which is just another thing that's truly odd. Being able to say that."

"True." Siena chuckled. "But I didn't want to risk Jamie overhearing."

"Overhearing what?" Jessie asked.

"Well." Siena took a deep breath and forced herself to sit a little straighter in the uncomfortable chair. "I know you and Jamie cut off your parents several years ago."

Jessie confirmed with a nod when Siena paused and looked pointedly at her.

"Well, I know it's not as though I need to ask permission or anything, but…" Why the hell was she babbling? She wasn't a babbler. Perhaps spending so much time with Jamie had rubbed off on her as much as Siena seemed to have influenced Jamie.

"Oh my God!" Jessie squealed and jumped up from her chair. She raced around her desk and wrapped her arms around Siena.

The entire reaction to words Siena hadn't quite managed to say yet stunned her into stillness for a moment before laughter escaped through her mouth.

"You're going to propose right?" Jessie moved her head back but kept her arms around Siena.

Siena lifted one arm at the elbow—her bicep still gripped by Jessie kept the rest of her arm pinned to her side—and gently patted Jessie's strangling forearm.

"Yes, that's definitely what I'm wanting to do."

"Well, if you are wanting my approval or anything, first Jamie wouldn't care either way and you totally don't need it. But yes, I can't wait to have you officially as my sister-in-law. And oh, that means Harley will be my niece! This is the most exciting thing."

Jessie finally let go of Siena and wandered back to her side of the desk.

"I'm glad you approve. But," Siena swallowed audibly, "permission wasn't exactly what I came to ask."

"It wasn't?" Jessie looked confused.

"Not exactly." Siena put her hands together and wrung

them as she searched for the right words. "The proposal." She winced. She was doing an awful job at this. Not that the first time she'd proposed had gone any better.

"You want help with proposing?"

Siena chuckled nervously. "Yes. I want to propose in a way that shows her just how much she means to me. How much I want to know everything about her, past, present, and sharing her future."

"Awww." Jessie nodded, her face breaking into a wide smile.

"And I want to show her that family can be both blood and found. Not just one or the other."

"Ah." Jessie nodded knowingly.

They hadn't exactly discussed the issues Jamie faced from how she and Jessie were brought up. But they had all skated around the topic more often than Siena had expected over the last twelve months. It was an issue she could see Jamie wanting to work through but not quite having the confidence and enough feeling of value within herself to address it yet. Siena knew it wasn't her place to fix Jamie. She was perfect and didn't need any fixing. But she wanted to offer as safe a place as she could provide. And Jamie deserved the world.

"All right. Any idea when you were thinking of doing this?"

"Well, it's her birthday in a few months, so I was hoping to get things figured out for then. It's September thirteenth." Siena looked up to find Jessie smirking.

"I may be familiar with that date."

"Right, of course you are." Siena shook her head. Long ago she had stopped seeing them as carbon copies of each other. Beyond their initial, and yes identical looks, their identities were entirely separate and different from the other.

"So, have you got any ideas?" Jessie asked.

"A few," Siena replied, a smile dancing on her lips. "But you know her better than anyone else. Any chance you might have some ideas of what she might expect, or have ever wanted in a proposal?"

She saw the sparkle in Jessie's eyes and knew she had definitely come to the right person about this. It surprised Siena how much the two of them seemed to have in common. At first it was hard to see beyond the physical similarities between Jamie and Jessie, and then not to think of Jessie as simply Harley's teacher, or Jamie's sister.

Sometimes Siena still failed at that, but Jessie and Jamie weren't just twins. Jessie was the closest thing Jamie had ever had to a friend. Even if she still dismissed Jessie's love at times for something Jessie had to do as family.

"I have so many ideas." Jessie beamed. "But we can't do it here. The janitors will be in soon, and I need to get out of here."

"That's okay. I have to get going soon as well. But I wanted to get started on it all, and asking you in person was necessary."

"Thank you." Jessie's eyes glistened.

"I wouldn't dream of doing it without you being involved, or at least knowing about it first."

"I am so excited and can't wait to get into the nitty gritty with you. Message me, and we'll find a time to get together."

Siena had a bounce in her step as she walked out of the school and headed home. It had gone so much better than planned, and seeing Jessie so excited and happy for Jamie filled Siena with such love for her future sister-in-law.

Assuming Jamie said yes.

———

Over the next few weeks, surreptitious texts and phone calls were exchanged. Siena found her mind wandering to different ideas and possibilities of how and where she would propose to Jamie.

There were the usual settings—beach, romantic restaurant, up in a hot air balloon. But nothing seemed to fit or feel quite right.

Whenever she would question if she even knew what the hell she was doing, Jessie would tut-tut her and spark the excitement back into Siena.

Siena loved Jamie, but she wanted this to be perfect for them.

Jessie: You and Jamie are two peas in a pod. Perfect doesn't exist. You've both been around the entertainment business and airbrushed photos for far too long.

Siena: Ha! Maybe.

It was after a particularly excited Jamie came home from work one day, positively buzzing about the latest drama to do with one of Ingrid's clients, that Siena got the best idea yet for how to propose in the grandest of ways to Jamie.

When Jamie went for a shower, Siena quickly typed out a message to Jessie.

Siena: Drama. We need to add some juicy drama. It's what she lives for. And it would make the entire experience catered just to her.

Jessie: Oh brilliant idea. I love it.

Siena: She'll like it right?

Siena didn't enjoy the way she questioned herself in ways she never had before when it came to this proposal, but despite Jessie's scolding, she couldn't shake her desire for this proposal to be absolutely perfect. It would be the last one she ever did. Jamie was her forever, and that needed to be honored in every way possible with each step forward in their relationship.

Jamie came out of the shower, water drops still beading across her collarbone above the towel she had wrapped around her body.

"What are you doing?" She smiled and flopped down on her back on the bed beside Siena.

Siena's mind threatened to fizzle out at the expanse of bare legs that hung over the edge of the bed.

"Work stuff. Shouldn't be long." Siena jumped off the bed before she got any more distracted. She was finally onto something for this proposal, and if she looked at Jamie any longer, all ideas would vanish, never to be returned.

It blew her mind that the mere sight of Jamie could still cause her such distraction. But she couldn't imagine ever getting sick of touching her, making love to her, ravishing her until she screamed her name and lost her voice. She'd only lost her voice once, but it was something Siena aimed to achieve again and again during their life together.

"Oh, all right then." Jamie's eyes radiated a sadness that Siena would ease later, but right now she had to get this figured out. She was tired of planning. She just wanted to propose.

In her office, she looked at her phone again.

Jessie: Absolutely. Can you use something plausible from work?

Siena: Definitely. I think I know exactly who I can ask a favor of to make it look more legitimate than she could imagine.

Jessie: Bunny and Piper?

Siena: Half right :-)

Jessie: Excellent. You work on that end, and I'll keep working on getting the ring sorted.

Siena: Thanks, Jessie. You're the best.

Jessie: Gotta work hard to keep up with Jamie.

The last text was joined by some laughing winky smiley faces, and Siena knew Jessie was trying to play into the myth Jamie always had that Jessie was the perfect golden child. But this wasn't the first time the joke had fallen flat.

From the outside looking in, it was obvious to Siena that the environment the twins had been brought up in had managed to create a competition between the two of them. As though neither of them had quite felt like they were good enough when they had an exact copy of themselves deemed better to compare themselves to daily.

"Babe?" Jamie knocked on Siena's office door.

Siena jumped and muttered a curse before she stepped to the door and opened it. Disappointment pooled in her belly as she noted Jamie's pajamas were on. Not that it had ever stopped them, but it did seem to be a step backward from the half dry, naked Jamie who had sprawled on the bed beside her.

"Hey." Siena smiled. It dropped almost instantly as she took in the expression on Jamie's face. "Is everything okay?"

"I don't know. Is it?"

"Huh?" Siena could have smacked herself in the forehead for that inarticulate response.

Jamie shook her head. "Sorry, it's nothing."

"Hey," Siena pulled Jamie back as she tried to walk away. "Baby, please don't do that."

"Don't do what?" Jamie asked, cold fire sparking behind the crystal of her eyes.

"Don't dismiss what you're thinking or feeling. Please tell me what's wrong."

Jamie's shoulders dropped, and the defensiveness she had carried with her since Siena had opened the door dropped away. "I just had this feeling you were hiding something from me, and my mind kind of spiraled I guess."

"Oh." Siena cradled Jamie's cheek in her hand.

Jamie pushed into the touch and closed her eyes.

"I'm so sorry, but please trust me. I only left the room because I couldn't concentrate on what I needed to work out with your gorgeous body laid out so temptingly beside me."

"Really?" Hope flared in those beautiful eyes. Eyes Siena would willingly gaze into for forever. And hoped to.

"I'm insatiable when it comes to you. Haven't you figured that out yet?" Siena asked.

Jamie smiled, and a small chuckle escaped her lips. "I may have suspected once or twice over the last year."

"Suspected?" Siena feigned insult. She removed her hand from Jamie's face and pressed it, spread, against her chest. "Well, we just might need to do something to amend that."

"Oh really?" Jamie laughed, that cocky smirk lighting up her entire face once more.

"Mommy?" Harley's panicked voice came from the bedroom down the hall.

"Go." Jamie's face instantly shifted from seductress to stepmom.

Siena couldn't love her more. She kissed Jamie's lips hard and fast, a promise of things to come, before she raced down the hall to Harley's room.

If she ever had any concerns about Jamie truly being her person and the person she could spend forever with, they vanished every time she saw her interact with Harley. Or like tonight, the way she reacted with Harley's concerns always coming first. Never hesitating and never expecting Siena to have to choose between the two of them.

They were already a family, and Siena couldn't wait to make that as official as she possibly could.

Jessie had also become the most loved Aunty Siena could have ever hoped for Harley. The woman spoiled the girl, and Siena saw the love shining from Jessie's eyes. She'd also seen the sadness at times when Jessie thought no one noticed.

Maybe once the proposal had been figured out, Jessie and Siena could get to know each other better, and Siena could help to understand the most important person in Jamie's life. Just as Jamie understood Harley and made every effort to make sure Siena's daughter knew how much she was loved and wanted when she was at Siena's.

"Mommy." Harley wrapped her arms around Siena's neck and buried herself into her mother's chest.

"Another nightmare, Batman?" Siena asked softly as she brushed her fingers lightly through her daughter's sweaty hair.

She felt the nod and the shuddering breath from her daughter and held on just a little bit tighter.

"Mommy, can you stay in here with me tonight?" Harley asked as she yawned, her eyes and body already growing heavy and limp in Siena's arms.

"Of course, she can," Jamie said as she stood in the doorway of Harley's room.

"Are you sure?" Siena mouthed.

Jamie smiled and nodded.

"Mommy Jamie." Harley yawned and wriggled back into her bed, pulling Siena down to curl around her as she did.

It didn't take long for Harley to fall back asleep. Siena uncurled herself from Harley's body, waiting to make sure her daughter remained peacefully asleep, and slid out to find Jamie. She found her in the kitchen, leaning against the island counter and flipping through a gossip magazine.

"You really are obsessed with the tabloids, aren't you?"

"Of course. Who couldn't love the drama?" Jamie looked up, a smile wide but natural over her face. "Is Harley okay?"

"Yeah. Are you sure it's okay I stay in there tonight?"

"Of course," Jamie said, eyebrows narrowed as though trying to work out why Siena would even question that. "And I know she didn't mean Mommy Jamie when she said it before, but it sounded so adorable."

"Look at you liking kids."

"Nope." Jamie shook her head as she wrapped her arms around Siena's body, Siena's arms instantly going around Jamie's neck. "I don't like kids. But I do like Harley, and Rebel is a total hoot."

"Rebel is crazy."

"I know." Jamie laughed. "That's what I love about her. My mini me in the making."

"You can only hope. God, I love you."

"I love you, too. Now go make sure that cute kid of yours is okay. She needs her mommy, and she needs to know she's never second place to anyone."

Siena hadn't really understood how amazing Jamie was about her parental responsibilities, but that one sentence made things fit into place a whole lot more.

"You aren't second place, either. You know that, right?"

"I know." Jamie smiled. "You've never made me feel like I am."

"Good." Siena returned to Harley's room, curling around her daughter and ensuring she got some nightmare-free sleep.

thirty-eight

"Shit, Jamie's home early. This is definitely the way to go. All right, you're the best. Bye."

Jamie heard Siena's rushed words as she opened the door. Despite how easily Siena had brushed Jamie's concerns away without making her feel unheard, something was definitely going on, and the panic building in Jamie's chest threatened to overwhelm her.

Today of all days. And work had gotten weird and even a little uncomfortable. Jamie loved her job, most of the time, but there was something going on between Ingrid and her business partner and Jamie got the impression it wasn't good. The tension between the two of them was filtering through the office, and the vibe had gotten harder to ignore.

"Babe." Siena's face bloomed into excitement to see Jamie, but her words still echoed through Jamie's head.

"Who were you talking to on the phone?"

"Work stuff, nothing important."

"It didn't sound like work stuff." Jamie knew she sounded like a petulant child, but today had been harder than she had expected.

"I promise, I'll tell you all about it after dinner, but right now…" Siena walked over to the couch and from behind it she pulled a beautiful bouquet of flowers. "Happy birthday, babe."

"Oh my God." Jamie laughed at the sheer size of the bouquet. "It's as big as my head."

"Well, it's a rose for every month."

"Every month of my life?" Jamie laughed again, struggling to hold the weight of the thing when Siena handed it to her.

"No." Siena wrapped her arms around Jamie's waist, leaning back from the flowers between them. "Every month since we first met."

"Oh." Jamie blinked and stared at the arrangement of different colored roses she held in her arms.

"I love you, Jamie, and ever since that moment, my life has changed."

"For the better?" Jamie questioned, hating how much she still needed that reassurance.

"Oh most definitely." Siena took the flowers from Jamie and led the way into the kitchen. "Let me get these in some water for you, and then I'm taking you out for dinner."

"You are?" This was the first Jamie had heard about it.

She knew Siena hadn't forgotten her birthday. She had made Jamie breakfast in bed before she had raced off to work that morning and promised a present tonight. But Jamie had almost convinced herself that Siena hadn't even gotten her a present yet.

Right now, she still wasn't entirely sure.

Siena had been a lot more distracted over the last few weeks, and Jamie had felt it like a reminder of the past. It wormed its way into her fears.

"Of course I am. I know I've been extra busy with work lately." Something darker shadowed Siena's eyes for a moment before she shook whatever it was away. "But it's your birthday, and I want to spoil you rotten."

"Oh, do I have to change into something nicer, then?" Jamie looked down at her work attire and worried at the casualness of the outfit. At least in relation to whatever fancy restaurant Siena obviously had in mind.

"Nope. What you're wearing is perfect." Siena smiled as she finished with the flowers and gave Jamie a proper welcome home. Their lips slid across each other's, and soon Jamie forgot all about the crappy things from the day and lost herself in Siena's kiss.

"We better get going." Siena stopped their kissing, but her lips remained on Jamie's, the movement of her speech tickling Jamie's lips.

"Do we have to?" Jamie purred, pressing her body a little closer to Siena's.

"Any other day, I'd say no. But it's your birthday, and I want to show you off to the world."

"Hmm." Jamie's mind ticked over.

What in the hell did Siena have planned? First, she assumed a fancy restaurant, but now… Show her off to the world? Jamie felt lost.

"It's okay. Trust me, I've got you."

"I trust you. But that doesn't mean your secret plans aren't terrifying me." Jamie chuckled, feeling the last of the tension from the day melt away.

The phone call she had overheard could have been nothing. She had returned home early and maybe Siena was just talking to Tori or something and wanted to make sure all her attention was on Jamie when she got home.

It didn't seem entirely correct, but then again, it didn't feel out of the realm of possibility either. She pushed away her internal critic and focused on the positives. Siena had made plans for her birthday, and who cared if the plans had only been made today? People forgot things all the time, and with the amount of work Siena had, Jamie was happy she'd been able to finish work early enough to take Jamie out for dinner.

When they arrived, Jamie turned to Siena, eyebrows furrowed and a question on the tip of her tongue. Siena laughed, threaded Jamie's arm through her own, and walked toward the tapas bar.

"Trust me, Jamie. You're going to love tonight."

"You're demanding this trust a little too much lately, Ms. Frazee."

"Well, Ms. Kettlehouse…" Siena purred back, instantly willing to fall into the sexy and playful banter of the past. "I'm not the one who's given you any reason not to trust me."

"*Au contraire*," Jamie retorted as they stepped inside and were surrounded by the ding and clatter of the busy tapas bar. "You're an entertainment manager. I have zero reason to *simply* trust you."

"Hmm." Siena's eyes smoldered as they turned to Jamie before turning back to the counter where she gave her name, and they were quickly led to a table.

"This is the same table," Jamie said, unsure if it were coincidence or not.

"It is," Siena said with a smile and glistening eyes.

Not a coincidence then.

"You're recreating the first time we met?" Jamie's stomach tightened at the mixed emotions she had from that night.

"Well, some of it." Siena smiled, and Jamie's underwear grew wet at the look Siena gave her.

"You're such a romantic." Jamie laughed, unsure if she was being sarcastic or not. Maybe a bit of both.

"You don't like being here?" Siena asked, but there was something in her eyes, deeper and darker that held an understanding of Jamie. It sent shivers up her spine.

"It was a rather fantastic night if I remember correctly. For the most part."

"I know." Siena reached over the table and took Jamie's hand. "But tonight is all about changing the ending."

"Oh really?" Jamie's eyes widened, and her face couldn't hide the hope and enjoyment of this moment that she felt inside.

"Really," Siena said as she moved back for the three waiters who piled up the table with plates. "But why change how good the night started?"

"You're definitely the sappy one in this relationship." Jamie laughed. But the warmth in her chest reminded her how little she minded this in Siena.

"That's okay. Love does tend to bring out the sappy in us mere mortals."

They laughed and ate, and Siena confessed that the person who had stormed out on her that night wasn't a girlfriend but a pushy client who had invited herself to dinner, and then threw a tantrum when Siena did not bow down to her unethical demands.

"Oh my God." Jamie laughed. "That makes so much more sense now. I thought I had recognized her as well, but not enough to consider she might actually be in the industry."

"I haven't seen much from her since. I took her off of my books the next week when she not only went against my advice but name dropped D.Y.K.E. Management in a public lie."

"Ooh." Jamie hissed in a breath. "That wasn't a clever move."

"No, no it wasn't." Siena leaned back in her chair as though trying to stretch her stomach.

Jamie surveyed the table, impressed at how much the two of them had gone through while they talked. The waiters came and took away the crumbs they'd left of the meal.

"Jamie." Siena took Jamie's hands in her own as she spoke.

The trembling in Siena's fingers made Jamie look up into

Siena's eyes. Worry curled around her chest as unshed tears pooled there.

"What's wrong?" Jamie leaned forward, fear flooding through her.

"Nothing." Siena managed to laugh, though a few tears slipped from her eyes. "Nothing's wrong. Nothing's been wrong since the moment I told you the truth about not wanting anything casual with you."

"Why are you crying?" Jamie asked, her voice hoarse and foreign to her ears.

"Because I love you more than anything else in this world, and I want to have a drink with you."

"A drink?" Jamie's head couldn't keep up. She had no idea where Siena was going with any of this, and her mind whirled with possibilities. Very few of those would meet with Siena's approval with her *no negative thoughts about yourself* mantra.

"Yes."

Siena moved back again, and a waiter placed a shot glass in front of Siena.

"I've loved you for so long, I hardly remember how it feels not to love you, not to be with you and share my life with you." Siena kept talking as the waiter remained silently in his place by the table.

Jamie noted another shot glass on his tray, but he hadn't moved to give it to her or to step away.

"Jamie." Siena nodded and finally the waiter placed the shot glass on the table in front of Jamie and moved away. Siena raised her glass, and Jamie looked down to pick her own up.

And then she froze.

Her mouth fell open, and all the worries and fears fell into place. Had Siena been on the phone to someone here, organizing tonight? She looked up and all the emotions on Siena's face made sense.

"Oh my God," Jamie managed to stutter out.

"Will you marry me?" Siena held up her shot glass, her shoulders stilled as though holding her breath.

Jamie scooped up the glass and clinked Siena's own waiting in the air. "Of course I will."

Siena's questioning expression morphed into pure bliss.

They took their shots, Jamie carefully ensuring the ring in her glass stayed in the glass before she put the thing back down, and Siena moved out of her chair, scooped up the ring and put it gently on Jamie's finger.

"I love you."

"I love you, too," Jamie said as their lips met, and they held each other as though they might literally never let each other go again.

"The night's not over," Siena whispered into Jamie's ear, pulling her lobe into her mouth.

Jamie moaned and closed her eyes. "No?"

"I believe room 312 is waiting for our check-in."

"What?" Jamie laughed, joy and pleasure fighting it out within her.

"Mm-hmm." Siena nodded and took Jamie's hand, leading her toward the exit, a nod over Jamie's shoulder to the man behind the counter and they were gone.

Siena had barely stepped through the door of room 312 when Jamie grabbed her and pinned her to the wall, kicking the door closed behind her.

"This time," Jamie said as she nibbled her way along Siena's jawline and down her throat. "I get to play first."

Siena groaned her agreement.

Jamie's body and heart were on fire. She would get to marry the woman of her dreams, the woman who made her wet on a daily basis, the woman who made her the best version of herself, and the woman who believed in her while also refusing to take her shit.

Jamie's breath increased as she found the hem of Siena's shirt and danced her fingers up to Siena's breasts. The shock of skin made Jamie's breath catch.

"No bra?" Jamie asked as she cupped a breast, fondling it as her fingers found the nipple and rolled it until it pebbled, making Siena's breath increase.

"You don't approve?"

"Oh, I highly approve."

Jamie made short work of Siena's shirt as she pulled it off and found the perfect body of her fiancée beneath. It'd take a while for that truth to truly settle in, but she was looking forward to it. Siena's hand tangled into Jamie's hair as she took one nipple into her mouth while her other hand slid down Siena's body and moved just a fraction into the waistband.

"Bed?" Siena panted out.

"All in good time," Jamie murmured around Siena's breast.

She unzipped Siena's pants and pushed down both pants and underwear, helped urgently by Siena's insistent hands.

"Eager are you, Ms. Frazee?"

"For your touch, Ms. Kettlehouse? Always."

"Good, now turn over."

"What?" Siena opened her eyes, and she looked at Jamie, her body stilling.

"You heard me." Jamie smirked. "Be a good girl and turn around for me."

Siena pulled Jamie into a deep tongue-fucking kiss before releasing her and slowly turning around to face the wall.

"Such a good girl." Jamie stood on tiptoes to whisper into Siena's ear. "Now let's see just how much of a good girl you can be."

Siena groaned as Jamie pulled Siena's naked ass against her crotch, pulling Siena away from the wall just a little.

"Hands on the wall," Jamie said as she held onto Siena's hips, ensuring she didn't step any closer to the wall. Siena did as requested, and Jamie felt the pool of heat drench her underwear. "You're so fucking sexy."

Jamie ground her hips in slow circles against Siena's ass as she snaked one hand around Siena's hip and played with the wet curls above her clit.

"Oh, fuck." Siena moaned as she pushed her ass hard against Jamie's crotch.

Jamie groaned in reply and nearly gave in immediately, but she was enjoying this far too much. With one hand still gripping Siena's hip, Jamie continued to tease Siena as her fingers brushed through wet curly hair, drawing closer to the heat that radiated from Siena's opening.

"Please," Siena begged, the word coming out long and guttural.

"Good girl. Beg for me." Jamie kept grinding circles against Siena's ass, her own need building and throbbing between her thighs.

"Oh baby, please, please fuck me. Please." Siena begged and despite Jamie's enjoyment of it and desire to make it last longer, her own craving to be inside Siena won out.

She circled Siena's entrance with her fingers.

"Do you want me to be inside you?"

"Yes. Oh fuck, please, please, yes."

Jamie slid two fingers easily inside, and without any more intelligible words, she fucked Siena against the wall until Siena came with a loud scream and a shaking of her legs.

"Oh God." Siena laughed as her legs wobbled.

"Come on, baby." Jamie led Siena to the bed and gently pushed her onto her back.

"Give me a second, and then it's my turn."

"Oh." Jamie laughed and shook her head. "No, it's not. I believe from memory, it was three orgasms."

"What?" Siena asked.

But before she could do or say anything else, Jamie dropped to her knees and shoved her face into Siena's wet pussy.

She would make sure that tonight, they did it right. And no one would leave here without being fully satisfied.

———

thank you!

Dearest Reader,

Thank you so much for reading this beloved story. It means the world to me! When I first met Siena in **Taming of a Rebel**, I knew that she needed her own story. This book has been a long time coming!

I love the push and pull of these two mains, the extreme opposites finding love in the midst of unexpected ways and with no intention of falling in love, either of them.

I really hope you enjoyed these two characters and this story as much as I did. I'd love it if you'd leave a review or a rating for the book! Every single one of those helps books get noticed by other readers!

You'll get a free copy of **Made You Look** when you do sign up for my newsletter, a novella all about Aili and Birch, and just how their love story starts.

If you haven't signed up for my newsletter yet, you can by going to: https://qrco.de/MYLnewsletter

or scanning the QR code with your phone

I love keeping in contact with readers, so send me emails or get hold of me on social media anytime.

And I always love a good dad joke. Send me your best!

Til the sun shines again,

Eada

Eada Friesian is an author of snarky sapphic women who fall in love hard. She loves all the characters and relationships she gets to play with and the best friends she makes with each new book she writes. She fell in love with the genre years ago and could never leave it. Who would? Now that she's authoring her own books, she hopes to bring a fresh flair to the sapphic book world.

Eada lives in the mountains, camping her life away with her partner and horde of animals. She has her family right by her side as she strives to live her best life authentically as an author, a parent, a spouse, and weird person. She loves the smell of campfire, the taste of a completely charred marsh-mallow for a s'more, and living off the land with very little people around her. Of course, none of this last part is true, because Eada is a pen name, and the identity of the person(s) behind her remain hidden.

facebook.com/sapphicsnarks

instagram.com/sapphicsnarks

reamstories.com/sapphicsnarks

Do you believe in soulmates?

Tori Frazee is unapologetic when it comes to falling in love before she's thirty. When her marriage ended amicably, she knew she had to get back into the game to find her soulmate and have the family she wanted. Running face first into a cold but frazzled funeral director and a rebellious toddler at the grocery store isn't how she expected to find love, and Miranda certainly isn't her soulmate. Or is she?

Miranda Hart doesn't believe in love. When she's saddled with her flakey sister's kid, she has a choice to make—step up to break the cycle and keep her niece from being another victim or continue to live through her work. When she meets the cute, down to earth Tori, she can't help but wonder if maybe she does want more than her career.

When opposites attract, steam rises, especially with an ice queen in the mix. Will these two single parents break down their preconceived notions enough to find a family they can rely on?

If you love sensual, steamy age gap, ice queen, sapphic/lesbian romances, then this is the book for you.

Read it today!

Taming of a Rebel

When opposites attract, steam rises, especially with an ice queen in the mix. Will these two single parents break down their preconceived notions enough to find a family they can rely on?

Love and Cherish

Will they put aside their differences long enough to ensure their boss survives the gala unscathed? Or will the mounting tension between them erupt in unsuspecting ways?

Spicy Sapphic Christmas

Will Bunny risk her career for love? Will Bea get out of her own way to open her heart? Will Piper and Jo admit their fake relationship might be real?